JUN 2 0 2021
JUL 2 0 2021

Crossing Second Narrows

a novel

BILL SCHERMBRUCKER

*For Virginia
Hope you enjoy!
Bill Schermbrucker*

iUniverse, Inc.
Bloomington

Crossing Second Narrows

Copyright © 2013 by Bill Schermbrucker

Illustrations and Cover Image: Pat McCallum.
Cover Design: iUniverse.
Author Photo: Sharon Schermbrucker.

All rights reserved. No part of this book may be used or reproduced by any means, graphic, electronic, or mechanical, including photocopying, recording, taping or by any information storage retrieval system without the written permission of the publisher except in the case of brief quotations embodied in critical articles and reviews.

This is a work of fiction. All of the characters, names, incidents, organizations, and dialogue in this novel are either the products of the author's imagination or are used fictitiously.

iUniverse books may be ordered through booksellers or by contacting:
iUniverse
1663 Liberty Drive
Bloomington, IN 47403
www.iuniverse.com
1-800-Authors (1-800-288-4677)

Because of the dynamic nature of the Internet, any web addresses or links contained in this book may have changed since publication and may no longer be valid. The views expressed in this work are solely those of the author and do not necessarily reflect the views of the publisher, and the publisher hereby disclaims any responsibility for them.

Any people depicted in stock imagery provided by Thinkstock are models, and such images are being used for illustrative purposes only.
Certain stock imagery © Thinkstock.

ISBN: 978-1-4759-6490-5 (sc)
ISBN: 978-1-4759-6491-2 (hc)
ISBN: 978-1-4759-6492-9 (e)

Library of Congress Control Number: 2012922656

Printed in the United States of America

iUniverse rev. date: 3/1/2013

A Note to the Reader:

This is an autobiographical novel. The names of institutions and some public figures are real, but the main characters are fictional. They are not intended to and do not represent real people. Minor liberties have been taken with times and locations.

BILL SCHERMBRUCKER
SATURNA ISLAND BC
JANUARY 2013

"What the automobile did for America,
in the first half of the 20th century,
the University will do in the second."
—Clark Kerr, President,
The University of California at Berkeley, 1968

"It seems to me that the primary function of a university in a sick society, the function which society should be asking the university to perform, is dissent: dissent from all the received diagnoses which have failed. That is the only way that society can get its money's worth from the university in our days."
—C.B. MacPherson,
Convocation Address, Memorial University Newfoundland,
22 May 1970

"We cannot exclude the other any more."
—Ulrich Beck,
CBC "Ideas," 12 December 2007

Acknowledgments

I wish to thank several friends and associates who read all or part of this book over the years and offered helpful suggestions: Bob Camfield, Jean Clifford, J. Marc Côté, Graham Forst, Will Goede, Maria Hindmarch, Crystal Hurdle, Crawford Kilian, Rolf Maurer, Ellen McGinn, Rachael Preston, J. Anne Roberts, Sharon Schermbrucker, Karl Siegler.

The editors at iUniverse have been most diligent and helpful.

The quotes from Tom Wayman in Chapter 21 are from his *Did I Miss Anything? Selected Poems 1973-1993* (Harbour: 1993) and are used by permission of the publisher.

The quote from George Stanley's "Letter from Berkeley" in Chapter 23 was originally published in *The Georgia Straight* and is used with the author's permission.

The quotes from the *I Ching* in Chapter 21 are from the classic translation by Richard Wilhelm, and Cary Baynes, (1967). *The I Ching or Book of Changes*, with foreword by Carl Jung. 3rd. ed., Bollingen Series XIX. Princeton UP (1967), (1st ed. 1950).

I am grateful to the British Columbia Arts Council for a writer's grant which enabled me to complete this book.

Rashid Hassan smiles out in a disciplined pose from the 5 x 7 photograph on the wall beside my desk. It was very thoughtful of his girlfriend Jenadie to give it to me after Rashid disappeared, and I've hung it beside my desk every place I've lived, ever since. It's still painful to look at but it composes the memories of that exciting but unruly time into something bearable. Rashid's strong white teeth and dark beard, his meticulous lips gleaming (perhaps from the juice of the grapes my girlfriend Caroline went out and bought for us in her political naïveté). Rashid smiles out at the world without a hint of irony, and whenever I look at him I feel a small rush of liveliness and gratitude to have come up against him. Jenadie wrote a dedication across the bottom left corner, but the ballpoint ink has faded completely over the years. I turn the frame into the light to read the shadowed grooves: *"For Alistair, whom Rashid respected because political disagreements were always discussed intelligently—for his friend."*

"Discussed intelligently?" Holy God! "One day I may have to shoot you, Sahib." Is that any intelligent way to talk to a friend, a guest in your own apartment?

Strangely enough, I felt then and still do that it was. We came from different parts of the old British Empire, Rashid and I, from India and Kenya, and perhaps we should have been enemies, but we were not. It was a defining moment of my life when I sat on the floor across from him one cold winter's day in Edmonton in 1969, and he spoke with unsmiling logic about the need to shoot me. For now, the three of us, Rashid, Jenadie, and I, could sit companionably on the Mexican blanket eating chicken curry in their fresh, warm, high-rise apartment, safe from the freezing temperature outside, and conduct a civilized debate about student participation in the governance of the University of Alberta; but that a more widespread revolutionary Day of Action must inevitably arrive on a national and world scale when he would have to order one of his henchmen to put a gun to my head and pull the trigger. And I think he definitely meant it. The civility and warmth of our conversation covered a cold menace as threatening as the brutal looks exchanged on the train, between the young General "Strelnikov" and the romantic doctor-poet Yuri Zhivago, in the movie of Pasternak's novel about the Russian Revolution. Or, in our times, the sinisterly gentle smile on the face of Osama Bin Laden, describing himself as "a poor slave of God," as he launched suicide bombers in jet planes into the New York Trade Center's twin towers.

Rashid blinked momentarily. If he was shocked to realize that the words coming out of his own mouth might end up with my brains splattered on the wall—I was as shocked to hear him say it. But there was no way either of us would have let these emotions show through our smiles. He had too much discipline for that, and too much was at stake; and I had grown numb from my own state of exile from Kenya. "One day I may have to shoot you." Spoken with chilling politeness, then adding with a playful grin, "Sahib!" Smile, smile. Friends, after all.

Perhaps it would not be a bullet through my head, but at least to be stripped of possessions and sent away. I didn't think he was joking, as Jenadie later insisted. I believed it because I had lived through civil war in Kenya just as he had lived through the bloody partition of India and Pakistan. I know what it feels like to have your neighbours murdered and then to be no longer welcome in your mother country because of the colour of your skin. In the 21st century, my remaining cousins in Zimbabwe are living through it still: Dispossession, rape, genocide and mass murder, torture of priests and journalists, but my one dear cousin hangs on in Bulawayo, stubbornly believing there has to be a place for her and her children in the land of her birth, as I used to in Kenya. All but one of my cousin's children have taken the hint and fled. And when I was reading a column recently about the Middle East ("Thugs are back at the helm of Iran's government"), one sentence came very close to home, and reminded me of Rashid: Global Network's Jonathan Manthorpe wrote, "Hojjatieh believes the appearance of the Mahdi, . . . which will finally bring peace and justice to the world, can be hastened by creating chaos."

"Creating chaos"? The natural destruction of whole cities by hurricanes and tsunamis seems less sinister to me than a deliberate and man-made chaos. But chaos is what Rashid sought, and for reasons that he explained patiently to me, again and again.

For over fifty years now, Rashid Hassan has sat like the ghost of some strict teacher on my shoulder watching every word I write. His subject was not the English language but the grammar of political change, taunting "The Establishment," working to break the old order and bring about a new distribution of power and to give tongues to silent voices. If that sounds like political claptrap to you, let me just say that I know very well the bullets and blood reality of it. I saw enough dead bodies in Kenya during Mau Mau days to last me forever.

Five years later, in April 1974, we saw that newspaper picture from the surveillance tape showing the sexy 20-year old heiress Patty Hearst ("Tania"), standing guard with her feet planted assertively apart and an automatic rifle in her hands in the Hibernia Bank in San Francisco, while her "Symbionese Liberation Army" colleagues clean out the vaults. How that story would have pleased Rashid! I can see him now, with a grin of triumph, contemplating the kidnapped and supposedly brainwashed daughter of the newspaper billionaire William Randolph Hearst, with her finger on the trigger of the loaded gun, while middle-class America cowers and trembles on the bank's cold floor. (Rashid, with his slight Indian accent: "*Wery* subversive, man! Excellent!")

I could begin this story with Rashid's chilling threat to shoot me. But before that collision there was Jenadie, and without her I wouldn't have met him, so I'll start with her: nothing cold about Jenadie! She was always hot, like the flames in her bra-burning barrel.

"There never *was* any bra burning in the Sixties," my wife Laura objects to me the other day, "I heard this woman on the CBC, Cynthia Heimel. She says *one* woman may have burned *one* bra at the Atlantic City Miss Universe pageant, and that was it. The rest of the bra-burning stories are a fabrication of the male media."

"Oh yeah?" I said. "Maybe Cynthia Heimel is one of those Americans who think that history only happens in their country? She should talk to my friend Jenadie MacIlwaine."

How unexpectedly things change! After teaching high school for five years at home in Kenya, I came to Canada brimming with excitement, in September 1964, a couple of weeks ahead of my wife and kids, to begin graduate school at the University of British Columbia. I needed to get a masters degree to hold on to my teaching position, as the winds of change worked against white Kenyans.

I was stunned by the beauty of Vancouver and charmed by the novelty of it all: wood frame houses that felt live under your feet as you climbed a front step, not the solid, cool stone I was used to in Africa. The unfamiliar everything of Canadian speech and culture ("Look in the meer," "Would you like an awnge?"). I began to write poems, and walked everywhere, and took colour slides of the Fall maples on Main Mall, the UBC Rose Garden, the panoramic view across English Bay to the North Shore mountains, blue and inviting in the unpolluted air. I sent the slides home to my parents in Kenya so they could see what a spectacular place I was living in. After that flush of enthusiasm over the scenery, I began to immerse myself in cultural events. One day in 1966 I went with my fellow grad student, the poet Stephen Scobie, to listen to Leonard Cohen sing in the auditorium of the UBC Education building. Cohen wowed the standing-room crowd with his low-timbred, drawn-out singing of "Suzanne," "The Sisters of Mercy," and "Hey! That's No Way to Say Goodbye." Stephen stood in line with his copy of *Beautiful Losers*, and the great man signed it to him "with love." Just a bar of Cohen's music today, just one or two notes of that gravelly voice especially now singing "Allelulia," will take me back to those halcyon days at UBC in the mid-60s. They were so exciting!

My wife and two young sons arrived, and after a year in married student housing, we rented a house in leafy Kitsilano, and were happy. But by October 1967, that happiness collapsed. I was 29 years old and my marriage was over. A widening rift between Imogen and me had reached a crisis stage, ("You bastard!" she screamed as she hurled the heavy black phone across the kitchen at my head), and with my compliance she took our kids, and went back to Africa. I had no idea when I might see them again.

The bleakness that descended on me then was mirrored in the weather: Vancouver was drenched. It rained non-stop for forty days before the sky eventually cleared. One afternoon, just as it was getting dark, I was driving home from the campus in my old Austin A50, when I saw a tall blonde, in a red sweater and jeans, thumbing a ride at the bus stop outside University Pharmacy. I stopped. Hitch-hiking was a fearless way of getting around then.

"Thanks," she said, climbing in. "Look how clear and beautiful the North Shore mountains are above the city lights, after all this rain!"

We had one of those quick conversations in which you reveal yourself to a stranger you think you'll never meet again. In the minutes it took to drive to Tenth and Alma, I poured out the sorry story of my failed marriage, my pain at not seeing my children because they were in South Africa, and my financial mess.

"It's very difficult to be a graduate student and make support payments," I complained.

She laughed, showing long white teeth.

"At least you don't have all that marital fighting to get through every day now!" she said. "This'll do fine."

I wondered what she knew about marital fighting.

"I go down as far as Trafalgar," I said.

"Okay! Then I'll ride a few more blocks with you."

Suddenly, she swivelled in the bucket seat and confronted me: "So what do you think of John and Bobby Kennedy?"

"I don't pay much attention to American politics," I said.

"Politics has become global now," she corrected me bluntly. "I have to say I admire Bobby *a lot!*" (*"a laaht!"*) He's the only one with the intelligence and the political will to pull the U.S. out of Vietnam. It's a terrible tragedy that JFK got shot, and I don't know if Bobby has the political charisma to carry on his work. Right here."

I dropped her at Bayswater, and she thanked me for the ride and walked briskly down the wet lane. Gone from my life. Parking at my rented house near Kitsilano High School, I felt perked up. This chance encounter with a lively young woman had unburdened me. I forgot about my troubles for the moment and whistled as I cooked dinner in the empty house, while Bob Dylan wailed away in the background about the times changing, and doing whatever you think you should do. I was struck by the contrast between Dylan's songs of isolation and turning away from the world, and the hopeful willingness which my hitchhiker had shown to engage in public discourse—why, she was positively romantic! I felt the pull of both forces. Part of me wanted to curl up and lick my wounds and take care of myself while ignoring what was going on in the rest of the world. Another part still responded to the memory of JFK's cry, "Ask not what your country can do for you but what you can do for your country!" As a student of the English language, one of the things I could do for my country—for the world—was expose the lies that the American Press was manufacturing for home and Canadian consumption: there wasn't an American war going on in Vietnam, we were told every day, it was just American "military advisors" helping the Vietnamese preserve democracy. Like hell! Even the Kenyan papers had been telling the truth about that for months.

After dinner, I opened a beer and switched on the small Woodward's Transonic black and white TV, and by coincidence it was a program on the Kennedys' political lives. The American accents reminded me of my hitch-hiker.

A week later, I saw her again, hitch-hiking along by Saint Anselm's church. There was traffic behind me on University Boulevard, so I swung into the church parking lot and beeped my horn, and she ran up, cradling an armful of books.

"How *are* ya?" she asked, with the smile and warmth of an intimate friend.

"I'm fine. How are you?"

"In a total dilemma! I came out to Vancouver from the States, to get away from the man I lived with, and now he wants me to come back to him."

"Where is he?"

"Syracuse, New York. But only till the end of the semester. The U.S. is kicking him out, and I don't know where he's going next."

"Why are they kicking him out?"

"Rashid's from India. They're not renewing his student visa, and they don't have to give specific reasons for that. 'National Security.' His cousin's at Berkeley and the FBI's after *him*."

"Berkeley? So he's been demonstrating against the Vietnam war?"

"Think the U.S. can kick out all the people protesting the war? Wouldn't that leave the country pretty fuckin' empty! That's not why they're after him. Rashid's part of the radical movement in the States. It scares the shit out of the Establishment. And it excites the hell out of me! My family is moderate and liberal, but the radicals are more interesting and crucial. That's why I'm in such a dilemma." She laughed again, that sweet, energetic ripple, zinging out and resonating in me. Jenadie was always so full of life!

At Bayswater, she invited me in for a cup of coffee. It was one of those typical 1960s Kitsilano student apartments, a low-ceilinged bed-sitting room roughed in by amateur carpenters in the basement of a house, with a kitchen nook at one end and a half bathroom across the cement floor on the other side of the gas furnace. But it had windows above ground and more natural light than most.

"So what's your name?" She handed me a chipped mug of Maxwell House instant.

"Alistair Randall. And you?"

"Jenadie MacIlwaine. I've seen you having lunch in the Grad Centre."

"Oh. I didn't notice you."

"Men are not very observant."

"What kind of a damn stereotype is that!"

So began a steady current of friendship and argument. We not only lived within a few blocks but found that our offices at the university were adjoining, in those old wooden tar-paper Army huts behind the Education building that were supposed to be replaced by permanent buildings in the 50s but were still standing. I would finish my day's quota of studying for the Ph.D. comprehensives, or marking papers for my class of English 100 students, and walk by the Anthropology hut and stick my head in the door. They didn't hole up, those Social Science Teaching Assistants, in single monkish offices like we did in English. They took the bear pit approach to grad-student life, everybody in on the discussion, with cigarettes and coffee and yackety-yack. Often I'd have to lean in the door and wait for Jenadie to finish an argument when I came to pick her up: "Listen," she'd be saying, "Lyndon Johnson doesn't give a *shit* about the Vietnamese! Only reason the U.S. is over there in the first place is to protect oil interests."

"So you don't believe the domino theory?"

"*Oh come on!* You think when the North Vietnamese win we're going to have communist hordes crawling up English Bay and take over Canada? Give me a break! It's not about communism, people. It's about oil." She stared around, but nobody had an opinion to contradict her.

In the car, she dropped her political obsessions for a few minutes, like someone coming home. She would sit recovering from whatever excess of passion had driven her argument in the bear pit, as we moved down the road. Then, when we talked, it usually began with personal stuff, like brother and sister checking up on one another.

"Guess what?" she said one day, eyes alight, as she climbed into the car.

"Let me see," I said, letting my hands fall limp on the steering wheel and staring at the horn button. "You're getting back together with Rashid?"

"How did you *know* that?" she asked, leaning forward and peering into my eyes, incredulous. "I talked with him for two hours on the phone last night. I've decided. I'm going in December."

"Are you sure you're doing the right thing?"

"I don't *know*, Alistair, *I* don't know." Her voice twisted with indecision.

"Let's go out for dinner," I said. "I know a place on Commercial Drive. The guy cooks for you, and then he sings while you eat. It's fun."

"Okay!" she said, buzzing with excitement. "We'll go Dutch. But I need to wash and change. You can come in for a minute and turn your back."

At Orlando's, waiting for our pasta, Jenadie took a sip of Chianti and said, "The thing is, is that Rashid always wants me back, but when I'm with him he's always screwing around. I couldn't take it. That's why I came to Vancouver. It seemed as far away as I could get in North America and still go to grad school. Now he's chasing after me here. I should have gone to Alaska!"

"Maybe that's what men do. Chase after women."

"Yeah, but when they get them they're never content. They always have to have more. Why is that?"

"I don't know. Tommy Douglas said that men chasing after women is like dogs chasing after car tires: what do they do when they catch them?"

"Who's Tommy Douglas?"

"Leader of the New Democratic Party. The founder of Medicare in Canada."

"I don't know Canadian politicians."

"Oh, but 'politics is global now.'"

"Touché!" She laughed her irrepressible laugh, eyes sparkling with energy.

Orlando brought our fettuccini, and as we started to eat, he hung his guitar strap round his neck and began to sing.

"How do you know about places like this?" Jenadie asked. "You're so sophisticated, you English. I'm from Michigan. I grew up on a farm."

"I'm not sophisticated, nor is Orlando," I said. "It's movie music he's singing, Tchaikovsky's *Italian Song*. Sophistication, hell! That's just marketing."

"Don't be such a cynic, Alistair!"

"Oh, I do like the music."

"Me too."

On the way home, I told her, "It irritates me that you think I'm English, Jenadie."

"But you have an English accent."

"No. I come from Kenya. If anything, the English are our enemies. Britain betrayed us."

"You're a colonialist! A settler!"

"I'm a citizen of the Republic of Kenya," I said huffily. "My family has been in Africa probably as many centuries as yours has been in America. Now the wind of change is blowing up into a goddamn cyclone, and there are too few of us to withstand it. They could pack all the whites of Kenya into London overnight, and they wouldn't have to lay on an extra bus. The guarantees that were supposed to be there for us when the British negotiated independence have disappeared."

She was silent for a while, turned her head and looked out the window. I drove on through the slushy streets, wondering if I should point out her double "is" usage in the restaurant, "the thing is, is that," or just accept it as one of the inevitable degradations of the English language.

Suddenly, Jenadie swivelled in her seat and confronted me. It was a move I was beginning to get used to. "Listen," she said, "we're having a rally against Dow at noon tomorrow outside the library. You gonna come?"

"What's it for?"

"We're going to picket the Faculty of Engineering. Dow are coming in the afternoon to recruit graduating students and we're going to stop them."

"I have a pile of essays to mark," I said. "And it's been weeks since I did anything on my dissertation."

"Suit yourself." She sank back in the seat.

"Why would you want to block recruiters anyway? Seems stupid."

"Oh really?" She swung round, on the attack again. "Dow Chemical manufactures Saran Wrap, right? *Well isn't that so nice!* But they also make fucking napalm. How civilized is that? The sweet folks at Canadian Dow are this very minute concocting a barbaric mix of diesel and petroleum gel for the U.S. Air Force to go and drop on women and children in Vietnam. Do you know how napalm burns, Alistair? At 1,000 degrees Celsius, it consumes human flesh in seconds and turns living bones straight to charcoal."

That night, I lay in bed and thought, "If people don't stand up and be counted, what's freedom for? But I have the essays to mark, the dissertation. . . . I have problems enough. Besides, people need jobs and the whole idea of blocking recruiters from coming onto the campus seems just plain uncivil. But what about napalm? . . ."

I never did join the Dow pickets.

When the term ended, Jenadie phoned and asked if I could drive her to the airport. In the car, she reached into the glove compartment for something to write her address on and pulled out a crumpled piece of blue paper.

"What is *this*, Alistair Randall?" she said. "An unpaid parking ticket? Oh, I'm shocked!"

I smiled sheepishly.

"You don't mean to tell me our good little colonialist is beginning to resist authority? There may be hope for you yet!"

After she had checked in for her flight, she turned and hugged me.

"I'm going to miss you," I said. "I wonder if we'll ever meet again."

"Promise to write," she said.

"You promise to write!" I countered. "You'll be so taken up by your new life with Rashid, I won't even cross your mind."

"You get yourself a girlfriend, and stop being like that!" Jenadie said. "Of course I'll write!" Our eyes met, and the pact of friendship was sealed.

Standing on the observation deck, I watched her cross the tarmac and then climb up the stairway into her plane, a tall, proud woman with a firm stride. She stopped at the top, turned, and waved. I couldn't tell if she could see me, but I waved back.

In a few short weeks this accidental friendship with Jenadie had grown so important. We were a couple of lonely-hearts who had become supports for one another, instead of tumbling mindlessly into bed.

I drove home feeling empty again. I knew I had to do something over Christmas, but I had no desire to reach out to anyone, or be reached out to.

I had a dream that night of an actual trip I made with Imogen, soon after we got married: we drove in my little Morris Minor up to a farm at Kipkabus in the Uasin Gishu district of Kenya to visit old family friends, the Trails. ("Please *do* come!" Joy had said in her deep patrician voice, when I phoned to invite ourselves. "We would *love* to see you both!") We arrive at dusk in the chill highland air and a servant in a white *kanzu* takes our suitcases into the thatched Elizabethan stone house. Inside is dark wainscoting of African mahogany, and a creaky wooden staircase leads up to the guest bedroom with its dormer window. We eat dinner and retire, exhausted from the dusty journey over corrugated roads. In the morning I wake early and throw open the mullioned window, and stare out at Joy's extensive garden and the Kikuyu grass lawn sparkling with dew, and I remember my mother once telling me that it was Joy Trail's ambition to cultivate as many as possible of the plants listed in Jex-Blake's *Gardening in East Africa*, the Kenya settler's horticultural bible.

Ring-necked doves are crying their onomatopoeic Swahili name *ndu-tuu-ra! ndu-tuu-ra!* as the dawn breaks. Before breakfast, Joy guides Imogen under a bright pergola of Golden Shower climber to begin a guided tour of the garden. Alan beckons me with a single word "Come," to join him in the rattly farm Ford. He doesn't speak, as we drive around to the dairy, and the cattle food store and the farm blacksmith's shop, except to exchange Nandi greetings with the labourers. He stops on a little knoll and gets out, and I follow. He signals with his eyebrows for me to look at something. At first I cannot tell what Alan is showing me. Then he kicks the little mound of earth and rotted wood in front of us and says, "This is all that's left of the mud hut we lived in when Joy and I first came here in a donkey cart from Eldoret." Satisfied that I have seen what he wanted to show me, he smiles and climbs back into the car to drive up to the house for breakfast. What I understood is that Alan was showing me evidence of his life's work of building a flourishing farm.

Joy Trail had a cousin who lived in West Vancouver, and I was supposed to look him up when I came here. Call it envy or bitterness, but I had not done so. I wondered how long the Trails would survive on their Kipkabus farm. "We want you to stay and to farm well in this country!" President Jomo Kenyatta said to a meeting of white settler men and women, soon after his release from seven years in jail for his leadership of Mau Mau. "Continue to farm your land well and you will get all the encouragement and protection of the government." The crowd of settlers present, who had earlier called for Kenyatta's execution, now stood up and cheered after his remarks, shouting in unison the country's new motto, *Harambee!* (let's all pull together). But in the end it was a message that few whites believed.

After Jenadie left town I felt oppressed by my empty house. The daily conflict with Imogen was gone, but I missed my boys. I would lie on the sofa staring out at the huge yellowing leaves on the maple trees across the street and listening to the Beatles' *Sergeant Pepper's Lonely Hearts Club Band*. The music didn't make me any less lonely, but it paced the heart till I'd feel my energy returning, and I'd get in the car and drive to the university and work on my thesis. The black flip-top cardboard box I'd made to hold the index cards with my notes on the one hundred novels and twenty books of critical theory I'd had to master for my comprehensive exams remained my treasure chest of ideas, now that the pressure of the exams was over and I could slow down and think more creatively. I'd pull out a card and read the notes I'd written on it, and my mind would wander off on a search.

After the Comprehensives comes the thesis or dissertation, and that's what I was working on now. You have to make an "original contribution to knowledge" to get your Ph.D. and my contribution would have to do with the concept of "defamiliarization." I was going to try and show how certain modern novelists—William Faulkner particularly—were not just being obtuse when they chose to tell their tales using complicated and extraordinary styles. Because they weren't just telling a story; they were deliberately undermining our accustomed vision of the world and presenting a radically different way of seeing things. I knew I was onto a workable idea, but now I had to make it into a convincing argument. I was glad my office was tucked away in a remote part of the campus where I didn't meet people and could think and finish my degree. I had internal distractions enough to deal with—or ignore.

My eldest son's seventh birthday was coming up. I typed a little story to send to him, and by the time I finished I was in tears. I was not yet 30, and an emotional mess. The marriage of eight years was over and my wife had flown back to Kenya briefly, then gone off to South Africa to stay with her parents, taking our children with her. Everything was on hold. I would finish my Ph.D. and then go back to Kenya, and get a job at the University of Nairobi, and help to build the new country. As for the marriage, "consider your children," my father had written, and I wrote straight back to him that they were exactly who I was considering. No, there was no mending this marriage. I knew that from the day she threw the telephone at my head. I knew it for certain when she took the car one midnight and didn't return for several hours. Eventually, around 3 a.m. she arrived escorted by a gentle Vancouver city policeman with his hand on her arm, who delivered her quietly to the front door and explained that the car had spun a full 360 at the intersection of 16th and Blanca. "You folks should maybe think about getting some counselling," he said.

Counselling, hell! We had tried that, sitting patiently in the shrink's office, sometimes alone and sometimes together, while he sat there writing, writing, as though his carefully pencilled letters on the yellow pad could somehow bring order and balm to the mass of seething emotions that coursed through each of us like a civil war. Eventually he recommended separation. No, the very morning after Imogen's spin-out, as I walked up 16th Avenue past Lord Byng High School to retrieve the car, knowing the marriage was over, I thought that if it was going to happen, we might as well split up now while we were still young enough to start fresh lives, and not try staying together "for the sake of the children."

After Imogen and the children left for Africa, her father had written to my father to say, "apparently, they are not one another's cup of tea," and I felt grateful for his understanding, but it didn't bring consolation. Imogen and the kids were surviving physically in South Africa. We exchanged a couple of guarded letters in which divorce was mooted. And I tried to focus on my academic goal, to master all my sprawling research notes and thoughts, and make my "contribution to knowledge." One day my dissertation would be written, and bound, and placed in the UBC Library. And even though I suspected that the only people who would ever read it would be other Ph.D. candidates looking for ideas for their own dissertations, or else just checking my format to follow it, nevertheless, the process of creating it in solitude, and preparing to defend it publicly in front of a panel of examiners was a challenge that I was enjoying, and in which I was determined to succeed. When I had first talked to Dr. Robbins, then acting-Head of the English Department at UBC, about doing something on Lord Chesterfield's *Letters to His Son*, the old prof nodded his approval; but when my favourite young American mentor Lee Whitehead heard that, he scoffed in his polite Mormon manner and said, "No, man! Do something fresh and new. Look at that mind-blowing essay you wrote for me on Sartre and the American novelists! Do something that'll open a whole new window." So that was the task I had set myself: to pick three or four complex and visionary twentieth-century novelists, Patrick White, Faulkner, D.H. Lawrence, Virginia Woolf, Malcolm Lowry perhaps, and try to illuminate what they were doing, through defamiliarization theory.

There was a bright graduate student named Pam Green who had been recruited from England to become a candidate for the English Department's brand new Ph.D. programme. We were all somewhat intimidated by having this star brought amongst us, but one day at lunch in the grad centre, she told me she was leaving. "I thought it was going to be great here, but it's not. The UBC English Department is very pedestrian. Very, very pedestrian!"

Her words upset me, and I was determined that I was going to find brilliance at UBC, no matter how many "pedestrian" profs I had to avoid. Later, there was a rumour that Pam Green had had an unsatisfactory affair with the prof who recruited her, but I never knew what truth there was in that.

The end of my marriage wasn't the only emotional disturbance in my life. Every few days I'd receive another aerogram from my ailing father in Nairobi, with the 50-cent stamp showing the black, green, red and white colours of the proud new Kenyan flag. I didn't answer them. How do you explain marital break-up to a parent? I was not about to invent blame, and I didn't know how to comfort him. In any case, my marriage woes were a distraction from what was really worrying him: He had once been an idealistic believer in a great future for Africa—he spoke at a dinner once about creating a "United States of Africa"—but now he had been reduced to thinking there wasn't even any future for white people in Kenya. He had gone up there full of hope and energy straight from university in Cape Town in 1928, and helped to develop the vibrant and proud community of Eldoret. And in Nairobi, after the War, he worked hard to build a law firm and ended up as President of the Law Society of Kenya. Now it was all coming apart as the British hastened to divest themselves of their empire. "I always thought this country would see out my time," he complained, "but the British Government seems absolutely determined to abandon everything we've built up over the years."

One day, I was up at the campus working in the office when the sound of a key in my door startled me, and then it opened. A heavy-set man with thin hair stood there with a broom on the cold brown linoleum. He seemed as surprised as I was.

"Is *Chrees-mas!*" he said accusingly, in a mid-European accent, as I looked up from my desk. "Why you are here? You should be with family."

"Why are *you* here?" I countered, but after he'd gone I packed up and left.

In my head, the Beatles chirped merrily about loneliness and losing your hair. The last of the Fall colours had long departed from the trees, and the streets of Vancouver were mushy and cold.

Kind acquaintances phoned to invite me to join their Christmas dinner parties, but I lied that I had already made other arrangements. I fastened the elk horn buttons of my duffel coat and went walking on the cold, empty sands of Kitsilano Beach and got through the nights sipping beer in front of the TV. If things became too miserable, there was one steadfast pair of friends I knew I could always rely on, to go to and share my sorrows: Yudel Rabinovitch, a fellow graduate student, and his wife Helge. They were an incongruous couple, a small Jew married to a blonde German Mennonite whose people had been expelled from the Ukraine, and perhaps because of their histories they were deeply empathetic people, supportive and non-judgmental.

Back a few years when I'd first known him, Yudel had been rocked by three tragedies in a row: one was the suicide by poison of the sad husband of a fellow graduate student of ours, devastated by his wife's having an affair. Another was a suicide attempt by one of Yudel's friends who jumped off the Burrard Bridge and landed in the parking lot. He survived, but was left a paraplegic. And the third, the one that really shook everybody on the UBC campus, was the death of Kaspar Naegele. He was an innovative faculty member, a controversial dean and founder of the Arts One program. Something went wrong, and he ended up in the psych ward of the Vancouver General Hospital. Then one day the news came out that Kaspar had somehow fallen from a tenth-floor window at the hospital. Yudel and I sat through the sombre memorial service held on campus, and the collective tide of emotion was overwhelming but there was no explanation given about the death. As we left the building, Yudel began nodding slowly in his ironic way and said, "Yeah . . . yeah . . . some things can never be understood." People wrote letters to the paper and poems about the death of Kaspar Naegele, but it seemed to me that there was an odd tranquillity and guilty acceptance of the event, as though we all were somehow complicit in the crushing out of this creative spirit. It's a wound on the psyche of UBC which may have faded from memory but has never healed.

At any rate, I got through the Christmas break without having to go and cry on Yudel's and Helge's shoulders. Just knowing they were there for me was enough.

Then, one afternoon in the new year, the phone rang.

"Alistair, this is Jenadie. Guess what? I'm back in Vancouver, back at UBC! I'm sharing an apartment with a couple of other grad students. Marianne's in English. She knows you."

My heart began racing.

"Where are you, Jenadie?"

"We have this great place, the second floor of a house at Third and Trafalgar. Walk over and have supper with us. Marianne's making lasagna. Follow the path round the side of the house and pull the string hanging down from the upstairs window. That's our doorbell."

Her nasal twang sounded so American, so foreign, but by God I felt the power of family in that voice. I felt alive again. I wondered how things had gone with Rashid. I jotted down the street number, put on my coat and walked to the liquor store on Broadway. I stood in line for two bottles of Lindeman's Hearty Burgundy and arrived at Jenadie's new place in a few minutes.

It was a big, maroon-shingled, three-storey house on a corner lot. I found the string and pulled it and heard goat bells clatter up above. Jenadie met me at the front door with a bear hug. "Happy New Year, Alistair! Come on in."

Oh, that Marianne! She was in my Modern British Poetry seminar which met in the prof's living room in Dunbar, and every time I sat near her I would lose concentration on Yeats and Eliot and company. She was a tall, fleshy woman of twenty-five, a flute player with a scornful laugh and eyes of crystal that seemed to look right into my soul. A teenage rush came over me whenever her gaze brushed my face. She used to be dropped off at the seminar and picked up by a sandy-haired Geography student, and I had seen her kiss him on the cheek before getting out of the car. I assumed they lived together. Now she was Jenadie's new room-mate. I felt my heart beat.

"How was Syracuse?" I asked.

Jenadie's eyes fell immediately.

"Ask her about Buffalo!" Marianne teased.

"Stop it Marianne!" Jenadie protested, but with a look of collusion.

The third room-mate, Karen, was reserved and tranquil.

After supper, Marianne went into her room to study, and Karen played the piano quietly in the living room. I sat with Jenadie in the kitchen.

"So?" I asked. "What happened with Rashid?"

"Catastrophe. Don't want to talk about that, Alistair. I'll tell you some other time. He's so deeply involved with the radicals that he hardly even noticed me. I decided to come back and finish my degree. What have you been doing? How's your thesis?"

"Sprawling!" I said. "I'm having a struggle to keep my mind on literary criticism. There's too much crap going down in Kenya and my people are packing up and leaving the country. Also, I'm worried about my father's health. It's going to take me another year at least to pull the thesis together."

"Your father's old enough to worry about himself," Jenadie said. "It's you you should be thinking about."

We talked and finished the wine, and I went home around midnight feeling light and tingling. A dry snow was falling, and I whistled Beatles tunes as I walked down the muffled streets.

That night I had a recurrent dream, revisiting something that actually happened when I was fourteen: I am riding my bike past the Kiambu police station, several miles northeast of Nairobi. The security forces ambushed some Mau Mau in the forest the night before, and we heard the shooting. A barbed wire screening compound has been erected next to the police station, with dozens of Kikuyu men inside in ragged clothing, squatting on their bare heels, waiting to be interrogated by the police team. Suddenly I look down and see four dead bodies lying in the dust inside the compound, propped up against the barbed wire. They have not been cleaned up, and glistening flies buzz noisily at the bullet wounds. I have witnessed road accident victims before, but these are the most shocking corpses I have ever seen. I stand on the pedals of my bike and tear home as fast as I can, down the tarmac Kiambu-Muthaiga road, and in through the rows of coffee trees to our house, panting with shock.

I woke early next morning, filled with adrenaline and ready to do something about my future. I knew what my dream had told me: My future lay in Canada. I phoned the UBC English Department and got an appointment to see the Head. In his office, I explained that I needed more time to finish my thesis and I needed to earn enough money in the coming year to live and support my children.

He lit his long-stemmed Dunhill pipe and walked to the window, shading his eyes with his hand as he gazed out over the campus lawn.

"That shouldn't be a problem, Mr. Randall. I've read your file, and it's outstanding. I have no hesitation in offering you a sessional lectureship for one year. That pays six and a half. You'll teach three classes. Come and see me on the first of August, I'll tell you what they are."

"But Dr. Durrant, can one actually be a grad student and a sessional lecturer at the same time? I think I've read somewhere that the university has a rule about that."

He smiled. He was the new Head, also from Africa, an immigrant from Pietermaritzberg. "Not to worry," he said. "We can bend the rules a bit. Consider yourself hired."

I walked out of the Buchanan building floating on air. *Just like that!* I muttered softly. *Got a job teaching at the university, just like that!*

I imagined myself picking out several dark, expensive bottles of *fino* and *amontillado* sherry and inviting select groups of students to my place for literary conversations on Friday afternoons.

Back at the house, I found my landlord, Mr. Bennett, sitting on the front porch. He liked to come round each month to chat while he collected the rent.

"Still haven't had a haircut, Alistair? Where's your family these days? I don't see them around."

"Gone," I said. "They're in South Africa. The marriage is over I'm afraid."

"Oh dearie me, that's too bad! It's very hard on the children."

"I know Mr. Bennett, but we tried to fix it and we couldn't."

I braced myself for criticism. I had had that already in letters from Kenya: "Divorce is only a sticking plaster....," "It seems to me when a man's made his bed he ought to lie in it...." But Mr. Bennett just looked at me with kind Canadian eyes.

"You know," he said, "people can survive some pretty difficult things. During the Great Depression there was only one source of hope for me, boy, and that was the fish. I rode the rails out here, and there was nothing doing, except briefly in 1936 when Mayor Gerry McGeer floated the Baby Bond and put men to work building the new City Hall on Cambie, and the fountain at Lost Lagoon. Otherwise, nothing. You'd knock on doors and offer to chop wood or scour the pots in exchange for a bowl of soup, and that way you kept alive—barely. But one thing there was was the fish, eh? Some days you could walk across English Bay on the backs of the salmon! I managed to get hold of a rowboat, fourteen-foot clinker-built, and I spent a whole year rowing right around Vancouver Island with thirty-pound test lines tied to rubber strike bands on my knees. I caught salmon, and I'd row over to a packer vessel and they'd pay me two cents a pound. That's how I got through my Depression, son. You'll get through yours."

"Come in, Mr. Bennett," I said. "I'll write you a cheque."

He came into the living room and halted abruptly. "Cripes!" he cried. "What's this?"

"A new painting by a friend of mine," I said.

"It shouldn't be on display," he said, "or at least he should have painted it draped." He pointed to the crotch.

"You don't see the beauty of that body?"

He leaned forward with an urgent whisper: "What I see is some tart putting her twat up for any fellow with a hot prick!"

I laughed. He was an amateur painter himself, and we often had brief conversations about art and literature. I enjoyed the monthly visits when he would tease me for my beard and shoulder-length hair.

"Well, at least I got a job for the coming year, Mr. Bennett," I said. "Sessional lecturer at the university."

"There you go, boy! See now? Good for you."

After he left I studied Mark Vance's nude on my wall. Imogen had encouraged Mark to display his work, and she even took his drawings to a frame shop on Tenth Avenue and got them ready for a show. No show had yet materialized, and now Imogen was gone back to Africa, but that heavy, warm nude figure on my wall, with the head turned aside, faceless, gave me an odd sort of comfort: she represented the presence of the female, my mother, Africa, Imogen herself, all gone from me now, but the female power somehow internalized. I was surprised to realize that I was feeling full of hope.

3

For a few days I worked away undisturbed, reading and trying to get ideas to coalesce for my thesis, and then Jenadie phoned to invite me to a party. When I got there, the first person I saw was Marianne's sandy-haired geographer. I felt a hollow twinge at his presence. But I stuck out my hand and he shook it.

"Hi, I'm Alistair."

"The famous Alistair from Kenya," he said, with what might have been a sneer. "My name's Mac."

"Mac joined us on the Dow picket line," said Jenadie, "and he's a fucking Liberal!"

"Oh yeah? Do I wear a label?"

Mac and Jenadie moved off, arguing, to the kitchen. I took my six pack of Toby Ale into the kitchen, opened one and put the rest in the fridge. When I turned around, I was face to face with Marianne, my heart fluttering.

"I'm glad you were able to come," she said. "It's nice to have some human beings here among all these flaming radicals."

"Radicals?"

"Didn't Jenadie tell you? This isn't just a party, Alistair. She's recruiting people for kaywo."

"Kaywo?" It sounded like Tupperware, but I suspected something more weighty.

"I guess she *didn't* tell you. Watch out! She's already got me committed to the anti-war rally next week."

Jenadie came and grabbed me by the sleeve. "There are some people I want you to meet," she said, pulling me through to the living room.

"Paul, this is Alistair."

The short, freckled man wearing a sports jacket squeezed my hand and practically barked at me, "How do you do, sir!" His accent was American. He was in his twenties but had deep furrows in his brow, like a very old man.

What's going on here? I wondered. This guy was hopping with nervousness.

"And this is Viviana," said Jenadie.

The tiny, dark-skinned Mexican woman smiled, showing perfect teeth. "I'm very pleased to meet you," she said in a formal monotone. Jenadie smiled and moved off elsewhere.

"Where have you guys come from?" I asked

Paul's eyes shifted quickly.

"California," he said. "We're draft-dodgers—I am. My wife is not an American citizen. We're really grateful to the Committee."

Committee? Then I understood: "Kaywo." CAAWO. The Committee to Aid American War Objectors.

"Where are you staying?"

Again, his eyes shifted. "We're sleeping in our V-volkswagen at the moment. But we have some possibilities."

"Well look," I said on impulse, "My house—I'm living on my own right now, and I have a couple of spare rooms. Want to take a look at it?"

"That's extremely kind of you, sir," Paul said.

"Paul! Stop calling me 'sir,' would you? Want to come by tomorrow afternoon about two?"

"We can be very grateful," Viviana chipped in with a smile.

In another room, I heard voices rising in volume against one another, culminating in an accusatory shout about "yellow-bellied runaways," and then the sounds of scuffling. Evidently someone had come to the wrong party, and Jenadie pressed through to the conflict. Pretty soon, quiet returned, but a residual tension was in the air and I decided to go.

As I was leaving, I told Jenadie that Paul and Viviana were going to look at my place, and she said, "Good! I was hoping you would do that." Then she turned away with a slight frown. "Alistair, you're not to let them stay more than four days."

"Four days?"

"They have to keep moving till they find jobs and become independent. They can't just settle down and get comfortable. That's the Committee's policy."

"That's brutal," I said.

"Yes, but it makes sense, Alistair."

That night, I lay in the upstairs bedroom, listening to the silence of the house. Soon there would be people here again.

Promptly at two next afternoon, an old dark green Beetle pulled up in front of the house. Oh dear! "Sleeping in our Volkswagen." I had envisaged a Kombi van.

"The two of you can sleep in that little bug?"

Viviana grinned. "We are both very short."

"Come on in."

I showed them around. There was a chair in the living room, and an old two-piece sectional sofa I had picked up at Klassen's secondhand store on Broadway for $18. The dark-stained fir floors were bare of rugs, and in the kitchen there was a mix of ancient pots and pans from the Salvation Army. The bedrooms had beds but nothing much besides. "This is it," I said apologetically, as they came down the staircase back into the kitchen.

"It's great," said Paul.

Viviana was quite excited. She reached beside the stove and grabbed the broom. "Is very useful to have a woman in the house!" she said, smiling broadly, and made a couple of sweeping motions.

"Where's your stuff?" I asked.

"In the car," Paul said.

I went out to help them carry it in. With the three of us, it took only one trip.

―――

My new house mates occupied me, and I didn't think about Jenadie, but a couple of days later, there she was, on the front page of the *Province* standing tall in a loose shirt on the back of a flatbed truck. The headline read, "WOMEN BURN BRAS!" and the woman beside Jenadie was holding a flaming bra over a smoky barrel. I read the story.

"'The bra as it now exists is a symbol of men's oppression of women's bodies,' says Miss Jenadie MacIlwaine, speaking for a group calling itself BRASH. 'The name expresses our goal,' Miss MacIlwaine said, 'to turn these bras to ash.'

"Asked if most women wouldn't prefer to wear their bras rather than burn them, Miss MacIlwaine said, 'Women should have freedom of choice about that. Underwear should feel good to wear rather than be sexually enticing. For years, the so-called foundation garment industry has been squeezing women's bodies into shapes for men to gawk at. Women should be designing bras for women's comfort, not for men's eyes.'" The police had issued a traffic ticket to the driver. He had pulled the truck across the intersection of Georgia and Burrard and then hidden the keys. A tow-truck removed the flatbed, and once the roads were clear again the police left without making arrests. I dialled Jenadie's number. It was busy, so I walked over to her place and jangled the goat bells.

"Congratulations!" I said. "That was a hell of a stunt. And I actually agree with you."

"So you don't come out for napalm, but you come out for bras! Alistair, you're such a hypocrite!" she teased, but with a hard glint in her eye.

"No, seriously," I said, "it's always struck me as a ludicrous tease, those cones on Jayne Mansfield and Marilyn Monroe with their tight sweaters. I grew up with bare-breasted African women all around. It seemed natural. It wasn't until it dawned on me that the women of other races covered themselves that I began to think of breasts as sexual. When I first went to England, in the Underground elevator at Russell Square station, there was this life-size poster of a woman wrapped in a Zorban towel, and you could see the guys in the elevator sneaking glances at her cleavage. I thought. 'This is obscene. Using breasts to sell towels.'"

"What a naïve upbringing you had. But all right Alistair! Your consciousness is rising."

"How come you got a *guy* to drive the truck?"

"Bob was the only one we knew with a truck licence. We don't *disapprove* of men, you know. Just male chauvinists."

Back home after supper that night, we watched the TV news and saw Jenadie again.

Paul said, "I guess we'd better be moving on."

"How come?"

"The four days are up."

"What four days?"

"The Committee—"

"Who are they to tell us what to do? You want to stay here, you stay as long as you like. I'm happy to have the company. Not to mention the refried beans."

Viviana grinned broadly. In the four days, I had not seen her touch the broom again, but she had certainly cooked. It was a strangely unnerving thing for me to have them in the house: fugitives from the tentacles of American military justice. I wondered what my scrupulous lawyer father would think of me harbouring law-breakers. Another part of me didn't care. The delightfully unaccustomed sound of Spanish, and the warmth and innocence of my new house mates, had livened up my solitude. From time to time, especially when there was wine, Paul and Viviana would break into childlike song *("Estabamos cortando rabanos, unos cortabamos, otros cantabamos . . .")* and I began Spanish lessons that way

"We really appreciate being able to stay here," said Paul. "I'm sure I'll land a job soon."

"Take your time, man. Sergeant Pepper's not so lonely anymore."

4

Jenadie came to dinner the following week. She stopped in the doorway, looking at Paul and Viviana.

"You know the Committee only allows—"

"Fuck the Committee!" I said.

She widened her mouth and eyes in mock horror. "My, my!"

I poured her a glass of wine. "You still haven't told me what happened with you and Rashid," I said.

"What's to tell?" she said. "Same old story, and an agony of indecision. The more I fend him off, the more he chases after me. He's on his way here."

"Now?"

"He's driving right across the goddam continent from Syracuse to come and convince me to go back to him. He's supposed to arrive later tonight. He'll probably phone when he gets in."

"Then I'll get to meet him finally!"

"I doubt it. He's too jealous."

"Of me? Why?"

"Men are very possessive. Any male friend of mine is a potential threat to him."

"Jenadie, enough with these potted generalizations about men! We guys are getting a bit sensitive about stereotyping women, but you march right on with yours: 'Men are not very observant'; 'Men are very possessive.' I understand you told Marianne the other day to watch out for me because 'Divorced men are clingy.'"

"All absolutely true!" Jenadie replied, with a taunting laugh. "Can't men deal with the truth?"

Paul said nothing, but I noticed Viviana was nodding brightly.

During dinner, I listened while Jenadie and Paul talked about the Vietnam War and what else we in Canada might be able to do to assist the draft-dodgers. Then the phone rang, and when I answered a quiet, formal, East Indian voice asked, "Hello, is this Alistair?"

"Yes, is this Rashid?"

"Yes. I believe Jenadie is visiting with you. May I please speak to her?"

"Why don't you come over and join us?"

"Thank you, but I'm rather tired," he said. "Could I speak with her?"

I handed her the phone, feeling uneasy at his icy manner.

Jenadie talked to him briefly and then said she had to go. I offered to drive her, but she said she'd rather walk. At the front door, she rested her forehead on my shoulder for a moment.

"Wish me luck, brother," she said. "I have a feeling things are either going to be fantastically happy or horribly sad."

"Either is better than lukewarm," I said.

After she left, Paul said, "I don't get where Jenadie's coming from, you know? I don't mean her clichés about men–she's just razzing us there–but about society, you know? She's not a Marxist. Where does she get her progressive ideas?"

"Her parents have a social conscience," I said. "They live on the family farm down in Michigan, and her father is an executive with the Ford Motor company. But they believe in helping less fortunate people. They have a section of the farm laid out for inner city people to use for vegetable gardens."

Jenadie's departure left an absence in the evening. Her energy was a catalyst, and without it we were quieter. Viviana tidied the kitchen and went off to bed. Paul and I did the dishes and then sat at the kitchen table, and I opened the last bottle of wine.

"How did you get drafted, Paul?" I asked. "If you feel like talking about that."

"It was bizarre," he said. "I get the interview summons, right? It says bring your draft card to this address in L.A., and I come there paranoid, thinking they'll arrest me."

"Why would they arrest you?"

"They give us all a form to fill out, and the last question says, 'Any Other Relevant Information?' so I write down, 'I am a practicing Marxist-Leninist,' and I hand it in.

"Half an hour later, they call my name. By that time I'm just baked man, shaking. I go in there and the guy gestures to a chair. I sit down, waiting for cops to come in and cuff me while the guy reads my file. You know what he says? He says, 'Take this voucher to the Washington Hotel, Mr. Bowles. They'll give you a room for the night. Please be here at ten o'clock tomorrow morning for your interview?' *Shit!* I write on their form that I'm a communist, so they give me a bed for the night at the George Washington Hotel!"

"What happened at the interview?"

Paul tried to laugh, but no voice came out. He shook his head from side to side, taking sharp, short breaths like silent laughs, dismissing my question. "No interview, man! I went back to my mom's apartment, and I said, 'Viviana, let's clear out of the country fast!'

"She said, 'Mexico?'

"I said, 'FBI are all over Mexico. At least in Canada we might stand a chance.'"

"'Bowles.' Is that your real name?" I asked.

"What do you mean?"

"Paul Bowles is an American Beat artist who lives in Morocco. I thought you might have adopted it as an alias."

"Of course it's my real name." He looked slightly offended.

The phone rang. It was midnight. I picked up and a young male voice apologised for the late hour and asked to speak with Paul Bowles.

I handed Paul the phone and went to the bathroom. I heard him exclaiming, and when I came back he cried, "You're not going to *believe this* man! My induction papers have just arrived at my mom's apartment in California. They've drafted me into the fucking Marine Corps!" There was a naked look of fear on his face which reminded me of poor whites I had met while visiting my uncle in Southern Rhodesia, with no family, little to fall back on.

"Is that so unusual?"

"Oh, man, the Marines are the military's cream of the cream. They take one in fifty from volunteers who wait in line to get in. And they've *drafted* me into the Corps, knowing I'm a communist! It's a death sentence. Talk about a sick joke!" He shook his head again from side to side, drawing in little breaths. His freckled face was pale with anxiety, the deep furrows fixed in his brow.

"Looks like you did the right thing, coming up to Canada."

"No kidding! I'm wanted now. They'll be looking for me."

"Who was it that phoned?"

"My buddy Lawrence. Didn't you meet him at Jenadie's CAAWO party?"

"No. Is he a draft dodger too?"

"Yeah—well, no: he actually deserted. He was inducted already, and he decided to go AWOL. He took his dad's Cadillac, because he thought it would be easier getting across the border if he looked like he had money."

"He stole his own father's car?"

"His dad's cool. He's going to phone him tomorrow collect from here, if that's okay with you."

So, next morning after breakfast I met Lawrence, a tall, clear-skinned youth with a suave manner, who looked athletic though he chain smoked 100-millimetre Belvederes. While he called his father from the kitchen, Paul and Viviana and I went to the living room and shut the door. But his voice became agitated and we couldn't help overhearing. His father had found him a lawyer who promised to get him off the charges.

"You're not listening to me, Dad! Don't you get that this is something I *have* to do?" Lawrence shouted. "The United States of America is not my country anymore. I don't agree with what they're doing in Vietnam. I've made my choice."

In silence, the three of us stared at the bare floor while in the kitchen Lawrence listened to the phone.

Then he shouted, interrupting his father: "Dad! Dad! I love you and Mom! But I don't *want* to come back. I'm not an American anymore, Dad. Don't you get it? I'll never enter the States again in my life. I've torn up my citizenship, abandoned it! I've turned my back on the U S of A."

When he came into the living room, lighting a fresh cigarette with shaky hands, Lawrence was smiling bravely. He had a more confident and sophisticated Californian manner than Paul, but I didn't entirely trust him. "I think the line was tapped," he said. "There were clicks. I'm sorry about that. We should have used a phone booth."

He exhaled a huge cloud of smoke. "Mister R," he said to me, "would you mind if I borrow your daily paper?"

I left them poring through the Help Wanted columns of the Vancouver *Daily Province* and drove up to the university. I wondered if the FBI would be tapping my phone from now on. I wondered what Jenadie had decided to do.

In my windowless office, it was difficult to concentrate on Viktor Shklovsky's theory of defamiliarization, but I forced myself: *"The business of the artist is to record the sensation of things as they are perceived and not as they are known."* It was a brilliant idea, so simple and yet so revolutionary. I thought of the Expressionist painters opening their eyes for the first time back in the early part of the century. *The cow is black and white? The grass is green? No! That particular cow is flecked with orange. That stretch of grass is full of purple streaks.* "To record the sensation of things as they are perceived and not as they are known" –that's what D.H. Lawrence was doing writing about the plumed serpent, and the escaped cock, celebrating the erotic body. That's what Faulkner was doing with Southern history, sitting in the back of a railcar, as Sartre said, watching the blind future turn into a conflicted and visible past for people who imagined themselves to be free, and scrawling it out in complicated sentences that sometimes ran on for pages. And Patrick White, with his truncated syntax and satirical phonetics, skewering Australia in ways I didn't yet comprehend, in his fictional Sydney suburb of "Barranugli." When I got back to the house that afternoon, I found Paul, Viviana and Lawrence, still sitting round the kitchen table, drinking tea. Three pairs of eyes looked up at me in a nervous silence.

"Jenadie came by," said Paul. "She returned two of your books. She's gone back East with Rashid."

"She's up and left already?"

"Yup."

I was shocked—no, alarmed would be a better word: since losing my marriage and, increasingly it appeared, my country, I had developed a kind of shockproof, stoic shell about events unless they were immediate threats to my safety. I was alarmed for Jenadie because she was making the same damn mistake again, reversing her course on an impulsive decision. She had done it in December and here she was a few months later doing it again. As her friend, I had a duty to speak my mind, like she did so readily for me.

I dialled. Her roommate Karen answered and said that Jenadie had already left town but Marianne was here, did I wish to speak to Marianne? "No, thanks," I said and ended the call ("Divorced men are clingy"? Huh!)

"I better get going," said Lawrence and left.

I took a shower.

"Paul, Viviana," I called, and they emerged from their bedroom, looking anxious as though they were about to be evicted. "Let's go out for dinner."

We went to Orlando's, and Viviana loved it. She sang along with Orlando, and he glanced over and smiled at her. Then he came over to our table, switched from Italian and sang a Spanish song for her. She got up and danced to it, her little dark figure whirling around like a gypsy, and her heels smacking the floor. Paul smiled affectionately as he watched her, his frown-lined head bobbing up and down to the music. For a few moments the turmoil of war was forgotten. Our insecurities were somewhere else, and we were insulated here in Orlando's warm and friendly *cantina* on Commercial Drive, eating and drinking and dancing like happy peasants.

"We must to do that again!" Viviana said emphatically, on the way home. "We do that on Friday nights, singing, wine and food!"

"Yo soy un hombre sin-cer-o," Paul sang softly from the back seat, *"de donde crecen la palma...."*

Later that week, I came home from the campus, and as I parked Paul burst out to meet me on the porch. It was a moment of such emotion I will never forget it—the light in his face: even his ancient forehead creases seemed to have unfolded.

"We've found jobs, man! All three of us. Viviana's hired as a manicurist at a hairdresser's downtown, and Lawrence and I are counsellors at Brown Camps for emotionally disturbed children."

"Well, well!" I said. "Let's go celebrate!"

Paul's look was hesitant. "It's not quite a done deal," he said. "First we have to get letters confirming that these employers will hire us, and then we have to go down and cross the border, and enter Canada again."

I stared at him, nonplussed. "You mean to tell me you're proposing to go back down into the United States? Where there are federal warrants out for your arrest? You're out of your frigging tree, man!"

"I think it'll be all right," he said. "The Committee will help us. Their people will keep watch and tell us when the barriers are down in the Peace Arch Park. Then we go down and cross through the Canadian side, hang a U-turn in the park, and then come back and re-enter Canada."

"What if the barriers are not down?"

"We have a picnic in the park and wait till they go down."

"What if you cross and then find the barriers are up and they stay up?"

Paul considered for a moment. "I guess in that case we'd abandon the car in the park and walk back across the grass through the Canadian entrance."

They phoned the Committee, and the Committee phoned them back. Then one morning they climbed into Lawrence's father's conspicuous gold Cadillac with the yellow on blue California plates to go to the border.

"Phone me the moment you're through," I said. "Stop and phone me from White Rock."

All morning I waited, and no call came. I had visions of them being gunned down by the FBI in the Peace Arch Park. Shortly after noon I heard a car tire nudging the curb and went to the window and saw the Cadillac.

We held the party down, because Paul was to begin his first shift that night at the Brown Camp. But over a modest bottle of champagne, the four of us sat around the kitchen table while Lawrence excitedly retold how the Canadian immigration officer had made a mistake in his calculation.

"'You don't have enough immigration points,' he says to me. 'You only have forty five points.' And I think *'FU-UUCK! Now what?'* And then he says, 'Oh, I forgot your ten points for High School graduation. Fifty five. No, you're fine, sir. Sorry about that.' And I could've fuckin' kissed him, man!"

That Sunday night, I took the three of them out for dinner, and we were buzzing with excitement. Orlando played *"Guantanamera"* and we all sang with gusto. A pair of tall guys in sharp grey suits and Cuban heels came in, and Viviana, seeing them, cried excitedly, "Look, Paul! Latin men!" She went over and danced with them, showing the vitality of a whole new life beginning. It was late by the time we got home, and Viviana was over the top drunk. She stepped out of the car and her heel gave way, tumbling her onto the lawn where she lay groaning. Paul was miffed at her for getting so drunk and wouldn't help, so I carried her in, light as a child. What a day! The buildup of anxiety finally over. Landed immigrants! I didn't blame Viviana for getting drunk. I wished I had achieved such security for myself.

Next morning, after Paul had left for an early morning shift, Viviana came and knocked urgently on my bedroom door. "Alistair, please, can you drive me to work? I'm so late."

As I drove her downtown to The Vikings hairdressing salon on Seymour, she leaned forward and towelled her hair. "I had to wash," she said. "Paul is mad with me! I got drunk last night, *señor!*"

"I know you did."

"But I was *so* very drunk! I threw out."

"You threw up?"

"On my hair. I had to wash." She gave me a little guilty smile, innocent and charming.

That night, I said, "Listen Paul and Viviana, why don't you guys stop looking for a place of your own? I want you to stay in my house, okay? *Nosotros son un familia.*"

"We can split the rent three ways," Paul said.

"When you get paycheques, we can talk about splitting the rent."

Viviana grinned, and one could see the Indian bone structure in her face. "You are very kind, *señor! Muy simpatico.* You are my brother, *hermanito!*"

"*Hermanita!*" I replied, and she hugged me and Paul together and kissed my cheek.

Things settled into a routine for a while. Lawrence would show up most days, ostensibly to read my paper, but I knew it was more than that. Paul and Viviana took turns cooking, hamburger and refried beans every night, and I got on with teaching and managed to finish a draft chapter of my dissertation.

Paul's job at the Brown Camp for disturbed children was an emotional disturbance in itself. That's why the draft dodgers were able to get work there—nobody else would do it. They paid him $200 a month, and out of that he had to pay $40 for mandatory staff group therapy sessions. It was a relief for him to get away from therapy and breaking up teenage masturbation parties, back into the world of ideas. For me, he was a political curiosity: he was the first communist I had ever known personally, and the first white man I ever met who referred optimistically to the Mau Mau in Kenya as "freedom fighters" and "cadres" instead of "terrorists." I listened to him uneasily, but we didn't clash. There's a line in the Bible that has always resonated with me: "Be not forgetful to entertain strangers; for thereby some have entertained angels unawares." I never thought of Paul and Viviana as angels—especially when he told me about how the Mexican *putas* used to soap and wash his genitals before getting down to business—but I was certainly glad to have them stay with me for a while. We three had the security of one another, and my Spanish vocabulary grew steadily. To this day, whenever I hear a snatch of Spanish sung or spoken, Paul and Viviana come immediately to mind. *Mi familia, mi compañeros!*

With his first paycheque, Paul went down to the Army and Navy store on Hastings and bought fishing gear, and a little inflatable boat for $19.99. He borrowed my Austin and took Viviana up to Cheakamus Lake, near Whistler, where he had heard there was good fishing. They had to hike in from the end of the road a few kilometres to the lake but they caught so many rainbow trout that they decided to deflate the boat and hide it underground, and come again when next they had an opportunity. A week later they were back at the lake, digging out the boat, when a black bear stepped through the trees and confronted them.

"Alistair," Paul recounted, "Nature just took over, man, real raw! You've read that book *The Territorial Imperative*, about apes barking? I barked, man! It was reflex. My shoulders went down till my fingers were touching the ground, and a sound came out of me like I've never heard from any animal, wild or tame. I blasted that sucker so loud he turned tail and fled. When we got to the lake, there were a couple young guys camping in the lean-to shelter, and I asked them, 'Did you see a bear?' They said, 'A black bear came running through here at ninety miles an hour! What did you do to him?'"

As Paul told the story, Viviana was holding his hand and stroking his arm. Her hero, all five foot six of him, a little guy with creased and freckled face, whose chain-smoking father had died in Paul's infancy of emphysema, leaving him alone to care for his mother and battle the world. Listening to the story, I felt a witness's bond with him. He had encountered death and survived it—no, chased it away—and through his telling I had participated in his existential moment. *"And all shall be well,"* the mantra played in my mind, *"all manner of thing shall be well."*

"Where were you in this?" I asked Viviana. "Did you bark too?"

She grinned her Inca grin at me, and the light gleamed on her dark pupils.

"I was there," she said. "I di' not make any noise."

~~~

A postcard arrived from England, the Bodleian Library at Oxford. Jenadie was there with Rashid. He had won a post-doctoral research fellowship. Then came a second missive from Oxford, a desperate aerogram: life with Rashid was absolute hell, a living divorce. The separation the year before had destroyed their trust in one another. *"I want to get out now but can't,"* she wrote. *"Alistair, I can't imagine living without him. In so many ways we make a beautiful couple. You know, it's that I don't have the courage to jump headfirst anymore. Remember I told you I would be fantastically happy or horribly sad with him and I was willing to take the chance? I don't dare anymore."*

What did that mean? Was she planning to stick with him or break away? I couldn't interpret it. I wrote back: "Hang in there sister, and listen to your heart. There'll always be a place for you to crash in my house."

After I had walked down to mail the letter and come back to the empty house—Paul and Viviana were away at work—I felt the twinge of solitude again and phoned Marianne. "The number you have dialled is not in service," said the harsh, mechanical voice. So even that temporary household had disintegrated with Jenadie's departure.

Next day, I got a letter from my father. There were age squiggles in his handwriting:

My Dear Boy,
It is becoming increasingly clear that there is little future for us in Kenya. Rory Mitford-Barberton, who was born in Kitale and has worked in the Kenya Police for ten years and took out citizenship, applied for a senior police position which was advertised for "Kenya Citizens." He didn't get it. It went to a 'Mkamba fellow with no police experience. When Rory pressed them to find out why, they eventually told him the job was only for "Kenya citizens of African origin." In other words, black. "African origin," in your case over the past few centuries doesn't

count. Your Kenya citizenship will mean nothing. It goes by skin colour.

Perhaps you have a future in Canada—who knows? But for us, it is time to leave Kenya with heavy hearts. Britain has been duplicitous, not the good people of Great Britain, but the Colonial Office and especially the Labour Party. There were supposed to be some minimal guarantees for us after Independence, but there is sweet blow-all. They're washing their hands, and those of us who were induced to come and settle here and put our lives into building a country have been sold out with a frozen smile. I've decided to move back South, where there is some hope of a future for us. As for you my boy, apart from your domestic troubles, I can only advise you to look most attentively to the future and choose your path with the greatest possible care.

I wish I could feel better about all this, but I don't. Sixty years of fine development work and administration in this country is going overboard. And the damn fool socialists in Britain think the blacks are going to step in and just pick up the reins and keep the thing we built rolling along happily without us. Well they've got another think coming! I'm afraid we are going to see chaos and corruption as the African continent reverts to darkness, all in the name of "freedom." What a pity! What a damned shame.

I must say I am very tired of it all.

And what are you doing with your life, Alistair? Everything I've worked for all my life you seem to be throwing away. It boggles my mind. I have no way of understanding it.

love,
Father.

P.S. I am sending under separate cover a book by Arthur Culwick whom I know slightly. He's worked in government for years in Tanganyika and wrote an important anthropology textbook with his wife. Pay particular attention to the picture he paints of a future Kenya under African rule. Perhaps you could apply for immigration to South Africa?

P.P.S. Alan Trail died on Wednesday. He and Joy were down staying at the Nairobi Club, and he had a heart attack and went in minutes. He thought he had indigestion, but it was heart. Joy is packing up the farm to sell for whatever she can get and heading South.

While I read my father's letter, Bob Dylan was croaking away on the record player about a hard rain going to fall, and then he picked up the melody on harmonica, like a thin siren. When I finished reading, I decided I wanted to get back to playing harmonica myself, like I used to as a teenager, and I went down to Woodward's and bought myself a little G sharp Hohner. I was sitting on the sofa finding the notes for "Hard Rain" when Paul and Viviana arrived home from work. At the sound of the music, Paul froze in the doorway. He had a fugitive's intuition.

"Something wrong?" he asked.

"No," I said. "I've decided to apply for landed-immigrant status."

"Good!" said Viviana. "We take you to Orlando's!"

"Not yet," I said. "When I get my status. If I ever get it."

Soon afterwards, the book arrived from Father, and I read it dutifully. It was titled *Britannia Waives the Rules* and had gone through nine private printings in Rhodesia in sixteen months. You could feel the author's hot-headedness all right. He had been an administrator in various East African colonies and predicted catastrophe following the granting of independence. He accused the British politicians of being ostriches with their heads in the sand, bent on appeasing the Afro-Asian bloc. He said he was writing for those betrayed by British policy in Africa: "the farmers and their wives in isolated homesteads, the businessmen and typists in the towns—in short, those among whom I live and call my friends, and whose interests my colleagues and I have tried to protect—ineffectually, I fear—those who will now have to carry the can, the ones who will be robbed, beaten, raped, murdered if the balloon goes up."

I put down his thin, raging text and thought of my black students back in Kenya who were already becoming the new leaders. I knew their optimism and gentle good manners and shook my head at the disparity between Culwick's vision and my own experience. Their names came cascading into my memory: Elijah arap Soi, head of Livingstone House, who advised me how to succeed as an Assistant Housemaster by always keeping a little formal distance from the boys, James Mageria, a brick of a guy who later joined the Kenya Police, Joseph Muturi, my Sir Toby Belch and Falstaff in the plays, James Gatanyu, another of my Shakespearean actors who gladly took on female roles despite the ribbing he got for it, Kibiebei arap Ng'eny, Head of Francis House who would later become Speaker of the Kenya Parliament, whose father walked barefoot ahead of me down a path from his hut in Nandi-land to show me the cliff where he "threw his enemies over," as his son translated for me; Samuel Mwaura who won an overseas scholarship and was studying now in Ottawa, Shem Oduor, the super-intelligent School Captain who yawned unabashedly and fell asleep in the front row in my General Paper class, Wilson Ngoka who sat patiently in the dust for seven hours awaiting my visit to his family in Ukambani when I had to detour because the road was washed out, and who, for a prank, got about forty village children to line up by height and shake my hand, pretending they were his siblings (and now, as I write, Dr. Ngoka is a prominent Nairobi gynecologist). Job Watene, my careful library assistant who stayed on at the school for one whole vacation to help me reclassify all the books on the Dewey Decimal system; wise *mzee* (old man) Sitswila Amos Wako who was determined to become a lawyer and later joined my father's old firm and is today the Attorney General of Kenya, Ali Mude Dae Mude who became city editor of the *Daily Nation* and later a Diplomatic Secretary in Sweden and then Kenya's Ambassador to Ethiopia, Akach, who sealed the window and door cracks of the theatre dressing room so he could keep the light on and study all night long; Chesaina, Mburu, Kipsanai, Ngumbi, God! all these names of boys tumbling through my mind and breaking my heart because I might never see them again; Amos Olando who met the Olympic qualifying time of 9.6 seconds for the 100 metres, and then broke the callused sole of his foot by hitting the pole vault box too hard and sat keening and rocking in the front seat of my Morris Minor, holding his split sole together to reduce the bleeding, while I rushed him to Kikuyu Hospital for stitches; Peter Alexander Karobia who wrote political plays and once threatened me with a panga and got expelled finally for his inability to conform to school rules; Donald Kiboro—Oh Kiboro! *Pole Bwana* (I am so sorry): who could forget your magnificent underplayed hauteur as Malvolio and now I hear you are dead, aged what, less than 40? *Pole rafiki.* Odhiambo, "that *black* boy" the other students called him, to my amusement, with the darkest skin and whitest eyes and a heavenly tenor voice (and here in Vancouver another Odhiambo, David

Nandi from Kisumu district, has been making films showing black and white bodies intertwined, and has published a novel in which the main character writes a graffito on a big building on Venables Street in East Van: "GO BACK TO EUROPE!"—what to make of that?); Eric Kotut, another Head of House, whose little sister about ten years old came out to greet my Morris Minor with an enamel washbasin and a towel and a bright cherubic smile, when I visited the family homestead down the dusty Rift Valley road near Marigat—Christ . . . would all of these fine, strong, gentle people be insufficient to prevent Kenya from becoming corrupted by dishonest officials and overrun by marauding gangs, as Mr. Culwick predicted? All of them deserve books of their own, and only Ali Mude has written a novel, that I have seen (*The Hills Are Falling*). And what about my colleagues, the teachers, Ishmael Omondi with his buck teeth, Robin Hood, Ben Ogutu, Ken Woolman, Paddy Lewin, Lazarus Munuve, and Jim Swift who now lives in Port Alberni BC, Alan Sanders and David Odongo, Shadrach Opiyo the School Clerk and Tailor, and Nimrod Mbogua, the humble carpenter with his great long tooth—was it all for nothing, what we built as a team at that national school, Alliance, with its boys from over 50 tribes? Would the country just sink into darkness and decay as the whites fled and the blacks tried ineffectually to take over?

I showed the Culwick book to Paul and he turned several pages at random, reading a few lines here and there.

"This guy's just mourning his past life," he said. "Don't let him get to you. He's a whining White Russian."

"You think I should go back to Kenya?"

"Why not? They'll need you there to build the new country. What are you worried about?"

"No, Paul!" Viviana interjected. "Alistair must stay in Canada, like us. He can build this country here."

"Culwick may be right," I said. "Maybe the new governments won't be able to keep control. He sees marauding gangs everywhere. You know, at Kenya's Independence celebrations, the President appealed to all the ex-terrorists still hiding in the forests to come out. 'Come out! And take your place as heroes! Freedom fighters!' I was there. I saw and heard it. But they paid no attention. They had gotten used to living in the forests and stealing out at night to raid the farms and villages. In the end, Jomo Kenyatta had to send in his military chief, ex-Mau Mau 'General' China, with the new Kenya Army to bring them out.

"Even if I went back to Kenya myself one day, Paul, there's no future there for my kids."

"Your kids are in South Africa."

"I want to get my degree finished and find a job and try to bring my kids back to Canada."

The doorbell rang. It was Mr. Bennett.

"I'm afraid I have some unsettling news, son. My wife has decided to retire from Brown Brothers Florists, so we're giving up the apartment downtown and moving back into the house at the end of the month. You'll have to vacate by then."

After he had gone, I fell into yet another wave of depression. That old wooden house on West Eleventh Avenue was the one place in the world where I still felt secure. The Bennetts were my connection to old Vancouver, when "you could walk across English Bay on the backs of the salmon." And now they were moving back into "my" house. I lay in bed that night feeling usurped.

When I told Paul and Viviana we were losing the house, they promptly went out next day, and by the afternoon they had rented a one-bedroom basement suite in Dunbar. I told them to take the two-piece sectional and anything else they wanted. As for me, I was frozen in indecision. The end of May was close, and my bank balance was running low.

I had been invited to a party a few blocks away, at the Vances', and I decided I might as well go. Wilma Vance was a poet I had met in grad school, and Mark was a painter and art teacher—it was his nude on my wall that Mr. Bennett had gotten upset about. When I arrived at the Vances' house, a young man dressed in blue denim including a waistcoat, was swinging slowly back and forth from the ornately carved front door jamb, a bemused grin plastered on his face. I waited.

"You going to let me in?" I said.

"Not until you give the password."

"Cool," I said. "Ozymandias. Abracadabra."

He shook his head.

"Supercalifragilistic," I said. "Flying purple people-eater."

He shook his head and kept swinging like a monkey.

"Lucy in the sky," I said, and he came off the jamb and bowed me in.

"With diamonds!" he said. "With diamonds!"

"Alistair," I said, offering my hand.

"Davie," he said, taking it.

"And what do you do?"

"I play," he said, the grin never leaving his face.

I took my bottle in to the kitchen, and there stood Hannah F., the tall, voluptuous, princess of the UBC English grad school. I touched her soft lips with mine and asked in the swirl of patchouli oil, "Who's that stoned character at the door?"

"You don't know our Davie the film maker?"

I felt a little foolish. Just about the whole Kitsilano artist scene was there. George Bowering was wandering around looking disdainful and smoking an Old Port cheroot, and Stan Persky was holding forth in the kitchen in impassioned political speech. The fresh new poet from Montreal, Simon Du Lac, had everyone's attention with a discourse on Blakean aesthetics in the dining room. Gathie Falk arrived, followed by Bill Reid and his latest. For a while, the venerable Jack and Doris Shadbolt made an appearance. I felt more and more out of place and wished I was back in Nairobi or at the Kiambu Amateur Dramatic Society amongst my own people. I ended up in the back yard at the picnic table, where Wilma Vance was talking to a bunch of wannabe writers.

"Where do you get your ideas?" one eager young woman asked.

Wilma just eyed her silently with a deadpan look for a second.

"And how are you," Wilma asked me, in the lull that followed.

"I'm losing my house in two weeks," I said. "I have to find new digs."

"Why don't you rent our upstairs suite? It'll be available in August."

"That would be great!" I said. "What do I do in the meantime, through June and July?"

"Can't help you with that," she said.

"Maybe you could pitch a tent in a provincial park and live there till August," Mark Vance suggested.

I left the party early and walked home feeling like a refugee.

Next morning the UBC English Department secretary called and said the Head needed to see me again.

"I'm more sorry than I can express, Mr. Randall," Dr. Durrant said, "but I thought you should hear the news at once. It's a bit of a bombshell, I'm afraid. The Registrar has ruled against us. If you're hired as a sessional lecturer, he will not register you as a grad student."

"Oh damn! If I'm not registered as a grad student my visa will expire."

"I can still offer you a double teaching assistantship, and you can be registered, but that will only bring in $3000. You said you need more than that."

"Family to support," I said.

"Yes." He frowned, perplexed, and lit his pipe.

"Listen, there are some new two-year colleges starting up around the Lower Mainland," he said. "Why don't you see if you can get something there to make up the shortfall? You can use my name as a reference."

This time as I walked out of Buchanan, I was in a rotten panic. Nowhere to stay, not enough income, no real job, marriage in ruins, immigration status temporary, Father's life falling apart. . . . Our lives in Africa finished, casualties of history. I went to the typewriter and banged out a résumé, put on my best tie and coat and drove around Greater Vancouver and dropped off job applications at the three new colleges.

In my uncertainty, waiting for replies was an agony. I sat in the kitchen and listened to Simon and Garfunkel's "Scarborough Fair" from *The Graduate,* but the delicate list of herbs ran counter to my dark mood and I decided to take Mark Vance's improbable suggestion and get the hell out of town and live in a tent till August. I phoned the colleges where I'd applied and left the Vances' number. I cleaned the house and returned the key to the Bennetts, packed my few possessions into the Vances' basement and told them I'd call every few days in case there was news. Then, on the 1st of June, I set off for the BC interior with my tent in the trunk of the Austin and my plywood rowboat on the roof. It felt like a journey into the unknown.

Lac le Jeune was pristine, and no one else was there. A rough dirt track led in to the undeveloped provincial campsite in a pine grove. I found a spot right on the water's edge where someone had nailed some boards across two logs lying in the water to make a crude dock. I pitched my tent, heaved the boat off the roof racks and put it in the water, and rowed out trolling a fly. I caught a couple of rainbow trout, came in and tied the boat back up at the dock, cooked and ate the fish, and slept. Next morning, coffee, then out in the boat again. I had brought a notebook for ideas for my dissertation, but I didn't write a thing in it. I slipped into a slow, past world where everything was simple and the waters were full of fish. Occasionally, I'd drive to Kamloops to see a movie or buy groceries and a case of beer, and the corrugated washboard dirt road had the feel of home: it reminded me of the little murram roads in the Uasin Gishu district where I was born. Every few days I'd phone the Vances collect and ask for Alfred Prufrock, and Wilma or Mark would tell the operator that Mr. Prufrock was out of town and, no, they didn't know when he was expected back.

In the middle of July a Volkswagen Kombi camper came puttering down the track and pulled up close to my tent, and I groaned. But the guy turned out to be a great companion. His name was Gustav Erikson from Copenhagen. He'd had a heart attack and had sold his tool and die-making business and was driving slowly round the world recuperating. I would row quietly around the lake with him trolling wet flies, or sit by the fire at night swapping tales of Africa and of the Second World War. He had been in the Danish underground until he was captured by the Nazis.

"Look," he showed me a crisscross of faint scars on the backs of his hands.

"Torture?"

"When they found I was tool and die maker, they broke the bones one at a time, till every bone was broken. Both hands."

"And you didn't give them any information?"

He glared at me, until I looked away from his eyes.

"Let me tell you something," he said. "When you are in Danish Resistance, out at night for a parachute drop from the British Mosquito bomber, and you have your colleague standing behind, guarding you, yes?"

"Yes," I said.

"There comes no Nazi there!"

"I'm sorry," I said, looking up at him again.

"Ah, you cannot know. You are too young. You can *not* know."

"I can try to imagine," I said.

"Imagination?" he said, weighing it sceptically, and looking down at his scarred hand. "And knowledge? They go together, I suppose."

I didn't try to make any response to that. It sounded wise, but I didn't know what it meant—not then.

On the 30th of July, I called collect for Prufrock from the phone booth in Kamloops, and Wilma accepted the charges.

"Alistair!" she cried excitedly. "Get down here right away. You've got an interview at eleven o'clock tomorrow morning, at Capilano College in West Vancouver. I've been frantically waiting for your call!"

I sped back to the campsite and packed up. Gustav helped me lift the rowboat onto the roof racks.

"Now you'll just have to cast from the shore," I said.

"It's what I expected," he said with a shrug.

I opened my fly box and picked out some Doc Spratleys and chironimids for him. I shook his hand gently, thinking of those broken bones.

"Goodbye, Gustav. It was a privilege to meet you. Thank you for helping to defeat the Nazis."

"Goodbye to you too," he said. "Then you try to make the world a little bit better, yes?"

I drove through the night to Vancouver. Printed in my memory was Gustav's affirmation: *There comes no Nazi there!* And later on, his comment about knowledge and imagination began to make sense to me. I was glad for that accidental meeting.

My weeks of insecurity up at the pristine lake had been an unreal vacation. Now I was full of energy and ready to get back to the real world.

5

"Norman Bull." The short, stocky man with no-nonsense black-framed glasses, extended a muscular hand across his desk and gripped mine firmly. "I'm the Dean of Instruction. Take a seat." He pointed me to a chair across from him and studied my letter of application.

"Africa, eh?"

"Yes." Was that good or bad, I wondered.

"You've taught at several different levels in the education system?"

"Yes. My last job in Kenya was Sixth-Form work, which is like first- and second-year university here. It was a new initiative in the country to expand the top end of the school system prior to Independence. Six of us were hired into that school to create the Lower and Upper Sixth Form, which was like a separate college built onto the top of the school. It was an exciting opportunity and the students were very keen. I think that kindergarten and first year of post-secondary are the most exciting students to teach, because their minds are the most open."

"Hmm. So you like being in on the start of new things?"

As I flowed nervously on, responding to this, his eyes moved methodically across the paper, line by line.

"What was this night school where you taught in Cape Town?" he enquired.

"It was a free school where we taught English one night a week, in a church annex. It was operated by the Student YMCA in conjunction with the Anglican Church."

"Who were the students?"

"Anybody could come. Everyone from non-literate housemaids to businessmen."

"Was it a paying job?"

"No. It was a public service, and one little gesture against racial segregation. Our students were all black and so-called Coloureds. They were very appreciative, and I enjoyed the experience greatly. Unfortunately, one of our YM members turned out to be a police informer and the Secret Police raided us and shut us down. But I think I learned as much from that teaching experience as I did in a year of teacher training."

Mr Bull sat back in his chair and eyed me with interest. "What *did* you learn from it?"

"I learned that you have to work with each student individually, however many there might be in the class."

"Very good!" He put down my application, took off his glasses and swung them once around in his hand. He leaned back again in his swivel chair. I seemed to have passed a test.

"Community colleges are a new kind of institution for British Columbia," he said, as though speaking to a colleague. "We are not going to blindly follow the universities with our academic curriculum, and we're totally unlike the Ontario colleges, which are mainly technical institutes. It's a chance to do something entirely fresh, more in keeping with the times. First of all, we're going to be organized in a somewhat democratic way at this college. Instead of Department Heads we'll have Co-ordinators, sort of a *primus inter pares*. You know Latin I see."

"First among equals."

He nodded and talked on for a while about the Co-ordinator system and then suddenly sat straight up in his chair.

"Another major difference from the universities," he said, "will be our approach to teaching. Most universities have a research orientation and they're far more interested in their top graduate students than the sweaty undergrads. Think of education as a train pulling out of the station. At the university, they leave it up to the students to get aboard. Here, we want to make darned good and sure that every student has a chance to board, before the train pulls out."

"Adapt the teaching to reach students at different levels of ability?"

"Exactly! The traditional university attitude is, 'Here's the information. You learn it. If you didn't get it, too bad. You didn't make the grade, bye-bye.' My idea is that the College will take some responsibility for the learning to occur."

"So if the students don't learn it's the prof's fault."

"No, I'm not talking about namby-pambying them. But *some* responsibility. What we don't want is self-important scholars standing on a podium lecturing into a void as so often happens at the universities. Think of the train. We want everybody on board."

"Sounds good to me!" I said. "In a small way, I suppose that's what we were trying to do in Cape Town."

"A comprehensive community college should have room for every kind of student," he declared. "Everyone from the straight A, disciplined, academic genius born into a wealthy family, to the trapped divorcée who got pregnant at sixteen and has spent the last ten years waitressing to feed her kids and she now wants something better out of life. Within the comprehensive college, people can get started and find where they want to go: Academic, Career, Vocational courses, all within the same institution. They might start out in one direction and move to another without having to change school. I see education as enablement, not a set of hurdles." He paused, and I could tell this was a set speech. I was reminded of lunch lectures at the Nairobi Rotary Club my father had taken me to. He rambled on for a while about "community."

"Right, then!" he said with an air of conclusion, and nodded. "We'll be in touch."

I moved my stuff from the basement into the Vances' upstairs suite that night, and the next morning my friend Ross Fraser phoned from Castlegar to say he had to come down to Vancouver and asked if he could stay with me overnight. He had been a graduate student with me at UBC and had left to take a job at Selkirk College that had just opened in Castlegar. When he arrived, I told him about my interview.

"Have you got the job?"

"I sure hope so. He said he'd get back to me. All I need is two classes of English 100 there, and that'll give me enough income with the two TAs at UBC."

"You know what," Ross said: "I think today the community colleges are the place to be."

Crossing Second Narrows

"You're happy working at Selkirk? I thought it was just a temporary job till you get a Ph.D. and work in a university."

"No. I doubt that I will ever get the Ph.D. now. There's something so fresh and lively about Selkirk—I can't tell you: I love it there! The community colleges are going to change the face of higher education."

Next morning while I was in the shower, Ross answered a phone call asking for me to be at Capilano College at ten o'clock for another interview with Mr. Bull.

"How many classes would you be willing to teach here, Mr. Randall?" the Dean asked as soon as I sat down.

"Two if possible," I said.

"Two, yes. But I'm asking how many would you be willing to take?"

"Well . . . I guess as many as you offer me."

"That's settled then. You'll teach four classes and be the English Co-ordinator, and we'll pay you for five, which is a full load, so you'll have to drop your teaching assistantships at UBC."

I climbed into my car thunderstruck. I had a full-time job! But as I drove back home across the Lions Gate Bridge it began to sink in that now I would no longer be spending any time on the UBC campus. My only connection with UBC was my incomplete degree: "ABD" –all but dissertation. I felt like a traded hockey player. After four years of feeling at home on the leisurely, isolated Point Grey campus, my loyalty was now going to be to a totally different institution. Out of the weeks of shifting insecurity, I had suddenly acquired a fresh identity. English Co-ordinator of a brand-new community college, no less. Well, good! I preferred teaching to research anyway. The image I had composed of sipping sherry with a select group of students in my book-lined study faded away, to be replaced by . . . what exactly? Mr. Bull's train and a station full of sweaty bodies.

I had not asked him about salary; I trusted him.

When I got home, Ross had left. There was a bottle of Canadian Club standing on the kitchen table with a note under it: "Thanks for the bed. Congratulations, Co-ordinator?"

Around midnight, feeling somewhat Canadian from having sampled rye whisky for the first time, and figuring Ross must have made it home by now, I phoned him in Castlegar.

"How the hell did you know?" I said. "Did they tell you on the phone they were going to offer me the Co-ordinator job?"

"It wasn't hard to guess, my friend! They don't spend half an hour explaining the Co-ordinator system to you, then call you for a second interview at ten a couple of mornings later unless they mean business."

"I don't know how you could have been so sure of yourself."

"You're going to enjoy that job, Alistair. It suits the Kenya settler in you. Start from scratch and build something. If your college turns out anything like mine, you'll find it pretty exciting."

Next morning, I drove to the College at nine o'clock and started pulling together my department. Faculty hirings. Book lists—oh, shit, we had no bookstore! Dean Bull and I drove down to Eaton's department store in Park Royal and finalized the arrangements he had started for college textbooks to be stocked there. Course outlines. It was such a rush of excitement and novelty. It kept me so busy over the weeks ahead that when a card arrived from Jenadie postmarked Edmonton with exciting news, it barely registered:

Alistair:
Rashid has a one-year teaching appointment here at the U of A. Isn't that fantastic? You'll have to come and visit us. It's going to be such an interesting year!

I put her postcard of the High Level Bridge on my mantelpiece. If ever I glanced at it, it was merely to think of Jenadie and Rashid being very far away. Edmonton, Alberta . . . they might as well have been on Fogo Island or in Timbuctu as far as I was concerned, because Capilano College absorbed my full attention.

Mark Vance had access to an old letterpress machine owned by the UBC prof Peter Quartermain, and for my belated birthday present, he printed me a hundred pages of beautiful, watermarked linen bond paper with the letterhead:

Alistair Randall,
Co-ordinator of English
Capilano College, 1750 Mathers Avenue,
West Vancouver, BC.

6

"Ladies and gentlemen . . . congratulations!" Dean Bull greeted the fifty-odd college faculty. We were crowded into a room in the basement of the West Vancouver High School, on Mathers Avenue. This was the college headquarters for now, one room for the faculty, and one for the administration, though we would soon have a two-story wooden portable of our very own out on the lawn. Classroom space was scattered over the North Shore in high schools at night, and in church basements, and the old Squamish Library. It was Monday, 19th of August 1968, and classes were due to begin in three weeks time.

"Congratulations! You are in on the birth of a completely new kind of institution for this province. With your help, Capilano College will be a community campus for the 1970s, a people place, flexible, dynamic, and responsive to the real educational needs of the community. Not a top-down institution, but as far as possible a bottom-up, non-hierarchical college. We are going to transform post-secondary education in this province for the brightest young minds, as well as make it available to certain classes of students for whom it was out of reach before: mature entry, single parents, part-time students and so on.

"Now, I've got good news and bad news for you. The bad news is that we've been planning for 350 students, and so far more than 600 have applied for admission, and they're still coming!"

"Holy shit!" cried Andrea Halvorson, a tall, vocal blonde from California, which drew a checking glance from the Dean. A buzz of tribal electricity infused us all, like a winning team.

"What's the good news?" I called out.

He smiled, his face round as a ball topped with a fringe of white hair. "The good news," he said, "is that we operate under a funding formula from Victoria. The more students we enrol, the more money we get to run the College."

"What about class size?" I said. "That means we'll have to hire some more faculty?"

"It does indeed. The ads are in tomorrow's *Sun* and *Province*. Co-ordinators can expect to give their time to assist in job interviews beginning next Monday. This Friday's the closing date."

By week's end, 765 students had applied and been processed and 551 actually admitted to the College. I was phoning all kinds of people I knew, and by the following week's end we had hired an additional seven faculty in English alone. Most were graduate students at the universities, teaching one or two classes for us.

Since there was nowhere to eat at the school, most days for lunch a group of us would drive down to the George Café, a greasy spoon on Marine Drive at 16th and talk excitedly about the College. The core of this group was in the English Department, Barnet Nolan, Thelma Smith, Max Odegaard, Andrea Halvorson—all part-timers with four-fifths teaching loads. The College Council had been so nervous about commitment that they had allowed the appointment of only two full-time faculty out of the hundred or so now hired, myself and the Co-ordinator of the Early Childhood Education program. We two had one-year appointments. Everyone else had one-semester contracts with no guarantee of anything beyond.

One Friday, I decided to hold my English Department meeting over lunch, but the George was too small so I asked Dean Bull if he knew of a suitable place.

"Ripp's Diner," he said. "'The Garden of Eatin' on Lonsdale in North Van."

"'The Garden of Eden'? What sort of place is that?" I asked.

"'Eatin'!" Bull said emphatically. "If you want a place that's down to earth and inexpensive, that's it. Perfect for your purpose."

For a second I thought of asking him to join us, but then decided we would be better off on our own.

We assembled at Ripp's Diner and found the place buzzing with activity, but we managed to snag a large double booth and had the waitress bring in a table to extend it. The decor was pre-psychedelic shades of brown, and the menu, painted on wooden panels above the serving hatch featured such delicacies as "Salisbury Steak with Mashed Potatoe and Pea's," and "Liver and Bacon with Fry's and Gravy." It was partly self-service, and as I set my plate on the Formica table and slid back onto the stuffed orange Naugahyde bench, I realized that Bull had been right: this was the perfect place for the English Department to get down to business without academic airs or pretensions. Around us, families were eating, and here and there an overalled tradesman or truck driver sat at a solo table.

"When we get our own campus," Thelma Smith said quietly, "we should demand a faculty club and dining room."

"Hell no!" said Max Odegaard, glaring at her. He wasn't actually a draft dodger but had left the States for similar reasons: his father and mother had been persecuted by the McCarthy Committee in the 50s and hounded out of Hollywood as pinkos. "I wouldn't want any special privilege stuff. No faculty club or parking, no faculty washrooms. I would prefer to acknowledge our common humanity with the students and support staff and administration." He bit into his burger and chewed determinedly.

Thelma smiled and canted her head. "That will certainly make the place more interesting," she said, seeming to concede his point with a few quick nods, but I was already learning not to trust her smile completely. Thelma had her Ph.D. and several years of university teaching, and I was rather surprised that Dean Bull had picked me instead of her to be the Co-ordinator. She had asked me privately how Max came to be hired, since he had only a bachelor's degree, and I put her off, telling her Bull had hired Max before my appointment. But if I had my reservations about the candour of Thelma's smile, I soon grew in admiration for her drive and tenacity. She was a champion of student rights—especially women's—and was not intimidated by authority. She and her husband had parted company, and she had four young children to bring up on her own.

"What interests me most about the College," I began "is that we have the freedom to decide what courses to offer and how to structure them. Since we've all been hired so close to the beginning of term, I've decided that to get started we'll just use the UBC model: Literature and Composition in the first year; short stories and poetry in the first semester, novel and drama in the second. And in second year, the survey course from Beowulf to T.S. Eliot. But during the coming year we have an opportunity to create a whole new syllabus-"

"'Themes in Contemporary Literature,'" Andrea Halvorson interjected.

I nodded. "Over the coming months, I want you all to be thinking right outside the conventional patterns."

"'Literature of Civil Disobedience'"? Max Odegaard suggested.

"'Women and Literature,'" said Thelma.

"I think it's going to be very interesting to see what kind of students we attract if we break away from the traditional university offerings," said Barnet Nolan thoughtfully. "We might attract dropouts, or *crème de la crème*."

"Or both," I said. "*Crème de la crème* who find the universities too hide-bound and want something refreshing."

I was happy with this meeting. Everyone seemed excited by the novelty of our situation, even though none of us at that point expected to stay at the College very long. We thought it would just be a temporary job, before we went on to teach at universities.

One afternoon as I walked back to the car from lunch at the George with Peter Hansen, an American draft dodger who had been hired in Economics, I asked him what he was writing his Ph.D. dissertation on.

"Zee Ee Gee," he said.

"What's that?"

"Well, you know Zee Pee Gee, don't you?"

"Zero Population Growth. Sure," I said, resisting correction of his American pronunciation, "Paul Ehrlich. The population bomb mushrooming exponentially, and we have to radically reduce it if we're ever to survive."

"Exactly. This is a similar idea applied to economics. Zero Economic Growth. See, capitalism is a cancer. It knows nothing other than growth and expansion. I think your friend Paul Ehrlich said something like that. 'People who boast about their economic growth remind me of cancer patients who are proud of the growth of their tumours.' The beast eats and moves on, and we're left with excrement. In the end, everything on the earth will be consumed, nothing left. The only possible way for humans to survive in the long term—let alone animals, and trees and other life forms—is to develop a model of economics based on zero growth. Balance. What the Greeks called '*harmonia*.' But this is heresy to all existing economic theories."

"That's really ambitious, Peter!" I said. "How do we possibly get there?"

"Don't know if we can! Never been tried. You probably have to demolish the existing capitalist structure and rebuild from the bottom up, with real human values instead of private greed."

"How do you destroy the structure to begin with?"

"You serious?"

"Yes, Peter, I want to understand."

"Well, first of all you have to be prepared to break the rules. Come with me."

He turned and walked into the Owl Drugstore, and I followed him.

"Lift something," he whispered.

"*No!*"

"I'll show you."

I stopped in front of the magazines and watched out of the side of my eye. Peter took a bottle of Aspirin from a shelf and dropped it into the pocket of his brown corduroy jacket.

"We better be getting back to work," he said loudly as he walked towards me.

On the sidewalk, he marched along for half a block before turning to me with his fist clenched like a small boy.

"That's it!" he crowed. "That's the way we do it!"

"That's ridiculously *childish*!" I said forcefully.

"It may seem childish to you, but I mean it symbolically. Only way!" he said. "Hit them in the belly, in the profits, where it counts." He took the Aspirin bottle from his pocket and dropped it in a green litter bin on a lamppost. I looked around to see that a store clerk wasn't following us. How could he jeopardise his tenuous position in Canada by committing a crime?

"I don't know about that, man. Stealing Aspirin's not going to change the world."

"Mighty oaks from little acorns grow," he said. "The point is, you have to be willing to fight the bastards, resist and break the rules and maybe even break the law as I just did. Look at what the tobacco industry is doing to people's health! And it's got a passel of corrupt scientists shielding it from consequences, lying under oath that there's no proven connection between tobacco and ill health. You're not going to get them to change their ways by sitting down and having a civil discussion with them, are you? It's going to take a war: direct action, demonstration, confrontation and eventually powerful lawsuits. But you've got to commit yourself. I'm in it for the long haul. How about you?"

At the College I was completely occupied, but at home I missed my two little boys terribly, and after a couple of glasses of wine in the evening, I would often get weepy and start writing poems for them on the typewriter, which inevitably ended in the waste basket next morning. My replacement "families," first Jenadie, and then Paul and Viviana, had come and gone in quick succession. I missed the political arguments with Jenadie and with Paul. There was a woman named Yvonne whom I'd known as a grad student, and I called her up once and invited her to go fishing for kokanee salmon on Jones Lake, but in the boat we fell into that charged sexual banter that boys and girls engage in at church camps, and I didn't ask her again.

Desperate for company, I tracked down Marianne's phone number at her parents' house in Calgary and called her. She told me she had broken up with Mac, her Geographer: "He's too young for me," she said. So the following Friday I drove up to Calgary and booked into a cheap hotel. Next morning, I was woken very early by the sound of a marching band, and went to the window and saw smart police officers with shiny instruments leading a parade of kids through the deserted dawn streets. Seeing the big officers smartly devoting themselves to the task of honouring these little kids brought a lump to my throat.

I called Marianne, and she seemed astonished that I had arrived in Calgary. However, she gulped down her surprise, recovered her composure and invited me to come for lunch. So I duly went, and met her mother. I told them about the marching band.

"Ah yes," her mother said, "that would be the annual march-past of the Calgary School Crossing Guards. It's quite a touching scene, isn't it?" She smiled, and I felt comfortable in the house.

But I could see from her nervous eye-movements that Marianne was flustered by my presence. She invited me to drive her up to Banff National Park for a hike, and we stayed the night in the segregated wooden dormitories of a camp there. Next day, after our hike up Iron

Mountain, while I was filling up at the gas station, she took out her flute and played the *adagio con grazia* theme from the second movement of Tchaikowsky's *Pathetique* symphony. I finished pumping the gas and sat mesmerized by the passionate strains of her flute, amid those huge, snow-covered mountains. I got back in the car and asked her if she would come down and visit me in Vancouver. She looked at me, put her flute to her mouth, and began to play a melancholy tune I didn't recognize. I waited for her to finish, and when she had, she took the flute away from her lips and told me no, she wasn't ready for another relationship. She thanked me for visiting her, and said goodbye. She had already arranged a ride back to Calgary with a woman she met in the dorm. I turned westward and drove through the night back home, heartbroken by this lightning attempt at courtship and its equally swift rejection. Even today as I write this, I Google Tchaikowsky's *Pathetique* and listen to a clip of Pierre Monteux conducting the Boston Symphony, and it's a significant moment of my own life I'm listening to: intense and sinuous musical beauty in the Banff Esso station, and then the long descent back to the coast, tormented by the echo, and the quick glimpse of Marianne's bare white shoulders when I went to wake her up in the women's dorm. Back in Vancouver on Monday morning, a letter arrived from Kenya. My father and stepmother had finally packed up and were leaving the country for good. His heart was giving out, and not just metaphorically. I felt numb and disconnected.

At the College, Barnet Nolan asked me with an expectant look of excitement if I had seen the Kenya runners beat Jim Ryun in the 1500 metres at the Olympics.

"Talk about teamwork! Jipcho holds the lead all the way till he's spent and then Keino breaks ahead. Three thirty-four point eight! New Olympic record. I was sure the Americans would take the gold. Make you feel proud?"

"It was a good show," I said.

My heart *had* stirred as the two triumphant Kenyans coasted for an extra lap around the track with their arms in the air, coming down from their miracle race, and the crowd went wild. I even felt a twinge of African pride and solidarity when Mamo Wolde from Ethiopia won the marathon. But I also knew Graham Nottingham who had helped train the Kenya athletes, and who had left the country now. Keino's kids might have a future in Kenya. Not Graham's, not mine.

Sometimes, I went downstairs and talked to Wilma Vance when she wasn't busy writing. She had published three books of poetry and I found her uncompromising and self-centred, which were things I had been trained never to be. Her self-possession and intensity excited me and reminded me of D.H. Lawrence's *Fantasia of the Unconscious*, his tough preachments about taking care of yourself and not giving in to social pressure. ("Alone. Alone. Be alone my soul…. and don't take fright at the pop of a light bulb.") Wilma had a kind of intensity about her that put some people off, unlike her husband, who was genial and good-humoured with everyone.

One Sunday, Mark Vance and I went fishing at Anderson Lake and spent the whole day exchanging only a few sentences. "Marriage is fine," Mark said, as we were driving home, "but it would sure be nice to have a holiday from it once in a while."

I was having a terminal holiday from mine all right, and I was not enjoying being alone. I was fine at work, but at home I sat most of the time alone, watching TV programs like *The Ed Sullivan Show* with Topo Gigio, his silly mouse, and the legs of the June Taylor dancers making kaleidoscopic patterns of flesh.

I had written to my old friend Andries Krige in Cape Town and sent him a photo of myself. Now he wrote back saying, "I don't understand why you've let your hair grow like a woman's—and why the hell are you wearing that Moroccan bead round your neck? Are you trying to prove something?"

I didn't reply. I put Kris Kristofferson on the record player and sang along to "Jesus Was a Capricorn," while I prepared material for my classes.

At the College, Dean Bull would call me into his office for Co-ordinator business, and afterwards he'd lean back in his chair with his hands behind his head and talk about other subjects. It was comforting, like a gab session with the village elder. He seemed to enjoy my company.

"Do you ever miss Kenya?" he asked one day.

It was a question I was asked often and never knew how to answer without pouring out my guts and leaving the questioner wishing he or she hadn't broached the subject. So I would usually just reply, "Not really." But Bull deserved a fuller answer.

"Consider this, Mr. Bull," I said. "If a civil war, or the Canadian courts, removed your right to live in your home and it was taken over by the natives, would you miss it?"

Bull moved his head from side to side, as though weighing opposing answers, before replying, "Hypothetical question, son. Never going to happen here. "

"Civil war is unlikely," I conceded, "but you never know what the courts will do."

"Whatever the courts say, you could never pack all the Canadians who immigrated here from Europe over the centuries onto ships and send them back to Europe. It's inconceivable! And the government is making it even more so by encouraging mass immigration from the Pacific Rim. Believe me, those immigrants are not going to let go of what they find here. No, son, it ain't going to happen."

"That's what we thought in Kenya," I said. "My father's generation were encouraged to settle in Kenya and build the country, and after World War Two they recruited more settlers. But when the African political independence struggles happened, the British sold us all out in the end."

"Well, those pioneers and early settlers took their chances. Anyway look, you'd better just finish your degree and settle down here in Canada. I'll vouch for you with Immigration." Bull sniffed, done with that subject. He slid a copy of the magazine *Performing Arts* across his desk to me.

"What do you make of all this public nudity, Alistair?" he said. "I find it hard to comprehend. In Third World countries, people are dressing up in finery and doing their freedom dances. But in the West have you noticed the mania people have for taking their clothes *off*? I've never seen anything like it! People stripping off buck naked."

"It's become the chosen form of protest," I said. "It's an obsession."

"Damn right it is! Look at that."

I picked up the copy of *Performing Arts* subtitled "Morality" on the front cover—with the "o" replaced by a fig leaf: "M rality." I opened it and glanced through a piece by Mavor Moore: "The arts and letters seem to be in a race these days to get our private parts out in the open," he wrote, but this wasn't smut or obscenity, he claimed, "the usual underground septic tank into which most men and women guiltily dip from time to time: the smoking room joke, the filthy postcard, the naughty novel, the peep-show." No, it was a truly revolutionary movement in society to cleanse sex of "the taint of obscenity."

"Who's this Moore guy?" I asked.

"My God! You're finishing a Ph.D. in English at UBC, and you sit there and ask me who Mavor Moore is! He's a well-known Canadian playwright and theatre producer," he said. "You haven't learned a whole hell of a lot about this country, have you? Stuck out there in the ivory towers at Point Grey."

He twirled his glasses by the temple. I knew he had been a high school English teacher, then the Department Head, and then he had moved to administration in the night school system. When the College opened and he got the job as Dean of Instruction, I suppose it must have given him a jolt of excitement. Despite his conservative mien, he had progressive ideas about education. And now this streak of nationalism showed. I could see that he envied me running my brand-new college English Department.

"I keep telling you, we have to hire some Canadians, Mr. Bull. Meanwhile, you'll have to fill me in on Canada," I said. "I know about the naked Doukhobors."

"That's not new. They've been doing that for donkey's years."

Well it was new to me. In Duthie Books' front window I had seen Simma Holt's *Terror in the Name of God* on display and when I went in and opened a copy, I was astonished at the pictures of big, fleshy, middle-aged Ukrainian women, standing with droopy cellulite bums and breasts naked in front of the cameras, their burned-out houses in the background.

"Did you read what happened at Lords cricket ground in England, the other day?" said Bull. "A guy ran across the field stark naked before ten thousand spectators during the England versus West Indies Test Match!"

"They call it 'streaking.' I think. Mavor Moore is right," I said. "Stripping off your clothes is symbolically connected to getting rid of hypocrisy."

"Really? Well, let's get back to business. . . ."

Following this particular conversation, there were more stories of nakedness, men—and women—streaking in public all around the world–Lords, Wimbledon, even women stripping off at soccer matches. And the movies: *Taking Off, Adrift, Without a Stitch*. I went one night to The Varsity Cinema to see *Out of Touch*, a realist film which followed a group of actors playing themselves, moving through talk therapy, water therapy, finally nude therapy. By the end, the husband of the beautiful fashion model who had been the first to undress, still had his boxer shorts on, and two naked women sitting on the pool edge urged him to take them off. He confessed he was embarrassed about the size of his penis. "Let's have a look!" the women said, and finally he dropped his shorts. The camera stayed still, no prurient closing in. "That's fine!" "It's very nice!" the women reassured him, and he broke and cried like a baby. The group gathered round and held him in the water, as he poured out years of bottled-up jealousy about his wife. After the show, people in the audience relaxed, and looked about them. They seemed to be longing to reach out to one another, a network of strangers, over the back of the seat or the one ahead.

Outside the theatre, I bought a copy of *The Georgia Straight*, Vancouver's then radical little underground newspaper that the cops kept closing down, which has now become a fat 136-page entertainment guide full of advertisements. It had a nude cover, and naked women on inside pages and some naked men. Then one night, I was sitting down to supper when Jenadie called from Edmonton and told me to watch the CBS news at six o'clock and call her afterwards.

I took my plate into the living room and turned to Channel 12, Bellingham, Washington, and adjusted the rabbit ears. I saw live coverage of a demonstration at the Atlantic City Beauty Pageant: A convoy of yellow rental buses was pulling into a hotel parking lot, and women passengers disembarked, then formed up on the tarmac chanting:

> "Atlantic City Is a Town with Class!
> They Raise Your Morals and They Judge Your Ass!"

One woman began to fumble under her shirt, and pretty soon she was swirling a bra above her head. The camera panned, and there was a sullen, heavyweight male security guard with his hand on his hip, staring down two women who held up cardboard posters. One read "WELCOME TO THE MISS AMERICA CATTLE AUCTION." The other showed a large photograph of a woman, naked under a cowboy hat, kneeling up with her back to the camera and her body marked off with butcher's chart lines labelled "CHUCK," "RIB," "LOIN," "RUMP," "SHOULDER," and "SOUP BONE." She was looking back over her shoulder, deadpan at the camera from under her Stetson, and the slogan above read, "BREAK THE DULL STEAK HABIT." In the background, you could see glamorous contestants in chic pastel swimsuits teetering on high-heeled sandals as they hurried to the safety of the poolside dressing rooms.

"The Women's Liberation Movement has decided to mount an assault on the Miss America Beauty Pageant," said the network commentator. "We're bringing you live coverage of this event, as it unfolds today in Atlantic City, New Jersey."

The camera cut to a smoking oil drum. Women paraded past it and threw things in, a steno pad, a bra, a copy of *Playboy*, high-heeled shoes.

"These instruments of oppression are going into the freedom trash can!" a woman's voice said.

The camera panned to two women kneeling down, with their arms round the neck of a bewildered sheep. As a crown was placed over the dazed animal's ears, a woman with a loud-hailer shouted: "We are crowning this sheep 'Miss America' to indicate that all the misguided young women contestants in this so-called beauty pageant are oppressed and being judged like animals at a County Fair."

"And there you have it," said the anchorman, wrapping it up. "Women in Atlantic City, New Jersey, expressing their desires for unbound freedom, by taking off their brassieres . . . and crowning a sheep!" He smirked.

"You idiot!" I said aloud. "It's not a soap opera!"

I picked up the phone and called Jenadie back.

"Alistair! Did you see—"

"I watched it! You know, when I was an undergraduate we had scavenger hunts, and on the list of things you had to get was always a bra, and it was so *embarrassing*! And here are these women marching tall in public for the cameras and swinging their bras around like lassoes!"

"Some people say that women going bra-less is nonsense," she said, "but the manufacturers are taking it seriously. Get this: Maidenform sells fifteen million bras a year, and now three million of them are 'natural look.' I'm doing a feature story on the bra-less revolution for the *Edmonton Journal*."

"You got a job!"

"I did! One article at a time. It's not much, but it might grow."

"That's great, Jenadie. I got a job too, teaching full-time at a college."

"Fantastic! Tell me all about it."

"It'd cost too much. I'll tell you when I see you next."

"So you're not going back to Kenya?"

"Not right now. I've applied for landed immigrant status."

"Great! Anyways, how the hell are you? I want to see you."

"Lonely," I said.

"That's what happens when you get divorced, buddy. Come up and visit us, you hear? Can you come up at Christmas?"

"I'll try. By the way, you should add public nudity to your article."

"Don't say you'll try! Tell me you promise!" she insisted.

"Things are too hectic and uncertain here. I'm the Department Co-ordinator, you know! But I will try my best."

In the following days, the bra stories kept coming. North America was fixated. On TV, there was more commentary on the Atlantic City protest, and I hurriedly scribbled notes for Jenadie's article. A Maidenform executive explained that the traditional bra made of cotton broadcloth and giving a pointy look to the breasts was still available to those who wanted it, but Playtex announced they'd studied shifting sales patterns and decided to market the 18-hour bra. "It's a very functional bra for women who need good support," she said. The President of Lady Suzanne Foundations had the last, smiling word: "We are actually expecting a tendency for profits to increase," he announced, "because it's slightly cheaper to manufacture the 'no-bra-look' bra."

"You appear to be winning!" I wrote to Jenadie. "The industry is turning its attention to women's comfort. The manufacturers are falling into line and making money. No more Jayne Mansfield cones!"

And then the first semester of the new college finally began. I went to my first English Composition class and looked at the bright, expectant faces: mostly late teenagers, but a couple of middle-aged women and one man. I asked the students to write for twenty minutes on any subject they wished. I took the papers home to read that night, with some excitement to find out who my students were and what they were thinking, but even that pursuit was jostled aside because the first paper I read began: "The girl sitting next to me in the pink sweater isn't wearing a bra! I don't know how often you have that kind of luck, Professor, but it's never happened to me before. College life is going to be a real gas.

It's going to be a ball!" Primly I wrote in the margin: "How does not wearing a bra suggest a ball?"

Next morning, *The Daily Province* reported that in Florida girls were showing up at high schools without bras. In Jacksonville, a Vice-Principal took the girls into his office one by one and made them jump. If their breasts bounced too freely under their sweaters, they were sent home and told not to return till they were properly dressed.

The nudity stories kept coming, too. Every day in the newspaper there were reports of taverns and beer parlours across the continent featuring topless or stark naked dancers. In Chicago, the cast of *Hair* took off their clothes, dozens of them all naked on the stage, swaying in unison and singing ecstatically about Abe Lincoln, "emanci-motherfucking-pator" of the slaves. And at the Fillmore East in New York, a group called "Living Theatre" walked naked in amongst the audience chanting "I AM NOT ALLOWED TO TAKE OFF MY CLOTHES." I dutifully clipped that story from *The Georgia Straight* and mailed it with a bunch of other stuff to Jenadie.

Life at work was a whirlwind of excitement. How thrilling it is to be in on the start of something new, especially something that's succeeding beyond expectations! Faculty would converge on our basement headquarters at around 4 pm every day as the last of the high school students cleared out, and our classes ran non-stop from 4:30 to 10:30, four 90-minute periods back to back, with most instructors allowing ten-minute bathroom breaks in the middle. Yatter yatter! We may not have had a building to call our own, but the life was there: students full of excitement and hope, faculty full of dreams–many of them PhDs, but in the years to come they preferred to stay at the College instead of moving to a university; quite a few of them American draft dodgers, intent on building a more humane country than the one they had turned their backs on. Maybe Ross Fraser had been right: building the College did suit the Kenya settler in me.

There were walls of ignorance and prejudice too, amongst the students. One night, I was teaching a class on writing in a church basement we used as a classroom in North Vancouver District, and I had brought a record player and the soundtrack of *Hair* to have them analyse a couple of songs. One young man, pushed over the edge by the track about decorative dress being typical of males in most animal species, suddenly scraped his chair back loudly and declared, "I'm really sick of all this faggot stuff!" and stormed out. We heard his motor cycle start and rev loudly, and listened to him roaring off down Berkley Road, never to return to my class. Another time, an earnest young Mennonite boy suddenly complained, as we were discussing immigration, "Well, the East Indians are just *taking over* the Fraser Valley!" What to say to that? I smiled at my elegant young Sikh student and risked saying in an emphatic voice, "Jasbinder! Kindly advise your people to *stop* taking over the Fraser Valley!" Whether the discussion that followed made any changes to anyone's thinking, I will never know. You do your best. . . .

My life also meant meetings. Individual office-hour meetings with students to discuss the course and what I expected in their essays. Meetings with my four full-time American and British faculty and the Canadian part-timers, to try to figure out how to build a distinctively Canadian English department. Meetings with the Dean and the other Co-ordinators.

In October, Dean Bull rented the cabins at Paradise Valley north of Squamish for a weekend retreat to discuss the future. Students, faculty, administrators, support staff, council members, all bunked down in the little rustic cabins under the evergreens. We watched the eagles glide majestically, searching for salmon in the Cheakamus River, as we sat in circles on the cold grass listening to one another's dreams about a new kind of college where higher learning would flourish free of the traditional pomp and restrictions and elitism. And in the late afternoons we took time off and fooled about like children. We hit softballs on the river banks and played "Kick the Can" in the woods.

On the last day of the retreat, Dave Marsden, the Vice-President of Student Council, stood on a chair with a loud hailer and announced, "Ladies and gentlemen, we are going to finish the retreat with a relay race. There will be two teams, Gophers and Chipmunks, equally represented by faculty and students, and by women and men."

I looked around but couldn't see any teams. "Where are they?" I yelled.

Suddenly people were screaming, "Oh my God!" as they put their hands to their faces. To my left, a couple of naked men had burst out of the bushes and were streaking down the river bank in front of everybody.

"I can't look at this!" a student shrieked and bent down and turned her back, but turned again and looked.

There was Barnet Nolan from the English Department plunging his large bare feet recklessly between harsh stones, as his orange-tufted genitals flipped about. I didn't recognize the other, dark-haired guy, presumably a student. They reached a cover of evergreens on the right side, holding out their wooden batons, and now two naked women leapt out and took the batons and continued the relay, back to where the men had come from. The crowd went wild. The faculty woman was Gretchen Brandt from Chemistry, tall and skinny with startling white bikini marks, and she easily outdistanced the student, Caroline Bell from one of my classes, whose plump, suntanned breasts swung back and forth as she pumped her arms to run. Into the bushes they went, and it was over.

"The Chipmunks have won," Dave Marsden announced solemnly. "The Gopher team has placed an excellent second!"

Everyone laughed and crowded round the excited runners, draped in blankets now and sipping hot drinks. Standing next to Dean Bull, I asked, "Well, what did you think of that?"

He raised his eyebrows and smiled grimly. "I believe you used the word 'obsession.' You seem to have got that right. I cannot imagine students and faculty running around together naked, in my day."

"In your day," I countered, "I cannot imagine a college administrator setting up a weekend retreat for students and faculty and support staff and administrators all mixed together discussing things on an equal footing."

"Oh, I don't know," he demurred. "I think of the colleges at Oxford and Cambridge."

"Is *that* how you think of Capilano?"

He didn't reply, but from the look in his eye I saw I had touched on something.

Then we climbed aboard the buses and cars and went back down to finish the first semester, carrying in our minds the startling images of the naked runners. It wasn't just Caroline Bell's top that had no bikini marks: she was tanned all over. There was something daring and exhilarating about the memory.

Dear Alistair,
Yes! Please do come and visit us in Edmonton! Something very strange is going on, and I don't understand it. Rashid is so busy all the time with department meetings and the political shit, that we never seem to have much time together, and even when we do, we get into these arguments, "struggle sessions," he calls them, that never seem to end. I don't know if I'm going crazy or what. But in any case, it would be nice to see you. And nice to have an ally here, where all the people we know are Rashid's friends. Come up for Christmas (although don't expect turkey and cranberry sauce).

This is a very weird city. The university is full of political refugees of one kind or another—not just American draft dodgers and war objectors, but exiles from South Africa, casualties of the India-Pakistan war, Chileans . . . you name it. Very interesting mix! C'mon up and see!

Love, Jenadie

As soon as the grades were in on Monday 16th December, I lingered in Dean Bull's office.

"What's up?" he asked.

"I was thinking of driving to Edmonton for Christmas."

"Hmm," he frowned. "The College closes only from the 24th to the 29th. But I'll tell you what, Alistair: I've worked my butt off and so have you. I'm taking my wife to Hawaii for two weeks on Thursday. Let's get everything that needs doing done in the next couple of days and then you be in my office at 9 am on the first Monday in January, and we'll pick it up from there, no questions asked."

As I was leaving his office, Bull called me back. "Have you seen this stuff about the Mohawks blocking the bridge in Cornwall?" he asked.

"Yes, I believe they're calling it trespass on their reserve."

"Well, you've experienced this kind of thing in Africa. Do you think the Canadian natives are ever really going to try to kick the white man out of this country?"

"Anything is possible, Mr. Bull," I said, "even such an unthinkably huge dislocation as that. But I believe you're safe. It's a question of numbers."

"Damn right!" he said. "Although I think they have a point too. Your people must have had a lot of pluck in Africa. Well, enough of this. Go get ready for your trip."

So the following week, after finalizing the semester section plan with Bull, I phoned the Frasers in Castlegar, threw my sleeping bag onto the back seat of the Austin and set off on the TransCanada, and then the Hope-Princeton Highway. The heater wasn't working, and it was a freezing winter, but Mark Vance had lent me a catalytic tent heater, and I figured I'd be okay.

As I drove, I kept fiddling with the radio to follow a live broadcast about the fantastic American adventure of landing a man on the moon, but through the mountains of Manning Park there was no reception. In Castlegar, Ross and Judy and I ate steaks and drank wine and went walking by moonlight in the falling snow. We threw snowballs at one another in the schoolyard. Next morning, I picked up three cold hitch-hikers and slithered up the Salmo-Creston highway where there had been a heavy snowfall, past stalled cars and tracks where vehicles had gone right off the road. In Cranbrook, I stopped at a hamburger joint and bought a round of burgers. The two young women hitch-hikers went off to the bathroom together, and the young man pulled out his wallet and slid his I.D. across the Formica towards me with a crafty smile. I stared at the plastic Alberta hunting licence and wondered what he expected me to say.

"They think I'm 21," he said.

I saw his birthdate was 1949, which made him only 19.

"What's the big deal?" I said.

"They wouldn't let me fuck them if they knew I was younger than them."

"Little rooster!" I said. "You don't have to boast about it!"

When we set off again, the hitch-hikers huddled together under a sleeping bag in the back seat. With four people breathing in the car, the windshield frosted up on the inside, and I had to use an ice scraper to keep a clear strip so I could see to drive. Already, the sun was down.

At Fernie, as I pulled out of the 24-hour gas station, the motor quit. I stood under the hood thinking my way through the fuel and electrical systems, and the hitch-hikers got another ride with a truck. One of the girls called out, "Thanks for the burger." Then they were gone, and I wasn't sorry. To just leave home and go hitch-hiking down into the States till the money ran out, smoking dope and having sex with one another . . . they made me jealous.

I took off the distributor cap and saw that the moving contact arm of the points had slid up on its pivot, and the holding circlip was missing. I scoured the carpets until I found a bobby pin and cut a bit off with pliers and made a crude replacement. This worked, but the metal was too thick to stay in the narrow groove, and before I got to Fort Macleod it came off and disappeared into the distributor, and I had to make another. When I opened my door to get back in the car, the latch froze open. So I lowered my window a crack and tied the door shut with a work sock. The wind whistled into the car, and it was bitterly cold. By the time I reached Calgary, I had made four circlips and there was nothing left of the bobby pin. My fingers and toes were numb. The temperature was -30°F. Driving in at midnight on the neon-lit main drag, I saw with relief a "24 Hours" sign at a Shell station.

"There's no mechanic," the attendant said.

"I can do it," I said, shaking with cold. "I just need the warmth. Can I put the car in your bay?"

"We're closing," he said.

I pointed to the "24 Hours" sign.

"It's Christmas Eve," he said. "That's the one day of the year we close at midnight."

"No room in the inn," I said.

It was a lucky shot: he smiled.

"How long do you need? Twenty minutes?"

"Fifteen," I said, "once I find a bit of wire."

He raised the door of the bay for me, turned all the outside lights off, and came and watched.

I showed him the problem and asked, "You got a junk box?"

He walked away and came back with an old Lucas distributor.

"Oh man, perfect!" I said and removed the points circlip and put it on my distributor. I oiled the door lock and made sure it was working. I was done in five minutes.

"Merry Christmas, man, and thanks a lot."

"Merry Christmas to you."

We shook hands and I was on my way to Edmonton. I drove slowly, aiming to arrive around breakfast. Near Wetaskiwin, my fuel gauge was on empty, so I stopped to put in the two gallons I always carried in the trunk. The key wouldn't turn in the locking gas cap, so I blew into the lock, bringing my mouth closer and closer, until it was touching. I gave the key slit a good warm blow and then I couldn't move. I felt really stupid, lips frozen to the metal like a cow's tongue. I tried to think of what to do and in the end just pulled away, leaving strips of skin on the lock.

In Edmonton, I stopped at the first phone booth and Jenadie gave me directions to their apartment. It was a new building, still incomplete and constructed beside the railway line. I found it and parked and could hear the rumble of a train underneath as I picked my way in the clean smell of fresh concrete through builders' rubble to the elevator. I pushed the button for the fifth floor.

"Oh my God!" Jenadie cried as she opened the door, "What happened to your mouth?"

"It's nothing," I said. My lips had stopped bleeding, and they didn't hurt.

"Rashid had to go to an emergency strategy meeting with a colleague. He'll be back at lunch time."

"On Christmas Day!"

"Christmas is the same as any other day to him. But you're here! All right! Merry Christmas, Alistair!" She threw her arms around me. She seemed excited and really happy. "Let me get some ointment for your mouth."

It felt strange to be there. I had known, the moment I read her letter of invitation, that Edmonton was where I belonged over Christmas. Jenadie had exerted a family pull, tugging my heart. But here, she was part of a couple, and I'd never even met Rashid. I felt intrusive entering his brand new apartment through the fresh cement smell and being greeted so warmly by his lover, when he wasn't present.

I sat down and began to pull off my gumboots, but the left one was stuck. My foot was frozen to the sock, and the sock was frozen to the boot. Eventually, when I got it off, I washed my feet and put on fresh work socks. I sat in the dining nook and ate the scrambled eggs Jenadie cooked, and then she showed me to the spare bedroom. I put my head on the pillow and was soon dreaming again of the old days in Kenya—an oath-taking ceremony, then the Ruck family murders: hacked to death by the Mau Mau, a tricycle on the lawn amid the dismembered bodies of Dr. Esme Ruck and her husband Roger, and their six-year-old son Michael's bedroom in bloodstained turmoil. The Kiambu police station with the four terrorist corpses propped up against the barbed wire screening enclosure. I felt the chill of horror at those grisly cadavers, heads lolling in different directions, fixed in rigor mortis, the gory limbs and blood-soaked rags arrayed in a brutal demonstration. The prisoners squatting on their heels in the wire cage all huddled at the far end, away from the dead. Gazing back at the bodies as I stood on my pedals, I noticed again how the grey-black skin of the dead Kikuyus had turned purplish in death, bruise-coloured. Bluebottles gorged noisily on the clotted wounds. I pedalled away from the police station as fast as I could, under the big gum trees along the golf course on the road to Nairobi.

I woke with a shock. A small, bright-eyed man was standing over my bed, with a mug of coffee, his beard full and intensely dark against the pale skin of his face.

"Alistair? I'm Rashid. Would you like to have some coffee?"

"Thanks. Nice to meet you finally. *Salaam aleiko!*"

"Huh!" He laughed and shook my hand. "You say that strangely!" he said. "*Aslaam alequ. Alequ aslaam!*"

"We have our own ways of saying things in Africa."

He sat on the edge of the bed, and, after expressing concern over my lips, began asking me about my trip.

"Yes? You could fix that distributor? So you are a mechanical genius!"

"Oh no. That's pretty simple."

I was astonished by him. He was right there. A real person—small, only about five foot four, but with a presence that radiated energy. Before, he had existed as an abstraction, a potential enemy with an icy cold voice over the phone. I was Jenadie's friend, and this was the guy who was screwing her and just might be screwing up her life. But as we talked I felt more and more at home with him.

When we sat down to eat I said, "I came here expecting to find a stranger, Rashid, but I feel we have a lot in common."

"Why not?" he said, with his slight accent ("*Vvy* not?) "We are both products of British colonialism. I come from India, you from Kenya, but we share many cultural facets."

He was wearing a striped elastic cotton belt with three coloured bands and an S-buckle. Just like my uniform belt at Parklands Primary School, Nairobi.

"You're both men, dammit!" Jenadie laughed with bright scorn and swung her long, blonde hair over her shoulder. "It's got nothing to do with colonialism!"

Rashid looked at her and sniffed.

"I'm going to take a shower," he said. "Alistair, you know what is the thing I appreciate most about North American life, high-rise life anyway?"

"Showers?"

"Exactly man! The hot water never runs out! You can shower all *day* if you want, in a high-rise. Hot tap is limitless. That's what I call luxury. What are we going to eat, Jenadie?"

"I haven't planned. And I have to go out and do a couple of things. Shall I try to pick something up? Everybody else in this town is sitting down to Christmas dinners, and I doubt if anything's open."

"We have chicken in the freezer. I'll make dal, and chicken curry."

"You want to come with me, Alistair?" she asked.

"No, I'll sit and read the paper while Rashid has his shower. Then he can teach me Indian cooking."

Rashid grinned revealing perfect bright teeth. "I won't be long," he said and disappeared into the bathroom.

I sat and read the paper, which was full of stories about the record cold weather. Exactly a year before, the janitor had tried to send me home from my UBC office on Christmas day. Now I was with people who cared even less than I did about social conventions. I felt at ease.

"Okay, Alistair!" cried Rashid, as he emerged from his bedroom freshly showered and combed, in clean jeans and an immaculate white denim shirt.

"The secrets of curry?" I said.

"No big secret to curry, man," he said, taking chicken from the freezer, "as long as you remember to burn the cumin seeds and use real *garam masala* from India, not the bland stuff they sell here as 'curry powder.' But let me show you the secret of dal."

He was being charming, as to an old friend, but underneath that, I'd catch the occasional, momentary, deadpan look in his eye as he observed me privately. And I was sussing him out too. In my African past, Rashid would have been sealed off from me by derogatory terms, *Chut, Hindee, Jundi-wallah*. Times were changing. I had never been a personal guest in an East Indian's home before—let alone one in which he was sleeping with my white "sister." But here I was.

"The secret to dal is ghee!" said Rashid. "Do not stint on the ghee."

I had never heard of dal before.

The phone rang. He stood still and looked at it while it rang three, four, five times.

"Maybe it's Jenadie?" I said.

"She wouldn't be phoning."

"You're not going to answer it?"

"I'm talking with *you*!" he said.

And when it stopped ringing, he nodded his satisfaction.

I had never before seen anyone sit and watch their phone ring and not answer it.

"Ghee is a kind of fat?" I said.

"Buffalo butter, clarified. Here of course we have to use cow butter. Although I have heard of some local fellow who is marketing actual ghee from American bison, if you can believe it. Edmonton is really a very groovy place you know, Alistair. One can get anything! Everybody is here, all kinds, microcosmic city of the future. There are a great many refugees of one sort or another—people for whom there is no place in the country they came from. There's a lot of building going on, construction of a new society."

"You extrapolate *all of that* from a rumour that some guy is selling ghee in Edmonton?"

"Heh-heh," Rashid chuckled. "Sorry man, getting rather carried away! Anyhow the point is, the butter—doesn't matter—cow butter fine! Clarified, that's the thing! And use *lots*! My mother taught me."

He unwrapped half a pound of butter, cut off a large chunk and threw it into a pot on low heat.

"You don't worry about what the fat does to your body?"

"Oh," he groaned. "Some of those nutritionist writers don't know what the bloody hell they're talking about."

"In Africa," I said, "the fat is usually considered the best part of the meat. A few years ago, I visited one of my students, Makau, very poor, in a remote village in Ukambani, and his mother made chicken soup for my visit. She stood at the fire and carefully spooned off all the fat into a bowl which she then served to me as a special honour."

Rashid threw his head back and chuckled like a tickled kid.

"You ate it?"

"What else could I do, man? I took the spoon and ate it. Beautiful, clear, yellow chicken fat. *'Tamu?* Is it good?' 'Delicious,' I told her. *'Tamu sana, Mama ya Makau!* Thank you very much.'"

Rashid chuckled again and, remembering the event, I laughed with him. Our eyes met, and we both knew that we were laughing about the comedy of good intentions running afoul of cultural difference or mistranslation. Like *"Ich bin ein Berliner!"* the discredited story of John F. Kennedy's trying to express solidarity with the residents of Berlin by calling himself a jelly doughnut. I told Rashid the joke about the Catholic priest in Kenya who wanted eggs, *mayai,* for breakfast, and asked the waiter to bring him two *malaya*, prostitutes.

"Well, tonight we have Bihari chicken curry," Rashid said. "And for you, Alistair Sahib, we will reserve the special fat!"

I sat in the dining nook while he slid around the kitchen on thin, brown Moroccan sandals. He was slim and compact, his movements direct and graceful. But it was not cooking that he talked about, unless I asked. He kept up a steady patter of politics.

"Pierre Trudeau is fucked, even within the Liberal Party," he said. "Cult of personality, with no consultative process. He should have realized, as soon as women began to throw flowers at him, that he was on the wrong track."

"I *like* the man, Rashid! Anyone who can stop and take on the Press, turn reporters' questions back on them, and make them laugh, deserves our respect."

"Okay, so he has a pinch of humour."

"I understand Trudeaumania! I'm part of it."

"Didn't I say, 'cult of personality'? You prove my point, Alistair. Roses in the lapel, what are they? It's my understanding that Trudeau actually had an important political opportunity for the Liberals, and he flubbed it. Lester Pearson deliberately brought him into Ottawa from academe as a bilingual francophone intellectual, to unite the country and defeat the separatists. Unfortunately, he has so much ego that he won't succeed. Wait and see, man."

"If you think liberalism is not the answer for this country, Rashid," I said, "what do you see as the answer?"

He paused. "To which particular question, sir?"

"Oh, enough politics for one night!" I said. "I brought a bottle of Scotch. Let's crack it."

"I second that!"

By the time Jenadie came home, we were looped and ready to eat.

"You shouldn't have waited for me," she said.

"Of *course* we waited for you!" Rashid and I chorused.

8

That was Alberta's coldest winter in half a century. The *Journal* had certificates printed up for people to hang on the wall. "I Survived 40 Days of below 0°F Weather in Edmonton, Alberta!"

I went out one morning with Rashid to get the paper and as we stepped from the Strathcona Apartment building, I cried, "Argh! The hairs in my nose have frozen stiff!"

"You just walked through a change of one hundred degrees Fahrenheit, my friend!"

On the street, pedestrians wrapped scarves across their mouths to protect their lungs and angled shoulder-first into the wind.

For a week, I stayed with Jenadie and Rashid in that half-finished high-rise building, noisy with the sound of tools and the trains rumbling below. We played three-handed bridge, and cooked and ate, and endlessly talked. For me, it was an astonishing immersion course in radical leftist thought. I can still hear Rashid's patient voice lecturing me: "It's not a matter of seeking peace. It's a matter of *enhancing the contradictions* until conflict is precipitated, otherwise there's no change in the power structure. . . ."

"It is necessary to find forms of struggle appropriate to the level of revolutionary development in any particular sphere. . . ."

"What does that mean in Canada?" I asked. "I take it there's no point in blowing up public buildings here yet?"

"Exactly!" said Rashid. "Such a strategy might be appropriate at this point in a context like South Africa. The masses there are ripe for revolution, and many are willing to die to effect changes. Your example is precisely what the African National Congress *has* done. They have restricted their bombing to symbolic targets. Power pylons, telephone lines, that kind of thing."

"Why take symbolic action?" I said. "If you're going to bomb you might as well bomb."

"Oh *Alistair!* Come, my friend. Human history is very largely composed of symbols! Look at Ghandi and salt, look at the Boston Tea Party, look at—I mean look at your own history, Kenya: what do you think the Mau Mau did? They brought about independence!"

"Maybe. Maybe they delayed it."

"Okay, maybe. But how did they function? Were they a big fighting force? No. They were a bunch of half-dressed ragamuffins living in the forest. Did they capture a single town, or derail any train?"

"No."

"No. They did it by raising international consciousness. The press helped them by popularising the words *Mau Mau* and *Uhuru*, and a few pictures of victims' corpses in the newspaper, and stories about oath-taking ceremonies. All symbolism, and voilá!"

"I guess," I said reluctantly. I told him about that display of corpses I had seen outside the Kiambu police station.

"That is strategic, graphic symbolism from the other side, to terrorize the Kikuyu." Rashid said. "Both sides understand the value of symbols. In South Africa, so far, the movement has avoided confrontations leading to deaths. Except of course for those unfortunate individuals who get caught and executed by the regime."

"So what is the appropriate level of struggle in Canada? Try to recruit and double the number of Marxists in the country from six to twelve by next year?"

Rashid grinned sweetly. "Don't be confused by terminology, Alistair. Each situation has its peculiarities. The goal is to enhance the contradictions until people see what is at issue and then they *realize* that there is no middle ground. That's the key thing. You are on one side or the other, man. Eventually, there comes a showdown."

"But I don't get what kind of showdown you are looking for in Canada. Civil war?"

"Not particularly." He smoothed his tidy black beard several times with his right hand. "Don't even talk about Canada," he said. "Too big.

Talk locally. Talk Vancouver or Edmonton. A single campus. U of A, let us say."

"All right, what's the goal at U of A campus?"

"Hmm." More stroking of the beard. "Here we are actively promoting SDU objectives."

"'Students . . .'?"

"'For a Democratic University.'"

"What does that mean? Students get to vote on . . .?"

"It means students take part in running the university. They become involved in the design and implementation of their education. Participation and responsibility for all decisions. Ultimately it means parity. Total equality on every committee and board of the university."

"Students on the Board of Governors?"

"Yes! But not just membership. *Parity.* Fifty per cent."

"*Half* the members of the Board of Governors should be *students?* Give me a break, Rashid!"

He stared at me in silence for a moment, his face patient and determined, without a smile. "I am totally serious, man. As we democratize the university, changes will start to spread through other institutions. Once people have had the experience of democratic participation in their schooling, they will start to expect it everywhere else, in their workplace, in the communications industry, and the marketplace—even in their shopping, so on so forth."

"Democratic shopping?"

"Sure! Look at the way they make you line up at the liquor store like supplicants and sign a little chit to get a bottle of wine. Once we begin to democratize society people are not going to put up with that sort of moralistic, feudal bullshit. They'll demand open liquor stores with aisles and aisles of bottles to choose from."

"I don't know about that. If the Liquor Control Board ever does that, it'll be to cut staffing expenses and maximize profit. Well, I can't get my mind around that SDU one, Rashid! Students governing the university?"

"Don't even call them students, it's demeaning. *People* in charge of their own education. Selecting what is important for them to learn. Yah?"

"How do they know that, if they're ignorant to begin with?"

"Human beings are extremely capable and imaginative, once you free them from the shackles and fog of consumer capitalism and empower them with choice—"

"I don't know, Rashid. I've been appointed Co-ordinator of the English Department at Capilano College. I think it's the faculty who should be deciding which books the students are going to read. I don't think the students can. They don't know enough!"

"And that's because you are an incorrigible imperialist!" Jenadie interjected with a taunting laugh.

Rashid grinned wickedly and leaned towards me. "She may be right, you know. Incorrigible. One day I may have to shoot you, Sahib!" he said.

I blinked.

"Oh yes? Do you have a gun?"

"Tell him what Ché told you," Jenadie said.

"Ché Guevara is the most radical guy I ever met. Won't even wash, y'know? Comes from a wealthy Argentinian family, but he won't sell out to capitalist values even by using soap, man! He told me our duty is to begin the revolution. 'Get a gun,' he said, 'and be prepared to fire the first shot.'"

I looked at him looking at me. Deadpan. For a cold and hollow moment, I wondered if theoretical political talk like this might really lead one day to killing in Canada.

"Ché's dead now," I said.

"Yes. American bastards murdered him, so now the peasant farmers are hanging his picture up in their houses next to Christ. He may be gone but he won't be forgotten."

Jenadie said, "I'm getting cabin fever in here. Let's go out for lunch."

"Why don't we phone for pizza?" Rashid said. He seemed at ease in the apartment.

"Let's go to that Chinese place," said Jenadie.

"Yah, yah! Did you know, Alistair, there's a very good Chinese restaurant here? Moon's Café. Edmonton is a great place, once you get to know it."

We went down to the underground garage. Rashid held out his keys to me. "Could you drive? I'm not confident in the snow."

I got behind the wheel of his enormous '65 Chevrolet Impala with worn-out suspension and crunched slowly down the snowy streets, following his directions to the restaurant. Once we were seated, Rashid began to ask me about my job.

"You are Department Head?"

"Co-ordinator," I said. "We don't have Heads or even Chairmen."

"'Co-ordinator.'" He mouthed the unfamiliar word which was too new then to even be in the dictionary—I had looked for it, to see if it had a hyphen, and not found it. "So, co-ordinates. In other words no sub-ordinates, no hierarchy."

"Exactly."

"And you are elected to this position?"

"Appointed by the Dean."

"Oh," he said dismissively, "so you still have Deans etcetera. In other words it's simply window dressing. Different names but the power structure is still in place. University issues orders, you all jump to obey."

"Not exactly."

I was annoyed at his referring to the college as a university.

"Comprehensive community colleges are not as traditional as the universities," I said. "They are much more exciting and lively. We already have some participatory democracy. I have just struck a Curriculum

Committee to revise our course offerings. Six people, three faculty and three students, with me as a non-voting chair. So, I guess that's parity."

"Good for you, Alistair," said Jenadie brightly, then switched to sarcasm: "And I bet you hand-picked the student reps? All goody two-shoes, huh? No noisy radicals."

"Wrong!" I said. "The students were elected at an open meeting, and one of them, Rod Marining, is pretty forceful and, I would say, radical."

"Very good," said Rashid. "Interesting! If students are really able to change the curriculum, that sounds potentially very subversive to me. Excellent!"

"Come on, Rashid! What's good about subversion?"

"Alistair—" he said impatiently, with a confrontational look, and then broke off and looked away out the window, avoiding being personal. "Societies change, yah? The world is in constant flux. Systems become rigid, become oppressive. In our time, capitalism has done that in a very obvious way. It's destroying humanity because it has turned us into nothing more than alienated consumers of manufactured product. Two billion pieces of plastic shit sold? Only question is, 'How to sell more?' In such a situation, subversion becomes a constructive and necessary thrust. To discard financial profit as an index and rediscover real human social values."

"Huh! The last guy I heard talking like that ended up showing me how to shoplift a bottle of Aspirin from a drugstore!" I said. "I mean, okay, but what has all that got to do with universities and colleges? They're there for innocent young people to begin to come to grips with the world, to learn. What is the point of subversion there?"

"My friend," he said, "universities and colleges are social laboratories. Innocent, hell! People are allowed to try out ideas relatively freely on campus. But the Establishment in Western capitalist society has hijacked the universities. It's put them in a stranglehold and made them serve the profit beast. The only new thinking allowed in the universities now is technological: find new methods of making more money more quickly! Look at who gets appointed to the governing boards? Conservative pillars of the capitalist system, and the occasional token oddball thinker. No truly fresh thinking or values can emerge from Western universities now. They are assembly lines. That's why I say perhaps the new colleges as you describe them may be a beam of hope. I mean think how *slowly* even simple curriculum changes are made in the typical university. It takes two, three years to get approval for a single new course. Everything has to grind its way through departmental subcommittees, the Dean, the Senate, so on so forth. Why? Deliberately cumbersome in order to squelch any tendency towards radical innovation. The whole purpose of Western universities today is to maintain the status quo and prevent meaningful social change."

"Wouldn't it be wonderful," said Jenadie, spreading her hands and looking up with a zealot's gleam in her eyes, "if we could completely disengage the educational system from the military-industrial complex! Just imagine if universities and colleges were actually free to allow people to think and learn, instead of being used as screens for employers. Education would cease to be just a grading system and really help people grow into fuller lives!"

"I don't see how you can get rid of grades," I said. "Don't people either pass a course or fail it?"

"Well then move to pass/fail system!" Rashid said.

"The only people who need the A's and B's and C's," said Jenadie, "are the employment officers at General Motors. Let them conduct their own fucking grading system with skills and aptitude tests!"

Rashid frowned slightly at Jenadie's excessive emotion and asked if I knew about the takeover at the Hornsey College of Art and Design in England. I shook my head.

"It was very interesting," he said quietly. "After about six weeks the authorities crushed it, but maybe they can't really crush it. Maybe the groundswell of student unrest and revolt now is a hydra-headed thing. Crush it in one place, it will rise up in another. The Sorbonne, Berkeley, Hornsey, here at U of A, or at your little college down on the wealthy North Shore of Vancouver.

"What was interesting about Hornsey was that there was minimal planning, minimal political theorizing. Students and lecturers just moved in and took over the main buildings. Art students are not usually political–they're too busy doing their individual thing. But these people at Hornsey were so sick and tired of having a top-down educational design imposed upon them that they just took the place over. They kicked the administrators out of their offices, took over the telephone switchboard, and made sure there was a plentiful supply of food, round the clock. Nobody went home to sleep. They crammed into the meeting rooms night and day, six- seven-hundred at a time, and talked for days on end. See, they didn't really know what they wanted, and the Press mocked them as a bunch of naughty children, but they persisted, and even though they were crushed in the end, some very radical and important documents came out of it."

"Show him the posters!" Jenadie said.

"Yah! Yah! I'll show you back at the apartment."

On the way back, driving was made difficult by a dense fog of frozen exhaust fumes hanging in the air. I hunched over the wheel, nervous of the unfamiliar power steering and the wobbly suspension, and listened to Jenadie and Rashid rattle on behind me, analyzing and redesigning the world. Rashid was explaining that the one good thing about capitalism was that it had an inherent tendency towards inflation which kept the struggle going between the owners and the workers, so that the workers could keep trying for a fairer share of the pie. This evolved into an argument about the Quantity Theory of Inconvertible Paper Money or something like that, which completely lost me.

"Look at these, Alistair," Rashid said, coming from his bedroom with a roll of papers which he laid out on the carpet, with knives and forks to hold them down. They were black and white linocut prints issued by the "Association of Members of Hornsey College of Art." One showed a gigantic fist in the air, powerfully strangling a delicate flower, and the slogan read "power must not crush." Another showed a huge, fat flea swollen from sucking some amorphous body: "BUREAUCRACY MAKES PARASITES OF US ALL."

"I like this one the best," Rashid pointed: Large hands were pushing tiny struggling bodies into a machine consisting of a pair of rollers, and as they came out the other end they flopped into uniform cube-shaped boxes on an assembly line and were carried away. The slogan read, "Don't let the bastards grind you down!"

"This was the most popular one," Rashid said. "People were coming in off the streets to buy it. When I was there, some girls, thirteen or fourteen years old in their neat little school uniforms, came in to get copies to put up in their classrooms."

A day or two later, I was alone in the apartment with Jenadie when she asked me point blank, "So what do you think of Rashid now that you've met him?"

"I like him a whole lot," I said. "But his political commitment scares me."

"He would never really shoot you!" she laughed.

"I think you're wrong about that," I replied.

"Come on, Alistair, where's your sense of humour?"

So I laughed with her, but my laugh felt shallow.

"Who's not facing the truth now?" I taunted her.

"Oh," she replied breezily, "somebody once told me that you don't really face up to the hard truths in life till your parents die, and mine are still very much alive. Rashid's father died when he was young, so he's more of a realist than I am."

The night before I left, I went out and got the ingredients for a farewell breakfast. Early next morning, I baked the scones, whipped the cream, sliced the strawberries and poured the champagne and orange juice mimosas. We ate, and then it was time for me to go.

"Alequ aslaam!" Rashid said, as I stood in the door of the apartment.

"Asante sana!" I replied.

"What is that?"

"In Swahili, when you've had a good conversation, you say thank you."

"Asante sana!" said Rashid.

"Thanks for coming," Jenadie said and handed me a paper bag of fruit.

"Look at that!" I said. "*Padkos*, food for the journey. Old Afrikaner custom. 'Politics is global now,' remember? Not quite the same thing with language and culture yet, thank God."

Jenadie hugged me long and hard.

I began the drive home in a windy snowstorm. It was hard to make out the edges of the road, and I crawled anxiously along in second gear. At Wetaskiwin, I saw a ghostly figure standing at the side of the road, wrapped up in a long woolen coat and a Russian *ushanka* hat with earflaps, holding himself closed against the swirling cold. I stopped and rolled down the window.

"Want a ride?" I shouted.

"You going to Banff?"

"I'm going through Fort Macleod," I said. "I'll drop you in Calgary."

He shook his head.

"Calgary's two thirds of the way, man!" I yelled. "You rather wait out there for a one-shot ride?"

No response.

"You hungry?"

He nodded.

I reached into Jenadie's bag of *padkos* and pulled out a banana. I tossed it to him, and it landed a couple of paces away from him in the dry snow. He looked down but made no move.

"Better pick it up before it freezes," I shouted.

He shook his head. "Bananas are okay," he said.

I cranked up the window and drove off leaving him clutching his sides in the snowstorm. Crazy bugger!

At Red Deer, I pulled into a gas station, handed the young kid my keys, and asked him to fill up. I remembered that my spare can was empty.

"Could you open the trunk and fill the red can too, please?"

I went in to find the wash room.

Back on the highway the snowstorm became a whiteout. I put on my headlights, shifted down to second gear again, and crawled along.

I didn't mind going slowly. I had a Shell card for gas, but not enough money for a motel. I thought, *If I just drive slowly all night, I'll get to Castlegar in time for breakfast.* So, wearing gloves, hat and overcoat, with Mark Vance's catalytic heater barely keeping off the chill, I drove through the invisible snowy landscape, tense against accident. Occasionally, a truck came by and showered me with blinding road muck, but there were no other cars. My mind kept rolling back through the conversations. Something had happened to me, cooped up all week in the Strathcona Apartment with Jenadie and Rashid, the construction workers pounding above completing the building and the trains rumbling below. A window had opened in my mind. Universities serving the beast of capitalist profit! I resisted the idea even as I succumbed to its truth. And what if we could liberate the communications industry also, as they had suggested? Purge television of the garbage that now filled the airwaves and put on quality entertainment and information instead. The image of Rashid was vivid, perpetually talking, as his compact dark figure moved swiftly around the apartment on thin sandals. He smiled, he grinned, he joked: but underneath it all was a steady intent: question everything, undermine assumptions, subvert the status quo. Yet he managed to present these ideas politely, in the British debating manner, without a personal quarrel. And then, that moment, as we squatted companionably on the carpet eating curry together at the low table, when he leaned forward and grinned at me: "One day I may have to shoot you, Sahib."

It had grown dark at the Fort Macleod turnoff, and as I swung west on Highway 3 the snow fell heavier in straight diagonals. I began to realize that this was actually dangerous. If the Austin crapped out, there was absolutely no traffic coming by.

So what? The catalytic heater would keep me alive till morning. I'd be better off than that idiot at Wetaskiwin with his frozen banana.

But what if the heater runs out of fuel?

I contemplated turning back to Fort Macleod for a can of white gas, but my brain seemed to be frozen and the more I contemplated turning back the further west I kept driving, as though drugged by motion. I strained to peer through the blinding reflection of the headlights thrown back at me by slashes of snow in front until the tension was too much to bear. I pulled up, let go of the wheel and relaxed my shoulders and took a deep breath. I turned the headlights off, and in a minute or two my eyes adjusted. Then, with only the parking lights on, I crawled down the middle of the road towards the Crowsnest Pass, hoping that no other driver in all of Western Canada could possibly be fool enough to be doing the same thing, coming the other way.

The road climbed, and eventually the falling snow thinned and I was able to put the headlights back on and drive normally again. It became a clear, starry night, brutally cold. On one bend, I glimpsed six or seven horses standing immobile in a field. They seemed iced over, frozen dead. The gas gauge was hovering close to empty, so I pulled up and shined the flashlight onto the map. I took my glove off and reached down to touch the catalytic heater. It was completely cold now.

I had enough gas in the tank to make the all-night station at Fernie. Plus the two gallons spare in the trunk. I drove on through the looming, moonlit mountains and hamlets, thinking of the historical booklet I had picked up in Hope and just read, about the miners buried alive here years ago in the Frank Slide. I was glad of the companionship provided by an occasional porch light or the fogged, yellow glowing windows of a mobile home. It was after midnight, and most places were dark.

With the catalytic heater out, the windshield began to ice up inside. I scraped for a while but then opened the window a crack to let in fresh air and found that worked better, despite the bitter cold.

At Fernie, a shock: the all-night gas station was dark. No one inside, no light on. Damn it! On the way up, I had specifically asked, and the attendant serving me had said, "Yes sir! We're open twenty-four hours a day." Then I realized it was New Year's Eve. Across the street, I saw a light on in a café, so I walked over. At the sound of my gumboots on the wooden steps, the light went out, and I heard a scrambling inside. I shined my flashlight and rapped on the glass.

Eventually, a man in a green plaid shirt came to the door, cupped his hands and looked at me through the pane. He called back over his shoulder, "It's okay, guys," and the light went on again, and several men gathered round a card table.

"We thought you were the Mountie!" the man said, opening the front door.

"I was wondering if I could get a cup of coffee," I said, my teeth chattering, and my toes aching and going numb.

"We've got beer in the fridge, if you like. Quarter a bottle."

"No thank you. Listen, west from here, where's the next gas station that'll be open tonight?"

"Cranbrook. Come inside and close the door. It's forty-four below for Christ's sake."

"Harry, are you in or out?" a voice called from the card table.

"You *sure* it's open, eh?"

"Yeah. Guys, there's gas all night at Cranbrook, right?"

Several voices affirmed it.

"Even though it's New Year's?" I called out.

"Oh yeah."

"I gotta get back to the game," said Harry.

"Thanks a lot," I said and walked to my car.

You better figure this out right, boy! a voice inside me said. *Otherwise you could end up stone cold dead.*

Fernie to Cranbrook was just over 60 miles according to the map. The Austin did at least 25 miles to the gallon, so the two spare gallons would give me 50.

So drive till it runs dry, and as long as you've covered 10 miles, you can put in the spare and be safe; if you've done less than 10 miles when it runs out, put in the spare and drive back to Fernie and knock on somebody's door.

I reset the trip recorder to zero and drove off, very chilled from the stop. The car ran well, and I felt relief as the 10 mile figure showed on the trip recorder, and then 20, and then 30. Amazing. I thought I might even make it all the way to Cranbrook on the tank, without having to use the spare at all.

On a long curve, the motor finally quit. I slid the gear into neutral and let the car slowly crunch to a halt. The trip recorder read 37 miles. I opened the trunk and reached in to lift out the spare can.

I knew immediately I was in trouble. The flat can was far too light. Damn! That kid in Red Deer knew nothing about filling a gas can. He must have stuck the nozzle in once, and as soon as the automatic mechanism kicked shut, he must have pulled out and screwed on the cap, instead of withdrawing the nozzle progressively at each shutoff, making sure he squeezed the can full.

"It's your own damn fault! You should have checked," I said aloud, and the deserted, snowy road swallowed my words.

I shined the flashlight into the can and estimated I had maybe one gallon of gas in there. *Don't guess!* Shivering, I stepped carefully in the deep snow till I reached a pine tree, broke off a twig, shook it free of snow and ripped off the needles. I measured the can. It was slightly less than half full.

So . . . 25 miles to the gallon, half to three-quarters of a gallon . . . you can go somewhere between 12 and 18 miles. And Cranbrook lies 23 miles away. Twenty-three miles plus. Well, that's better than the 37 back to Fernie. How much of this road ahead is uphill, and how much down? Can't you bloody well remember?

What I did remember was the chilling sight of those car tracks going off the Salmo-Creston highway, on my way up.

I poured the contents of the can carefully into the tank, waiting for the very last drop. The nozzle rattled against the filler tube, and my body was shaking with cold.

Prime it! said a voice in my head. *Otherwise you could end up with a dead battery in this cold, and that would really be the end.*

Without removing my gloves, I opened the hood and reached in for the manual override on the fuel pump and pulled it several times till I heard gas swish into the carburetor.

The car started promptly. I drove at a steady slow speed and eased up the gas pedal at every opportunity. I switched off and coasted down hills.

Suddenly, I caught a glimpse of bright orange and white lights! It had to be Cranbrook, that long main drag with gas stations and hamburger joints on either side.

Then the motor died again.

By the time the car came to a rest, I was in a dark valley. I tried to estimate how far off those lights had been. A mile? Two? Maybe three? It was such a clear, cold, brilliant night they could have been as far as five miles away.

I got out to start trudging down the road with the empty can, when the inner voice said, *Hold it boy.*

I got back in and sat shivering. My watch said 2:45 a.m. Five or six hours at least before any vehicle was likely to come along. Forty-four below zero. In all my life, I had never been in such a cold temperature. Stay in the car, or walk? Movie images of the frozen corpses in *Doctor Zhivago* flashed into my mind. Could a person walk even one mile in this cold? I contemplated the end of my life. No more seeing my two boys. No more excitement of building Capilano College. No trips back to Africa. No more dinners and singing at Orlando's with Paul and Viviana. Never again would I stand in front of a class of students and challenge them by defamiliarizing their comfortable assumptions. No more anything. . . .

And then I remembered the little Swedish Optimus stove that I used when I went fishing. It was under my seat—at least it *should* have been: I wasn't taking anything for granted any more.

I nudged my gloved hand under the seat, and it bumped into the stove. I unscrewed the cap of the brass tank and shined the light in. It was full of white gas, about eight ounces.

Do I put it in the car, or in the catalytic heater?

The car. If there is any chance of getting to Cranbrook, that's better than freezing in the car so the snow plow crew can find you dead in the morning.

Carefully manoeuvring the stove, I poured the precious little glugs of fuel into the Austin's tank, primed the carburetor, and started the engine. Within a couple of minutes, I saw the lights again. Two miles off at the most. I decided to speed up for maximum coasting whenever it quit.

And it did. I was doing 50 miles an hour, and my heart was racing with the danger of a skid, when I lost power. I slid into neutral and hung onto the wheel. I coasted all the way down that lit strip of road and swung into the ESSO station, right to the pump. I could feel the blood pumping through my arteries. I got out, walked shakily into the attendant's booth, and spotted a carafe of old, black coffee. I warmed my hands on the glass carafe, poured bitter coffee down my throat, and narrated the tale of the past few hours to the teenaged attendant, who kept interjecting, "You're *kidding!*"

I paid for the gas with my last ten-dollar bill and made it to Castlegar at 9 a.m. It was Wednesday, the 1st of January. Ross and Judy were up and waiting for me with pancakes for breakfast. I ate and then went to the bed in the spare room, put my head down, and crashed in a dark, dreamless sleep.

When I got home next day, there was a telegram from my stepmother.

"FATHER DIED TODAY OF A TIRED HEART."

Damn it! He had made it out of Kenya, got to South Africa, and died.

Trembling, I called Paul. Viviana answered the phone.

"Hermanita," I said, *"mi padre e muerte!"* I began to shed tears.

"Ah, no, no, *señor!*" Viviana said. "You stay right there, we are coming now!" So Paul and Viviana arrived in their little Volkswagen, and we sat and talked for hours and drank wine. By the time they left, I was empty of emotion. All the while I had been struggling with my important but foolhardy journey to Edmonton and back, my father had been battling death and lost. I felt a shiver run down my spine, because now I realized that the cautioning inner voice I had heard out there in the cold, as I struggled to extricate myself from the mad danger I'd placed myself in, was Father's.

Goodbye Africa. Two hundred and fifty-two years my family had been there. Time to focus on becoming a Canadian and start a whole new life. Make my own contribution to the old Dominion of Canada. Break through the walls of convention and timidity and help empower my students to take control of their lives and build a vibrant modern country, intelligent, creative and proud.

9

Despite my pending immigration status, I should have found a way and just flown to Cape Town for my father's funeral. The College would have gotten along without me for a week, and somehow I could have scraped together the $2,000. It was an enormous sum of money at that time, four months' take-home pay, but I know now that I should have done it. Then, I did not consider it necessary. I called my brother Cal in England, and through the crackle and delays of the radiophone, we agreed that our stepmother and her children could handle the arrangements without us. I suppose that was part of my practical father's legacy to me: to think that the importance of a funeral lay in the handling of arrangements. I repeatedly put calls through to my stepmother in Cape Town, but after a day of sitting waiting for the Montreal international operator to call me back, I gave up trying.

Stoically, I sealed up my emotions, and threw myself into work, and was glad when the spring semester began.

"It's a pity your father never saw you doing this job," Wilma Vance said one day.

"Why?"

"You remind me of your tales of him when he was a young settler in Kenya. People here don't understand Africa you know. They think the whites in Africa sit around their swimming pools all day, calling to servants to bring them fresh drinks. They don't know about the tough business of development."

"Some of them did sit around. Nobody I knew had a pool, though on my godparents' farm we could swim in the green scum in the cattle water tank."

"I see you rushing about, I listen to you banging away on your typewriter upstairs, and racing out of the house to the College, I get quite jealous of you."

"It doesn't feel like being a settler," I said. "It feels more like being a freedom fighter, trying to deal with the universities."

"Because you're fighting old ideas."

Wilma with her poet's insight had penetrated to the nub of my situation, and I felt gratified by her recognition; yes we were pioneers, and it was damned exciting!

The day before classes started, the English Curriculum Committee met to discuss new course proposals.

Student member Rod Marining began. "We'd like to offer a course called 'The Canadian Imagination.'"

"Fiction?" I said.

"All kinds of writing. C.B. MacPherson, Marshall McLuhan, Margaret Atwood, David Suzuki. Not only literary texts. Scientific and general cultural works too. Here's the draft outline we've put together." He passed copies round the table.

I swallowed silently, read the outline, and listened. It was a fascinating idea, but after a while, I grew impatient.

"Your discussion about whether to begin in 1867 or 1900 is minor!" I said. "What is the generic nature of the course? What about transfer credit? I'm the one who's going to have to go and negotiate with the universities."

"It's *our* course," said Rod.

"They have to approve it though, or our students will lose credit when they transfer there."

"No kidding! They can do that?"

"Absolutely Rod. And that means a multiple set of negotiations! At UBC and UVic, the Department Head decides, so it's quick. At SFU there's a Curriculum Committee, and a parallel Student Curriculum Committee and the decisions could take forever. And then there's Notre Dame."

"So what?" Rod said. "You're just bitching, Alistair. Isn't it the same process for any course?"

"I'm not just bitching, Rod. A course like 'Introduction to Fiction' will be accepted, because it fits their existing categories as a course in literature currently offered at SFU. But 'The Canadian Imagination'! How do I present that? Is it an English course, or Philosophy. They don't have an Imagination Department."

"Maybe they should."

I swallowed again.

"Just because the universities don't know what pigeon-hole to put it in doesn't mean we shouldn't offer it," Andrea Halvorson said.

"That," said Barnet Nolan.

"What?" Andrea turned to him.

"'Just because . . . *that* doesn't mean,'" he said.

"Oh, for Christ's sake!" Andrea scoffed.

Someone called the question on approval of the course, and all the hands went up in favour.

"Fine," I said. "But I warn you getting transfer may be slow."

"So what?" said Rod. "The point is, is that we want the course!"

I looked at Barnet to see if he was going to correct the double 'is,' but he held his tongue. I remembered him running naked down the river bank, his genitals jumping around above ginger pubic hair, and I wanted to laugh at the contrast between that frivolity and the seriousness now.

"Without transfer credit," I said, "who's going to enrol?"

"They're public institutions same as we are," said Rod. "They can't withhold credit! Can they?"

"The way they see it, they want control over the coursework for a degree they award."

"Then let's us award the degree! Fuck *that* noise."

"We're not allowed to award degrees," said Andrea. "Rod, there's no point offering a course that nobody enrols in."

"Okay, look," said Rod, "we've approved the course. Let's wait and see what happens about transfer. We can put it in the calendar but we don't actually have to offer it until we want to, once the university dinosaurs eventually come around to giving it credit."

There was a good solution! The rest of the new proposals were more straightforward. I thanked the committee and asked for a motion to adjourn.

"Not yet," said Andrea, "I'd like to talk about second year."

"What about it?" I asked.

"Well, we're stuck with this major British authors course. Why shouldn't we offer Canadian Literature?"

"Or American," said Thelma Smith.

"What's wrong with the major authors?" asked Barnet Nolan. "Students should be exposed to a common core of great literature."

"Defined by who?" said Andrea. "For one thing, they're all men. Were no women writing in England in 1600?"

"Queen Elizabeth," said Barnet with a muddled frown.

"Oh right! And don't let's forget Lady Mary, the Countess of goddamned Pembroke!" said Andrea sarcastically.

Max Odegaard looked from one to the other, puzzled. "Andrea," he said quietly, "what do you want to do, rewrite the history of Western Civilization?"

"I just think," she said, "that because women's voices have been suppressed and censored for hundreds of years is no good reason to continue to ignore them—'*that* is no good reason,'" she corrected herself, glaring at Barnet.

"What?" Max asked. "Go dig up forgotten women's manuscripts and make them required reading?"

"Why not?" Andrea shot back. "If they're good."

"I think we should have a course in World Literature," said Trevor Easton.

I decided to close off the discussion.

"I'm not about to enforce any regulation limiting which authors you put on your reading list," I said. "Put anyone you want, provided you can justify it on literary merit."

Silence. Fine, a compromise would do for now. I could feel a seed had been planted. There was a war beginning to be waged between the traditional elements in the universities, and us cocky upstarts in the colleges. And I was right in the thick of it. On the one hand I had to restrain my faculty and warn them of the dangers of moving too quickly; on the other, I was secretly cheering them on and trying to open pathways for their new ideas to emerge and crack the solid grey walls of the universities. And the universities held all the power: they didn't even have to debate us on the issues, because they held the trump card. They could simply withhold or delay the granting of transfer credit, and then all our imaginative new ideas and courses would fizzle out and come to nothing. I remembered the words of Pam Green: "Very pedestrian."

A few days later, Dean Bull called me into his office.

"We've decided to reorganize," he said. "We'll devolve some of my responsibilities onto senior co-ordinators. I'm offering you the job of Co-ordinator of Humanities, with three Co-ordinators reporting to you: Modern Languages; English; and Fine Arts, Philosophy and Theatre lumped together."

"So I give up being English Co-ordinator?"

"You can do both if you like."

"Fine. I accept."

"Good." He smiled. "Now the first thing I want you to do is go up and see the Head of Theatre at UBC about transfer for our Theatre course. He's being sticky. And while you're there . . . take a look at this."

He handed me a letter from the UBC Registrar saying that their English Department had no equivalent for Trevor Easton's proposed second-year World Literature in Translation though they did have a third-year course offered in the Comparative Literature Department.

"But the *Colleges Act* won't allow us to give third-year courses, so that blocks transfer!"

"Exactly," said Bull with a frown. "Catch 22."

"I'm getting so sick of this run-around!" I said. "I'll go see the Dean of Arts himself."

"Good man!" Bull said.

On the appointed day, I drove down University Boulevard, past construction billboards with graffiti reading: "ABOLISH ENGLISH 200!" and advertising a student Unity Rally. I found a free parking spot on the highway and foot-slogged in to the Theatre Department. The legendary Darcus McAuley was sitting at his desk with papers. When his secretary announced me, he looked up, acting surprised. I took a deep breath.

"Yes, yes, Mr. Randall," McAuley fussed through a straggly mustache. "It's to do with a regional college is it not?"

"We're going to offer a Theatre course at Capilano Community College," I said. "I'm the Humanities Division Co-ordinator and I'm here to arrange the transfer credit."

"Yes, yes," he fussed. And then, leaning forward, "Have you a degree, Mr. Randall?"

"Several," I said. "And you?"

He didn't hear that.

"Masters?" he said.

"Two of them."

"Doctorate?"

"Almost finished."

"Not one of those Florida things?"

"UBC."

"Ah!" He smiled.

There was a pause. Then he leaned forward with a pained look and said quietly, "This Theatre course you want to give. Why?"

"That's our choice," I said.

"You do mean Theatre, not Drama?"

"We teach Drama in the English Department same as you. This is a Theatre course. Speech, Movement and Acting."

"*Why* though! The Vancouver area produces possibly one competent actor every two or three years. And to have all you regional colleges churning out students—it's plain silly."

"Possibly. But that's our decision."

"What I'm going to suggest," McAuley said, putting his hands together in an arch, elbows on his desk, "is that you run your course for a couple of years. Then send me the *curriculum vitae* of the person you have teaching it, and we'll come down and take a look and let you know about transfer credit."

"Our students are not guinea pigs, Dr. McAuley!" I said heatedly. "Do you suppose I could advertise a course with no transfer credit and get students? Nobody would enrol! They may be going to school for the joy of learning, but they also need to get degrees."

"And *we* are the ones awarding the degrees."

"And don't you realize that soon about half of your senior students will have taken the first one or two years of their degrees at a community college—where, incidentally they will have had instructors more highly qualified and experienced than the teaching assistants here?"

McAuley blinked.

"I'll give the matter some thought," he said. "We'll let you know."

I marched from his office in the Freddy Wood Theatre, muttering, "Bloody old fossil!" I was due to meet with the Dean of Arts, and I was looking forward to it. I decided to go in there and relate to him word for word what had just taken place, as an example of the impediments we faced. I didn't know this new Dean. I still felt part of UBC but now also an outsider.

"Dean Kenny is expecting you." The secretary pointed me to a large wooden door. I pushed it open, entered, and froze.

Inside was a boardroom with seven people seated around a huge oval table, waiting. Dean Kenny, tall and looking majestic in an academic gown, rose to greet and introduce me.

Head of Comparative Literature *how-do-you-do*, Head of English *yes-we-know-one-another, hi Geoff*, Women's Adviser to the Faculty of Arts . . . .

I spent a long and difficult time in that room. I had thought I was going in to have a personal conversation with the Dean and get some understanding from him of the transfer barriers confronting us, and some action. Instead, I faced a panel of examiners it seemed. I told them about the World Literature snafu, and they nodded wisely, and someone muttered, "Difficult." I repeated to them the scene just played out with McAuley, and they exchanged knowing looks. I staggered out two hours later and realized that I had brought them my problems and they had cooed their sympathy but would probably do nothing to help. They had used me as an exercise in thinking. I had been ushered in to represent "the regional college problem" in front of a surprise jury. Did I pass? Was I guilty or not? As soon as I got back to the College, I knocked on the Principal's door.

"Dr. Forrester, I want to address the College Council on the problems of transfer."

"Very well," he said. "I'll put you on the agenda for next meeting."

Then I went downtown and had a rare steak and two glasses of red wine at Mr. Mike's, and on to a movie, Jack Nicholson in *One Flew Over the Cuckoo's Nest*. I was there in the asylum all the way with old R.P. McMurphy, fighting the grey authorities. Afterwards I went to a beer parlour.

It was past midnight by the time I parked at home. I tiptoed up the icy steps of the Vances' house and found the front door locked. Twice I tried the handle. No, it was definitely locked. I was locked out of my home!

I stood back and wondered what to do. Through the front pane, the faded pink blur of Wilma's dressing gown appeared, and she undid the deadbolt and the chain.

"Remember when you first moved in here," she said, "we told you if you're going to be out late you can ask for a key?"

"I guess I forgot," I said. "I'll get a key cut."

She frowned. "I'm afraid that's not an option."

"I see. Well, sorry. Thanks for letting me in."

I went upstairs agitated. It had seemed like a great idea, renting an apartment in the Vances' house. They were interesting people and they attracted all kinds of freethinkers and artists. Nobody wasted life in that house sitting in front of a TV set—they didn't have one.

But now it was time to get out. The Vances didn't need me there; they needed some quiet student's rent, as a mortgage helper. I couldn't possibly live my life doing battle with powerful universities by day and having to look ahead to curfew time and ask for a key to tiptoe home late. I needed a place of my own. I would ask my friends at the College to look around for a small house that I could rent.

Dear Alistair,
When are you coming back to Edmonton? It was really lovely having you here, and Rashid talks about you all the time. He imagines what you would say in certain discussions. It's quite rare that he likes my friends, so it made me feel particularly good that you two got along so well. Sometime in April there is a conference in Victoria; hopefully we could drive out and spend time in what looks like utopia from here in the middle of the prairies.

Have you read The Golden Notebook by Doris Lessing? Although I'm fascinated by the woman's life in the Communist Party (her reactions to the political group) and somewhat interested in her struggle to be independent while wanting to be married, I can't decide if it's too good. Guess I'll reserve judgment till I finish it.

How is the thesis progressing? You said you had finished a draft of your chapter on D.H. Lawrence while you were here . . . did you do any more with that? Are you still planning to stay in Canada, or are you going to go back to Africa? Any word from South Africa from your kids? When is the divorce final? Miss you Alistair, do write soon.

love, Jenadie

P.S. Of course Rashid sends his best but if I waited for him to write it would be months before I could mail this off to you.

I put her letter down with a panicky feeling. *You're never going to get your thesis finished because you allow the College to swallow too much of your time,* I told myself. *What choice do I have right now?* said an answering voice. *The transfer battles are on, and for the students' sake we've got to bloody well win them.*

During a day-long articulation meeting at UBC, one grave professor took me aside at a coffee break for a confidential word: "We're actually in a partnership," he said. "Your students become our students. We have to work together."

"That's exactly right!" I said emphatically. Was the message finally getting through?

"In fact," he continued, "I've been thinking, it might be a better idea to transfer the whole of the lower division to the junior colleges and have third year as the starting level in the university."

I looked at him in astonishment. "Interesting plan George, but it has a serious disadvantage from your point of view."

"What's that?"

"You guys pack fifty students into an English 200 class, or a hundred and fifty into Psych 100, and that way you can afford your graduate seminars of ten or twelve students. Your lower division is your tax base; give it to us and you'd lose half your fee income and have to lay off almost half your faculty."

"Oh, really?" He frowned in that childlike, perplexed manner of the academic who purports not to understand gross worldly matters. "Naïve twit!" I told my department. "He was hoping to rid himself of the burden of teaching first- and second-year students, so he could concentrate on his majors and cosy grad seminars and thesis supervisions."

Andrea hooted: "You know what those old fogeys at UBC said when Simon Fraser was being built? They said why not let the new university handle all the undergraduates, and turn UBC into a purely graduate school. Somebody even put up a proposal to helicopter UBC grad students back and forth to teach the undergraduates at SFU! Bunch of pigs!"

I restrained a smile. Andrea's frankness was refreshing, but she did spill over.

After the department meeting, Max Odegaard took me aside.

"Sonia's found a house that might suit you. It's in Deep Cove, close to us. Come and take a look. She's making lunch for us."

He drove me out to Deep Cove where Sonia had a tuna salad waiting, and then we walked over to see the place on the hidden part of Panorama Drive. It was ideal. A small cottage with two bedrooms, and a huge stone fireplace in the living room built of smooth river rocks.

"Look at the floor," said Sonia. "This must have been a summer cabin originally, one big room. See where the front and back extensions have been added on?"

"How much is the rent?" I asked.

"Ninety," said Sonia.

"That's only fifteen bucks more than I'm paying for my little upstairs suite!"

We returned to Max and Sonia's and I phoned the landlord and took the place.

"Oh good!" said Sonia. "And you must come jogging with us. We go twice a week before breakfast."

"With the dog?"

"Yes, with the dog!" Sonia replied, scratching her languorous-eyed Labrador, who looked as though he knew we were talking about him.

"Dogs outnumber people in the Cove," Max commented dryly.

As we drove back to the College, I felt a tremor of excitement, the pleasure of belonging in a new neighbourhood, a community perhaps.

I went to the Dean's office for an afternoon meeting he had called.

"You're the first one here," Bull said as I sat down across the desk. He leaned back in his swivel chair and sucked on the temple of his glasses, frowning at the air in front of him. "We've got a slight hassle with the West Vancouver Fire Chief. He wants no more smoking in the high school classrooms."

Alarm bells went off in my head.

"You can't deny college students the right to smoke," I said.

"I know, but West Van Senior Secondary lends us their classrooms to use at night, and in the morning the high school kids come in and there are butts around."

"Has the school complained? What do you think?" I asked.

"It don't make no never mind what I think, Alistair," Bull replied, sounding like some TV cartoon character. "The Fire Chief's requested me to order no smoking in the classrooms. I knew there'd be resistance, which is why I've called this meeting."

"So if someone signs up for Anthropology 100 at the Lonsdale campus, they can smoke in class. But if they happen to take it at West Van, they can't?"

"That's right."

"Instructors too?"

"Yup."

"Oh, that isn't going to go down," I said. I had an image in my mind of Andrea Halvorson, standing in front of her class waving a cigarette as she moderated the energetic discussion taking place. "We'll have a demonstration on our hands. Can I talk to the Chief?"

Bull looked at his watch. "He'll be here any moment."

"I'll be right back," I said and walked down to my office to get some paper. Andrea's door was open.

"Want to come and help me deal with the Fire Chief?" I asked.

"What's his problem?"

"Smoking."

"Ah no! What a turkey."

I took her in to the meeting. "Is this okay?" I mouthed to Bull, indicating Andrea, and he raised his eyes to the ceiling and gave a little shrug. The other two Division Co-ordinators were there, and the Fire Chief in gold-braided uniform. Handshakes all round, shifting of chairs.

"I appreciate your coming over to discuss this matter, Chief," Dean Bull began.

Inside my head, a small devil was laughing at this lunacy. *A bunch of grown men and women with enough education to run a small republic, and here we are sitting around discussing the question of lighting up cigarettes in class.* Then I remembered what Rashid had said about the importance of symbols. This was not about cigarette butts and matches any more than the Boston Tea Party was about tea leaves; it was about empowerment. In Québec, that week, two people walked past a mailbox and a bomb blew up and killed them, because the mailbox had a little metal crown on it and the letters *EIIR*. In 1968 smoking in class was still a symbol of adulthood.

"It's essential we reduce the fire hazard!" said the Chief firmly.

If smoking at West Van was a fire hazard, why not also at the other locations—our portables were surely more combustible? Was it the smell, or the bad example to high school kids, or was it the Chief being pig headed?

"What exactly *is* the danger?" Andrea asked bluntly, echoing my thoughts. "Suppose a piece of paper in a classroom were to catch fire by accident. The desks are steel and Arborite aren't they? And the walls are concrete. What's going to burn, Chief? The metal window frames? The glass?"

The fire officer's face clouded at her. After a few minutes of uptight discussion, I concluded it wasn't him. The high school administrators were too cowardly to front up and were hiding behind the Chief. Evidently the presence of a college with its culture of lax rules and freedoms within a tighter, more controlled high school was a problem. Smoking was a small symptom of the friction.

"Let me propose a compromise," I said. "How about if the College provides those little crinkled tin ashtrays, and the people who smoke are responsible for cleaning up after class? If they don't clean up, they lose the privilege. Could we try that for a couple of weeks and see if it works?"

Silence for a moment and then the Chief said, "Seems reasonable."

The meeting ended and I stood up feeling heady. Amazing what a tiny success will do for you. Settling over disposable ashtrays!

"Thanks for coming," I said to Andrea as we walked out, but the Dean called me back in.

"There's another little problem at the high school, Alistair," he said. He took off his glasses and leaned back. "Your friend." He nodded to the closed door.

"Miss Halvorson?"

"Apparently she swore at McMurtry, the Vice-Principal. In front of students."

"Our students?"

"High school students."

"All right. I'll take care of it."

"Good man." He smiled pleasantly and told me a joke about the new jumbo jets controlled by computers, "and nothing can go wrong–can go wrong–. . . .'"

I laughed dutifully and walked down to Andrea's office.

"You had a problem with the high school Vice-Principal?"

"That asshole! Has he complained?"

"What did you say to him, Andrea?"

"My alternator was on the blink, so I couldn't switch off my car, and my muffler's fallen off. I had to run into the school office to get my briefcase which I'd left in a classroom. I parked in front of the school, and he comes out and starts yelling at me. I told him I'd just be a couple of seconds, but he screams at me like a Nazi."

"What time was this?"

"Around three."

"So the school buses were pulling in? And students all around? What did you say?"

"I was really mad at his behaviour. I said, 'Fuck off, you pathetic little chauvinist!' Something like that."

"God! Do you want to keep your job?"

"I suppose I'm going to have to write him a note."

"We'll have to go and see him. Maybe grovel a bit."

"Alistair, I'll *see* him. You can do grovelling if you want."

I phoned for an appointment and we walked over. The secretary ushered us into a drab office with family pictures in pewter frames on the desk, and there sat the V-P in an expensive charcoal suit.

"I'm afraid my temper got the better of me the other day, Mr. McMurtry," Andrea said. "I do apologize."

He listened with a dour face and left a guilt-inducing silence.

"I suppose we all have our bad days," he said and proceeded to lecture us on the necessity of decorum. "Well, I appreciate your coming over," he said at last. "I'll consider the matter closed."

As we rose to go, he said quietly, "May I have a word with you Mr. Randall?"

Andrea stopped, glared at me, then went out and closed the door.

"Regarding the Fire Chief and the smoking problem," McMurtry mumbled.

"We've met with the Chief," I said pleasantly. "I believe we've got the problem solved." He waited for more, but I wouldn't give it. Since he hadn't had the balls to be direct with me but had hidden behind the Fire Chief, I let him swallow some of his own medicine. "He'll be in touch with you," I said.

"What a power trip!" Andrea said, as we got into the car to go for lunch. She lit a cigarette and rolled down the window. "And exactly what did that pipsqueak have to say to you that was not suitable for my woman's ears? Huh, Alistair? First the frigging Dean does it, and now him!"

"It wasn't about you," I said. "It was about the smoking."

"And what did you tell him."

"I told him, 'Fuck off, you little shithead.'"

"You did not!" She slapped my leg.

We drove down the hill in high spirits.

With all this trivia going on, it was a relief to get into a classroom, where nobody could interrupt me and I could enjoy teaching. I loved walking in and challenging the students to think freshly about things. There was anger in class then, some of it resonating from the protests of the War in Vietnam. The students would challenge one another, "You're full of shit!" or "You're copping out!" but that didn't upset the tenor of the class as much as it would today. More disturbing to them was the idea I promoted of querying any information they received, and testing its provenance. Where did the information come from? Through what filters? "On his first voyage round Africa in 1497-99," wrote a student, "Vasco da Gama lost 50% of his crew to scurvy." I read the sentence out in class and asked, "How reliable is that information? Who was on board the ship, calmly recording these events and making the specific medical diagnoses of cause of death, while sailors were collapsing–and remember, friends, this happened or perhaps did not happen over 450 years ago?" To my dying day I will relish the memory of my young student Bettina Andrews from Prince George in Northern B.C., standing up outraged, her hands on her hips protesting: "What you're saying is: we can't believe *anything* we're told!"

In addition to these delightful freshman classes, I had the privilege of a small second-year group—*we* had given *them* transfer credit for their courses elsewhere. One night, in English 201, we were discussing the super-rational horse-like Houyhnhnms in *Gulliver's Travels* which Swift uses to show up the wickedness and irrationality of humans.

"How would it be if all the people of Vancouver were Houyhnhnms?" I asked. "How would that affect parenting for example?"

Blank stares. My mistake: too general a question.

"All right, suppose you're a twelve-year-old kid in a Houyhnhnm Vancouver, and you go to the P.N.E. with your friend, and you stay too late. Ten o'clock at night, and Playland goes dark. What would you do?"

"You'd phone your parents," said Eileen, a middle-aged mother who sat in the front row and took copious notes.

"Why?" I asked. "Since all of the adult Houyhnhnms form a pool of parents, and parents are interchangeable for any rational purpose, why wouldn't you just knock on the door of the first house you came to and ask to sleep there for the night?"

"*Far out!*" cried my Québecois student who had arrived late and sat towards the back of the room, his eyes glassy as usual. "*Far out!*" he repeated. "That would be a great *société!* I want to live there!"

Eileen swung round to face him. "Thank you very much Jean-Pierre, but I happen to want to know where my kids are sleeping at night!"

"Really?" Jean-Pierre taunted her. "You know where your kids are at?"

"Of course I do!" said Eileen. "Even when my husband and I take a trip to Hawaii, we make sure that the children are fully supervised."

Jean-Pierre laughed scornfully. "Lady!" he said, "I doubt if you have taken any real trip in your whole life!"

"All right," I said, "let's get back to *Gulliver*."

That night I lay in bed and wondered, painfully, how my own kids were doing. I thought of my father's stream of letters, how he always made a point of writing to me whenever I was away from home, sometimes even twice a week. I couldn't do that. And, I rationalized, my kids probably would be mystified by it if I did. Communication with my children was something vital to attend to, but not right now. Like any other immigrant, I needed to establish a secure home base to live in and maybe bring them to later. Meanwhile, I sent support money; birthday cards were about as much communication as I could handle emotionally.

After the next 201 class, Eileen hung back and dawdled putting her books away while the others left.

"Uh-oh," I thought, "she's going to complain. So damn what? I can't control it if Jean-Pierre comes to class stoned."

Sure enough, she approached the table at the front and began trying to overcome internal obstacles and speak. By now the room was empty except for the two of us.

"Um, Mr. Randall, Alistair, I was–do you ever accept personal invitations from students?"

"Within limits."

"I was wondering if you would like to come to a cocktail party with us?"

"Us?"

"My husband and a few friends. I don't know your situation–you're welcome to bring someone. You have such a different perspective than what we're used to."

"That would be very nice, Eileen. It'll just be me."

She walked away with a confident stride.

So, on a Saturday night soon afterwards, with a map open on the seat, I made my way through the twisting rocklands of West Vancouver, where every house and mansion is architecturally positioned for the best possible view, westward to the Gulf Islands, or northwest over Queen Charlotte Channel to Bowen Island and beyond. I steered my old Austin up a long driveway off Caulfeild Wynd and parked, and as I walked through the landscaped front garden to the heavy door with its dark mahogany panels, I felt in a familiar place. I could have been in Kenya, passing St. Paul's Church in Kiambu, coming under the big old gum trees that edged the long third hole of the golf course along the Nairobi road, and then up the other side of the valley, entering the farm house of Solleys' coffee plantation. Same low *macrocarpa* ground cover. I pressed the illuminated doorbell, and chimes jangled within.

Eileen opened the door, glanced to see if I had a coat, and took me in to introduce me. A nod here, a word there, and diffident smiles. I was soon bored and wished I hadn't come. I found myself talking to their English nanny.

"People eat the most *extraordinary* things for breakfast!" she said. "Kidneys? Liver? I'd rather have a nice fresh apple!"

A nice fresh apple, yes! What a relief from the pressure of politics, of the times we were living in, of napalm and the Vietnam War.

When the nanny had gone, I was chatting with a tall woman named Marjorie when all of a sudden I must have pressed her button.

"Are you one of these communists?" she asked.

"No," I said. "I'm not any kind of -ist, except maybe an environmentalist."

"But you academics are all so anti- everything."

"Well, I'm anti-capitalist. See those beautiful Gulf Islands in the distance?" I pointed. "Imagine the future when they're buzzing with personal helicopters, and used car dealers with strings of neon flutterflags."

"I'm back at university for my masters in Zoology, now that we have an empty nest," she said. "My husband's a successful engineer so we don't need the money, but I've got a job as assistant to a prof at UBC and it's so exciting. However, I do find that everyone I talk to on campus is so cynical, so negative, and opposed to everything! There's no upbeat."

"There's a lot of shit in the world to be opposed to, Marjorie," I said, and she blinked.

"We seem to live in an age of unrelenting cynicism and protest!" she complained. "I saw these idiots from a group called the National Organization for the Reform of Marijuana Laws in the States, marching around like fools for the TV cameras, chanting, 'NORML! NORML!' Here in Vancouver, I've seen brainwashed wealthy kids from West Van sitting on the courthouse steps in filthy torn jeans, smoking pot openly. We had that Be-in at Stanley Park . . . the Smoke-in at Gastown . . . it just goes on and on. High school students protesting about the curriculum, and vicious prison inmates parading themselves before the TV news cameras like damaged victims!"

I bantered back and forth with her on politics, and capitalism, and the environment and I thought she was fine. Working on a campus was luring Marjorie into arguments and making her think. But I sighed for her future in this rich, muffled, suburban world, if she kept it up.

"Have you ever seen a Möbius strip?"

"Beg your pardon?"

I realized that the man standing beside my chair was addressing me.

"This is my husband," said Marjorie. "Alistair, Bernard, Bernard, Alistair."

I nodded to him, but he didn't shake my hand. He repeated his question forcefully. I wondered if he was drunk.

"'A Möbius strip'?" I said. "Is that a comic?"

Turning to Eileen's husband, Bernard said, "Can you get me a piece of paper and scissors and a pencil, Ken, and some scotch tape?"

We watched him cut the paper into inch-wide strips, then tape them together into one long piece and then he gave a turn to one end and brought it over and taped it to the other, making a loop with a twist in it. He handed it to me.

"How many sides does this piece of paper have?" he asked.

"Two."

"All right," he said. "Draw a line. Hold the pencil point lightly on the middle of the strip on that glass table, and pull the paper through."

I did, and when my pencil line came round to where I had started, I took it off and examined it. The pencil line was on both sides of the paper. "Fantastic!" I said.

"A single-plane object–a Möbius strip," he said. "Now, what will happen if you take the scissors and cut along the pencil line?"

"You'll get two loops."

"Try it," he said.

I picked up the scissors and began cutting, and as I made the last snip the two halves fell away and became one long loop without a twist.

"Incredible!" I said.

"How many planes?"

"One, again, I suppose!"

I pulled the thin loop through under the pencil tip, and this time it marked the paper on one side only.

"That's absolutely ingenious!" I said.

"Now you know something you didn't know before," Bernard said. He walked to the closet by the front door and took down a long green coat and folded it over his arm. He turned around and clapped his hands. "On your feet, woman!" he said. "Time to hidey-ho!"

Marjorie jumped up like a huge rabbit, holding her paws together, dancing her feet up and down a couple of steps as he threw the coat over her shoulders, cloaking her. They said goodbye and were gone.

"I like your friend Marjorie," I told Eileen. "But she'd better turn her mind off, or that marriage will never last."

"Bernard was furious with you!" said Ken. "Good thing you'd not seen a Möbius strip before!"

I left the dinner party feeling dismal. I went to my typewriter and pounded out a ten page letter to Marjorie about how unrestrained capitalism was destroying the world.

Next morning around seven o'clock, the phone rang.

"Alistair, we've got to do something about this British Properties municipal covenant that excludes Jews and Asiatics."

"What?"

"We've got to protest it!"

"Andrea do you mind if I call you back after I get a cup of coffee? This is Sunday morning, and do you know what time it is?"

While the coffee was percolating, I thought about the conversation with Marjorie, and felt pulled to her side for a moment. I looked at my letter to her on the table and wondered if I should mail it.

I downed half a cup of coffee and called Andrea back.

"What are you proposing?"

"I did one for you, guy, with the Fire Chief. It's payback time. Here we are in the late twentieth century perpetuating a racist exclusion from the dark ages. If you're a Chinese- or Japanese-Canadian, you can tend the gardens for the people in the British Properties, but you can't own a house or even sleep there! And no Jews allowed."

"What the hell does this have to do with you or me, Andrea?"

"You're the Department Head of a community college which allows this kind of crap to happen!"

I sighed. "*I* am not *allowing* it to happen!" I said. "And I'm not the Head anyway, I'm the Co-ordinator."

"What are you doing to stop it?"

"It's not my job to stop it. I'm doing my job. Teaching my classes and coordinating the Division and the Department. Trying to negotiate transfer credit."

"Alistair, you can't just teach people how to avoid comma splices and sentence fragments and then cash your paycheque and go home. You live in the world, don't you? I'm getting up a picket line at the West Van Municipal Hall. Are you in?"

"Oh, right! Just this one thing?" I said. "Or next week will you be calling me about some other cause?"

"Shit, yes! The nuclear tests on Amchitka Island have got to be stopped."

"Oh really! Amchitka Island, huh."

I thought she was ridiculous, imagining she could stop nuclear tests. How could I have suspected that a scant two years later ten thousand high school students would be converging from the suburbs, marching over Lions Gate Bridge, Granville and Burrard Bridges and the Georgia Viaduct, into downtown Vancouver to protest outside the U.S. Consulate-General's office? And the *Phyllis Cormack*, a small halibut fishboat renamed for the occasion, would sail up to Alaskan waters and put itself in harm's way from the 5-megaton blast, with Rod Marining, alumnus of Capilano College, on board, while the longest telegram in world history, containing 188,000 Canadian signatures was delivered to the White House in Washington, and over a thousand United Churches in Canada from Atlantic to Pacific to the Hudson's Bay tolled their bells in solidarity, and conducted prayers for the safety of the twelve brave men aboard that little vessel, renamed the *Greenpeace*.

The day we stood with our picket signs that read "WEST VAN MUNICIPALITY RACIST," and the scowling councillors ducked past us, was also the day after young people on the North Shore threw one of their legendary "parties." A hundred and fifty rambunctious teenagers crashed the house of some unsuspecting parents vacationing in Hawaii. Police were called, and rocks and bottles were thrown, and it ended up with one officer losing an eye and a police car being burned. That story bumped our picketing of the West Van Council from the front page of the newspapers.

But a short while later, Andrea showed me the inside page of the *North Shore Citizen*. At another meeting of the West Van Council, the covenant excluding people from residing in the British Properties on racial grounds had been "legally vacated."

"We done good, bro'!" she said and put her arm around me and kissed my cheek with her big, red, luscious lips, leaving no mark.

My letter to Marjorie sat on the kitchen counter for a few days, and then I put a couple of stamps on it and marched down to the mailbox at the end of the street.

Yudel Rabinovitch, my good friend from graduate school, helped me move to the cottage in Deep Cove. With his big Plymouth, and a U-Haul trailer hitched onto my Austin for the bed, the kitchen table and chairs, and Murchie's tea boxes, we made the move in one trip. After we had carried in the last box, we sat on the floor and I opened a couple of beers.

"Gonna need some furniture in here," Yudel said.

"A bed, a kitchen table—what more does one need? A jug of wine, a loaf of bread and a Thou."

"Could use a sofa."

"You don't appreciate this hardwood floor?"

"It could use a rug."

"All right," I said, "I'll buy a rug."

"You know," said Yudel, "I never thought I would be friends with you."

"Why's that?"

"Remember what you said after my first presentation in the novel seminar?"

"Not exactly. Something about Monk Lewis' contribution to the Gothic Novel?"

"You do so remember! I finished reading the paper. Prof Gose looked around the room. You were the first to speak. You said, 'In spite of everything you've done, I don't believe you've actually defined 'the

Gothic Novel." I thought, 'Whoah . . . what kind of a schmuck African fascist is this!'"

I laughed.

"You don't believe in direct argument?" I said.

"There are ways of getting a point across. . . ." Yudel sat there with his hand circling to complete the thought. And he smiled at me. "Anyhow, Alistair, I'd better get going."

Everybody hugged in those days, but Yudel was more into a kind of nineteenth century "Pshaw!" After I thanked him for his help, and he'd pshawed me off and left, I sat on the floor in front of the cold fireplace and felt the emptiness of my new space. It was so quiet I could hear myself breathe.

I set up my TV rabbit ears and watched the CBC News, and then prepared for bed. Oh, dear! I suddenly remembered that there was no key to the back door. My new landlord had told me when I picked up the front door key and wrote him a couple of cheques that the previous tenant had left the back door unlocked and that I would need to get a skeleton key at a hardware store, but in the move I had forgotten. I thought of rigging a teabox and a chair to block the door from any intruder trying to open it, but the dimensions didn't fit, so I just left it unobstructed. I went into the little front bedroom and lay down, remembering Wordsworth's line, "open unto the fields and to the sky." I would sleep in an unlocked house, just as Joy and Alan Trail had slept in early Kipkabus days, unprotected from persons with murderous or felonious intent. *Breathe easy, man,* I told myself. *There are no Mau Mau here.* In that mood, I slept.

A great metallic crash woke me, and I hopped out of bed and followed the noise to the back of the cottage. The garbage can had been tipped over, and with the back porch light on I could see two large raccoons and several smaller ones out on the grass yard inspecting their finds. I grabbed a spatula in the kitchen and went out and chased them away. I put all the garbage back in the can, shoved a couple of large stones on top, washed my hands, and went back to bed.

The next time it was a light thud that woke me. I made my way quietly and saw the raccoons were back, and a big fat one was sitting on the garbage can. I watched as he picked up a stone in his paws, lifted it away from the wooden platform the can was sitting on, and dropped it with a slight thud onto the grass. I took the hatchet from beside the back door and chased the animals noisily out of my yard, then bungeed the garbage can lid securely on and turned off all the lights. But I suspected they would be back, and sure enough, in a few minutes, the big fat fellow came gingerly towards the door, so I switched on the back porch light. He stopped in his tracks and waited, but after a minute he advanced towards the door and put his hands up to form blinkers on either side of his head and nosed up to the glass pane to get a good look inside. He appeared so human that I burst out laughing. This little scene of comic relief set the tone for my stay in Deep Cove. Despite the ups and downs that lay ahead, it is still that ludicrously anthropomorphic sight of the raccoon approaching my back door using his hands as blinkers that remains most vividly in my mind. I felt some empathy for him, in his search for food. Knowing the garbage can lid was secure, I retired to bed for the third time and slept easy, untroubled by any further thoughts of thieves and felons.

Next day, the phone rang for the first time. I picked it up, assuming it was still connected for the previous tenant.

"Hello."

"Hello, Alistair?"

"Yes."

"Rashid Hassan calling long distance. I was wondering, I've got an interview tomorrow at Simon Fraser University, and I need some place to stay overnight."

"Great, Rashid! Give me your flight number and I'll pick you up. First visitor in my new house!"

"Actually I'm driving. I'm in Kamloops already" (kam-LOOPS he pronounced it). If it's okay, then, can you give me directions?"

I gave him exact directions, but he seemed uncertain.

"I don't understand about the narrow bridge."

"Rashid, as you reach Vancouver, the freeway ends and becomes a street called Cassiar. Stay on it, and it puts you on the Second Narrows Bridge. Get off at the first exit and keep on the main drag, and that will bring you to Deep Cove. Then make the turns I told you. Okay?"

"Yah. But . . . I'm not sure."

"Listen, if you get lost, just stop and ask someone how to get onto the Second Narrows Bridge. Okay? You have to cross the Second Narrows Bridge. From there you know what to do."

"Okay. I should see you . . . some time around six, seven."

It was one o'clock. I put the roof racks on the car and whizzed over to the Odegaards'.

"Sonia, could you come and help me buy some stuff for my house?"

She grabbed her purse eagerly. "Shopping!" she said with a bright smile as she stepped into my car. "I *love* it! Especially when it's other people's money."

We bought a spare bed, and Sonia picked out a rug and curtains for the living room. Thank God for my Woodward's credit card and the old steel slot clamp-on roof racks. Irene Baldwin, the History instructor at the College, had promised me an ancient sofa they were throwing out, so I went and picked that up and vacuumed the dog hair off it. I picked up a skeleton key for the back door and got another front door key cut. By five-thirty I had the spare bedroom ready, curtains hung, curry and dal cooking, and beer in the fridge. Six o'clock: no Rashid. Seven, o'clock. Eight. Nine. I began to worry about an accident. With nothing left of its shocks, his old Impala was a boat that pitched and yawed down the road. I had horrible visions of little Rashid's dark, bearded head lolling against the steering wheel, with the smashed-up Impala stopped vertical against a tree in the Fraser Canyon, out of sight below the highway, and the river roaring underneath.

I began drinking wine.

I was hungry but didn't want to eat till he came. I turned on the TV and watched a program about the shooting of Martin Luther King, earlier in the year. Violence erupting all over the United States, many protesters killed, thousands arrested. Riots in the streets of Chicago outside the Democratic National Convention. Folk singer Phil Ochs arrested. And the cast of *Hair* singing in angry ecstasy, a happy birthday to Abraham Lincoln: *"Emanci-motherfucking-pator" of the Slaves.*

I dozed off.

A rapping on the loose pane of glass in my front door woke me.

"Rashid! What the hell happened to you, man?"

"Got lost."

"Didn't you stop and ask directions?"

"No—it's a long story."

"Well come on in. You hungry?"

"Hungry, Alistair. First I need to take a shower."

I brought the food on a tray to the living room and built up the fire to a roar. I could hear Rashid chanting softly as he showered. By the time we sat down between the fireplace and the sofa, on the red-brown-orange deep shag rug Sonia had picked out, it was midnight. I laid the plates on an old Murchie's tea box between us, and we tucked in.

"So what's this interview?" I asked.

He grinned, showing white teeth. "Probably bullshit," he said. "Still, interview is better than nothing. And I get to come and visit you." How it warmed my heart to hear his deep, accented voice again!

"Why do you say bullshit, Rashid?"

He stroked his beard quickly with a cupped hand, as though wiping food off it. "Mm, Social Science Departments in universities all over are in—not exactly crisis, but—a struggle. Edmonton, for instance, hired me because of my politics."

"I don't believe that! They must pay attention to academic achievement. You have a Ph.D. and you got that post-doc to Oxford. Don't tell me it's just political."

"In any case, there is a war going on in the universities, between conservatives and various innovative groups. On one hand the old guard want to maintain *status quo*, on the other side the radicals want to get rid of the old structures and let something new evolve."

"But if Edmonton hired you, why are you looking for a new job?"

"Position in Edmonton is just a one-year leave replacement. Beautiful irony is that the guy I have replaced, the Department Head, is an arch-conservative. Soon as he gets back from sabbatical and finds his colleagues have brought a Marxist into his department, the guy is going to throw a tantrum! I'll be out on my ear in no time flat."

"So you have nothing for next year?"

"Americans won't renew my visa. Edmonton is finished. I've got applications in at Guelph, Trent, Queens, Simon Fraser. *Something* has to come through pretty quick, or else it's back to Pakistan for me, willy-nilly."

"You don't want to go back?"

"Of course I do! Mother is there. But not yet. I'm not finished doing what I'm doing in North America. When I go back, it will be on my own terms. I don't want to bloody well be deported. Would you?"

"What *are* you doing in North America? I mean, you've finished your Ph.D. Why don't you go home and teach in a university in Pakistan or India?"

He looked at me, deadpan.

"Why don't *you* go home and teach in a university in Kenya?"

"For one thing, I haven't finished my Ph.D.," I said. "And for another, I don't think the University of Nairobi would hire me."

"Have you applied?"

"No point."

"Why?"

"*Mzungu*," I said and pointed to the skin of my forearm. "Or as the Kikuyu describe us, *nyakeru*, pinkskins."

"But you're a Kenya citizen, aren't you?" he asked.

"After Independence they announced a policy of Africanization. Government jobs would go to Kenya citizens only. Then this was modified to 'Kenya citizens of African origin.' I applied for a job at Voice of Kenya television. I figured I was the only person in the country who met the three published criteria: citizen, university degree, experience in broadcasting. I had all three. I didn't even get an interview. They gave it to a black guy with no degree. Kenya citizen 'of African origin.'"

"You consider yourself of African origin?"

"Christ, Rashid! After nine generations in Africa, two hundred and fifty years, am I African or what? Is Jenadie an American?"

"Interesting reverse discrimination," said Rashid "but probably just a phase. The Kenyans are going to need all the expertise they can get."

"It's more complicated than that," I said. "I did actually apply for a lectureship at the University of Nairobi, and they wrote back rather embarrassed because here I was, a native citizen, and they had already filled their vacancies for next year with imports from the U.K. So they offered me a research position at 60% salary. But that wasn't enough money to let me support my children. Also, the strongest voice in the Nairobi English Department is a Kikuyu writer, James Ngugi, a playwright and novelist, who now writes his name as Ngũgĩ wa Thiong'o, born the same year I was. He's on a crusade to promote indigenous African languages and literatures over English, and I don't think he accepts that native white Kenyans like me have a right to be there. He writes about teachers like me, who were producing Shakespeare and Greek plays in African schools, as robbing the Africans of their culture. Most white people in his writings are caricatures, exploiters and thieves. So I'd be walking into a guaranteed battleground."

"What's wrong with that?" asked Rashid with a grin. "I thought you liked to fight for your position. How else will you make your contribution?"

"It's an interesting thought . . . me up against Ngũgĩ. Agemates, which is an important concept to the Kikuyu. But it's bound to be one of those one-side-or-the-other situations, and I'm a middle ground sort of guy. I believe there's room for Shakespeare and the Greeks, *and* the African writers. The polarization would drive me to join his camp, but I don't think Ngũgĩ would want me in it. No thanks! Ironically, I have my classes studying one of his novels here: *The River Between*. I guess all of us these days are caught between changing worlds. Anyway, I've decided to immigrate if Ottawa'll let me. What about you? What do you need to finish doing before you go back to India or Pakistan?"

He pulled a piece of bread off the loaf and cleaned up his dal bowl, thinking. Finally he cleared his throat: "Before going back to the Indian subcontinent, Alistair, I want to have an established academic reputation. Whether that means the traditional books published, articles, papers at conferences etcetera, I don't know. Things are changing radically in academe, as you are very well aware. Right now, North America is the most exciting place for me to be."

"Tell me about this job interview."

"Good dal, Alistair!"

"Well, you taught me. I always pour on the butter."

"Clarified?"

"Sahib!"

Having finished his dal, he now ate curry and rice with his fingers, cramming it into his mouth with gusto. As the firelight flickered in his dark eyes I thought we might have been sitting round the fire in a simple village. I felt such a warmth at his presence—my brother, my family.

"Situation at Simon Fraser," Rashid finally answered as he wiped his lips and hands on a napkin, "involves a struggle over departmental procedure. Same sort of SDU power struggle we were talking about when you were in Edmonton. Only here at Simon Fraser the battle lines are drawn. Radicals outnumber the conservatives within the PSA department, but the university's faculty as a whole are majority conservative. So the department is up against the rest of the university. Should be volatile."

"Why won't you get hired? Why do you call the interview bullshit?"

"University administration are not going to want some dark-skinned fucking Marxist born in India and brought up on the Qur'an! They'd rather have a well-behaved WASP from Ontario who wears grey flannels and a blazer and tie to class, and calls the dean 'Sir.'"

"But it's the department that hires, huh? Not the administration."

"Deans have an influence. President. So on so forth. I'd be extremely surprised if they hired me."

I had vivid dreams again that night—all in Kenya. In one, I am sitting with my father in the dead of night in the Kiambu Forest with Home Guard-issued rifles across our knees. We are motionless, listening for terrorists creeping through the dark trees. All of a sudden, we hear shots, and tracer bullets rip through the wattle branches.

"Down flat!" my father yells at me.

"It can't be Mau Mau, with tracers Pa," I say.

"Doesn't matter who it is! Bullets are bullets. It's probably the bloody Lancashire Fusiliers ballsing it up again! Stay down!"

The firing stops. We lie there interminably, waiting for some explanation, which never arrives. When I look again, it isn't my father beside me. It's Rashid.

In another dream, I am walking on a grassy ridge near Mangu looking for the remains of Kihimbuini, the Kikuyu village which Richard Meinertzhagen wiped out in 1902 in reprisal for a white settler's murder. A big Bedford camouflage truck full of black soldiers rumbles over the ridge towards me. I run down a slope and reach a dirt track, and now a little blue Datsun pickup is racing along Serengeti Avenue towards the Thika Road roundabout with Rashid driving. There's no time to stop. He slows and signals me to jump in the back, and I jump in and cling on to the sides while we speed away, with the army truck chasing us. Eventually Rashid swings off sharply onto a smooth, grassy hillside and stops behind a stone coffee factory. We look back and watch, as the truckload of soldiers roars on towards Thika, past our hiding place. Rashid grins at me through the rear window and mouths the word, "Escaped!"

"For now!" I mouth back.

On the wall of the coffee factory is a painted metal sign: TARGET GASOLINE. Never heard of it—and besides, they don't call it "gasoline" in Kenya, but "petrol."

"Displacement dreams," Rashid said summarily, when I told him over coffee next morning. "But why you think *I* should be driving you to safety is beyond me. It's usually *you* who does the driving."

"Maybe you're saving me up to shoot me!" I said.

"You don't forget that remark, do you?" he laughed.

"It is a pretty memorable one!" I said.

He tousled my hair. "Not to worry *yaar*, we'll give you a slap-up last meal. Anything your heart desires! Strawberries and champagne for breakfast. Cuban cigar."

I handed him a front door key. He left for his interview, and I went to the College, where I found that trouble awaited me: In order to try to coordinate well with the high schools in our area, I had called a meeting of the high school English department representatives with our English faculty members. We'd had a cordial meeting of teachers and learned about the variety of requirements in the schools. In one school, the students graduated without ever having to write a whole essay, just paragraphs. When their department head realized how out of line his school was, he was shaken up and vowed to make changes. So I thought we had accomplished something tangible, in addition to simply getting to know one another. But apparently I had not done things the proper way.

Sitting on my desk was a note from Dean Bull: "Please get down to my office a.s.a.p."

I found him in there, literally twiddling his thumbs, leaning back in his chair and making small talk with one of the school district Superintendents, who was unsmiling and looked mightily aggrieved. With Bull smiling on, I proceeded to tolerate a dressing-down from this bureaucratic fart such as I had not experienced since I was a high school student in Kenya, when the Dean of Discipline called me into his office for some offence or other and told me I was a disgrace to my family name. I don't remember that offence, but I remember the feeling that my head was somehow becoming detached from my neck—and it was the same with this guy. On and on he went, about "the appropriate channels," till I was ready to stick my tongue out at him or spit on his shiny Oxfords, but I knew Bull well enough by now to read his signals, and his exaggerated affability was telling me to please not resist the man. I called a brief pause and went looking for Thelma Smith and brought her into the meeting. I knew she would have the right kind of education-ese to deal with this guy. She knew how to turn irritation into an articulate argument, whereas my instinct was to tell him he was full of shit and should get out of the way of the school and college teachers, and let us do our jobs with the students. Thelma managed to charm him, and by the end as we left the room she and the Superintendent were talking positively to one another about future meetings with the high schools.

"Well that was a crock of nonsense," I said to Bull afterwards.

"Yes, yes, yes," he said, "but we must maintain good relations with the school districts, for the good of the College. Thank you for holding your tongue."

Smoking, "the appropriate channels. . . ." I was beginning to get fed up with the co-ordinator business.

In the evening when I came home, Rashid was sitting cross-legged in front of the fire he had made, looking at one of my books about the Mau Mau.

"How did it go, Rashid?"

"Who is this guy Dedan Kimathi?" he asked, tilting the full page photo to me.

"A Mau Mau leader," I said. "That's a famous picture of him, in handcuffs if you look closely, taken on his stretcher when he was shot and captured. He's a hero now. They've named a street in Nairobi after him."

"He looks pretty wild!"

"It's the hair," I said. "Living for years on end in the forest and not using soap, they had to roll their hair in mud to keep the lice out."

"No, it's not just the hair, man, it's his eyes. What happened to him?"

"He was tried and convicted of murder and possession of firearms and sentenced to death on each count. They hanged him in '57, a few months after that picture was taken."

"What do you see when you look at this face?" Rashid handed me the book.

"He's definitely defeated," I said, "but you're right, there's something fanatical about the look in his eyes."

"I see courage," Rashid said. "He is down, but he's not out. They may kill him, but he sees beyond the present. He is confident of victory in the long run. You say they named a street after him?"

"Hardinge Street in Nairobi, named after a British Viceroy of India, is now Dedan Kimathi Street."

"Good."

He closed the book and put it back in my shelf.

"Excellent place you found here, Alistair. How much is rent?"

"Ninety a month. Now are you going to tell me about the interview or not?"

"Ninety is not bad! And you have landed immigrant papers, so on so forth?"

"The *interview*, Rashidi?"

"Mm," he paused and did three or four quick strokes of his beard. It was a characteristic habit of his, grooming his jaw to make a formal statement. As though everything he said was being recorded for posterity, so he had to mind his words. "Interview itself was fine. I'm not sure about the individuals or the politics involved. They are on the brink of confrontation with the administration. One guy suggested to me privately that if I were hired, I could stand aside from the fight. Meanwhile, the university is delaying the hire. So the interview wasn't official and there may not be a job. It's going to take months to find out."

"But they did talk of hiring you! Somebody did."

"I'm not going to start thinking it might happen, Alistair, because in all probability it's just bullshit. I'm not even sure I want it."

Next day he was gone, back to Edmonton.

A little later, Jenadie wrote:

Dear Alistair
Here I sit alone in the apartment! Boring 9-5 job in a government office. Come home to emptiness. Deserted! Three days ago, Rashid, after months of hearing the train rumble right under him—always going to parts unknown without him, just like all those songs about the call of the train whistle (only imagine how much more difficult to resist when the train is going right underneath you) well he heeded the call and travelled east. He knew if he went west I wouldn't have stayed here and been deserted. He thinks he can find a new life in eastern Canada— get a job, settle down, start over. I told him he can't run away, nothing changes because of that, but he wouldn't listen. He's determined to get a job either at Queens or Guelph. Of course he says that when he has money he'll send for me. . . .

I was visited again that night. This time it was that horrible thing I've had ever since childhood, when the Mau Mau first began their attacks, my goat's-blood nightmare:

I am captured and in a hut where an elongated wooden bowl containing goat's blood is being dedicated by a long-haired medicine man, a *Mundu Mugo,* wearing strings of beads and metal ornaments over his rags. As the *Mundu Mugo* performs his ceremony above the bowl, a terrorist leader in the darkness of the hut is repeating in Kikuyu, *"Tukurua na Nyakeru onginya muico wa thi. Tukurua na Nyakeru onginya muico wa thi angikoruo matigutucokeria Wiyathi na Tiri witu."* "We shall fight with the white man till the end of the world, unless he gives us back our land and freedom. . . ."

Hands seize my hair and yank back my head. The nauseating bowl is raised to my face. The warm, pungent goat's blood is poured into my mouth and nostrils. I choke and spit it out, but they hold me more firmly and pour it in. Huge clots of congealed blood slide down the back of my throat like slips of raw liver, and I am helpless. I am drowning in it, like the settler Meinertzhagen found staked out on the ground by villagers and drowned in their urine and feces.

I woke from this nightmare with a start, covered in sweat.

Time to make coffee, I told myself. *Forget* Africa, once and for all man! Get on and build Capilano College and let the past go. Let it go!

I pulled out my thesis notes and worked all morning on a new chapter on Faulkner's *As I Lay Dying*. I made good progress, and by lunchtime I was ready to get outside and do something active. So I ate a sandwich, threw my Swede saw into the trunk of the car and drove up to Indian River Road. Where the blacktop ended and the dirt track continued over the hill towards Sunshine, I pulled off into the forest and went looking for deadfall to saw up into rounds of firewood. I filled the trunk and drove it home and returned to get two more trunkfuls before darkness fell.

I built a huge fire, and roasted myself a steak on a skewer of fencing wire in the flames, and washed it down with red wine, and then more red wine. Tipsy, and exhilarated at being in my own new house in Deep Cove, I took a pad and began writing names, line by line: *Joy and Alan Trail, Cassie and Stanley Ghersie, Wing Commander and Mrs. Francome and Ian and Andrew. Mike Ingham, Ian Baldwin, Brenda Patterson, Jill Kennaway, Ian Bompas, Shirley Barratt, Jill Wood, Robin and Mona Stanley and Dibs, Nigel Challoner, Kibiebei arap 'Ngeny, Wilson Ngoka. . . on and on.* With dramatic, inebriated compulsion, I wrote down the names of everybody I could think of who had ever meant something to me in Kenya. Friends, family friends, important society members, students, colleagues, old girlfriends, the lot. Page after page, hundreds of names. And when I had finished, too tired to remember any more and needing to get to bed, I ripped the sheets off the pad, glanced over them briefly and fed them one by one into the fire, and watched the paper curl up and burn. Strangely elated, I fell immediately into a deep and dreamless sleep.

12

On a Monday morning in February, Dean Bull called me into his office. When I got there, he was on the phone but motioned me to sit down. As I waited, I realized he was talking with his wife about dinner. I couldn't help reading upside down the pencil list he was making of things to pick up on his way home: broccoli, avocado, wine.... "Alrighty dear," he said, twisting his slim silver pencil and parking it in his shirt pocket, "I'll see you around five." He tore the sheet off the pad and folded it behind the pencil, coughed once, and then his soft, domestic face suddenly became businesslike again. "Alistair," he said, "we're over the hump. It appears that the College is here to stay."

"Was there ever any doubt about that?"

Bull stared at me incredulous. "I guess you don't realize how precarious the situation has been, and all the preparatory work that went into getting us off the ground."

"Like what?"

"Like knocking on doors all over North and West Vancouver for the past couple of years. Plus Squamish. Plus Howe Sound. Four school districts!"

"You mean the residents had to agree to have the College here?"

"Of course they did! The community colleges are funded by Victoria, but Victoria collects the money from the community by a mill rate on the property taxes: so much per thousand of your assessment. First we had to get the local population to pass a referendum to have their taxes go up. We got it in three of the four districts, sixty-three percent, but it was a long, heavy haul. Next we had to attract students, and, as I say, the enrolment numbers are good, so I'm confident we'll stay in business. Now we have a little breathing space to think some more about the future. I don't believe we've given enough thought to the direction the College is going in."

"We just had the retreat at Paradise Valley," I pointed out.

"Oh lordy me! That was only a beginning, Alistair. That was just getting to know one another. The community college movement is going to change the face of higher education in this province. In the whole country perhaps."

I looked at him with surprise. The old night-school administrator with grandiose ambitions.

"What's on your mind, specifically?"

"A lot of things, actually. Tell me, did you ever fail a course at university?"

"No. I quit one once, but that was a different matter. It was an extra course I didn't need for my degree. The prof had his knife into me."

"I did," he said. "I flunked my required science course, Geology 100. You know what they made me do?"

"Repeat the year?" I guessed.

"Exactly! I had to repeat the entire cotton-picking year, including the courses I had already made A's in! That seemed grossly unfair to me and it still rankles! Recently I realized how some of those academic regulations and traditions are not as arbitrary as they might appear. The typical university system is designed not so much to help people get an education, but to weed people out."

"Yes, but we're not like that at Capilano. We're not going to require people to repeat courses they've already passed; we let them choose whatever they want to take, we allow part-time students."

"Mmer-mmer-mmer," he mumbled, floating his hand to and fro. "Yes and no, my friend. I believe we need to rethink the whole concept of admission to post-secondary education. Who gets it, who doesn't. A lot of fine potential students are losing out. Think of all those gifted single parents stuck in waitress jobs. Anyway, we need to hold another retreat! I've booked the UBC Forestry Camp for the first weekend in March. A hundred spaces. Do you want to drum up interest among the faculty? I'll work on the students."

I left his office thinking what an interesting mixture he was of the new and the old-fashioned. And I went about the College talking up the retreat. So, on the first Friday night in March, a procession of cars and buses made its way an hour's drive east to Haney. Surprisingly it snowed. In the big central log house, with a fire crackling in the fireplace, a mixture of people, about fifty students, and about fifty faculty, administrators and support staff, all sat around and talked about what the College might become. It was a heady, exciting atmosphere, with some alcohol, and, at the outer fringes, whiffs of marijuana. There were several College Council members there.

"What do you think of the idea of an open-door college?" asked Dean Bull, sitting with his suit jacket off in a lotus position before the fire. "No entrance requirement. No academic barriers. Anyone who is out of school for a year and is over the age of seventeen can come in."

"Oh great!" said Barnet Nolan, sarcastically. "No prerequisites? You want a student to sign up for French 100 and they've never taken a day of French in their life? Or Chemistry, or Math?"

"I didn't say *take* whatever they like, Barnet. But the door is open for anybody to come in. Once they're inside, we find what's appropriate for them to take."

"So we become a remedial institution. Upgrading high school dropouts."

"Not necessarily," said Bull. "Look, I'm trying to open a discussion here. Don't close it off so quickly."

He *was* wearing a tie even at the retreat and he had chosen to drive in every day to the sessions in his MGB sports car, rather than risk sharing a log cabin with us and the students, but his thinking was progressive. Behind his modest necktie lay the heart of a missionary, and his mission was to break old moulds and create a place where higher education was dynamic and exploratory.

"How about grades?" I said, remembering conversations in Edmonton. "Maybe we can get rid of grades."

"Another very interesting idea," said Bull. "I believe at Shoreline College, south of the border, they're using Pass/Fail. That takes away some of the rigid competitiveness and allows students to take more intellectual risks."

"What kind of risks do you mean?" Barnet asked skeptically.

"My father used to tell a story," I broke in: "At the University of Cape Town, his friend Knott-Craig, who later became the Registrar, sat to write his final exam in Economics. The exam paper required that you choose three questions. He wrote across the top of his answer paper:

'Attempting to address three questions in three hours will only produce superficial answers. I shall attempt to answer one question in depth.' He passed, of course."

"I approve of that kind of boldness," Bull said. "A Pass/Fail system might encourage it."

"At Shoreline they don't call it Pass/Fail," Andrea Halvorson interjected. "It's P and NYP, Pass and Not Yet Passed."

"Sounds like a kidney stone," said Bull and got a laugh. And the conversation kept vacillating like that, between new ideas punctuated by jokes.

All Saturday it snowed heavily as we talked and dreamed and argued, and after supper some of us went outside and began to throw snowballs in the bright moonlight. When I came back in, wet and cold, and stood in front of the blazing fire, I realized I had lost my watch. Damn! It was the Tissot my father had bought me from David Lyall Jewellers in Nairobi for my twelfth birthday.

"I'll help you look for it," said one of the students, Caroline Bell. She strode ahead of me, outside.

"I don't think we have a hope of finding it," I said despondently, looking around at the expanse of rough, bright snow.

"Don't be so negative! Over here. You were over here."

We looked in the broken snow, and sure enough, there it lay. Caroline snatched it up and held it teasingly behind her. I reached for it and she kissed me on the mouth. Next thing, we were rolling in the snow, and her tongue was in my mouth. Then I got up and we brushed ourselves off and went inside to warm up, our little fingers interlinked.

Later, at cocoa time, I found Andrea and asked her, "Do you think it's okay to have something going with a student?"

"A student? A sexual thing?"

"Could become."

"Not if she's in your class, Alistair!" Andrea said at once. "Otherwise I suppose it's okay. The bra-less Miss Caroline Bell huh?"

"She *is* in my class."

"Then absolutely not!"

I knew Andrea was right. Our fledgling Faculty Association had passed a number of policy guidelines, and one of them was that faculty should not enter into personal relationships with students, if this caused upset to any member of the class. So for the rest of the retreat I took care not to be alone with Caroline. But after we packed up on the last morning and I stood in front of the fire, she came up to me and smiled bashfully and said, "Could I bum a ride home with you?"

"Sure!" I said breezily. "I can take three people," and I went around offering until I got two other students in the car as well. I dropped the three off at various locations on the North Shore and went home, high on all the talk we had had. For many days and nights after that I remembered the excitement of that roll in the snow, the softness of Caroline Bell's cold, wet face, her tongue, the clean scent of carnations off her skin, the memory of her plump, sun-tanned breasts swinging from side to side as she ran the naked relay race at the Cheakamus River....

One night, Caroline phoned me at home.

"I've got my photographs developed from the retreat. I could bring them round. Would you like to see them?"

I was too weak to refuse. She drove up in her Volkswagen and we sat at my kitchen table with mugs of tea, looking at the pictures. My skin tingled when our hands accidentally touched. There was one snap of her and me with our arms draped over each other's shoulders.

"Do you work as well as go to school?" I asked, evasively.

"Yep. I work in the daycare at the North Shore Neighbourhood House. I love the kids, and it pays my tuition fees."

Then she looked me full in the face and said, "Alistair, do you ... want to go for a walk with me some time?"

I took a deep breath and sat up straight. "Caroline," I said, "I can't do this. You're a student in my class."

"I see." She looked down, thoughtfully. "What about after the semester ends?"

"That would be a different story," I said.

She gathered her photos and left, and in the days that followed I would see her in class with a coy secret hidden in her bright blue eyes.

At the next department meeting, Thelma Smith raised her hand to speak, and I nodded.

"In one of the discussions at Haney," she said, "I was disturbed to hear about some of the pedagogical approaches being taken to the teaching of English Composition."

I groaned inwardly. "Pedagogical" was one of Thelma's favourite words. It might do to mollify an aggrieved School Superintendent but it put me off completely. I sat there pretending to pay attention as she rambled on.

". . . and when people do things like bringing puppies to class as subjects for writing, I have to ask is academic writing really being taught? It seems to me more like show and tell in kindergarten."

"What are you proposing," Andrea Halvorson demanded. "That we go back to traditional grammar?"

"The new generative theories have killed traditional grammar," said Max Odegaard.

"Yeah but only wonky-eyed specialists can understand generative and transformational theory," said Andrea. "And the high schools seem to have absolutely given up any attempt at grammar. The English teachers are mostly playing tapes or showing films. My students can't tell a noun from a verb. Unless they're also studying French or German."

I listened to the discussion without interfering. My mind went off on another track As Co-ordinator, it was my job to approve people's course outlines, and I had adopted a wide-open policy: anything they could justify to themselves as enabling the students to learn and write passed my scrutiny. For myself, in literature classes I began by carrying my portable record player into class, and had the students analyze the structure of contemporary songs. I had had a great class with Judy Collins singing Joni Mitchell's "Both Sides Now":

"Can you see any progression in the three verses?" I asked, after playing the song.

"It moves from childhood to adolescence to adulthood."

"Well done! And the theme is?"

"Relationships. Love."

"Good. Does the mood change?"

"'Mood'?"

"Her feelings."

"Well, her imagination is strong as a child, like 'Ice-cream castles in the air.' And later when she's a teenager it's all romantic mush, and when she's old it's so dull. Trying not to reveal your feelings. And dumping them before they dump you."

"Right. And don't let on that you care about them. All the way from the child's bright visions to sexual politics?"

"It gets dull."

I was very happy with this.

Next class I brought in Gordon Lightfoot singing "Changes," all about the turning of the leaves from green to red, to brown and yellow.

"It's about the seasons, right?" I suggested.

"It pretends to be, but it's not!" said Jessica Phelps, the outspoken feminist of the class. "He's a typical male chauvinist trying to justify swinging, and failing to commit to a relationship!"

". . . and I take exception to your criticizing me for bringing an animal to class," I suddenly heard Max Odegaard say angrily, which brought my wandering mind back to the department meeting. "It wasn't a puppy, anyway, Thelma, it was a kitten and it led to some very fine writing." Jolted out of my reverie I called an end to the meeting.

As we moved out of the common room known as the Bull Pen, I asked Andrea: "Did you know that Gordon Lightfoot singing 'Changes' is a male chauvinist saying 'Use women and lose them'? That's what my student told me in class."

She eyed me strangely and punched my arm. "Don't tar my hero," she said.

"Who?"

"Phil Ochs wrote 'Changes.' He's coming to town to do a benefit concert for the *Georgia Straight* Legal Defence Fund. You want to go with me and hear him? Kurt can't stand him."

"Certainly."

On the day of the concert, I drove to Andrea and Kurt's place, an old farmhouse off the Loughheed Highway in Burnaby.

"We've got to get there early," Andrea said, climbing into the car. "It's going to be a sellout."

We reached the Garden Auditorium in plenty of time and got seats in the balcony. People poured in and soon the place was full. Scruffily dressed young men and women began to sit on the floor along the walls. Some of the overflow settled on the steps on each side of the stage. Stan Persky, the young radical student Vice-President from UBC, was the master of ceremonies. Three poets read briefly and then Persky led Phil Ochs up on stage. "Move off the dais, let's give him some room here!" he muttered to the people sitting on the steps. He took the mike and said, "Want you all to welcome, please, Phil Ochs!"

Through the polite applause Ochs came forward where the spotlight made his fringe of red-brown hair glow, and he stood smiling shyly in front of the microphone stands. A technician adjusted the mikes to his mouth and guitar. The crowd fell silent.

"Good evening. This is my first evening in Vancouver," he said with a little *ritard*, "Vann- Couver," and made it sound an innocent place. But then he strummed his guitar harshly twice. He announced that he had been to Canada, before [strum] "Toronto [broken chord] a lot, [plucked note] Montreal," [broken chords] "where all the extremists live." This last was meant to be a throwaway joke, but there was no rapport. The audience was waiting.

God damn it, I thought, another bloody American coming up here to tell us how to live.

Ochs must have realized that he had misread the crowd, for he launched immediately into a popular choice: "There but for Fortune." At the end of that number, through the applause a young man called out a question, and Ochs, raising a hand to shield his eyes from the bright spotlights, called back, "What's that?" and the question was repeated. I couldn't catch it, but it broke the ice. "I've been living in Los Angeles," Ochs replied, "and I haven't been singing much ever since Chicago. So if I don't remember the words you've gotta forgive me." He turned his face slightly, back to all of us. "I wrote these songs a while ago when I was but a kid, walking through the American wilderness."

He began a strong strumming, and spontaneous applause greeted him as people recognized his ballad about the murder of Kitty Genovese in Queens, which dozens of people watched from their apartments, and nobody went to help her. Through the clapping he sang about people ignoring the stabbed woman as they returned to Monopoly or *Playboy* and the Sunday *New York Times*, and marijuana.

I was uncomfortable. I didn't trust him, and the whoops and yells of the political in-group were pissing me off. I turned to Andrea and saw her face was transfixed. Her nipples were erect under her blouse.

"God, what an artist!" she said. "Do you realize this is spontaneous? He's got no set plan for this concert. He's communicating with us just as he finds us."

I cast her a skeptical look.

Phil Ochs kept harping on Chicago until I began to think that Andrea might be right. We had all been shocked and numbed by the news and seen the pictures of the Chicago police breaking up the "Get Out of Vietnam" demonstration at the Democratic National Convention, but Ochs just couldn't get over it. He could not get over the fact that Mayor Daley had turned the city police onto the left wing and Yippie demonstrators. Ordered to take their badges off to avoid identification, the cops beat and tear-gassed people in Lincoln Park, Grant Park, up Michigan Avenue to the Convention Center, clubbing and kicking and stomping as they went. Ochs asked us where all the people were who had promised to come to Chicago and didn't show up. But he ended by singing that he himself was in Detroit. Sporadic clapping. The audience didn't know how to take this twist. They applauded politely.

"That's about the Movement's psychology," Ochs said, and the groupies gave a few knowing yelps. He told us that Chicago was going to come to Vancouver, and we would all meet Mayor Daley personally, and then he said that at Chicago . . . something died, and it was America.

The crowd fell silent at this bitterness. And immediately he began to sing again, in a youthful, high, plaintive voice, his memory of the events that day in Lincoln Park. By the end of this lyric he had won me over. The aching sadness in his heart swept me with empathy. His boyish face so vulnerable, his voice so high and determined. He kept bathing us in his feelings, all circling around the damned Vietnam war.

The next song he dedicated to John Wayne and the film maker John Ford, saying that it was extraordinary that some of America's greatest artists were not especially intelligent. This brought a loud guffaw from Stan Persky.

Ochs shrugged, saying nobody could take these matters seriously, and then launched into a fragile, bleak tale about sailors' lonely lives, coming into harbour to whisky and women, and going back out again to continue their struggle at sea, battling the elements, one slip away from death.

Suddenly the mood picked up with rhythm as he sang Edgar Allen Poe's "The Bells," and a heavily bearded man with large black glasses stepped out behind him on the stage and joined in, briskly ringing two small silver bells.

"Good lord, it's *Ginsberg!*" Andrea whispered excitedly. "That's Allen Ginsberg! Can you believe this? The high priest of the Beats is here in Vancouver!"

Still merry with the bells, Ochs sang Alfred Noyes' poem, about "the Highwayman comes riding, riding, riding" towards "Bess, the landlord's daughter, plaiting a dark red love-knot into her long black hair." His voice slowed for the sacrifice as the woman pulls the trigger of the musket pointing at her breast to warn her lover of the ambush awaiting him. Phil Ochs had brought us all to tears. The woman sitting next to me was wiping her eye on the back of her hand.

As he sang the strange lyric "The Doll House," Ochs began a monotonous drawl on some of the syllables and the crowd chortled.

"I don't get it," Andrea said.

"He's imitating Bob Dylan."

"Oh, *Dylan*," she said dismissively.

"What have you got against *my* hero?"

"Shh!"

Ochs went back relentlessly to the war:

His voice grew more and more angry. Bitterness mounted to a patriotic climax or was it treason? He pledged allegiance "*against* the flag," and to the land. The applause was thunderous and insistent. Andrea took my arm above the wrist in both her hands and began squeezing it and letting go, squeezing and letting go, in the rhythm of a mother keening at the loss of a child.

Ochs stood in the bright light, gently thumbing strings on his guitar, and then, as the noise quieted down, he broke softly and lyrically into "Changes." I felt a disturbing disconnect between the anger in this concert, and the careful, quiet analyses my students had made of "Changes" with its seductive lyricism.

From those gentle rhythms, Ochs veered off again to the harsh strains of "Crucifixion," his elegy for the murdered leaders, John and Robert Kennedy and Martin Luther King.

Then, very quietly he announced that he would sing us a protest song, which he defined as something they don't play on the radio because they claim the guy can't sing and they play shit instead. He rambled on about the media, and the Vietnam War, and the Kennedy assassinations and said we were just helpless pieces of flesh surrounded by cruel machinery and terrible heartless men. So he said all we can do is turn away from filth and here was a turning away song.

As he talked, he had been worrying at a D note, and now he picked it insistently [ting-ta-ta-ting-ting-ting], followed by a trickle of seconds down to the G, and again, until some in the audience, recognizing and anticipating the song that was coming, began to clap hands:

Verse by verse, he sang the history of American wars, from the Battle of New Orleans to Hiroshima and the Cuban missile crisis ending each verse with the defiant chorus, *"I ain't marching anymore!"*

This last line was ringing in my head as we left our seats and made for the doors:

"Jesus!" I said to Andrea, as we came out of the building, "I've been to bullfights in Spain where my shirt stuck to my back, but I've never been through anything as emotionally wringing as that!"

"Didn't I tell you?"

"What did he mean when he called John Wayne a truly great artist? Was that straight or ironical?"

"Sarcastic!" she said.

"I honestly couldn't tell. It sounded like he meant it."

"Phil Ochs is full of contradictions. That's why you can trust him. Oh, what a tender man! He won't survive, you know? The war will break his heart, if the CIA doesn't assassinate him first."

For weeks and months to follow, every morning when I woke up, Phil Ochs' music was in my head. As I walked around, I whistled or sang bits of his plaintive melodies, and I heard the nuances of his voice, saw flashes of him standing alone in the spotlight, "turning away," standing against fraud, pledging allegiance against the flag and to the land. Even now, forty years later, and over thirty since he hanged himself with his belt in his sister's bathroom in Far Rockaway NY during the American Bicentennial hoopla, Phil Ochs stays imprinted in me, more than any other singer of the time, more than Donovan, more than Dylan, different from the Beatles and the Rolling Stones.

That night in the Vancouver Garden Auditorium, Phil Ochs added flint to my soul. And I think of that tender young man as a spark of light. I bought his records and played them incessantly. In all the dark times to come and the dark memories that resurfaced—like Kaspar Naegele's mysterious fall from that tenth-floor window at the Vancouver General Hospital—I leaned towards the lyrical truth of Phil Ochs' voice to remind me of our humanity, our vulnerability. The paroxysm of war shook us all then, as it shakes us today when the armies and the suicide bombers do their tragic business, and the body bags come home from Iraq to the USA, from Afghanistan to Canada, leaving scores of dead in those lands, and the enraged multitudes raise their fists and cry their bitter hatred against *Amrika! Amrika!* And how many people die each day in Congo or Darfur, unknown to anyone outside their own small circle?

Two letters arrived from Jenadie, the first an angry rant: Rashid had had an interview at Dalhousie University and was told a teaching job was his and they were just working out his placement on the salary scale. Five days later, he received another letter from them regretting that there were no openings at Dalhousie. *"Obviously the administration got word that Rashid was a 'trouble maker.' Bastards!"* Her second letter came the following day:

> *Dear Alistair,*
> *You won't believe this—well, I don't believe it, maybe you will. Rashid has been offered the job at Simon Fraser University. I practically screamed with excitement ... to return to Vancouver! To be with all the people there! To at last put down roots in familiar soil! Depends on many things, but we may move out in the summer. Rashidi is so excited. He was seriously thinking of returning to India ... but then Simon Fraser came through. So, if you hear of any houses for rent, keep us in mind. ...*

I called my landlord right away and asked if he had any other places for rent. He gave me the address of a two-bedroom Panabode house on West Keith Road in North Vancouver that would be available in August. I drove over and looked at it, called Rashid and Jenadie, and wrote the deposit cheque.

At the end of the semester, I was still full of adrenalin from Phil Ochs' declaration of the dawn of a new age, when I went before the College Council to ask for their help in the transfer battle. There were nine Council members present, seven men and two women, with Maureen Ingleton, the Principal's secretary, taking minutes. They listened to me without interruption as I poured out my frustration.

"Many of the people I deal with at the universities are progressive and open-minded," I said, "but there are also some real Neanderthals blocking the road. They don't respect the colleges at all—they put us down by stubbornly referring to us as 'junior colleges' or 'regional colleges' instead of community colleges. They don't care about the good of the educational community but are focused on preserving their own autonomy. They are narrow minded, blinkered parochialists. I have come to the conclusion—and I would like to suggest to the Council and to you as individual Council members that you go after your government connections on this—that the *only* satisfactory way to solve the transfer problem for college students in BC is by legislation. The universities can still retain their autonomy and set up any prerequisites they want for specific courses or programs, but they must give at least unassigned credit for all our academic courses. Otherwise, our students, instead of getting a degree after 120 credit hours, are going to have to take an extra course, or two, or three. An additional semester, an additional year. It's deeply unfair to them. Some of the university people I negotiate with pretend to be concerned, but they really just don't give a damn about it. They pass the buck. The only way to solve the problem is legislation. The provincial government should pass a law saying that as a condition of receiving their operating grants, all publically funded universities in BC must grant transfer to all eligible college courses. Thank you."

I sat down, feeling the heat in my face.

"Do we not have a provincial Articulation Board that oversees these matters?" asked one of the school board appointees.

"We do, but it's got no teeth," I replied. "All the Academic Board has the power to do is call meetings and serve coffee, in the hope that we'll talk it out and reach agreement. Let me give you an example of how that doesn't work," and I rehearsed for them the humiliation of my meeting with Darcus McAuley at UBC. "The man sits there and tells me to run our Theatre courses without transfer credit for two years, and then he'll deign to come down and inspect us and make a decision. That's totally unacceptable. That's what I mean by Neanderthals."

A pasty-faced business type in a grey suit, a government appointee to the Council, raised a finger, and the chairman nodded.

"I would hope that we can conduct these matters without resort to disparaging language."

"Forgive me, Mr. Campbell," I interrupted. "I take back 'Neanderthals.' Call them stick-in-the-muds. It's just that I'm so frustrated."

"I understand that," said Campbell. "But negotiations are best conducted with modest words, in my experience."

"I've already said I'm sorry," I repeated quietly.

"Yes. Now with respect to the transfer issue, it may be that we are dealing with a perception rather than a real problem."

Oh don't give me your stupid buzzwords, you asshole! I thought, but I leaned forward attentively as he spoke for several more minutes.

"As regards legislation," Campbell finished with a smug little smile, "I hardly think the Western tradition of academic freedom would be compatible with a provincial government endeavouring to impose laws constraining the universities to grant transfer credit."

"Why not?" My voice was loud and confrontational, and Campbell blinked twice. "New York State does it," I said. "California does it. By law, the State University of New York with all its many campuses and colleges, cannot require any student to take more than 120 credits to get an undergraduate degree. All of the state colleges and universities in California are governed by a similar law. They have to give transfer credit for one another's courses. What's wrong with British Columbia doing it? Don't we have the same resolve to stand up for our students as those two American states?"

No one answered. I looked around at them. *You bunch of overdressed chickens! Are you so afraid to stand up to either the government or the universities in case you fall out of favour and lose kudos and whatever little stipend they're paying you to sit at these meetings?*

"Thank you very much, Mr. Randall," said the chairman. "We appreciate your input and will take your remarks under advisement. I'll make sure the girl sends you a draft copy of the minutes to check the accuracy."

I turned my head deliberately to look over at Maureen Ingleton. She smiled back at me. "The girl." Thirty-seven-year-old mother of two. Pretty much keeps Capilano College running day to day. "The girl." *Fucking hell!*

"Thank you very much," I said and walked out.

The battles had exhausted me, but the excitement of dealing with my colleagues and the students buoyed me up, even though I was teaching four classes plus administering the English Department and the Humanities Division, and fighting the transfer battles with the universities. At the end of the semester I presented the Dean with our proposed revision of the curriculum, and he went over it carefully. He asked for explanations of several points, and finally initialled the bottom of the plan.

"That's it for me!" he said. "I am now off for two weeks! And by the way, the Council approved in principle the open door policy. Now we have to work out the details."

"Congratulations!" I said and shook his hand across the desk. I went back to my office flushed with success. In the coming year, we would have a whole new slate of first-year English courses—including "Themes in Contemporary Literature": the universities had hemmed and hawed but at last one of them, Simon Fraser, had finally granted it unassigned transfer credit as an elective—though not "The Canadian Imagination." That would have to wait a few years.

Next day, with Bull on vacation, I gathered my energy for one last push and went in to see Denby Forrester.

"That was a most forthright presentation you gave at Council," he said.

"Thank you," I said. "Now look, I want to ask you to think about reducing English Composition classes from the regular 40 to a maximum size of 25. There's a very heavy marking load. Much heavier than in any other course."

It took about twenty minutes, and to my amazement he agreed. I decided to leave it till after my vacation to deal with the new hirings. I was ready to goof off. I phoned Jenadie, and she invited me up to Edmonton. They were moving out of the apartment at the end of May but they had the use of a colleague's big old house beside the university for the whole month of June, and I was welcome to come and stay.

There were a couple of late final persuasive essays from my English 100 class, and I sat down to mark them. The Persuasive Essay question I had posed was, "At what other time in history would you have preferred to live, and why (or why not)? Try to convince me." Most of the answers came in nostalgically favouring the horse and buggy days before cars, or exciting epochs like the Italian Renaissance. But one young student knocked me out: "I would like to have lived in a truly romantic time," she wrote, "like the 1950s." I phoned and called her in to my office.

"Your writing is grammatically correct and the essay flows smoothly and coherently," I said, "so I've given you a passing mark. But you didn't actually succeed in persuading me, which is what I asked you to do. I *remember* the 1950s, Diana! *The Man in the Grey Flannel Suit*! The Korean War. The Iron Curtain. They called women 'dames' and 'skirts' then. Look at us today! We've seen the world from space and we're landing on the moon. There's liberation happening every which way. This is one of the most exciting times in history that I can imagine. And you want to go back to 1950?"

"But they had Elvis Presley," she said.

"Ah! Okay."

Many times, I thought of calling Caroline Bell but decided that since I had refused any relationship while I was her teacher, now that she was no longer my student it was up to her to initiate the call, if she so wished.

I did call Paul and Viviana.

"I know a great place to go fishing," I said. "Let's have a family reunion."

They were for it and arranged their holidays. So, in late May, I loaded my camping gear into the car, and my rowboat on the roof racks, and drove up to Lac le Jeune en route for Edmonton. Paul and Viviana came up in their Volkswagen, and we fished for three days and sang Spanish songs round the fire. I bought ice in Kamloops and packed it round several large trout and then we swapped cars and I drove on to Alberta in their Volkswagen, leaving Paul and Viviana with my tent and boat and Austin. The fish were still fresh when I arrived in Edmonton, and I made a stuffing of bread, celery and onion, and baked them, to add to the lamb barbecue which Rashid and Jenadie had planned for some of his colleagues.

Next morning, I woke in the basement bedroom to the sound of Rashid's voice: "Coffee, Sahib?"

I reached out for the mug, and he began to talk as though I'd never been away.

"Here, for example, Alistair, we had two sociology profs whom they tried to fire for advocating student participation in university governance.

But we protested. We rallied! Now the bastards are negotiating. Enemy attacks, retreat; but when the enemy retreats, chase him!"

"You think you'll get parity?" I asked.

He grinned, showing his white teeth in the dark room. "Not right away, but I can imagine it," he said. "I think U of A is going to get parity eventually."

"Doris Lessing says that when people can imagine something, it's bound to happen. I met a Danish Resistance veteran at a lake last year, and he told me that imagination is linked to knowledge. I'm beginning to understand that now. Wallace Stevens has a poem called 'Reality Is an Activity of the Most August Imagination.'"

"Sounds good! What kind of a poet is he, Marxist?"

"No. He was an American lawyer and a businessman. Insurance. You wouldn't think someone in that line of work would have such a high regard for imagination."

He raised his eyebrow at that but let the conundrum sit unexplored.

Later, Rashid asked me to drive him downtown in his Impala to do some shopping and pick up Jenadie from work. I got behind the wheel, and he climbed in the back.

"You like to have the white colonial bwana chauffeuring you, don't you?" I said.

"No, man, it's that I don't like driving," he said. "When I sit in the back, I can't see the road. You don't *mind*, do you?"

"It's fine, Rashidi. Why have you got your name tag here?" I pointed to the plastic plate stuck on the dashboard: "Dr. Rashid HASSAN."

"Soon as the term ended, those bastards told me to vacate the office. I thought at least I'll take my name. Does it give a bad impression to put it there? Vanity?"

I reached over and pulled the nametag off the dash, turned it upside down and stuck it back on again.

He cocked his head. "Ha! Much better!"

Jenadie brought home complimentary movie tickets to a sneak preview.

"Sneak preview!" said Rashid, excited as a small child. "I wonder what it can be."

"It better be good!" Jenadie said, as we sat in the dark, expectant hush of the theatre.

Suddenly the screen filled with bright blue and white mountain vistas and yellow fall leaves, and the voice of a cowboy was singing in the background about a little girl's fight for justice, and how it will happen eventually when she finds a man with "true grit."

Jenadie began protesting.

"Hush! Hush," Rashid urged, but there was no containing her.

"I can't believe this!" she called aloud in the filled theatre. "We come to a sneak preview, and it's *John fuckin' Wayne!*"

"Jenadie, be quiet!" Rashid said firmly. "We can talk about it later!"

He managed to shut her up, and for a couple of hours we sat and watched the movie, Jenadie letting out a snort from time to time. It was a classic American western from Saturday mornings of my childhood at the Capitol Cinema in Nairobi: innocent young girl with ranch in the mountains hires big tough John Wayne to track down her father's killer and accompanies him and the effete but handsome Texan lawman played by Glen Campbell. They cross rivers and survive gunfights and a pit of rattlesnakes and eventually the bad guys are brought to justice. The pioneer promise is fulfilled. The world is free once more.

I had expected a long discussion of the movie, but Jenadie was too disgusted to dwell on it. "It's sickening to think that kind of shit is being pumped into naïve farm boys who don't know their ass from a hole in the ground!" she said. "And it's all about Vietnam, it's about why the U.S. is in Vietnam."

"Beautiful mountains," Rashid suggested, winking at me.

"Yeah *right*!" said Jenadie cynically. "And where are all the Indians? John Wayne saves Montana, gimme a break!"

For that whole hot, lazy week in the borrowed old wooden house in Edmonton, we drank coffee and talked politics and went walking in the park. And at night when Jenadie was home, we got out the cards and played bridge. Rashid had a graduate student, Susan, who joined us as a fourth at the card table, and she was very good. She and I played partners and understood one another's signals perfectly, whereas Rashid and Jenadie tended to squabble.

"Two hearts is a forcing bid, Jenadie. You can't just *leave* me there!"

"But I only had nine points, and no hearts, just lots of clubs."

"So give me the damn clubs! If you had done that we could have made rubber."

Susan smiled at me and I smiled back, smug in our victory. I looked again and thought there was more to her smile.

Jenadie managed to get some free seats to the Edmonton Symphony, and one evening the four of us went.

"Look at that double-bass player," I whispered to Rashid. "He's playing in syncopation to the others, isn't he?"

"Which one?"

"Second from the right. With the light coloured instrument."

After a pause, Rashid said, "The black guy?"

I had not noticed.

I barely heard the music then, because there came to me with the shock of revelation, the very strange effect that Rashid had on me: For all our rhetoric about politics and colonialism, I lost awareness of race and colour around him. I had never had so close a personal relationship before with a person of a different race, despite the cultural kaleidoscope in which I grew up. In colonial Africa, everybody knew their place. If two people of different races stood on a street corner in Nairobi and talked to one another as equals, every passer-by would monitor the situation with a watchful eye. Around Rashid, ethnic difference seemed to evaporate.

My last night in Edmonton, Susan asked, "Could I catch a ride with you down to Vancouver? I've got a friend in New Westminster I want to visit."

She was lying, I could feel it.

"I'm meeting some friends at a lake to fish," I said. "I'm not going straight to Vancouver."

"I'm in no hurry," said Susan. "I love to fish!"

In the kitchen, Jenadie gave me a teasing punch and said privately, "Go with the flow, Alistair! Don't be so uptight." She laughed her taunting laugh, and I looked at her to see if she was actually flirting with me.

"I'm not uptight," I said. "I just like to make my own choices."

"That's chauvinist control talk!" she said. "And you don't even mean it. Why are you such a stoic, Alistair? You seem to have sealed off your emotions and just let things swirl around you instead of going after what you want." And from the look on Jenadie's face, I knew that she was teasing, not flirting. I was relieved.

"You might be right," I conceded. "Susan's a perfect bridge partner. It's just that when you sense someone has other designs on you, your guard goes up, or mine does anyway."

Whatever she thought about that, Jenadie said nothing more on the subject.

Early next morning, Susan arrived and we set off for British Columbia. All the way down, I gripped the Volkswagen's wheel too tightly and we talked politics.

"You have a saner view of things than Rashid," she said. "But I like to listen to his radical views. We Canadians are so fucking tame, we could use some shaking up."

"I don't know much about politics," I said.

"Sure you do! You're a classic small 'l' liberal. You believe in compromise and conciliation. You could have been born in the Ottawa Valley."

"Rashid and Jenadie regard me as a capital 'F' fascist," I said.

"They're razzing you, man! They like to make converts but your instincts are too strong for them."

"I don't know about liberal," I said. "Rashid and I are both children of the British colonies. He's on a high because his people have gained power, and I guess I'm shocked by the realization that mine have lost it."

"Democracy replacing colonialism is not a loss," she said.

"If it works it's not," I said. "How do you think India and Pakistan are doing right now? My father predicts total chaos in independent Africa."

"Don't you know about self-pride?" Susan asked. "People have to be in charge of their own lives, not have other people over them. That's the important thing."

"More important than running water, and hospitals, and roads and railways?"

"The infrastructure is pretty irrelevant if people have had their pride trampled out of them. Hope you don't mind if I smoke," she said, and lit a cigarette and cranked down her window.

It was dusk by the time we reached Lac le Jeune, and I was relieved to see the familiar green and yellow canvas of my tent and the old grey

Austin. But where were Paul and Viviana? I peered across the lake but couldn't see the boat.

"Where shall I put my sleeping bag?" Susan asked.

"Throw it in the tent. We'll figure it out when Paul and Viviana get back. I'm going to start cooking supper."

"It's so beautiful here," said Susan, sitting on a log, watching me at the fire. There was only one other tent along the lake, and the two guys there were quiet and unobtrusive. Susan reached out her long, thin fingers and combed them through my hair. I ducked away from her.

I was heating beans and hamburger meat, when Paul and Viviana rowed in, with six fresh rainbow trout. I scraped out the pan onto a plate and fried the fish instead.

After supper I saw Paul pulling a pup tent out of a bag.

"What are you doing?" I asked.

"I thought I'd pitch—"

"No way, man! We'll all sleep in the big tent."

I took him aside to go pee in the bush and told him, "For Christ's sake Paul, I don't want to be alone in the tent with her! I'm not interested. And she *is!* Next day, I decided to skip the fishing, and Paul and Viviana decided to keep my car and the boat, and drive up to Puntzi Lake for one more week. With the Volkswagen's windshield close to my face, I drove fast, hallucinating along the slow curves of the hot, dry sagebrush country around Cache Creek, then gripping the wheel as we bucketed through the sharp turns of the Fraser Canyon. Susan held firm to the passenger handle above the doorjamb.

"Why are you avoiding me?"

"I'm not avoiding you, Susan. I'm involved with someone else," I lied. "You're crowding my personal space."

"Oh don't give me that Edward Hall proxemics cop-out! I'm involved with someone else, too. So what? Haven't you ever heard of open relationships?"

"I've heard of them," I said grimly. "I'm not ready for one."

"So what *are* you ready for, huh? Monogamy? You were married before, weren't you? Serial monogamy? Fidelity? That's really quite cute."

I drove down the Fraser Canyon as fast as I dared and didn't speak any more. She continued with her monologue for a while, then lapsed into silence.

We came to the 264th Street exit, the beginning of home.

"Where shall I drop you off?" I asked.

She sulked and wouldn't reply.

"Your friend lives in New Westminster?"

After a while she said, "Could I come to your place?"

"No," I said firmly. I turned off the freeway at the New Westminster exit and pulled up on Royal Avenue at 6th Street.

"Where would you like to get out?" I said.

"This'll do," she said. She opened the door, swung her legs out and lifted her bag from the back seat.

"Too bad you don't have balls!" she said. "See ya, coward! Have an exciting life."

She slammed the door, slung her bag over her shoulder and walked off down the street. Her sandals slapped the sidewalk angrily, and her blue Indian cotton skirt swished from side to side.

Back home in Deep Cove I thumbed through the mail that had accumulated on the floor inside my front door and stopped at a small blue envelope with the address neatly printed by hand. Inside was a sheet of airmail paper.

Dear Alistair,
Where are you? The semester is over—or hadn't you noticed? I call your place and no one answers me. Are you dead?
CALL ME!
C.

I called, and in an hour Caroline was over for dinner.

An hour after that we were naked in bed together and seemed to stay there for several days.

"You're the best!" she said. "You're the best ever!"

One morning, the phone rang.

"Alistair? This is Paul. We're back, man, and guess what: I've landed a new job."

"Well done. Where?"

"In a furnace filter factory."

I lay there and listened to his excited explanation of how the furnace filters were good for the environment because they recycled waste sheets of metal that had been punched out to make bottle caps, and all the while Caroline was tickling me, until Paul eventually stopped and said, "Have I called you at a bad time?"

"I'd say it's a really good time," I said.

After a momentary silence, he said, "Way to go, *muchacho!* I'll bring your car and boat back this afternoon. Say hello to Susan."

He hung up before I could correct him.

14

Oh the "Summer of Love"!

The Mamas and Papas sang "San Francisco (Be sure to wear some flowers in your hair)." Sitting with my arm around Caroline, I watched on my little black and white TV, as the lank-faced Harvard professor advised the CBS host: "Turn on! Tune in! Drop out!"

"What exactly do you mean by that?" asked Walter Cronkite.

"The name of the game is to feel good," replied Timothy Leary earnestly. "The function of government is to get everybody high!"

We switched off the TV, stacked some albums on the stereo and went to bed, as Bob Dylan wailed insistently how everyone had to get stoned.

"Have you done drugs?" I asked Caroline.

"Tried a bit. I'm not interested."

"Me neither. The war in Vietnam has boggled people. They say they're dropping acid for new visions of the universe. I think they mainly want to get numb."

"Don't worry about it, babe," she said and reached for me.

In my new happiness, I whistled through the day, talked to people in grocery stores. In the Lions Gate Market, a tiny Japanese girl pointed at my small beard and said, "Mum, dat man look like a goat!" and I laughed with delight even as the mother hastened to shush her, and I told her to let her be. I stopped for hitch-hikers. One afternoon I picked up a teenage boy with long, dirty blond hair, thumbing from the Cove.

"What are you up to tonight?" I asked.

"Goin' to my old lady's place, we're goin' to get fuckin' wasted, man!"

"Your old lady?"

First I thought he meant his mother.

At the College, Andrea Halvorson handed me two theatre tickets. "Here, Alistair, comps. Go see this. Friends of mine from San Francisco are doing a piece of theatre that'll knock your socks off! It's been banned in the States."

Caroline said she had never been to a play except for a high school performance, and she'd love to go, so I took her to The Fisherman's Net on Granville for a shrimp supper and then to the Arts Club on Seymour Street, to see Michael McClure's *The Beard*. There was a lineup on the narrow staircase. I peered around some shoulders to try to make out what the delay was but couldn't tell. Slowly we ascended, and at the top of the stairs an usher held a velvet rope across the entrance. He let Caroline through, then pulled the rope across and cut me off.

"Oh, no, I'm with her!" I said and began to step over the rope.

Another usher, wearing a blue dress and a black mask, intercepted and took my arm firmly.

"You're with *me*," she said and led me off into the dim auditorium. I didn't know what was happening. She sat me down on a bleacher and touched me on the shoulder.

"This is where you are, and this is for you." She handed me a piece of cloth. I held it in the sparse light. It was a piece of blue velvet. I looked around but couldn't see Caroline. This was ridiculous! I sat fingering the piece of cloth, then put it in my pocket.

Suddenly, the lights dimmed right out and a movie flickered onto one wall. The frame shook, as though the camera was hand-held on a moving vehicle. I recognized Broadway, heading east through upper Kitsilano . . . left at MacDonald . . . right on Fourth . . . over the hill . . . down across Burrard, all the while the picture low to the ground and shaking. Under the Granville Bridge . . . right, up the on ramp . . . over the bridge, right at Seymour, a left turn, and then a quick right into the lane, and the camera is aiming directly at a wooden ramp against the wall of the Arts Club where we are and begins to ascend it.

In the auditorium two big loading doors swung open on the west side, and an actual motorcycle thundered in. For the next hour, characters representing Billy the Kid and Jean Harlow bantered about one another's sexuality, in language so frank and vulgar that some man behind me expostulated, ("They seem to have a very limited vocabulary!") and ending in a strobe light scene in which Jean Harlow lay back naked on the seat of the motorcycle and Billy knelt down, with his mouth going at her crotch.

The house lights came on dimly. The actors had vanished. The black motor cycle stood alone on the stage, a mysterious monument, evidence of the improbable drama that had just played itself out.

People were too stunned to move. Then the house lights showed dimly and brought back the ordinary world. People began to look around as though we had been collectively dreaming. I got up and pushed past shoulders till I found Caroline and we went down and found my car. For twenty minutes I drove through East Vancouver, over the Second Narrows Bridge to the Cove, with neither of us speaking a word.

We sat with wineglasses by the fireplace.

"What was all that about?" she asked.

"I don't know," I said and quoted from the play. "'Before you can pry any secrets out of me you must first find the real me. Which one will you pursue?'"

"Why's it called *The Beard*?"

"Is it pubic? They gave me a piece of blue velvet to hold." I reached into my pocket and gave it to her.

"All the men got this?" she asked, her lip curling in suspicion.

"I don't know."

She threw the piece of velvet into the fire.

In bed that night, when I started to stroke her shoulder, she turned so violently that she kicked me.

"I'm sorry," she said quickly. "I'm feeling. . . . Just hold me, would you?"

I lay quietly beside her all night. In the morning, I got up and percolated coffee and retrieved the newspaper.

"Caroline, come and look at this!" I called.

"What's up?" She appeared in the kitchen doorway in a brown and yellow pair of my cotton pyjamas, brushing the sleep from her eyes.

"The police have busted *The Beard* for obscenity!"

"I don't blame them. It was a hateful thing."

"Hateful?"

"It's written by a man who hates women."

I looked at her curiously–twenty years old to my thirty. Maybe I could learn something from her.

"I thought the play was about how we can't accept the fact that we are animals," I offered. "It's about revulsion and desire. How we feel uncomfortable with the fact that we can be seduced by mere flesh."

"Yes, Teacher," she said, and grinned at me without a smile.

We sat reading the newspaper story together, drinking coffee, when there was a sharp rap on the glass pane of the front door. We looked at one another guiltily. Caroline retreated to the bedroom and I went to the front door and held the curtain aside.

"Rashid! Jenadie!"

I pulled the door open, and shrieks of excitement sounded into the street.

"We decided enough of Edmonton," said Rashid. "Let's pack up and go to Vancouver. Bivouac on somebody's floor till the house is ready."

"Camp here," I said. "No problem."

"I'm only here till Sunday," said Jenadie. "I have to fly back to my job, till the end of the month."

Caroline came out dressed and I introduced them.

"I'm really pleased to meet you, finally," she said. "Alistair's found you a great little house. Listen, I'll be back in a minute." She slipped out the front door, and we heard her car start and drive off.

"You hungry?" I asked. "Shall I make eggs and bacon?"

"Eggs for sure. Not bacon," said Rashid.

"Oh, off course not, I'm sorry."

"It's not a religious thing, man. I don't like the smell of it."

"I'll make a soufflé omelette. How about that?"

"Sounds wonderful," said Jenadie.

"No trouble finding the way this time?"

"Second narrow bridge!" Rashid said and chuckled.

Jenadie looked from one of us to the other, and then the penny dropped. "What!" she accused Rashid. "You mean to say that time you got lost, you didn't realize that was the *name* of the bridge, and you didn't ask for help?"

"Yah! How I was going up to a policeman or somebody on the street and ask, 'Where is the second narrow bridge?' when I don't even know where the bloody hell is the *first* narrow bridge? Sound like a complete idiot!"

"So you drove around for hours! Men!" said Jenadie. "Can't manage the humility to admit they're lost!"

"Being lost is one thing," said Rashid. "Making a fool of yourself over a narrow bridge is something else! I didn't realize that 'narrows' was a noun. The bridge itself is quite wide."

"It's not just a noun," I said. "It's a historic name."

We were still laughing when Caroline arrived back with a crammed Safeway bag and busied herself at the sink.

"Ta-dah! Welcome to Vancouver you guys!" She stepped forward and gave her coy, canting smile as she produced a large glass bowl spilling over with a festive array of grapes, green, red, and a deep purple-black. Rashid and Jenadie blinked at it coldly, as though it held snakes.

"Well," said Rashid with a gulp. "Might as well *eat* them, now that you've bought them. Thank you very much!"

"What's the matter?" Caroline looked from face to face.

"The grape boycott," I said.

Again we ended in laughter. Jenadie had tears streaming from her eyes as she opened her camera case to take pictures.

"How were you to know?" she said, putting her hand on Caroline's shoulder. "Let's dive in and enjoy them! I haven't tasted a grape since the Sacramento march—what's that been, two years?"

Caroline looked abashed.

"How does it help to not buy grapes?" she asked.

"César Chavez is struggling to unionize the itinerant Mexican grape pickers," Rashid instructed patiently. "The boycott is a pressure tactic on the fruit growers."

"Maybe these grapes aren't from California," Caroline suggested hopefully.

"Where else would they be from?" said Jenadie with a sour smile. "The limited success of the boycott so far means the Californian grape farmers are having to sell off under cost to get rid of their harvest. You can bet your sweet ass, lady, Safeway isn't buying grapes from Spain or the south of France right now."

Caroline listened, looking from one speaker to the other.

"Are you guys radicals?" she asked.

Rashid nodded once, and his perfect teeth gleamed as he grinned at her.

"You know what it means?" I asked.

"Protesters," Caroline said.

"Sure," said Jenadie. "Against shit and corruption. We're going to change it and we don't believe in minor revisions. Redesign the whole system and get rid of capitalism and all its parasites and pigs. Rebuild a human world."

"'Radical' means 'to the root,' as in 'radish.'" I said. "Changing things from the root on up."

Caroline looked at Rashid with deadpan blue eyes. "Can you do all that?"

"We are living in very changing times!" he said. "You know what Clark Kerr said the other day?" he asked, looking round the table. "Something insightful. He said, 'What the automobile did for America, in the first half of the 20th century, the university will do in the second.'" He raised his bushy black eyebrows. "I think he is right, you know. In terms of transforming society."

"I hate to ask—" Caroline began.

"Clark Kerr is the President of the University of California at Berkeley," I said. "Berkeley and Buffalo are the main radical campuses in the States."

"That's where the changes begin," Rashid added, "and they *spread* outward." He stretched his arms and fingers emphatically.

"Speaking of change," I said, "I never thought I'd see oral sex on stage at the Arts Club Theatre."

"Okay, let's go!" said Rashid with a smile.

"Too late. The cops busted it." I showed him the paper.

"No, no!" He said. "It'll still be on. This is the play they busted fourteen nights in a row in L.A., and every night the company put it back on again. Let's go tonight!"

"Sorry, man, this is Canada. It won't be on. Anyway, bring in your stuff."

I settled them in to the back bedroom.

In the late afternoon, Rashid said, "I'm hungry. Don't you have some famous Chinese restaurants in Vancouver?"

So we piled into his Impala and I drove to Chinatown, to the Nan King. Hot-and-sour soup, beef with black bean sauce, honey garlic chicken, chilli tangerine eggplant, chow mein and chop suey—the dishes kept coming, and we washed them down with beer.

"To Rashidi!" I said, raising my glass. "Congratulations on getting the job. Here's to a long and brilliant career with your students! And to Jenadie!"

"To you two. To all of us," Rashid replied, with his beer bottle raised. "To the struggle! *Venceremos!* To a better world!" He drained the bottle.

"Let's drive home through Stanley Park!" Jenadie suggested as we got back in the car. "It's so beautiful on a warm night."

"We need more beer," Rashid said, so I stopped at the Denman Street liquor store, which was open till 9, and picked up a case of Old Vienna.

"Look, Rashid," said Jenadie as we rounded the curve at Lost Lagoon, "the lights on the water!"

She was in the rear, with her window rolled down and leaning her head out like a teenager into the warm night air. Rashid was lying back on the seat sucking on a stubby brown beer bottle.

"Who is this Stanley guy they named the park for?" he said.

"Lord Stanley was a Governor General," said Caroline. "We learned about him in Social Studies. He dedicated the park 'to people of all races, colours and creeds.'"

"Heard that kind of shit before," said Rashid.

"Can't you quit drinking and enjoy the view?" said Jenadie.

"Yah, okay," he said, contritely.

I parked at Brockton Point, and we strolled along the seawall.

"What time is it?" I asked.

"Almost nine," said Jenadie. "Who cares."

"The gun goes off at nine."

Rashid frowned. "Gun?"

"A ship's cannon," I said, pointing to the wooden enclosure. "Every night at nine o'clock they fire it off. It's a long tradition, back to the 1890s."

"What for?" said Rashid sourly. "Reinforcement of gunboat imperialism?"

"It was originally fired to sound the curfew on fishing in the harbour at six o'clock," I said. "The harbour's all fished out, but they keep up the tradition and fire it at nine as a time signal. It's electronic now."

"People need the government to tell them the time? Don't we have watches of our own?"

"You're in a damn fine mood, Rashid!" said Jenadie. "Let's get back in the car."

As we turned on the seawall, the gun went off, a loud, hollow explosion. We stood and listened to the echo ricocheting off the mountains of the North Shore and distant Burnaby. Rashid put his finger in his mouth and made popping sounds in mockery.

We got into the Impala, and I was backing out of the angle parking, when there was a sharp sound of smashing glass. I stabbed the brake.

"What the hell?" I swung around.

Rashid sat grinning like a naughty schoolboy. He had thrown an empty beer bottle out the window, against the stonework. I was shocked. I slid the car into gear and moved off.

"Nine o'clock Lord Stanley Greenwich Mean Time," Rashid announced, in an affected British slur. "Nine-oh-five and fifty-two seconds Rashid Hassan time! How you like my gun, Stanley Sahib?"

He pulled a full beer bottle out of the case and flung it hard out the window. It exploded on the rocks where the *Girl in Wetsuit* sculpture sits today.

"Rashid! You'll have cops after us," I muttered.

Jenadie pointedly ignored him. She leaned forward over the back of the front seat and began asking Caroline about her job at the daycare. I drove in silence. As we came off the Lions Gate Bridge I glanced in the mirror and saw that Rashid was asleep.

When we arrived at my house, Jenadie roused him, and they went straight inside and to bed.

"What an idiot!" Caroline whispered in the bedroom. "He may be some hot-shot radical political genius, but I don't go along with smashing beer bottles in Stanley Park. Children walk on the seawall!"

"They've been driving since Friday night," I said. "He's had a tough year, you know, a lot of insecurity."

"Right! So smash some bottles and cut people's feet. Way to *go*, big fellah!"

"I forgive him," I said.

"I don't."

"Well . . . love him anyway."

"Sure, babe, love's not the problem. Don't you think smashing bottles in Stanley Park is kind of stupid?"

"Whatever he needed to do," I sighed. "The park workers will clean it up in the morning, nobody's going to get cut. Would you feel okay about letting go of this?"

"Hh!" she grunted.

In the morning when I went into the kitchen to make coffee, Rashid was sitting immaculately groomed, in a neat green and black woolen dressing gown and leather slippers, engrossed in yesterday's newspaper.

"Hi," I said.

"Hi Alistair! I see the politician Tom Mboya was murdered in Kenya."

"Yes. There were riots in Nairobi."

"What did you make of the guy?"

"I met him a couple of times," I said. "Very intelligent and articulate. Very sophisticated. He was the best hope for a stable successor when Kenyatta dies. He's of the second largest tribe, the Luo."

"Unfortunate name. Everyone I've talked to says he's *Uncle* Tom, working for the U.S."

"Oh no! The Americans liked him because he was Westernised in education and manner, I don't believe it's because he was a tool."

"You think Kenyatta had him bumped off?"

"I doubt it. Maybe some of the other Kikuyu in the wings...."

So, our conversation resumed as though nothing had happened. I wondered if he even remembered smashing beer bottles in Stanley Park.

Sunday night Jenadie flew back to Edmonton, and Monday morning Caroline was off to work. For the next week Rashid and I spent time together in the house, hours of conversation. He was bracing himself to plunge into the Simon Fraser struggle. He would go off and confer with his colleagues and then come back and talk matters through with me. Caroline and I became the voice of liberal Canada for him, people he might one day "have to shoot" but, for the time being, a sounding board. By the evening of Day One he had made his first decision.

"There is no middle ground, you know?" he said, chewing for a while on a drumstick in case one of us might answer. "There is no fence to sit on, you know? Even Christ understood that—didn't he say something about one side or the other?"

"Pete Seeger," said Caroline.

"One side or the goddam other, man! My radical colleagues are suggesting that I sit out the battle. They say I'll be more useful as an uncompromised member of the department, a source of information. Who do they think they are kidding? Nobody's uncompromised. You are either on *one* side, or else you are on the *other*! Isn't that what Christ said?"

"Pete Seeger," Caroline repeated and sang softly: "'Which side are you on boys? Which side are you on?'"

Rashid listened to her and nodded. "By the way," he said, "give me your advice on this: A colleague at Simon Fraser is worried about Jenadie and me living together. Says the university could use this as grounds to get rid of me."

"Moral turpitude," I said.

"Is it? See, I don't know much about Canadian society. Is it acceptable for a prof to be living with a woman, unmarried?"

"'Acceptable'?" I said. "What kind of a goddamn Muslim are you? Debauch a woman and shack up with her without ceremony and then you claim to have the moral authority to profess your academic discipline to impressionable young students!"

He stared at me deadpan for a moment, till he realized I was putting him on. "Joking aside man, how is it here? Caroline? I mean in Edmonton we were in a high-rise at least while my job lasted, and that's more private. Here, in a house, what do you think? Is my colleague right or wrong? He says don't tell anybody."

"Jenadie's not your student, so that's not an issue. This is Vancouver in 1969, Rashid. Nobody gives a damn how you live your life. Nobody knows their neighbours. You do your job, and your private life's your own. 'The state has no place in the bedrooms of the nation,' to quote your favourite politician."

"Which one?"

"Trudeau."

"He said that? Huh. A redeeming feature after all. You don't think I should worry? But can't the administration use it to trump up something against me?"

"They'd have to use it against a lot of other people if they did! I think the last time a prof got fired for cohabiting with a woman was Ezra Pound in America in 1909. Today, in Vancouver, half the faculty probably live common law. Your private life has nothing to do with the university. If Jenadie was your student, or under 19, it might be an issue, but only if the relationship was making other students feel uncomfortable. You're worrying over nothing."

"Caroline is your student, right?"

"No," Caroline said firmly. "I was last year. Not any longer."

"So." He frowned and let the matter rest. "Another thing is, got to get rid of this car."

"Why?" I asked. I had come to like the sight of little Rashid in his big old boat.

"It's an embarrassment," he said. "Gas-guzzling Yank tank. I want something more modest, like your Austin."

So we went the rounds of the car dealers and Rashid traded in the Impala on a British Ford Cortina. I took a picture of him, with his elbow out the window. He smiled happily.

At the end of the month Jenadie came back down, and Caroline and I helped them move in to their new house. We were all drinking beer, and Jenadie put on a Melvina Reynolds song about people all living in identical ticky-tacky boxes, and about the university being just such a box.

Back in the Cove that night, I said, "Caroline, that song touched a nerve. From my first day as a freshman, I thought it was such a fantastic liberation and privilege to be at university! You know? No more polite restraints, the truth will out. Follow your instincts and damn the consequences. And all the time it's just grooming people to be polite and docile consumers. I'm beginning to think so."

"Right on, hep cat! Getting radical now! Smash some bottles for the revolution!"

She smiled at me, that coy, intuitive smile of hers.

"Come here, divine! Come here, you bag of flesh!" I said, alluding to *The Beard*.

I reached for her, but she pulled away and danced into the kitchen. She turned on Kitsilano 73 Radio CKLG and smacked her knees, drumming to the music of Blood, Sweat and Tears singing "Spinning Wheel."

15

I sat in Dean Bull's office, thinking how well his name suited the man. With his thick neck and shoulders, he had a prizefighter's mien, and a good thing too, for the College. I wondered how many people suspected that behind his conservative exterior lay quite a revolutionary mind, intent on changing the face of post-secondary education in British Columbia?

"Look," I handed him a paper showing my calculations. "With English Composition classes capped at 25 students, we'll need to hire two full-time English faculty."

He studied the paper. "Right," he said. "I'll place the ads, and you can receive the applications and make a short list. Then you and I will interview them together."

"Also," I said, "this is our chance to get some Canadians on board. You realize our English Department is made up entirely of immigrants? No wonder our new course in the Canadian Imagination was proposed by students, not the faculty."

"Never mind nationality," he said. "We'll hire the best candidates."

At the next department meeting, when I announced the new positions Thelma Smith asked, "Are we going to have a say in who gets hired?"

"I don't see why not. You can all sit on the short listing committee, and then the Dean and I will do the interviewing."

"Why can't we interview?" said Andrea.

"I doubt if the Dean would go for that, quite yet."

"Have you asked him?"

"No."

"Then I will."

I sighed. "It's too many people, Andrea," I said. "You need two or three people at a hiring interview. Not a whole panel."

"That could be fairly intimidating," said Barnet Nolan, the soft-spoken Mormon from Idaho.

"The process should be thrown open," said Andrea. "Get the students in there too. And the support staff—they're going to have to work day by day with the people we hire."

"You'd have the candidate facing a battery of twenty inquisitors!" I objected.

"Tough shit!"

"Why don't you trust Alistair?" Barnet asked her. "At least he gets to interview."

"It's not that I don't trust him, Barnet. It's that we should all have a democratic voice."

"Perhaps that will come," I said. "This is Canada and the College is not even a year old. Anyway, I invite you all to sit with me on the short-listing committee next Friday afternoon."

I looked around at the five faces, and they were downcast. Throwing in Canada had done the trick. All were expatriate Americans.

There were thirty-five applications for the two positions. All five new full-timers came to the short-listing, Barnet, Andrea, Max Odegaard, Trevor Easton, and Thelma Smith—at 45, the oldest member of the department, who had worked at several universities.

"How many are we trying to shortlist?" Andrea asked.

"For two full-time positions I think we need at least five. Let's see what's in the file. We might want to break it into three or four part-time positions, in which case we'll need a few more on the shortlist."

For two solid hours we sat and read the applications and settled on a shortlist of four candidates. Three Americans, one Brit—and, damn it, once again no Canadians. There was one promising Canadian: Sandra Atkinson. But she was only 22 years old and had no teaching experience.

"Her transcript is full of A's, and she's studied Canadian Literature and written a thesis on Leonard Cohen," I pointed out.

"We can't consider her," Trevor argued. "Either teaching experience is a criterion or it's not. She has none."

"She's been a teaching assistant," I said.

"We threw out several applicants who had only TA experience," said Barnet.

I looked at Thelma. I had noticed that she had voted only for women candidates.

"In view of the fact that we *are* planning to offer Canadian Literature, and she *does* have that background, and none of us do, we should keep her on the list for the time being," Thelma said.

"The criteria aren't written in stone," said Andrea. "We can do whatever we think is best."

So Atkinson made the list.

On the day of the interviews, Bull and I went through the first three before lunch. We developed a routine in which he would ask the questions about teaching at a community college, and I would ask the academic questions about English language and literature.

He drove me in his MGB to lunch at the White Spot at Park Royal. "I wouldn't have minded getting my Ph.D. in English," he said, as we looked at the menu. "Maybe I'll go back and finish it when I retire."

When we got back from lunch, Sandra Atkinson was sitting waiting. We settled into the office, Bull looking severe and venerable, with his whitish-grey hair and black plastic glasses that he would take off and swing by the temple while he leaned back in the easy swivel chair. I sat against the wall on an ordinary classroom chair, and Sandra Atkinson perched with her knees together in a short skirt on another chair in the middle of the room. She had startling, bright eyes and looked keenly intelligent.

"Do you want to begin?" Bull offered me, changing our usual order.

"All right," I said. "Ms Atkinson, tell us what novels you would put on a modern Introduction to Fiction course?"

"You mean I get to choose? There's no set list?"

"Absolutely. You design the course. You choose the books. It's not like being a teaching assistant."

"Canadian fiction?"

"If that's what you decide."

"Oh well, okay then! Well there's Leonard Cohen for a start, *Beautiful Losers*. And Sheila Watson's *The Double Hook*, and I'd love to teach Ethel Wilson's *Swamp Angel*...." As the interview proceeded, she was so bright and lively that I knew I wanted her on my faculty. So I began to push her, to convince Bull, thinking that if I got too tough his protective chauvinism would come to her rescue.

"What significant war themes do you see in Modern British poetry, Ms. Atkinson?" and so on. I grilled her about Anglo-Saxon rhythms, Milton's morality and the scope of Jane Austen's field of vision, and she answered all my questions with an energy I had seldom encountered. She talked like a river, the long sentences flowing unstoppably out of her mouth with nervous energy. I jumped from Shakespeare's language to George Eliot's prolixity, to Northrop Frye's categories, Leonard Cohen's antihero, Browning's dramatic monologues, Conrad's portrayal of women, Virginia Woolf, Margaret Laurence, and there was nothing she didn't have an immediate and voluble answer for. I went on far longer than usual, expecting any minute that Bull would quietly cough to shut me up.

But he waited. Then, when it was his turn, he began to grill her too. I was horrified: my strategy had backfired. "Oh shit, if he keeps this up," I thought, "she's going to break down and cry, and that's the end of her."

Dean Bull paused, sucked the temple of his glasses, leaned back in his chair frowning seriously, then put the glasses on the desk and linked his fingers behind his head, to begin a new line of questioning.

"Ms. Atkinson," he said formally. "You're young and rather inexperienced to be a college teacher. I would like to know how you would propose to handle disruptive students—I'm thinking particularly of aggressive young male students who might resent a young woman having authority over them?"

She looked at him for a moment and then said loudly, "FUCK OFF!" and raised her middle finger.

The Dean's chair landed upright. I blinked.

But she was not finished.

"'FUCK OFF!' this student said to me one day at UBC, and gave me the finger. I went straight up to him and said, 'You can leave this lecture room right now, or else I'm leaving. Which is it to be?'"

"This is when you were a TA?" I managed to ask lamely, recovering from shock.

"Yes. We looked at one another for a few seconds, and then he got up and gathered his books and walked out of the room, and I went on teaching. That's the only time I've ever had a disruptive student and I think I handled it quite successfully, don't you think so, Mister Bull? Mister Randall?"

"I should say so!" I laughed. "Why was he swearing at you anyway?"

"He hadn't read the novel we were discussing, but he kept giving his ideas, so I told him we weren't interested in his opinions until he had read it. Later, he came to my office and apologised and I let him back into the class if he promised to do the reading."

"Good for you!" said Bull, and I knew she was hired. We went on to the final interview.

In the end, we decided to hire Sandra Atkinson full-time, and two others half-time, Ellen Bennet, an American, and Douglas Boothby-Allen, the Brit.

"I'm very happy about Atkinson," Bull said. "She's got pep."

"Did you think she was actually telling you to F-off and giving you the finger?" I asked.

"I did! I nearly fell out of my chair! Is that what they mean by 'whole body language.'"

"I don't think we need to worry about 'erudite scholars lecturing into a void' with that one," I said.

He smiled, recognizing the quote from my own hiring interview. He looked at his watch. "Good enough," he said. "I'll write the letters tomorrow."

It was three-thirty. I said goodbye to him and went home.

I had cracked a beer when the phone rang and a soft male voice said, "Alistair Randall please?"

"Speaking."

"I'm sorry to bother you at home, Mr. Randall. My name's Malcolm Carter, and Dean Bull said I should arrange with you for a job interview tomorrow for one of the vacant English positions at Capilano College."

"I'm afraid we've completed the interviews," I said. "The decision has been made and the vacancies are filled."

"Oh, I know that, but he told me to get in touch with you and arrange an interview. I'm available any time tomorrow. The Dean will be in at nine."

Damn it, I thought. *There goes any work I was hoping to do on my thesis tomorrow.*

"All right, ten o'clock," I sighed.

I went in to the College at nine-thirty next morning and found in my mailbox Malcolm Carter's application, with a note from Bull clipped to it: "Too bad we didn't see this man. He's rather interesting, in his gentle way."

I stormed down to Bull's office.

"Did you tell this guy to phone me at home?" I asked.

"No. I told him he was too late for this round but that he could talk to you in case anything comes up in the future."

"God damn it! He fooled me. He's had the effrontery to call me at home and create an interview for himself. He's coming in at ten o'clock."

"Well," Bull shrugged. "We might as well see him since we're both here. I haven't sent the appointment letters yet."

At ten o'clock we interviewed Malcolm Carter in the Dean's office. He was an American from Chicago, patently gay, with a fine transcript. He had taught at two universities and had superb evaluations and letters of recommendation.

"Would you wait outside a minute?" Bull asked when we were finished. And when the door was closed he said to me, "Well what do you think?"

"He's great!" I said.

"Isn't he? Let's drop Bennet and Boothby-Allen, and take this guy full-time before one of the universities snaps him up."

"I agree."

"Good. Send him back in, would you? I'll make him the offer."

On the way home, I dropped by Rashid and Jenadie's. Rashid opened the door, and I saw behind him that the house was full of people.

"Sorry," I said.

"No, no, come on in," said Rashid. "This is my friend Alistair," he announced to the twenty-odd men and women sitting around on chairs and the floor. "He's our resident ex-colonial liberal. We can use him to test strategy. These are members of the PSA Department," he said to me. I nodded as each was introduced.

"We are discussing how to paralyse the campus, next week," Rashid explained. "We need something very dramatic to get attention, then I'm going to announce my decision on whether or not to join the strike."

"What strike?"

"Tk! Tk!" Rashid clicked his tongue. "We talked about it already, man."

"Where have you *been*, Alistair?" Jenadie exclaimed.

"The entire PSA Department, students and faculty, are intending to go on strike against the university, because the administration has refused to negotiate on decentralization of power to elected departmental committees including students."

"I knew there were battles going on, but nobody mentioned the word 'strike.' How does that work, anyway? You're not a trade union," I said, against a wall of unsmiling faces.

"Irrelevant," said Rashid. "What we are concerned with right now is planning an event for next week."

"I still say call a rally," said one energetic young man. "You don't have to mess around with happenings and guerrilla theatre. Put out posters and leaflets on Monday and hold a serious rally outside the Admin building. All you need is a megaphone. I move it."

"Second," a woman said.

Silence fell.

"We could block up all the johns with Jello," said a sombre voice. No one laughed.

"All right, let's vote," said Muriel Meyer, one of the rebel professors. "Who's in favour of Ehor's motion to hold a rally?"

Hands shot up around the room.

"It's time to strike down the ivory tower!" Al Waldie said, with his fist clenched. He was the elected Department Chairman, but the university had refused to recognize his election. "Time to restructure. Time for all our voices to be heard in the design of education."

Somebody tried out a chant: *"Re-struc-ture!"* In my mind's eye I saw cheeky barefoot Kikuyu children, in the months before Independence, standing along the Kiambu road outside Nairobi, giving the two-finger taunt to whites in passing cars and chanting, *"Uhuru! Uhuru!* Freedom!"

The meeting broke up and people left.

"Rashid," I said, "this is serious, man!"

"Very serious," he said. "Since April, administration has been trying to purge the department of radicals. Now they are threatening suspension of any faculty who go on strike."

"How many of you?"

"If I join the strike, six. Two others are on leave."

"Are you going to join? You haven't even taught a class yet."

Rashid gave his bandit grin. "What do you think?" he said.

"'One side or the goddam other,'" I quoted.

He nodded.

I told Rashid and Jenadie about Malcolm Carter muscling his way into a job at the College after the interviews were all over.

"You have to admire the guy," I said. "Without actually lying, he managed to set up an interview for himself."

"But he didn't go through the shortlist committee," Jenadie objected. "So why hire him?"

"He's the best candidate!"

"He circumvented the democratic process!"

"Smart!" I said.

"It's not ethical!" she cried, unsmiling.

"He is unfortunately a Yank," I said. "But I did manage to hire one Canadian, finally."

"Why should nationality come into the picture?" Rashid demanded with a frown.

"One out of seven, over zero out of seven, is hardly nationalism, Rashid. And it's not tokenism either, because she's bloody good."

"I have absolutely no interest in nationality," he said. "My perspective is entirely internationalist."

"That's not what you told me in Edmonton, my friend. 'Don't talk about the world or the country, talk locally.' Remember you said that?"

"Sure! Talk locally. But not only locals can do the talking."

"If you don't have locals talking, how do you find out what the local issues are?"

"Yeah but—"

"Yeah but—"

We both laughed.

"Oh, goodnight!" I said. "I'm going home."

He put his hands together and bowed.

"Aslaam alequ, Sahib!"

"Asante sana."

16

"When does the rally start?" Caroline asked, as I pulled onto the entry ramp of the Second Narrows Bridge.

"One o'clock," I said.

"Oh shit! Don't let's be late!"

"We're not going to be late, Caroline!" I said but I drove as fast as I dared. There were lots of cars but we eventually found a place to park. As we walked in, we could hear chanting:

End the Purge!

Re-struc-ture!

Behind the chanting, a tape of Phil Ochs was playing over the loudspeakers. Seats had been brought onto the paved area of the Convocation Hall and people were starting to gather. I took a leaflet from a student handing them out. Rashid's name was printed in bold.

Beside the microphone stand, Rashid and Jenadie were talking intently to other faculty members and student organisers.

"What are you doing here?" The hand on my elbow was Andrea Halvorson's.

"Oh hi! This is Caroline."

"We've met," Andrea said, and turned back to me. "God, isn't this exciting! But what *are* you doing here?"

"He's my friend," I said, indicating with a nod.

"Rashid Hassan is a friend of yours? You never told me! He's gorgeous. Introduce me."

"He's taken," I said. "That's Jenadie beside him."

"So what?"

"Andrea!"

Al Waldie took the mike and began testing. Phil Ochs was turned off. A student was setting up a music stand as a lectern.

"Good afternoon . . . .

"Good afternoon . . . ." Al shrugged and smiled and leaned forward and tried again.

"GOOD AFTERNOON PEOPLE!" Now his voice boomed into a feedback whine, until someone managed to turn it down again. The crowd hushed. "My name is Allan Waldie, and I am the elected Chairman of the PSA Department. It's great that so many of you were concerned and interested enough to come out to this rally." He glanced down at his speech on the music stand.

"As you know, a critical conflict has been developing between the administration of the university and the Department of Political Science, Sociology and Anthropology. More than a year ago, faculty, students and secretarial staff of PSA adopted a policy statement, which stressed three fundamental points:

"First, the need for critical social science. We must speak truthfully and openly about what is going on in the world, not participate in cover-ups and lies. We must work to achieve the full liberation of human potential.

"Secondly, participatory democratic control. We wish to replace faculty authoritarianism in the classroom and in the committee structures with parity, by which we mean . . ."

"This is really big!" Caroline whispered. "I can't believe so many people are here for this!"

Al paused and looked around to see how he was being received. Everyone was deadly serious. I felt strangely unreal, as though I was an extra on a movie set. It was obvious that Al had worked on this speech: he seemed to be reading it but the words were fluent on his tongue. The loudspeakers gave his voice a metallic sound, and the audience was hushed. He gripped the music stand again.

"Thirdly, integration of the university in the community. We are opposed to the notion of a university as an ivory tower set apart from the rest of humanity, in which social scientists work to serve the interests of the rich and powerful. We stress the idea of a university which is working with society to solve problems. To solve the problems *of* youth, not the problems *with* youth. To solve the problems of welfare recipients, workers, native peoples, and so on. We believe that the function of a university in the modern world is to work collaboratively, cooperatively, to improve the lot of all people and all groups in society.

"The administration of Simon Fraser University has resolutely opposed and undermined our efforts to implement these progressive ideas. In fact, the administration is embarked on a determined plan to purge the campus of all of us who hold to these views. Today, to address us on these issues, is our most recently appointed faculty member, Professor Rashid Hassan. Dr. Hassan."

Polite applause.

Then the chanters were at it again.

Rashid, five foot four inches tall, came forward wearing a white cotton caftan and sandals, with bare toes. He waited for the chanting to die down. Eventually he raised a hand, and the volume dropped off. He stroked his beard, adjusted his stance, sipped from a glass of water, and coughed.

A hush fell.

Rashid reached out towards the mike. A young man scurried forward at a low crouch and lowered the boom, bringing the mike closer to his face.

Pindrop silence.

"This university," Rashid declared into the mike, "belongs to all of us! It is OURS! We can do whatever we like with it."

Some people started applauding. Then silence returned.

"It must be made to suit our needs in the modern world. It must be restructured to fit the times. Those who resist change have a false set of values, a hidden agenda. They are wedded to the status quo, and they have no right to resist the vital changes of the institution in order to serve those hidden interests. Because the university DOES . . . NOT . . . BELONG . . . TO THEM! IT BELONGS TO US!"

A tide of affirmation rose in response, fists in the air, brave yells.

"It belongs to us," Rashid continued, "and we have the moral authority to do whatever we decide with it. If we wanted to . . ." he paused dramatically, lifted his right hand, circled it above, pointing into the steel, and glass and concrete overhead, "we could even BURN IT DOWN!"

A ripple of sound began in the bleachers and quickly built to a wave of laughter and excitement.

"Burn it Down! Burn it Down!" a chant began, and soon everyone had joined in, merry at the joke. Rashid grinned at them, turning from side to side, and to those behind him. Again, fists went up into the air. Rashid waited. Eventually it became quiet again, and he looked down seriously at the piece of paper on the music stand.

"As you know, last month Professor Allan Waldie was democratically elected as PSA Chairman. But the Dean of Arts, Dr. Marshall, refused to accept it and has declared the election illegal and placed the department under trusteeship of himself and certain others. This is a clear and unequivocal transgression of the democratic process!"

"End the Purge!" a voice screamed out.

Rashid waited for silence.

"Secondly, the university has refused to accept the recommendations of the departmental Tenure Committee with respect to two other faculty members. Also the university Tenure Committee and the Dean have placed highly unusual obstacles in the path of contract extension, promotion and tenure for members of the PSA Department. Clear obstruction and subversion of democratic process."

"Fuck the Establishment!"

Rashid glared in the direction of the yeller and waited for complete silence before continuing in a firm voice. He had such dignity about him, I was astonished at his power.

"It has become very clear to everybody now that the administration, supported by the more conservative elements amongst the faculty, is carrying out a witch hunt. They are attempting to purge PSA Department of radical elements, by provoking a confrontation. But our method is not confrontation. I repeat, NOT CONFRONTATION but dialogue. I say to President Barrington, 'Let us sit down and negotiate.'

"Mr. Chairman," Rashid looked over his shoulder at Al Waldie, "I move the following resolution before this plenary session. 'We call upon the President of Simon Fraser University to immediately enter into negotiations on four demands which have been made repeatedly in the past. One, rescind the quote-unquote trusteeship which has been imposed on the PSA department. Two, rescind the recommendations made by the undemocratic, so-called departmental and university Tenure Committees. Three, accept recommendations made by the legitimate elected Committee of the department. And four, undertake to foster encouragement by Simon Fraser University of experiment in decentralised organization and educational procedures. Finally, we set the date of 17th September 1969 for commencement of these negotiations in good faith, failing which, we hereby give notice of strike action by the PSA Department.'"

As he sat down the hubbub grew. (*Nego-tiate!*) The chairman had some difficulty recognizing speakers, and eventually a lineup was formed before a second, standing mike. For an hour, speaker after speaker poured out their passionate feelings, and eventually the vote was called. The resolution passed. The enumerators counted 36 opposed and then asked for the show of those in favour again. Several hundred hands went up, and the enumerators shrugged at one another and gave up counting.

Back at Rashid and Jenadie's, we opened beers and sent out for pizza.

"I loved that bit, Rashid," said Caroline: "'We can burn it down'!"

"Why was everybody laughing?" Rashid asked with a puzzled grin.

"The Mall and the Library, where you were standing, is all steel and concrete, not a wooden building," I said. "How would it burn?"

He paused to consider this.

"I suppose you could burn the books," he said. "Burn all the books inside and start again."

"Not such a great idea," I said.

"Oh no," laughed Rashid. "But it's one option! If we wanted!"

Later, as we were going to bed, Caroline said, "It's kinda weird, you know. There's all this gaiety on the surface. But the strike business is pretty serious, isn't it?"

"Deadly serious!" I said.

Things moved quickly after that. Simon Fraser University was on the front page of the newspaper all the time, and the editorial pages were filled with opinions. Rashid's time was taken up, and I didn't get to see them much, but one evening towards the end of August he phoned.

"I'd like to come and discuss something with you," he said. "You have some time?"

We sat on the rug, on either side of the Murchie's tea box before my fireplace, eating buttered corn and barbecued lamb chops. It was a hot evening, and I had left both front and back doors wide open.

Rashid's perfect white teeth munched determinedly down lines of corn until the cob was bare.

"There is definitely going to be a strike," he began. "What do you think will be the public's reaction?"

"Not positive."

"You think we'll get any support at all?"

"Sure. The old Vancouver commies'll support you in principle. They might even join your picket line. All six of them—or is it seven by now?"

"Don't joke, man. I mean from the public at large."

"I don't think so," I said. "Professors going on strike? Nah. Students—that's different. Students are allowed to protest and demonstrate. They only hurt themselves by delaying their education."

"Don't you think they *get* an education from the experience of taking political action?"

"Maybe they do."

He paused, eyeing the bowl of corn, chose another small yellow cob and buttered it.

"But professors, no. Why?"

He watched me with his eyes rolled up as he leaned over his plate and munched along a line of corn, waiting for my answer.

"I imagine the public thinks professors shouldn't use their students in that way. They have a responsibility. They're professionals. They shouldn't stoop to coercive measures and job action. They should use reasoning and negotiation to persuade."

"Quote-unquote professionals!" said Rashid, holding up the half-eaten cob. "To whom are such professionals answerable?"

"To their employers, and the profession. And the people they serve—in this case the students."

He finished the cob, wiped his hands, and stroked his beard several times and carefully put the next question phrase by phrase. It reminded me of Plato's dialogues. "Alistair, is there ever a situation in which professionals, acting out of dedication to their profession and service to the people they serve, go beyond the use of reason and negotiation and turn to coercive measures?"

"In war."

He frowned, surveying the bowls of food, but he was no longer hungry. "Apart from war?"

"Look, man, I don't know. You guys seem to be locked into something so bitter at SFU that neither side is going to give any ground."

"Yes, and who's got all the damn resources?" he asked with a sudden edge of bitterness. "Who can pay lawyers, so on so forth?"

"The university."

"Even the Faculty Association is on their side rather than ours. 'Because we are professionals'! Spineless bastards! *Acha*, okay: I did not come here to get carried away and waste your time. The question is, how do we get the public on our side? That's what I want to figure out."

"You would have to get the public to believe that the administration is hurting the university, and that you guys are protecting it."

"Which is precisely the case!" He shook his open hands in the air, in frustration. "Participatory government and decision-making are the way of the future—any social scientist who isn't asleep can tell you that. Even Japanese industrialists with their mildly democratic process of 'quality circles' amongst the factory workers know that. By resisting the inclusion of democratic processes in the running of the university, the administration is preventing students from preparing to run the world in the future. It's putting its head in the sand. By demanding that they open the process up, we are asserting and protecting the students' rights to understand and contribute to the world they live in."

"And you think you can persuade the public of that?"

"Have I persuaded you? At all?"

"Maybe a tiny bit, over time."

"What persuaded you?"

"Your persistence."

"So we have to keep putting out our message, that's your answer to me. More writing. More rallies. People will come to see in the end that we're right. But it's so bloody tiring!"

"Oh, you were expecting this to be easy?"

He grinned his grin, and then we opened beers.

"How's the house?" I asked.

"Fine, man, except the goddam shower drips."

"I'll come and fix it for you."

"Yah? You can do that?"

"Sure!"

Caroline's key sounded in the door, and she entered, home from a late staff meeting at the daycare.

"So, now you are living here full-time?" Rashid asked her.

She blushed. "I *guess* so!"

She went into our bedroom.

Rashid gave me a look that I couldn't interpret. His face was troubled, distanced, like a very tired man's.

At the College, at the first English Department meeting before the new semester, I sat at the head of the long table in the Bull Pen, and looked around at the relaxed and refreshed faces of the faculty.

"First I'd like to introduce our new members," I said warmly. "This is Sandra Atkinson, and this is Malcolm Carter."

After the smiles and hellos, Thelma Smith's face turned sour.

"Mr. Carter," she said, "please don't take offence at what I'm going to say. Alistair, I would like to know on what principle an applicant was interviewed and hired, without going through the short-listing process."

I groaned inwardly. Quarrels! Mediating with the Fire Chief was one thing, but handling objections of principle from Thelma Smith was not my skill. I could feel my mouth bunching up.

"The primary consideration is the good of the department," I said severely. "Mr. Carter came in at the last minute and managed to get an interview, and the Dean and I decided he was the best candidate for the job—together with Ms. Atkinson, of course." I nodded towards her, and she nodded back.

"How *could* he get an interview? He wasn't on the short list."

"I told you, Thelma. He applied after the short-listing was over."

"Then why wasn't he informed that he was too late?"

"Because that wouldn't have been in the best interests of the College. We're going round in circles here."

"Why didn't you advise us of his application or send it to us retroactively?"

"What would have been the point? By then he'd already been offered the position and accepted it."

"So our opinion doesn't count?" said Andrea.

"Did you hear me say that? I'm saying that in his case, circumstances made it too late to get the benefit of your opinion."

"Well, why wasn't he—again, Malcolm, I hope you won't take any of this personally," Thelma said.

"Oh, I'm not, I assure you!" Malcolm Carter intoned with a smile. "I probably agree with you!"

"Why wasn't he appointed subject to the department's ratification?" Thelma said.

I sighed. "Perhaps he should have been."

"I move we ratify the appointment of Malcolm Carter," said Andrea suddenly.

Thelma frowned.

"Second," said Barnet Nolan.

"Hold on," said Thelma. "How can we ratify an appointment when we haven't even seen the application? That's ridiculous."

"Any objection to them seeing your application?" I asked Malcolm.

"Feel free!" He spread his palms dramatically.

I marched down to Bull's office and made copies of the application. Silently, people studied them.

"It's been moved and seconded that we ratify the appointment. Any discussion?" I gave them about two seconds. "Those in favour? Opposed?"

The yes vote was unanimous, and the problem was solved, but I was still smouldering at Thelma.

When I stopped by Rashid's that evening, I told Jenadie, "You were right about the democratic process in hiring that guy. My department objected—or one person did. An American, of course."

"Well *good*!" she said. "The thing is, is that Canadians never insist on their constitutional rights!"

"They don't have any!" I said.

"What do you mean?"

"Canada doesn't have a constitution like the U.S. does," I said. "We operate at the pleasure of the Queen of England."

"No constitutional rights? You telling me if the Canadian police want to come into my house and search it, or arrest me, they don't have to have a *warrant*? They don't have to show *probable cause*?"

"Pretty much," I said. "There are some protections, but they're fuzzy."

"What a country!"

"Give it time, Jenadie," I said. "We just got the flag two years ago. We'll get a constitution eventually."

"This is after what, a hundred some years? Don't Canadians *care* about democracy?"

Rashid had been silent, looking distracted. Now he said quietly, "Canadians tend to trust their government. At least white Canadians do. The citizens of India were like that too after Independence. But not now under Mrs. Ghandi."

"How are things at Simon Fraser?" I asked.

Rashid's lips parted in a humourless smile. "Strike is set for 24th September. If Barrington has not agreed to negotiate on all four demands by then, we go out."

"What will you do?"

"Set up picket lines and an information centre. Of course a lot of faculty scabs will cross them. But more and more students are joining us. Hopefully we'll be able to shut the campus down. Al Waldie is trying to persuade the bus drivers' union to honour the picket line."

"But it would be illegal, wouldn't it, the strike? They can get an injunction?"

"Not before we stop the buses and disrupt the university. Once we've made the headlines with the pickets, I'll come back home and students will come here for classes."

"You're going to hold classes in here?"

"Certainly! Very old Oxbridge tradition. Meet with your professor in private rooms. Isn't it?"

Back at home, I was cooking supper for Caroline and myself, when there was a sharp rap on the front door.

It was Paul Bowles. His eyes were wide, and his face was pale.

"Alistair! I'm hot, man! Can I hide out here for a while?"

I closed the door behind him and brought him into the kitchen and gave him a beer. He let it sit on the table.

"You mind if we close the curtains?" he said.

I drew them shut. "What's up, man?"

"You know the place where I got this job?"

"The furnace filter factory?"

"I've been organizing the workers to get a union started, and now some big union bosses are after me! It seems I approached the wrong union, so the other one has their goons looking for me."

"Goons?"

"Is it okay if I hide out for a few days?"

"Where's Viviana?"

"She's visiting her family in Guadalajara. I phoned and told her to stay put till this thing's over."

Union goons in Canada? Had he been reading too many stories about Jimmy Hoffa?

Caroline came home and listened to Paul's story with disbelief.

"You haven't broken the law," she said. "You haven't done anything wrong."

After supper I called Rashid, and Paul and I went over there to talk with him. Rashid made a couple of phone calls and eventually patted Paul on the cheek and told him he was being paranoid, nobody would be out to get him. We drove back to my place, relieved.

Paul shook my hand and thanked me. I remembered that scared look he had had on his face at Jenadie's CAAWO "party," when he kept calling me "sir." He climbed back into his Volkswagen and went home.

"Do you really think it's all right for me to be staying here?" Caroline asked, when we were in bed.

"Jesus, not you too!" I said. "Everybody's on edge. Why wouldn't it be all right? You're twenty years old. You're not my student. What's the problem?"

"I just thought Rashid looked at me strangely the other day when he asked if I was living here."

"He's probably jealous!" I said.

"Rashid doesn't need to be jealous. He could have just about any woman he wanted."

"Including you?"

She gave me her canting smile and crooned, "I've got you babe!"

18

Simon Fraser University stayed front page news for several days following the rally. Barrington brought in more police, and the Homburg-hatted figure of the chief campus security officer was becoming a familiar sight. Students in the History and Geography Departments voted to support the strikers, so Barrington held a press conference: "These are not really History and Geography students," he announced. "They are actually PSA majors who happen to be taking an elective course in History or Geography."

The students responded by printing leaflets inviting everyone to a "mill-in" at the administration building. A huge crowd arrived, but they were barred from entering by a line of uniformed officers with walkie-talkies who would let people through only if they had appointments.

The students retaliated the next day by hiring five rock bands and held a loud concert for six hour s on the courtyard right outside Barrington's office. The *Province* front page headline read: "Rock Concert 'Completely Illegal,' SFU President Declares." But the accompanying picture showed that the power was with the students: the row of private cop hats between the crowd of dancing students and the concrete building behind seemed a desperate and flimsy defence. In a second floor window lurked the stooped silhouette of a figure I supposed was Barrington, watching, and isolated.

Back at the College, I got to my office one morning and found Malcolm Carter's course outlines in my mailbox for approval. The first one looked fine, until I came to the Grading Profile which read, "At the end of the semester, each student will assign him- or herself the grade that they reasonably feel they have achieved in this course." I looked at the other two outlines. The same.

"Sorry, Malcolm," I wrote, "we don't have self-evaluation here. You are required to mark and evaluate your students' work. Please revise."

I clipped on this note and returned the outlines to his box.

They reappeared a couple of hours later in my box with an answering note: "I am prepared to <u>mark,</u> i.e. <u>comment on,</u> and <u>evaluate</u> the work, but each student best knows what grade they have achieved."

I called an emergency department meeting, and discussion quickly deadlocked. Andrea Halvorson, Sandra Atkinson, Max Odegaard and Malcolm Carter favoured the motion permitting Malcolm to have student self-evaluation; Thelma Smith, Barnet Nolan, Trevor Easton and I were against it. Four to four.

"As chair, I'm going to break the tie and declare the motion defeated," I said.

"You can't do that!" said Andrea. "You've already voted! Only a non-voting chair can break a tie. You don't get two votes!"

Thelma Smith got up and went to her office and came back with a copy of *Robert's Rules of Order.*

"Here it is," she said, "Section 40. The Chair can vote to cause or break a tie."

"Isn't that for a non-voting chair?" Andrea insisted.

Thelma tilted her head back for a clearer view through her bifocals and turned the pages slowly.

"Why are we using an American book of rules to determine how to run our department meetings?" protested Sandra Atkinson. She looked left and right, but nobody answered her. She shrugged and was quiet.

"It seems to vary depending on whether or not there's a secret ballot," said Thelma.

"Let me see that," said Andrea. "Hnh, look here. It says clearly in Section 40 that a voting chair cannot vote twice."

"As far as I'm concerned, the matter is concluded," I said.

"Except"—said Malcolm Carter, pausing dramatically and looking around at each of us—"that I still intend to allow my students to determine their own grades."

"That would be improper," said Thelma. "We've voted against it."

"Very democratic!" said Andrea. "Where the boss gets two votes."

"Will somebody move to adjourn?" I said.

The motion to adjourn also produced a deadlocked vote, four to four, so I broke that too and we adjourned.

On the way home, I stopped at Rashid and Jenadie's with plumbing tools to fix their shower and get the latest news.

I knocked on the door, and Jenadie pulled aside a curtain. When she saw it was me, she opened the door and cried, "Rashid's been suspended. All six of them."

"Holy shit!"

I took the letter Rashid was holding out to me and read it closely.

"Came by Special Delivery about an hour ago," he said.

Dear Dr. Hassan:
This is to inform you that under Section 58 (1) of the Universities Act of the Province of British Columbia, you are hereby suspended from your position as Assistant Professor in the Political Science, Sociology and Anthropology Department of the University. You are hereby prohibited from taking part in any activities of the University or of the Department, including any teaching assignments, committee assignments, and the activities of any decision-making bodies of the University.

This suspension shall be effective immediately, and shall continue until further notice.

The grounds for this suspension are as follows:

1. *You have failed to perform your contractual duty to teach your assigned scheduled courses.*
2. *You have violated your duty to, and abused the trust of, your students, by failing to provide instruction in the courses for which they enrolled.*
3. *The facts giving rise to these grounds are as follows:*
   a). You have publicly asserted that you are "on strike."
   b). You failed to confirm that you would teach your regularly scheduled classes when so requested in a letter dated September 17th, 1969 from Dr. R.G. Marshall, Dean of the Faculty of Arts. You also failed to confirm that you

were teaching or would teach your regularly scheduled classes when so requested in a letter dated September 23rd, 1969 from Dr. J.J.W. Hendries, Vice-President of Academic Affairs.

c). You failed to teach your assigned course PSA 409, during the period September 18th to September 25th, 1969.

I am bound to inform you that under the terms of the Universities Act you have the right to appeal this suspension to the Board of Governors. Within fourteen days I will inform you of the Dismissal Procedures to be taken against you.

Yours truly,
Sheldon P. Barrington Ph.D.
President.

"It's draconian!" I said. "Meanwhile, are you getting paid?"

"He could have mentioned that, couldn't he?" Rashid smiled without humour. "As a courtesy? Bastard."

"I can just see his lawyers sitting down with him," Jenadie cried. "'Yeah, let 'em fuckin' sweat it!'"

"What are you going to do for money, man?"

"I think they'll have to continue to pay us until all procedures are exhausted," he said, "and we either win or we lose."

"We'll win!" said Jenadie, her face gaunt and tired.

"We'll see," said Rashid tranquilly and began palming his beard. I could see, from the tightness of his movements, how upset he was. "But you are right about 'draconian.' Barrington could have used the university's Statement on Academic Freedom and Tenure, which allows for suspension from teaching but not from committee work, until after a full hearing. He chose to suspend us under *The Universities Act* instead, which has sweeping power. It strips us of all university-related activities. We're banished from the campus, man. If I open the door of my office now, it's trespassing. He's pulled out the big guns."

"Damn bully!" said Jenadie.

"Then the overkill could backfire on him, couldn't it?" I said.

Rashid grinned. "He can't push us around!" he said. "Though obviously he's going to try. You know what? I salute the bastard for his honesty. At least we know he's not seeking a compromise. It's war, you know? Total war, till one side or the other is defeated. Didn't I tell you, Alistair? No fence! This side. And that."

"'Enhance the contradictions,'" I said.

"We have become the contradictions now! The radical right," he gestured with his left hand, like a thoughtful teacher considering the students. "And the radical left," he gestured with his right.

The phone rang, and soon Rashid became engrossed in a serious conversation. I heard him say excitedly, "There's no point appealing to Board of Governors! We need to go *directly* to hearings, with witnesses and evidence. Those bastards will delay as much as possible!"

After a strained silence, I asked, "Shall I do the shower?"

Jenadie shrugged. "Might as well. Thank you." She sat down and lit a cigarette.

I went into the bathroom and worked on the shower, resurfacing the tap seats and putting in new washers. The drip stopped.

Rashid was still on the phone. I wrote on a piece of paper, "*Nil ab illegitimis carborundum!*" and left it on the kitchen table and said goodbye to Jenadie.

On the road home, I thought to myself, "Malcolm Carter's grade profiles look like small potatoes now."

19

When I opened my front door, a gust of laughter came from within. Caroline and a couple of other young women were sitting around the kitchen table, drinking wine.

"Okay, here he is!" Caroline said loudly. "Come on mister, explain to these people why there's a strike at Simon Fraser University, and get me off the hook."

I stood with my briefcase hanging in my hand.

"Hi," I said. "Let me go and wash up."

When I came back, Caroline introduced me to Valerie and Elizabeth, both first-year Arts students at SFU.

"I come down from Kelowna to go to university, and I pay my fees, and there's a *strike*!" protested Valerie, her bright eyes wide with indignation. "I never heard of a strike at a university before! It's really screwing us up!"

"Keep your eyes and ears open," I said. "You're part of history. What's happening at Simon Fraser University is about as important as anything going on, on any campus today."

"Yeah! Well I wish they'd settle their stupid squabble and let me get on with my education. That's what's important to me. I don't need this noise! And they're all foreigners, anyway. Why do they bring their quarrels to Canada? Why don't they stay home and do their fighting there?"

"Valerie," I began patiently, and my brain was arranging a lecture on the value of participatory democracy on campus, the need to change education from elitism to an enabling culture.... But it was the end of a long day, and I remembered my own affront not so many months ago at the thought of picketing Dow Chemical. So I said, "Valerie, don't worry, it won't last long, and you can take it from me that you won't lose any credits. As for the foreigners, we're all foreigners here, you know, even the Indians. Let me pour you another glass of wine."

When her friends had left I said to Caroline, "I'd like to throw a party for Rashid and Jenadie. Take their minds off their troubles just for one evening. I'll invite some of my crowd. You want to invite some of your friends?"

"Sure! We'll need to buy a few things for the house."

"All right. Let's go shopping on the weekend."

"We'll get candles," she said. "I love candle light!"

Hand in hand, we walked down Lonsdale, into newly opened stores named "Orientique," and "Pier One Imports." There were brasses and bedspreads from India, posters of Krishna, and Buddhas of every size in brass and jade and sandalwood. The smell of incense permeated the aisles. We looked at candles and candle-holders, but in the end we crossed the road to Paine's Hardware and bought three traditional silver oil lamps with tall glass chimneys and wall brackets. We got a bamboo curtain to hang between the living room and the kitchen, and a large cane chair. We also bought two straight chairs at the Sally Ann and spent all of Sunday stripping them back to the original wood. I mounted the lamps, and we turned off the electric lights. It was cosy, and the smell of the burning kerosene reminded me of my childhood on farms in Kenya and Southern Rhodesia. We sat on the rug in front of the fireplace and made a list of food.

The party was a drop-in affair, starting at seven. We set out bowls of curried beef and chicken, tabouleh, dal, couscous, butternut squash, yams and sweet potatoes, bean and potato salads, caviar and crackers. Soon the house was crowded with people, and cars filled the driveway. At one point a police cruiser came prowling down the road and stopped, and I saw the two officers peering in the front window, but they drifted off again without bothering us.

Around eight, Rashid's Cortina arrived.

"Caroline," I said, "would you go and greet them and just introduce them by first names? Know what I mean?"

"Not heavies?"

"You got it. Let them have a night off."

It was a pleasant, relaxed party, and, late in the evening, when the first frothy hubbub had quieted down, people settled into two groups, one in the kitchen talking art and writing with Mark and Wilma Vance, and the other round the fireplace, talking politics with Rashid and the student Vice-President Dave Marsden, whom Caroline had invited, and who irritated me by constantly draping his arm around her neck. On the record player, Marilyn McCoo of The Fifth Dimension was singing about revelation and liberation.

A young man asked Wilma to read some of her poems, but Wilma said she hadn't brought any.

I took a couple of her books off my bookshelf, and plunked them on the kitchen table in front of her.

"Oh all right," said Wilma, and I turned off the record player and she tried to read for a few minutes. But it was too noisy, with people in the other room still talking so she stopped.

"Oh wow, that was so great!" said the guy who'd asked her to read. "I've never met a published author before."

"Reading doesn't work at a party." said Wilma. "I shouldn't have tried."

"Where do you find your *ideas*?" asked his girlfriend, in breathless wonder.

Wilma looked at the young woman kindly for a moment. "In my head," she said abruptly. Mark was lighting a joint, and Wilma went through to the other room. I followed.

"We are living in very interesting times," Rashid was saying. "You have heard of White Panther Party?"

Several people shook their heads.

"Guy in California—" he looked up at Jenadie.

"Sinclair."

"John Sinclair. I don't know about his politics, probably a pothead, but he's talking about the crumbling of the Western world."

Sitting cross-legged on the rug, with the firelight reflecting off his eyes and his fingers acting out his talk, Rashid had become a guru.

"Because it is already crumbling, he's calling for total assault on traditional Western culture by any means possible."

"Violent—" Wilma began.

"No!" Rashid cut her off with a hand chop. "He's calling for a totally free economy, free education, Rock 'n' Roll, drugs, and fucking in the streets. Did you read that article in *The Georgia Straight*, 'Sexual

Guerrillas'? Same stuff! End of nuclear family. End of sexual possession. California is the nucleus of a new movement that is going to sweep across the world. I think we must go there soon, huh, Jenadie?"

"Thank you, I think I'll stay here for a while."

"*I'll* go to California with you!" said a pretty young woman I didn't recognize, wearing a loose Indian cotton dress.

"So much for your plan of keeping them under wraps!" Caroline whispered to me. I took her arm and pulled her outside.

"I realized something, looking at him sitting there," I said. "The catastrophe that's happening to him at the University isn't a catastrophe at all, in his eyes. He's so excited by the changes sweeping across the world, that if he loses the battle on one campus, he'll just move to another part of the battlefield and continue fighting. I'm so glad we threw this party. I've understood that key thing about him! These Marxists have a lot of patience. They're sure their revolution is going to come in the end."

Long after midnight, when they were leaving, I walked with Rashid out onto the front lawn in the bright moonlight. The Cove was deathly still, not a tree stirring. I put my arm across his shoulder.

"You believe the times are changing *rafiki*?"

"We are at a turning point in history," he declared in a quiet, firm voice. "You know it when they start to change the names. You saw it in Kenya, huh? Terrorists become freedom fighters and now have their names on the street signs."

"That's right. Kenyatta Avenue, General Muinde Mbingu Street. What's changing here? Are they going to rename Vancouver Khatsalaano City?"

"Some of the radical students at Simon Fraser are trying to change it to Louis Riel University."

"They are?"

"Yah. LRU, didn't you hear that? Hang the guy for treason in one century, rename a university after him in the next. I told you, symbolic changes are more significant than anything achieved with guns."

"Hearts and minds?"

"Yah! That's why all the changes happening on the university campuses are keys to the future. American racial desegregation began at the University of Mississippi. Women's Liberation began on campuses. Decolonization movements—wasn't Kenyatta at the London School of Economics?"

"Yes."

"And look at the student strikes in France last year! I tell you, man, campus movements are changing the whole world. We are at a point of no return!"

His eyes were agleam in the moonlight, and he had raised his fist, underside facing forward. I reached over and turned his hand so the knuckles faced outward.

"If you're going to hit the enemy, make it hurt, Rashid! No soft punches!"

"Even the President of a conservative joint like UBC understands," he said. "Did you read about his speech to Rotary Club the other day? He said it's good for students to be protesting against things they don't like, because it shows they are thinking, and they will create the new society. Remake the world. President of UBC man!"

"Kenneth Hare said that? Sure you're not misquoting him? He's going through a nervous crisis with all the political activity at UBC. Anyway, he's a geographer, not in politics."

Rashid flashed his bandit grin. "Geographer, hey? Maybe he can recognize tectonic plates shifting when he feels it!" he said.

The Northern Lights suddenly flickered green across the sky, and then again, and again. I had seen this phenomenon only once before in my life, when I first moved to the Cove.

"Beautiful!" Rashid said softly.

I ran inside to call everyone.

We stood there, about a dozen of us, watching the magnificent spectacle in a silence punctuated with low exclamations. Caroline stood with me and put her arm around my waist.

When it seemed to have stopped, Jenadie turned to me with her American cackle of merriment: "Oh Alistair and Caroline, you really shouldn't have bothered to go to *all that trouble*! The food and drink and company would have been quite sufficient, without the fireworks!"

Laughing and in good spirits, the party broke up and everyone went home.

20

Next morning I crawled out of bed, leaving Caroline asleep, and headed for Marine Drive. My 12-year-old Austin had developed a bizarre electrical problem where the generator was actively discharging the battery instead of charging it. I had studied manuals and tried to solve the problem by reversing field coil polarity, but I was flummoxed and decided simply to buy a new car. Let the experts fix the problem. I had seen a near-new Austin A60 station wagon at Gordon Brothers on Marine Drive. They'd quoted me a good price, and the salesman had agreed to come in and make the trade on Sunday morning. He gave me $100 for my old Austin, which I left running on their lot, and drove home in the new one feeling like a prince.

Caroline was still in bed.

"Come see my car," I told her.

"What's wrong with it?"

"Come."

She came out in her robe, barefoot.

"Is this yours? Way to go babe!" She got in the passenger side and closed the door with a solid thunk. "British. Look at the wood, and smell that leather upholstery! And wow! It's got a cassette player."

"Get dressed," I said. "We'll go for a ride."

I threw my Swede saw in the back and took her on the Indian River Road to cut up fallen trees for firewood.

"Don't go and mess up your new car!" Caroline protested.

"It'll vacuum out," I said. "Cars are to use."

Later, when we were cleaning the house, she looked up at me with big round eyes from the kitchen floor where she was scrubbing the linoleum.

"At first I thought it was just about going to bed," she said. "I didn't realize it would get serious. Are we going to stay together?"

"I don't know," I said. "You want to?"

"We could get married."

"But I wouldn't want to have more children. And that's not fair to you."

She scrubbed for a while in silence, then looked up again and said, "My parents are taking me to Mexico with them for a week in October. You come too!"

"I couldn't do that," I said. "It's in the middle of the semester!"

She stopped scrubbing the floor and looked up at me, hurt.

"Anyone can take a few days off work, for God's sake!"

"*I* can't! I never heard of such a thing! I'm not a student like you and, what's his name, Dave Marsden. I've got responsibilities."

"Why are you bringing Dave into this?"

"He was all over you last night. I feel vulnerable when you're around guys your own age. I've noticed Dave looking at you."

"Dave *Marsden!*" Are you kidding!" she said with a grimace and scrubbed vigorously at the floor.

So, one Saturday in October, I drove Caroline and her parents to the airport, and came home to get ready for my Creative Writing class. The students were due to hand in their mid-term portfolios, and I had invited whoever could come to bring them to my house on Sunday morning, along with a potluck dish. By ten o'clock, eighteen of them had arrived, and we sat around and began to read the folders of poetry and prose. It was a pleasant experience, everybody intent on the work, and writing constructive comments. With us all crowded into the little house, there weren't enough chairs, but people were happy sitting on the floor, three or four squatting on a bed, some at the kitchen table. I had borrowed a 40-cup coffee percolator from the College, and its gurgling and the crackle of the fireplace were the only sounds to be heard as they all focussed on reading one another's creations. It took a full three hours to finish, including the seven portfolios from people who hadn't come, and by one o'clock we were famished. One student, Marti Wihksne, had written songs, and as they piled the finished portfolios on a table and began laying out their potluck dishes, he took out his guitar and sang.

Soon, the silence of intense reading was replaced with a relaxed hubbub of chatter and song and laughter. The noise grew until the morning's work session had been replaced with a party of friends. By three o'clock when the last of them had departed, I was exhausted but very happy with the experience. They were all serious about their writing, but the mood had been intimate, like that of an extended family circle. I looked at the pile of portfolios, only half of which I had managed to get through myself, and felt a positive desire to finish reading them—unlike most piles of marking.

The following Sunday, I picked up Caroline and her parents at the airport again, all tanned and lazy-faced.

I dropped her parents off, and when we got back to the Cove I said, "Caroline, you know, I have been thinking all week long about this children business. If we are going to stay together, of course you'd want children. I've accepted that fact. But not right away, okay?"

She stared at me and didn't say anything.

That night, in bed, she let me make love to her, but there was nothing coming from her.

I brought her coffee in the morning.

"I need to sleep in," she said. "I'm not going to work," so I left her mug in the kitchen.

I touched her head when I left. "Bye," I said. "See you this evening."

She grunted.

When I got back from work, she had cleared all her stuff out of my house. Where I had moved things to let her put hers in, there were now empty holes.

There was no note, nothing.

An hour later the phone rang, and it was her.

"Where *are* you?" I asked.

"I'm . . . at my place."

"Your parents'?"

"My own place."

"When did you get your own place."

"It doesn't matter."

"Caroline, what's *going on?* What's the matter?"

"I need space. I don't mean to hurt you, Alistair. I just . . . need my own space."

"Well are we going to still see one another?"

"I don't know. Maybe later. I need time."

"What's *wrong* Caroline? For God's sake tell me."

"There's nothing wrong," she said. "I just need to have my own space is all."

"You left your iron on the back porch," I said.

"I'll get it from you later," she said, "I have another one."

She wouldn't tell me where she was or give me her phone number. She said she'd phone me in a week.

That was a painful week to live through. When I wasn't at the College, I moped around at home listening to Gordon Lightfoot singing "Did She Mention My Name?" and waiting for the phone to ring, drinking coffee or wine. I sat at my desk amid all my thesis notes, but instead of working on it I rolled sheets of paper into the typewriter and wrote bleeding letters to Caroline, and then threw them in the fireplace.

One morning, on the way to work, I tortured myself by driving past the daycare, and when I saw her red Volkswagen parked on the street I drove on a block and had to pull in to the curb and get control of myself. All week long she didn't phone. I called Information and asked for a new listing, but there was more than one C. Bell and the operator wouldn't help me without an address.

She didn't phone.

After ten days had gone by, I phoned Paul and Viviana to invite them for dinner, but Viviana was still in Guadalajara. When Paul arrived, I told him, "Ever since I came to Vancouver, I've been saying that anyone who lives here and doesn't have a boat is crazy. I've got to buy a boat, man! The trouble is I've spent all my money on this car."

"Where's Caroline?" he said.

"I don't want to talk about it," I said. "I want to get a boat."

"Go to the bank," said Paul. "You've got a steady job. They'll be only too happy to lend you money. Where *is* Caroline?"

"That seems to be over. She went to Mexico with her parents, and something must have happened there. She's moved out to her own place. How are things at the factory?"

"Hasn't she phoned?"

"Barely. Forget her, Paul, she's in the past now. How's the union?"

He pulled my head down onto his shoulder and rubbed the back of it. "*Pobrecito!*" he said. "*Complicación de mujer?*"

"I'm fine," I said. "It was just so god-damned quick and unexpected! We were talking marriage. I had actually started negotiating having children. And the next thing off she goes and probably fucks some guy in Mexico, and that's that. It feels like having divorce papers served on you in the middle of a honeymoon."

"Come on, I'll take you out. Get you *borracho*, and we'll find some chicks to play with," he said.

"No!" I said firmly. "What I want to do is buy a boat."

"That's easy," he said. "Go ask your bank for a loan."

So next day I went to the Bank of Montreal and borrowed $1000. Then I went out and looked at second-hand boats. I found one I liked, and bought it, and was so excited I went round to tell Rashid and Jenadie.

Rashid opened the door.

"Come in Alistair. Shit," he said.

"What?"

"No students. I thought you were one. My students are caught between loyalty and their own interests. The university has offered to refund their fees, or switch their registrations to other courses. Some continue to show up each Wednesday afternoon and sit on my floor for the seminar. The course has been delisted, but I promised them when it is all over and we have won, they will definitely get their credit. This lasted for a while, but now the number has dwindled. You want to enrol?"

There was a knock on the door. Rashid opened it to a young couple holding hands.

"Ehor! Hélène! Come in. You've met my friend Alistair?"

They sat down, and we chatted quietly, waiting for others.

Eventually, Ehor said, "This is getting a bit silly, Rashid. With only two of us left, we'd better pack it in, eh?"

"I suppose. Let's have a celebration!" He opened a bottle of Scotch, and we all took a drink, passing it around from mouth to mouth in reckless camaraderie.

After the two young lovers had left, I said, "Come Rashid, let me take you for a ride."

"Where to?"

"I bought a boat. We'll go up Indian Arm."

"I can't swim!"

"I have life jackets, don't worry."

In the car, Rashid told me that Jenadie had talked her way into a plum job with the *Vancouver Sun*. She had gone off on assignment to northern Vancouver Island for a few days to do a series of articles on logging.

We drove to the Mosquito Creek marina, where I had rented a mooring for a month, and got into my boat. It had no name, only its registration number 6K 1439. It was an 18-foot cabin cruiser, scarlet and brilliant white, with sharp lines, fibreglass over plywood, big Johnson outboard motor, and a 3 hp Evinrude kicker. I helped Rashid tie his lifejacket, and we set off.

Once clear of the speed limit zone, I pushed the throttle lever and the boat leaped forward and up and instantly planed on the glassy sea.

"Shit, this thing really moves!" cried Rashid, grabbing onto the gunwale.

"Eighty-horse," I shouted back. "Fast as anything out here."

I steered towards the Second Narrows Bridge and we flew under it as traffic rumbled overhead. From the pocket of his duffel coat, Rashid produced the whisky bottle, and we each took a good swig. It was a bright, sunny day at the end of October, a typical Vancouver Indian Summer. The water was way too cold to think of swimming, but the air was warm. I cruised carefully into a cleft of rock on Raccoon Island, and we jumped ashore and I tied on some fenders and moored the boat to a bush. We spread a blanket on the grass and lay back basking in the weak fall sunshine, our eyes shut, talking, and passing the bottle back and forth.

"What will you do now that your students have drifted off?" I asked.

"One thing for sure—not going to stick around Vancouver. This campus war is damn draining, and I want to get on with research. I might go back to Oxford for a few months."

"Don't you have to be here for the dismissal hearings?"

"Whole process is stalled. Barrington's trying to wear us down, and we fight back as hard as resources allow and stall even further. There has already been one set of hearings held in camera, which is what AFT requires. For two days, the lawyers argued about procedure, and then the Hearing Committee announced its decision: No cause for dismissal."

"Terrific!"

"Not so fast! Appelgaard Hearing Committee announces no cause for dismissal so the very next day Barrington rejects the finding and claims that the Committee had not heard evidence and therefore the finding was invalid. He offered us quote-unquote proper hearings before a new Committee."

"He doesn't like the verdict so he demands a new jury."

"Nevertheless, we accepted! Under protest."

"How have I missed all this? I've been a bit strung out, Rashid, with Caroline and everything, you know."

"You and Caroline having trouble?"

I looked at his earnest face and felt tears well up in me. "She's gone man. It's over."

He looked away. "I can't say I'm terribly sorry, Alistair. She is not the one for you."

"Why?"

"Too young and unfocussed. Sea is full of fish, my friend. Don't let this upset you. You know, there is something I find absolutely amazing about you Alistair Randall: you get so worried when things don't work out. Failure seems to be much more important to you than success."

"Why do you say that?"

"Well, look at you: Successful guy. Father. College professor. Division and Department Co-ordinator. Lots of friends. Very capable— you can drive to Edmonton in a defective car through extreme winter conditions that would kill most people. Competent plumber—you fix my shower in a moment. Is that what you stress? No. You stress areas of your life where you feel that you have fallen short or it didn't work out. To me you seem obsessed with these points of failure."

I was silent. I wondered what he knew about Caroline that I didn't know.

He lit a cigarette, inhaled, and breathed the smoke out in short bursts. His face had the gravity of someone who has broken decorum to tell a friend an uncomfortable truth to his face. I watched the blue puffs of smoke drift away in the clear air. I had no answer. I needed time to think about his comment. I switched the conversation back again. With Jenadie away, it was a chance for me to understand without the clutter of emotions, the details of the unpleasant process going on at SFU.

"How did the Appelgaard Committee arrive at their verdict that there was no cause for dismissal?"

"They had a disagreement with Barrington about procedure, and the rest is a simple chain of logic." He sat up on the blanket and began counting mechanically with his fingers.

"One: Under terms of AFT, President can dismiss only if the Hearing Committee finds there is cause. Two: Hearing Committee can find there is cause only through a fair and just hearing."

"'Fair and just,' Okay."

"A fair hearing requires that there be a separation between prosecutor and judge. But Barrington said that *he* alone and not the Committee has the power to judge the meaning of the AFT Statement wherever it is unclear. So: no separation between himself as prosecutor and as judge means no fair hearing, therefore no finding of cause, therefore he cannot recommend dismissal. Follow?"

"That's your argument. What's his? Does he really have the authority to claim the hearings were not valid?"

"He has claimed it! In the newspaper and everywhere else. According to Barrington he doesn't even have to show up at the hearing! He calls himself a 'custodian' of the AFT document. And from his high and mighty 'custodial' position, he claims that since the Committee has not tabled any evidence its conclusions cannot possibly be valid. What an asshole! He thinks he's like a piece of rock. He sits there and watches the waves of democratic struggle crash on him. But you know what? Water always beats the rock in the end."

"'Had we but world enough, and time.' And what about money?" I was getting sick of the very sound of Barrington's name.

"I'm not worried," Rashid said. "They have to keep paying us till the hearings are over, and anyway I've got some research money saved up. And now Jenadie has this job, so we can pay the rent and eat, and that's all that really matters, isn't it? Survival."

"Not if you want to go to Oxford. Airfare and expenses."

"There are people there I can stay with."

"So you've accepted new hearings. When do they start?"

"Ah shit! Richard Duplessis is suing the university for acting illegally, so hearings have to wait until after that judgment is given, which won't be for several months. I have to be here for my hearing, but apart from that it's better to go elsewhere and get on with my work. I've started writing a book about reforms to land tenure in agrarian countries."

"Why can't the hearings begin anyway?"

"Because we have to wait for the judgment in Richard's case. He's arguing that the AFT document forms part of our contract of employment, and if he wins, that means Barrington acted illegally in suspending us under the Universities Act."

He stood up on a rock and talked over his shoulder as he pissed into the sea.

"There are going to be several sets of hearings. Al Waldie's is separate. Richard's would be separate. Muriel Meyer and I agreed to a joint hearing. Each Hearing Committee has to be struck. We provide a representative, Barrington provides his, then the two of them have to agree on a third who is the chair."

"And can they agree?"

"So far, no agreements. None! Ha-ha. And one Committee guy has died. Everything's in limbo. No hearings will get under way till next summer. Meanwhile, Barrington gives press conferences saying we have 'abused the trust' of our students. It's too bloody demoralizing, Alistair. I'm off to Oxford. I may even go to India and do field work. It's like your boat, you know? Boat gets you out of the shit, onto the water. Things look completely different, new perspective."

"How did you like going under the bridge?"

He chuckled. "This boat was a very good decision, *yaar*! You did the right thing here! How much?"

"He wanted a thousand and fifty. I gave him nine hundred."

On the way back, as we passed under the Second Narrows Bridge, Rashid tapped me on the shoulder and pointed up, grinning.

"It's gigantic from down here, isn't it?" I shouted.

I looked around. There was barely any tide rip, so I shut the motor off and let us drift.

"It's an *enormous* structure!" said Rashid. "And you don't realize how noisy it is."

"It fell down once."

"How?"

"They were constructing it from both ends and were almost joined in the middle, and they were backing a truck up on the south span, and it collapsed."

"Anybody hurt?"

"Nineteen ironworkers killed and I think one of the divers in the rescue effort."

"I wouldn't want to die like that. But look at that complicated design. It's so beautiful!"

"It's an engineering act of faith to build a bridge," I said. "You start at one end, the other guys start at the other. Hope to meet in the middle. And if something goes wrong.... They say every bridge takes a life."

"And this one took twenty. Well, what can one expect? Some die, others continue, eventually the job gets done. Like the revolution. You start out, and some people won't make it, but eventually the bridge is built. Eventually you are crossing Second Narrows. Ha!" he shouted.

"You like that idea huh?" We were drifting towards a grain ship at the Alberta Wheat Pool, so I started up the motor and opened the throttle.

"I like bridges," Rashid shouted. "When I was a kid, there was a bridge over a gorge near my village, and I used to climb up and hide under it when things became too difficult."

"'The world is too much with us.'" I yelled.

"Wordsworth!" he yelled back. "'Late and soon, getting and spending, we lay waste our powers.' You seem to be quoting a lot of poetry today. What was that other one, Andrew Marvell?"

"Not bad for a colonial boy from Bihar!"

"Listen Alistair, I was ten when India got independence. Ten years old but I knew all that English stuff."

"How about Tagore."

"Yah, yah! Remake the world. Such a dreamer! I read him in Bengali as a child, but at college we had to memorize whole chunks of *Gitanji* in English because he did his own translation. I guess they figured it would be an inspiration for us. But I can't remember anything now—oh yes!" He raised a finger: "'Grant that I may never lose the bliss of the touch of the one in the play of the many.'"

"The *what*?"

He repeated it slowly.

"Awkward and wordy," I said, "but the idea is nice."

"Liberal humanist shit for you," Rashid said. "Romantic individualism within the social revolution. No way! My Marxist colleagues would dismiss Rabindranath Tagore in a second. But I admit I like it too."

I slowed the boat to a crawl and waited for the following wave to surge us in to Mosquito Creek Marina. I was enjoying my new skill of driving a power boat. I nosed carefully to my berth, and we tied up and closed the canvas. It was dark by now. Rashid patted my back as we headed for the car.

"Good decision!" he repeated.

We picked up some White Spot hamburgers to take back to my place.

After eating, I took an old notebook from my bookshelf and read some Tagore to him: "The traveller has to knock at every alien door to come to his own, and one has to wander through all the outer worlds to reach the innermost shrine at the end."

"Yah! Yah!" Rashid scoffed. "That's Rabindranath Tagore at his very worst! Mystical journey shit! How come you have that? That's also from *Gitanji*."

"I was at Dartington Hall once, in Devon. I met Leonard Elmhirst, Tagore's secretary. They set up a centre there—"

"I know. Free school, art centre, woolen mill, so on so forth."

"That verse was framed in the library. I copied it down."

"Better you should learn his younger, revolutionary thoughts. Now you've got me started! 'When old words die out on the tongue, new melodies break forth from the heart; and where the old tracks are lost, new country is revealed with its wonders.' Unfortunately, Tagore got detoured along the way by narrow nationalist yearning, but he did start out with a truly radical instinct."

"Explain one thing to me, Rashid," I said: "Why does there have to be revolution? Wouldn't the world be much better off if we all put our energy into conservation and cooperation and coexistence? I mean that's what Dartington Hall was all about. Integrate all classes and occupations. Theatre next to the farm, next to the wool mill. Reverse the pollution and destruction of the environment, and gain control over population growth. Once we make progress at those things, we can then turn our attention to social justice. Revolution only produces more wars. Look at eastern Europe, look at Cuba, look at Biafra and the mess in the Congo."

Rashid shook his head with a sweet, cynical smile. "My dear, naïve friend!" He wiped a bit of mayonnaise off his lip and answered thoughtfully:

"How a person sees things always depends on where they are coming from."

"And, as you once said, you and I both come from the British Colonial Empire."

"Yah! Yah! But from opposite parts. You came from the ruling class and I came from the subordinate. In a way, I also came as a hanger-on of the ruling class—my father was a landowner. But we were not in charge. So, when ethnic violence erupted, my father was murdered by Hindus, and the British did nothing about it."

"Jenadie told me your father was murdered, Rashid. Tell me about it."

"*Thuggees* came into the house and hacked him to pieces. Middle of the night. I was seven years old, sleeping in the bed with him. Actually I have no detailed memory of it. Blotted out or something."

"Holy Christ! No wonder you don't trust the world."

"If it had been your father, we can be sure the British would have put troops in place to save him, simply because he was a white man—oh, even more if it had been a white woman—and track down the murderers. You may have grown up believing in the power and goodness of British colonialism. Whereas I was on the other side of the colour bar. Nobody did anything about my father's killers."

"You think the British are corrupt?"

"Compared to whom? The Portuguese? The Germans? Doesn't make a difference. All colonialism is self-interested and therefore evil. I've known that since I was a child."

"I can see why you think so. What I know about colonialism is that we spent our whole lives building a country out of chaos, only to be thrown out—Are you still hungry? I've got some hot and sour soup I could heat up."

"Great." He followed me into the kitchen.

"Don't tell me it was nothing but evil for Europeans to move to Africa and bring modern agriculture and medicine, and so on. Literacy. And put an end to slavery—which white people did not invent. Here you are an East Indian living in Canada as a consequence of British colonialism. Is that evil?"

"Oh Alistair, we can argue all night," he said wearily. "Let me give you a simple example. You talk of modern agriculture. Okay. Colonialism spread Western agriculture through the world, right? Good! But what are they growing? Cash crops for Western capitalist markets, while indigenous agricultural methods and needs are ignored. The result is a net *decline* in agricultural productivity, destruction of the soil, desertification and ultimately hunger and starvation—all in the interest of short term profits for the Western industrial complex."

"Would you prefer that people go back to wearing loincloths and digging the stony earth with pointed sticks?"

"Of course not. After colonialism, what should happen is a redistribution of land to the people as a whole, and the development of an agricultural economy which meets the actual food needs of the people. You only achieve that by a social revolution, and exclusion of the ravenous capitalist machine, by force if necessary. In Kenya what do they grow today?"

"Coffee, tea, pyrethrum, sisal—"

"Exactly! Do Kenyans eat sisal and pyrethrum? No. They should be growing rice, and beans and maize. There shouldn't be any thousand-acre estates devoted to a single crop. There should be small holdings on which families feed themselves, and sell the excess for profit."

"My friend Peter Johnson," I said, as I reached over to pour him more tea, "is a settler and citizen still farming in Kenya. He runs a dairy farm in semi-desert land, and provides Nairobi with cream—"

Rashid waved me down. "Nice guy no doubt! But that's an isolated exception. Thanks," he said as I put his soup in front of him at the kitchen table. "Look, I'm not saying that colonialism had nothing whatsoever good about it. What happens in history is a slow evolution of changes in the status quo. On one side are those who try to profit directly from those changes. Capitalists, stock market, currency traders, the whole rotten tribe of gamblers. On the other side are those like myself—you too—who try to change the image people have of the world, to bring about a more humane evolution, where power, profit and happiness are more evenly distributed among people rather than concentrated in the gated and barricaded mansions of a few rich pigs."

"I'm surprised you include me on your side! I thought you were going to shoot me!"

He grinned. "You are an educator," he said, "and I'm going to come to your class one day and see what you do. But I assume you are trying to change the received ideas of your students, to make them think and see the world in new ways."

"All I'm trying to do is get them to know the difference between *it's* with an apostrophe and *its* without one! Or spell *a lot* as two words instead of one."

"Liar!" he laughed. "Anyway, we are always talking about my affairs. Now tell me what you're doing. You said your Ph.D. thesis is about defamiliarity? What is it?"

As I answered, he leaned over the large bowl and slurped soup quietly into his mouth, avoiding his beard and keeping his eyes on me.

"Defamiliarization is a form of satire," I said. "The writer sheds new light on something so well known that people have lost sight of what it really is."

"Example?"

"Tolstoy on corporal punishment. In one of his stories, he remarks that bending people over to flog their bottoms with a cane is not efficient. You can cause much more severe pain by sticking needles into their finger joints, or squeezing their feet in a vice."

"I see. So instead of seeing physical punishment in a cultural context—like 'a good thrashing' or 'six of the best—'"

"Exactly. Tolstoy shows us that a beating is essentially nothing more than the cruel infliction of pain."

"Hmm!" Rashid laid down his soup spoon and smiled. "Pretty radical for a Russian land baron! Wow, this is good soup, man! Where did you learn to cook like this?"

"I didn't. You introduced me to the Nan King, and when I'm in Chinatown I get some hot and sour soup and keep it in the freezer."

Rashid grinned, obviously delighted to have been of use.

"Turning to practical matters," I said, "could you look after my cat for me next week?"

"Cat?" He blinked as though he had missed some logical segue in our conversation.

"I have to go to an articulation conference in Penticton, Friday night through Sunday, and my neighbour's away. You'd just have to come in once a day and feed her. You could sleep here if you like—the cat would love that."

"No problem."

I gave him a key.

"You know what?" he said, as he was going out the door. "This Caroline business, is it the first time a woman rejected you?"

"I don't know." I literally couldn't think for a moment. "Why?"

"Maybe white bwana is not used to being disobeyed."

"Ah come on, Rashid! You're not going to try and connect Caroline's flight with the decline of male imperial power!"

"Maybe—maybe not. Look, man, thank you for the boat ride, and all the food, and for the conversation. I appreciate the fact that you listen to me even though we don't agree. How do you say that in Swahili, *Asante bwana.*"

"Just *asante sana*. You don't have to call me *bwana*—unless you want to, that is. You know what the Duke of Edinburgh said to Jomo Kenyatta at the ceremony transferring independence to Kenya?"

"What did he say?"

"I was there. Just as the symbolic book called 'The Instruments of Government' was to be handed over ceremonially to Kenyatta, I saw Prince Philip lean forward—Kenyatta's not short, but the Duke is taller—he leaned over him, and later I read what he had whispered in his ear: 'Are you sure you don't want to change your mind?'"

"That is really funny!" Rashid said, with a grin as fixed as the one he had given me, when he said he might one day have to shoot me. "I guess the guy is a bit of a clown."

"Oh he is. And clowns have their uses, like Shakespeare's fools. But before we begin another argument, let me just say Rashid, it's a two-way conversation. Traffic runs in both directions across Second Narrows. Thank you, Sahib. *Dhanyavaad mera dost*."

༺ ༻

After he had gone, I turned in early, but late that night the phone rang and woke me. It was my former student, Dave Marsden, the Vice-President of Student Council.

"Alistair, man, I've got to see you right away. Are you going to be there for the next half hour?"

"Can it wait till after the weekend?"

"No. It can't wait."

"Okay."

I put on my dressing gown, and twenty minutes later he rapped on the front door. When I led him into the living room, he stood defensively behind the cane armchair, gripping its back. His arms were shaking. I felt a sense of complete unreality, once again like being an actor in a movie. He was a tall, strong man but he was quivering. I wondered what political mess he was in.

"What's up, Dave?"

"I don't know if you and I can remain friends after this."

"What's the matter?"

"I went to bed with— I *fucked* Caroline last night. Or rather, she fucked *me*."

I stepped over to him, smiling.

"Come on, man!" I ruffled his hair. "Caroline and I are not together any more. Why are you making such a big deal?"

He began to calm down, and I poured us each a glass of wine.

"Listen, Alistair, I'm relieved that you're not upset about this," he said. "I thought we were going to have to fight."

"What's there to fight about, man? So, are you and Caroline getting together now?"

"Jesus man, you haven't understood what I'm telling you! I never want to *see* the bitch again!"

I didn't wish to hear any more, but I couldn't help it now.

"What happened, Dave?"

"I was at this party in Kitsilano. She was drinking and you know what a couple of glasses of wine will do to her? She started dancing with me, and she got wilder and wilder, and then she whispered in my ear to come upstairs and into a bedroom."

I took a swig of wine.

"Why'd you have to come and tell me about this?"

"I don't know, man! It feels like a betrayal."

"I don't control her life, and anyway it's over between us."

"I know, I know! But—you know what it is? I felt . . . used, you know? It wasn't lovemaking, man. It was bad fucking. She was doing you, not even me. She was using me to give you the finger."

I looked at his devastated face and felt raw. Had she calculated that he would come immediately and tell me?

"Where'd you phone me from, Dave?"

"Park Royal."

"To Deep Cove in twenty minutes? You must have driven at seventy miles an hour!"

He came across the room and threw himself around me in a bear hug.

"I'm really sorry about this Alistair," he said.

"It's not your fault," I said.

We hugged again and then sat down.

"It's not as if she even enjoyed it!" he said. "She told me she's never had an orgasm in her life."

Now I definitely wanted him to leave, and I was glad when he did. I began rummaging around preparing for my trip to Penticton, but my mind would not shut it out. (*"You're the best! You're the best ever!"* The little whimpering cries of joy and release.) I went to bed hoping for a dark, empty sleep, not Caroline's mocking laugh coursing through my dream world. I swallowed a final glass of wine and set the alarm clock. I dreamed anyway, but it wasn't about her.

Rashid and I are flying side by side in long, frail gliders with stubby noses, high above the earth. There's an eerie sound of wind rushing over the wings, and we have to shout to hear one another. Far beneath us are miniature green fields and a meandering oxbow river. Ahead, near the town of Hope, a wall of blue mountains rises above us with clouds spilling over the tops. We are out of range of our launch crew and the landing field, and we cannot turn back. The wind is pushing us into the mountains and I'm scared. I suddenly remember that I need to explain something to Rashid. I try shouting an explanation but it's too complicated up here. I stab my finger anxiously at the mountains dead ahead.

"Not to worry!" Rashid calls across. "Thermals will take us over!"

"What's on the other side?" I ask him.

He turns to me. I can see his eyes through the screen of the aviator goggles and he sees me but he does not reply.

"What's on the other side?" I call again.

He turns to watch me. Our gliders are flying neck and neck, very fast, and I'm afraid to steer any closer to him in case our wingtips collide.

A third time I yell my question.

Now he breaks into a laugh and then calls back in a loud, clear voice: "Wait and see when we get there!"

The alarm clock started to ring and it took me several attempts to hit its button.

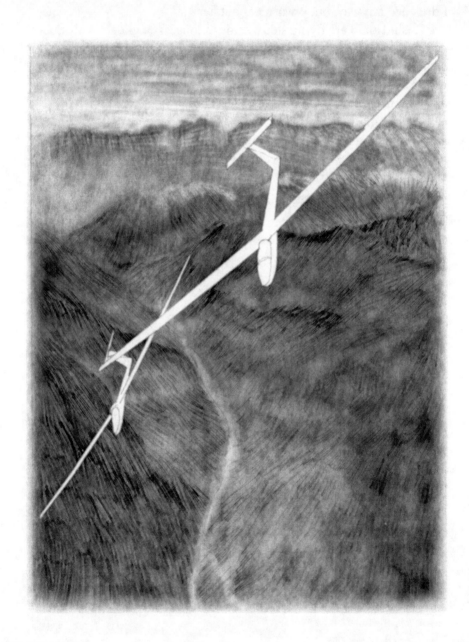

21

That morning, as I drove along the Trans-Canada through the lush, foggy dairy farms of the Fraser Valley, I tried to think what it would be like for a seven-year-old boy to witness his father's murder. He lies in the bed and the *thuggees break into the bedroom and start slashing his father. Brutal movement, sounds of struggle and cries of pain.* No wonder Rashid had suppressed the memory. Still, it was a night that must have moulded him. My mother's death from cancer when I was eleven was a bombshell all right; this was much worse. Rashid had stated theoretically the differences between us, both children of the British Empire, from opposite positions of power and privilege. What would it actually feel like to be him? I was not a radical. I wasn't driving to Penticton to blow something apart; I was driving there to put things together, to make connections, articulation. But that's because I believed that the world made sense, and British Columbia was as progressive a place as the Kenya I knew had been. For Rashid, Vancouver was part of the worldwide battleground. Enhance the contradictions and progress toward the eventual revolution. The future will be better than the past. Now I remembered what it was I needed so urgently to explain to Rashid in my dream: he had said at the party in Deep Cove, "we are at the point of no return," which means the triumphant point from which there's no turning back. But it has another shade of meaning too: the point at which you're running out of fuel so you no longer have the possibility of a safe landing.

Speeding along the freeway towards Hope past the exits to Chilliwack, I realized how close I had come to Rashid. He represented to me something lacking from all those relationships with people of other colours and cultures, amongst whom I had grown up and learned to say *Hello* and *Have a nice day* in a dozen different languages, but who remained on the other side of a barrier.

Not that I had lacked friendships with people of other races in Africa, some of them quite close, especially blacks. Playing with black children when we were too young to care about the difference, and then with the house servants: I used to read stories to Kibungi when he babysat me as a child, and eat *posho* with Obami in his room. Later, as an adult, I studied Sesotho under Professor Kunene at the University of Cape Town, and watched how carefully he crushed out his Craven A's in the sardine can ashtray in the seminar room. Later still, when I taught at a black school in Kenya, we reciprocated dinner invitations with black colleagues and their wives, Mwangis, Ogutus, and Simon Kithome. And I had warm relationships with my students in the Dramatic Society of all the different tribes, Kikuyus and Luos, Luhia and Maasai, Nandi and Wakamba. We all worked together as a team, far into the night, to rehearse and mount plays. Yes, I had known camaraderie with emotional ups and downs. But it was a camaraderie in which I was always aware of differences.

With Rashid there was a unique intimacy. Colour, accent, race faded away. Even when he threatened to shoot me—it wasn't a racial matter, it was politics. There had been that moment at the Edmonton Symphony when I realized that he made me racially colour-blind. Now I saw it was more than that. With Rashid, I let down my guard completely—no barriers at all.

And yet, on his side there was the devastating murder under British colonial rule, and the killers not pursued. I now wondered if my empathy had been totally one-sided, romantic and patronizing. When he joked about shooting me perhaps he really *did* mean it in his heart. Or had the brutality he had suffered steeled him so that he was able always to see the person and not simply a representative of some group. Perhaps that was part of the discipline that had become natural to him. Rashid's bandit smile, his white teeth gleaming, his intelligent eyes alight with humour and confidence. And behind that smile, I now knew, lay that night of violent intrusion and screams, and the sight of his father's inert and gory body. And then the long, lonely, difficult years of fatherlessness, and poverty, until the triumph of his educational successes, overseas travel, and now his tough intelligence and pure dedication to the radical cause.

I felt privileged and proud to have Rashid Hassan as my friend.

In Penticton, the articulation conference took place in a hotel where the indoor-outdoor carpeting smelled of beer, fish and cigarette smoke.

The tall blond man who was our host welcomed us and then said, "To begin the proceedings, we thought it would be a good idea to remind ourselves of what it's all about, namely the living language and literature. Would you welcome, please, the British Columbian poet, Tom Wayman."

A dark-bearded, curly-haired young man took the podium. He smiled nervously through gold-rimmed glasses, and nodded his head.

"Hi!" he said, opened a folder of manuscripts, and began to read.

His voice was clear, and his language fresh. He read about Kenworth trucks and Toronto streetcars, about pulling off the highway into a campsite, about people being on unemployment and making coffee, about the murder of Salvador Allende in Chile, about the poet Robert Bly and the occupation of a campus in California to protest Dow Chemical and the Vietnam War:

And Bly in the afternoon speaks softly
of a great despair in the land: like the deep snow
out of the lounge windows where he talks, easing down
on the hills and frozen trees. Only fifteen left and willing
to face the massed police and be busted, and Bly
speaks to them slowly, waving his red wristband of support
for the Milwaukee Fourteen, who napalmed draft records
months ago on cement in the sunshine. Bly in the evening
sighs as a wind, his sweet voice soothing
and crackling like a gentle fire in a grate somewhere
warm against a cold night. . . .

Great round of applause. Wayman drank some water and turned to another poem. He read about people bored with their industrial jobs who dreamed of dancing and began to tap out musical rhythms with their tools. He described a street of second-hand stores in the East End of Vancouver which I recognized immediately, right down to the engine blocks sitting on grass outside the car repair shops. In the discussion afterwards, I stood up and said, "That was a good reading, Tom! This is the sort of stuff I think our students should be studying."

A tall, grey-suited professor from the University of Victoria rose to contradict me: "Isn't there a danger in university and college teachers ignoring the canon of great literature and imposing their own idiosyncratic tastes upon students?"

Before I knew it, I was up and at the guy: "Whose taste do you want to impose on them? Don't you have the authority to judge what your students should read? You wait for some committee of foreign scholars at Oxford or Harvard to tell you what to do? In my department, I encourage people to teach what they enjoy. Joni Mitchell and Phil Ochs, and now Tom Wayman. Teach the stuff *you love*! Can you suggest anything better than that?"

No applause. But in the lunch break several people came and congratulated me on my position. Others avoided my eyes. A young prof from UBC with a strong Yorkshire accent came up and shook my hand. "Ee, I'm glad you told that old fart off!" he said. "Have you heard about this new woman we've 'ired at UBC from Yale?"

"No."

"She's absolutely terrific! She comes into class the first day and tells the students to arrange their desks in a big circle. Well, of course, you know the Buchanan building? They can't move 'em. ''Oo's screwed all these fookin' desks to the floor?' she says. 'Bring screwdrivers!' So the next day they bring tools and unscrew all the desks and put 'em in a circle. Janitors are goin' up the *wall* man! She's a real breath of fresh air, I tell you."

I drove home from the conference with a light heart. We were winning some ground against the grey authorities.

Phil Ochs sang about the dawn of another age, on the cassette player.

On my kitchen table, there was the key and a note from Rashid: "Sorry, man, cat is gone! Hope I didn't do anything to scare it off! Hope it comes back."

But she didn't. I never saw that old black cat again.

"Things aren't going too well for your friend Rashid Hassan, are they?" Andrea Halvorson observed, as we waited for the others to arrive at a department meeting.

"No kidding! The dismissal hearings are bogged down. Both the Simon Fraser Faculty Association and the Association of Canadian University Professors have refused to become involved. The Association had an investigation to see if the university or the suspended profs themselves were deliberately causing the stall. Listen to this": I opened my briefcase and read to her from the report:

> *"When the deep suspicions and differences gather as much bitterness as they have gathered over the past year at SFU, the dismissal procedures themselves can become a further means of pursuing the conflict. In Clausewitzian terms, the procedures become extensions of policy by other means."*

"You mean they hate one another's guts so badly that they use the hearings to continue fighting?"

"Exactly."

" I hear he's going to England."

"Yes, he's going to do some research. Jenadie's beginning to carve out a career for herself as a reporter. Anyway, everyone's here. Let's begin." I went through the formal agenda items and then invited further discussion.

"When are we going to be inspected?" Thelma Smith wanted to know.

"Inspected?" I countered.

"Isn't somebody going to come and sit in our classrooms and inspect our teaching?"

"You'll be *evaluated*."

"Oh bullshit, Alistair!" said Andrea. "'Inspected,' 'evaluated,' same difference. When is it happening? And are they going to give us any warning this time?"

"It's very unnerving to walk into your classroom and see Dean Bull sitting quietly at the back," said Trevor Easton. "It gives me the creeps."

"Forrester's worse!" said Sandra Atkinson. "That man's so big, he hunches his shoulders together and holds still to try to minimize his presence, which only makes him more conspicuous. He won't make eye contact with you and you offer him a class handout and he just looks down and won't take it. You get this eerie sense of being spied on!"

"Warning's a reasonable request," I answered Andrea. "Say a week's notice. And I think we ought to be able to choose which of them comes to evaluate us. How about I take it up with the Dean?"

"We ought to evaluate one another," Sandra Atkinson said.

"We certainly should," said Thelma Smith. "We should have a college-wide Faculty Evaluation Committee. Elected. They should receive evaluation reports and advise on renewal or non-renewal of contracts."

"And students should be involved," said Andrea. "There should be questionnaires for the students to fill out."

"Are you kidding!" said Max Odegaard. "You know what happened at UBC when they did student evaluations and published the *Black and Blue Report*? One prof committed suicide by jumping out of a window, and another was smeared so badly she couldn't face her classes and resigned. You want that?"

I let the discussion continue and listened. I had felt uneasy at the arbitrary power wielded by the Dean in particular. At the end of one semester Bull called in a Fine Arts instructor and asked her to explain a discrepancy in her grade book. Two students got the same score 73%, but she gave a B- to one and a B to the other. When he asked her for an explanation, she said the second student had worked harder. At the end of the semester, her contract was not renewed. Her Co-ordinator had not gone to bat for her, and I felt powerless to intervene. And in the case of a young instructor Bull had hired to teach Communications, he confided to me that he might have made a mistake : "She seems to be too pro-student," he said. "Yes, indeedy, we might have to let 'Miss Brighteyes' go." That casual remark made me really fume inside, though I didn't take it up with him because I knew I couldn't alter his course once he was set. There was no point trying to argue with him about how "pro-student" was "too pro-student" or what he even meant by the term. I went to find the "Miss Brighteyes" in question and invited her into my office, where I uttered some vague insinuations about protecting her rear and making sure her marking was rigorous and consistent and her grade books were in order, etc. She took the warning seriously and thanked me profusely for alerting her. Later, it occurred to me that this was precisely what Bull had expected me to do. In his own bull-like and chauvinist manner he was using me to give her what we now call "alerting and guidance"—or at least the alerting part of it—and apparently it worked: for the next thirty years or so her smile brightened the College and brought credit to it. Whatever quality it was that had given Bull his suspicions, she had obviously taken care of, following my warning. But that's not the way it should have been done. There should have been a formal process, not a private tip-off.

Of course, tensions between the administrators of a college and the faculty cannot be totally avoided. But when one of my English Instructors asked for leave in December, in between semesters with no classes happening, to fly to Switzerland for four days to get married, and the College Council imposed a deduction on her salary for each day she was out of the country, I wanted some way of resisting that stupid and vindictive decision, but had none. Going to bat for the faculty became my natural role. One time, faculty asked for the purchase of two of the newly available cassette recorders, but the "Media Centre" (a tight-ass librarian) replied in a memo that it was not possible within his budget. Outraged—these machines cost $68 each—I put a sign on my office door:

**"Capilano College Faculty Association Media Centre:
Sony TC60 Tape Cassette Recorders
Available Soon For Classroom Loan."**

The librarian capitulated next day before I even went to the Faculty Association for authorization and a $150 budget.

Back in the department meeting, I said: "Maybe faculty evaluation is something the Faculty Association should take up?" I looked at Thelma. She was the Vice-President of the Association, which so far had not done much. It had produced a code of ethics that said you couldn't come to work under the influence of drugs or alcohol; and it had proposed an idealistic salary plan whereby every employee of the College would be paid exactly the same amount, which Bull and Forrester had just scoffed at. Perhaps this Evaluation Committee proposal was something important which the Association could fight through. I decided to test the waters.

After the department meeting, I went to Bull's office.

"About future directions, . . ." I said.

He leaned back in his swivel chair and locked his hands behind his head. "My ideas, Alistair? Or have you come in here to lay yours on me, as they say nowadays?"

"I was thinking about the position of faculty," I said. "We don't have ranks as the universities do, and that's good: we're all just instructors. We have pay steps, which is fine by me. No guaranteed tenure—I agree with that. But these one-semester contracts are unnerving people. Nobody can get a mortgage with that kind of insecurity. What would you think of bringing in graduated multi-year contracts, contingent upon successful evaluation? You'd get appointed for a probationary year, and, if the next evaluation was successful, a longer term contract, and so on."

"Evaluation performed by whom?" he asked with his brows raised.

"Well," I hedged, "several people, really. There could be student reports, colleague, Co-ordinator, administrator, a whole package. The file would be submitted to an Evaluation Committee which would advise on reappointment."

"Who appoints the Committee?"

"A member could be elected from each department."

"No way! I'm not handing over my responsibility like that."

"All right, then you could reserve the right to disagree with the Committee. Or you could reserve the right to ratify its membership."

Bull took off his glasses and swung them round a couple of times in the air, then put the temple in his mouth and sucked on it. "Sounds like duplication of effort," he said. "And an awful lot of paper work. But it is an interesting idea all the same. I'll put it on the agenda for discussion at the next Co-ordinators' Meeting."

I walked out of his office feeling victorious and immediately began phoning my counterparts in all the other colleges in BC. By the time the Co-ordinators' Meeting came around, I had assembled a file and typed up a summary table of procedures used elsewhere. Most had arbitrary evaluations by administrators, but two had introduced democratic models. "There is no question, they're the way of the future," I said, and my fellow Co-ordinators looked at one another rather hesitantly.

Bull, as usual, despite his bullying ways, took the progressive view. "I like the sound of it," he said. "You people work up a detailed proposal and bring it back to the next meeting for discussion. If you develop something I find suitable, I'll be prepared to take it to Council."

"What about the Faculty Association," I said. "Shouldn't they be involved?"

Bull eyed me as though I were a child. "The Faculty Association is free to do whatever it likes," he said. "I'm the one charged with the responsibility for running the departments of this college. And by delegation through me, you, the Co-ordinators. Meeting adjourned."

Later that week, in the Faculty Association meeting, Thelma spoke in favour of the proposal for an elected Evaluation Committee.

"And we should have elected Co-ordinators too," said Andrea Halvorson.

Thelma smiled approvingly at her. "Let's take things one step at a time," she said. "I'll raise that with the Executive later."

The proposal was modified to allow for elected Evaluation Committees in each department, and the motion carried overwhelmingly.

I would go home from meetings at the College more exhilarated than exhausted. But my private life was dismal again. There was nobody to talk to. My heart was bleeding, and I still had no clue what had gone wrong with Caroline—and how she could have pulled that number with Dave Marsden was beyond my experience of women. The last time I talked to her, after I finally got her number, I phoned and she told me she wished I would go and walk on a beach somewhere and "be happy." I felt totally humiliated and too raw to even think of another relationship.

I spent time with my boat. I was paying $20 a month for moorage at Mosquito Creek and wanted to move the boat to Deep Cove, but they were asking $180 in advance for a year's moorage, and I didn't have it and was trying to figure out how to get it. One morning a letter arrived from the Royal Bank, and I opened it, puzzled, because I had no account there. Inside was a blue and white and yellow striped Chargex card with my name embossed on it, and a letter informing me that I had a credit limit of $300. It seemed a small miracle, a windfall. So I went to the Dollarton branch of the Royal Bank and borrowed $200 on the card and moved the boat up to Deep Cove. I would walk down to the marina on sunny winter days and putter around on the wooden floats for hours, fixing little things and chatting to the other boaters.

A letter arrived from Imogen's lawyer in Johannesburg. He proposed a support agreement of £300 per month for the kids plus £50 for Imogen and enclosed a detailed budget right down to the haircuts. I took my pencil and calculated the exchange. In Canadian dollars, they were asking for $850 a month whereas I was taking home $526. I drove to the UBC Library and looked up advertisements in the *Times Educational Supplement*. A Lecturer at the University of Witwatersrand was offered a gross starting salary of £3,200 which was £1000 less than Imogen's lawyer was asking me to pay.

Angrily, I sat at my typewriter and rolled in a sheet of paper.

"Dear Sir," I wrote, feeling lawyerly like my father, "I acknowledge receipt of your letter of the 13th. inst. . . ." but after ripping a couple of sheets out of the machine and starting over, I dropped the formal language and told him plainly he was asking for more than I earned. I offered them $300 a month which left me $226 to live on. Rent was $90, and my loan payments $50, leaving $86 for food and everything else. I figured I could get by. Damn! I'd forgotten, there would now be a monthly loan bill from Chargex. *Oh well,* I told myself, *it's nice to have the boat up here, but don't charge anything more on that card!* Newspaper editorials condemned the Royal Bank for their mass mailout of the cards, but it was too late. The age of Aquarius had begun turning into the age of plastic money.

As I sealed up the letter to the lawyer and walked down to the mailbox, I felt strangely peaceful. Although it had angered me to read his smarmy lawyer language, and his demands had unsettled me for a while, nevertheless I appreciated the advantage for Imogen that he had built in to the agreement: if she remarried, she'd lose only 10% of the support payments. The other 90% for the kids would go on for years to come.

A few weeks later, I got a letter from my stepmother saying she had heard that Imogen was having to get medical treatment for the kids through the welfare office. I threw this lie into the box with my father's old letters, feeling very alone. Paul and Viviana had saved enough money to go and explore the rest of Canada and decide where they wanted to live. They sent occasional postcards from Québec. As for Jenadie's old roommate Marianne of the crystal eyes, who had been in my fantasies for a while, she and her geographer, Mac, were now engaged.

One day, Andrea Halvorson phoned and invited herself over for tea.

The first thing she said when she arrived was, "You have a terribly squeaky bed."

I looked at her in astonishment. *Is she coming on to me?* I wondered. It seemed awful, like your own sister. Besides, she lived with her boyfriend.

"How do you know?" I said.

"I slept in it."

"When?"

"When you were at the articulation conference in Penticton."

I frowned at her. "What a dog! How could you do something like that? What about Kurt?"

"What's the problem, sweetie? Nobody got hurt. It's okay to swing a little. What Kurt doesn't know can't harm him."

"Well I'm shocked! I guess I'm pretty old-fashioned."

"Certainly. That's why I brought you these."

She pulled two books out of her bag and handed them to me. One was a paperback of the new best seller by Eldridge Cleaver, *Soul on Ice*. I put it aside. The other was *I Ching: The Book of Changes*.

"It always helps me when I'm in a rough spot," she said.

"You think I'm in a rough spot?"

"I see your face every day at the College, man!"

"I find Thelma Smith a pain in the ass," I said. "She watches everything I do and calls me to account all the time. One time she jumped in, when I had joked around with a student and managed to cause offence. Thelma offered to bring a 'sensitive, non-chauvinistic male' to the meeting I arranged with the student to hash the matter over. Of course the student didn't show up, just Thelma and me and the guy who was to be my model of non-chauvinism. It was only afterwards I realized that she had interpreted my usual energy as male chauvinism. I think she takes out her hatred of her ex-husband on me. I had one of those out-of-body dreams about her the other night: she was crouched over me with a dagger, as I slept against a wall, waiting for movement. I died, and eventually my body turned into dust. Thelma waited patiently with her knife. A piece of my cheek crumbled and fell, and at that movement she leapt forward to stab me."

"She resents the fact that you were chosen as Co-ordinator instead of her."

"Really? I never heard that. Do you think she'd make a better Co-ordinator?"

"I don't know. She'd be harder for Bull to control than you are. She thinks you got the job because you're a man."

"What do you think?"

"She's probably right. But I didn't come here to talk about Thelma." She put her face close to mine. "What's upsetting you so much? Caroline Bell with her round heels? Hm?"

"You're a fine one to talk!" I said.

"Honestly, you men! I can *not imagine* having an affair with a student! They're children. They don't know enough to interest me. All you care about is young flesh, huh? Serves you damned well right Alistair. Anyway, let me show you how to consult the *I Ching*. Have you got three coins? You've been bottling up your feelings. This should help you get in touch with yourself."

After she had gone, I decided to consult the book immediately. I asked aloud, "Can Caroline and I be reunited?"

Carefully I began to throw the coins and made the hexagram.

"Huan, 59, Dispersion," I recorded in my notebook. "See text. Very hopeful. The upper trigram is first daughter and the lower one second son. Note especially, 'When a man's vital energy is dammed up within him, gentleness serves to break up and dissolve the blockage.' And the gentleness is located in the upper trigram (Sun), the Gentle, Wind, the First Daughter.

"This hexagram has a double meaning. The first is suggested by the image of wind over water, indicating the breaking up of ice and rigidity. The second meaning is penetration; Sun penetrates into K'an, the Abysmal, indicating dispersion, division."

This is beautiful, I thought, magic!

Next I asked specifically, "Can the obstruction between Caroline and me be dissolved, to make for reunion?"

The coins gave me "Lin, 19, Approach."

"Approach has supreme success," the text said. "Perseverance furthers. . . ."

I phoned Andrea.

"Come and see what the *I Ching* is telling me," I said.

"It's incredible!" I said, when she arrived. "The book even knows that she's a first daughter and I'm a second son." I showed her my notebook, with my questions and the book's answers.

She pondered the writing.

"I mean, Andrea, I have never believed in mumbo jumbo, but this is so *informed*, it's spooky. Here, I'll do one now. I'll ask it if Thelma is right about me getting the Co-ordinator position because I'm a man."

I began to throw the coins and record the results.

"I don't know if I should tell you this, Alistair," Andrea said, after watching for a while, "but when you construct the hexagrams you're supposed to start at the bottom line and work upwards, not top down."

"Ah no! You mean they're all wrong?"

"Who's to say? Maybe for you they're right. Do you want to smoke a joint?"

"You go ahead. I don't do dope. Ah shit, what a letdown!"

I fetched her a cup of tea and said, "Dave Marsden came to see me the other day."

"He did?" She sucked in her breath and held it, studying my face. "Haa!" she blew it out. "What did he want?"

"He wanted to tell me that Caroline grabbed him at a party and practically raped him, then told him she's never enjoyed sex, never had an orgasm"

"No kidding! What did you do to her?"

"I don't think I did anything bad to her."

"Well somebody's hurt her and made her really mad."

"You think so?"

"You want me to have a chat with her?"

"No thank you."

While she fussed with her joint, I sat and thought about what had happened between me and Caroline. There had been that one strange incident in bed the night we saw *The Beard* when she kicked me away inexplicably. Maybe Andrea was right. She'd been sexually abused.

"Thanks for coming over," I said. "I think I'm through with the *I Ching* for now. Do you want to go out for a ride in my boat?"

"I didn't know you had a boat!"

"Yeah. I bought it when we split up."

"You *what?*"

"I went out and bought a little cabin cruiser."

"Men!" Andrea hooted. "What a classic!"

"Come on, Andrea! When shit like that happens you can't get bogged down in feelings. I have classes to teach and a department to run."

"If you don't confront your feelings by letting them out, *they*'ll end up getting bogged down in *you*," she lectured me. "You end up with cancer of the soul. You know what I think?" she said, her eyes glassy now. "I think you and Caroline Bell are both too needy. Each of you needs more than the other can give right now. She probably did you a favour by clearing out. It was a protective move for herself, but actually it protected you too. When you play on the same level as someone that much younger, you know, you leave yourself vulnerable to humiliation like this. I'll take a rain check on the boat ride, Alistair. I've got to get going."

After she left I felt really stupid to have been taken in by the nonsense of the *I Ching*. It had raised my hopes. I also felt disturbed by Andrea's accusation that Bull easily controlled me. Was I such a patsy? I ran through the six co-ordinators who reported to Norman Bull. Two had been "let go" from university jobs in unexplained circumstances. One was gay, and not very out about it. My immigration status was uncertain. Had Bull instinctively surrounded himself with a set of vulnerable minions, each with an Achilles Heel, to do his bidding under his control?

I poured a Scotch, put on my Fifth Dimension record and listened again to Marilyn McCoo singing in syncopation about harmony and liberation.

Soppy, remembering, "Approach has supreme success," I dialled Caroline's number.

"Hello," she answered in a guarded voice.

"Can I—, could we . . . have coffee some time?"

"Alistair, don't call me anymore, okay?"

"Oh, look, I'm sorry—"

"It's fine. It doesn't matter. Just don't call anymore."

"Okay."

She hung up.

I listened to records.

I played the harmonica.

I didn't call. ("Don't drink and dial!" I told myself.)

I felt so very bereft. I think I was as close to a suicidal state as I have ever come. I had nobody. My family in Africa was bitterly disappointed with me because of the marriage break up, and now this wall of ice had blocked Caroline off from me. And I felt guilty about all of it. It was all my fault. I should have worked harder to keep my wife and children together with me; I should never have become involved with a student, and her distancing herself from me was a self-redeeming move on her part. Andrea was right about that: we were both too needy, and at least Caroline had had the guts and strength to break it off.

Reaching around in this frigid emotional vacuum, I suddenly found a centre of warmth: it was the college! Despite my misgivings about how Dean Bull had chosen his co-ordinators, my soul leaned towards the college and I felt the power of family there: these were my people now, the ones I could call upon when I needed anything. Bull had become a substitute father figure for me, distant but secure, and fundamentally a loving, caring person. And all of us who had wound up working at Capilano, faculty, support staff, students, and the administrators, immigrants, American draft dodgers, a few qualified Canadians finally, were tied together by a bond of common purpose and enterprise. We were a new face of education in British Columbia: egalitarian, without ranks or privilege. Even the ridiculous proposition to have every employee of the college be paid exactly the same salary brought a smile to my face as I remembered Peter Hansen making that motion at a Faculty Association meeting, to wondering stares. We accepted our common humanity without ranks. We were family.

But even as I nursed these utopian thoughts, I remembered a conversation I had had with one of the secretaries at the retreat at Paradise Valley: It was the night after two exhausting days of discussions, and people were dancing. This young woman, Emily, who worked in the Career/Vocational Division was drunk and coming on to me. She kept taking my hand and dragging me out to dance. She had some bitterness bubbling up in her, and as we danced she began to taunt me: "You faculty think you're so clever!" she said. "You think we're all on the same level because you don't have a faculty club, and we all use the same washrooms, and nobody has special parking permits. And you don't insist on calling yourselves Doctor or Professor. And Peter was pushing that ridiculous notion that everybody should be paid the same. How stupid! The fact is there's no equality. You guys get to go and teach your classes, and the students all look up to you like gods, and then you can get in your cars and drive away. Whereas us—we're chained to our desks. We can move from the desk to the photocopy machine and the mailboxes—and, oh yes, we can go to the washroom. The fact is we hate the bloody students. All they ever do is come in and complain to us, and try to whine their way around the regulations. We're better off without them. The support staff are never happier than when the semester ends and the students all disappear!"

"Come on, Emily," I said. "You know that's not true. The faculty depend on you guys to keep the college running. Without you we'd have no students to teach." But even as I said this, I remembered that horrible moment when I was delivering my rant to the College Council on the university transfer problem, and the Council Chairman referred to Maureen Ingleton as "the girl." (*"I'll make sure the girl sends you a draft copy of the minutes to check the accuracy." "The girl." Fucking hell!*)

I had to admit to myself that for all our utopian ideas, there was no equality: the faculty had the freedom of artists, doing what they could to open up students' minds, while the support staff faced the drudgery of being tied to their desks and dealt mostly with complaints. As though to prove her point, Emily, dancing with me at Paradise Valley, suddenly hugged me tight and thrust her crotch against mine, and cried in tipsy desperation, "Come on man! There's got to be something there." That was the end of that dance.

Raw from this incident with Emily, I decided to bring up the general matter of campus sexual relations with Dean Bull. He sat in his comfortable position, leaning back slightly in this sprung desk chair, and slowly revolved a pen in his fingers. It was clearly not the first time he had thought the matter out.

"Alistair," he said, "when people work in close proximity to one another, some are going to get involved. That's human nature. In the College we have students young enough to be classified as children, and we have a duty to protect them. But anyone over 19 is an adult, and free to act as they wish within the limits of the law. What are the guidelines? Your faculty association has already established that if relations between a student and faculty or staff member—or administration member for that matter—are causing disruption in a class, then that's a problem that must be addressed. Thelma Smith helped me understand this issue. Did you know that she married one of her students at the University of Rhode Island?"

"No," I said. "I know she has children and is divorced."

"Well, he was her student, and as you know, she has a strong ethical sense. Talk to her."

But I had no desire to talk it out with Thelma.

One day there was a sharp rap on my front door. Rashid and Jenadie.

I looked at their smiling faces. "The university's backed down?"

"No way, man. Dismissal hearing starts next week. You going to come?"

"I wouldn't miss it," I said.

"I brought you this from England." He handed me a beer mug with the familiar Oxford crest of three crowns and the psalmist's phrase, *Dominus illuminatio mea*.

"Thanks, man. Oh, I've really missed you guys. Let's go out on the boat and barbecue lamb chops on Raccoon Island."

"See!" Rashid smiled at Jenadie. "What did I tell you?"

"It's winter, it's not even spring!" she protested. "You can't go out and have a barbecue at sea!"

"Come on," I said, "It's not cold. You'll see."

We got the hibachi and stuff for the barbecue and took the boat out to Raccoon Island. I barbecued the lamb chops right on the coals to a charred rareness. After we had eaten, we sat drinking Lindeman's Hearty Burgundy in the cold sunshine.

"What happened to Richard Duplessis' court case?" I asked.

"Lost it. Judge ruled the AFT document does *not* form part of the contract of employment." Rashid's cheery manner had turned serious. "Al Waldie's hearing has finished, and the Chairman promised they'd try to report next week, when Muriel's and mine begins."

"How did Al's go?"

"They let me cover it for the *Sun*," Jenadie said, "and then the bastards went and killed it down to a four-liner."

"What happened?"

"The hearing concentrated on the grounds for dismissal," she said. "Did he or did he not 'perform contractual duties'—given the fact that he *did* hold classes at his house? Did he or did he not 'violate his duty to and abuse the trust of his students'—given that he told them *exactly* what he was doing and why. Does the fact that he 'failed to confirm to the university in writing' that he was continuing to teach his classes mean that he wasn't teaching them? We'll know the answers next week."

"I hope they don't end up as a hung jury," said Rashid.

"Guess what?" said Jenadie brightly.

"What?"

"I'm going underground!"

"You're what?"

"I'm going to be doing some stories for the Vancouver Free Press."

"*The Georgia Straight*? I thought you were working for the *Sun*?"

"I was, but my stuff was too radical for them. I spent a long fucking week on Vancouver Island getting material for my series on logging, and my editor just axed the whole series. So now it's the *Straight*. And, Alistair, I want to ask you, there's a really interesting young guy working for the *Straight*. He's a poet from Montreal, Simon. He needs a job. He'd be a terrific teacher. How about it?"

"Well, we are probably going to be hiring again. Does he have an M.A.? Does he have any teaching experience?"

"Don't know. Can I give him your number? Talk to him, will you? He's published in the *New Book of Canadian Verse*."

"Oh, you must mean Simon Du Lac? Sure, give him my number."

"You won't regret it."

"Somebody gave you a good haircut in England, Rashid," I said. "But what is this colouring?"

I touched the grey strand at his temple.

He looked down humbly. His lips were shut. I saw that he was gearing up for the ordeal ahead.

"We're losing the sun," I said. "Let's go back."

"Yah," said Rashid and shivered. "I've got duty-free Scotch in the car."

22

Early next morning Jenadie phoned.
"Alistair! Have you seen the story in the *Province*?"
"Haven't read it yet."
"Take a look at page four," she said.
"Hold on."

I put the phone down and scanned the paper. Shirley Jean Sutherland, daughter of Tommy Douglas and wife of the actor Donald Sutherland, was charged with buying hand grenades for the Black Panthers from an undercover policeman in Los Angeles. That couldn't be it. . . .

Then I saw the headline: "**College Principal Rejects Draft Dodgers.**"

I read the story, while Jenadie's voice squawked away in the receiver on the kitchen table.

Denby Forrester had told a CKWX radio news reporter, "We don't want draft dodgers enrolling at Capilano College, and we certainly wouldn't have any of them on the faculty. If I found one, I would fire him."

I picked up the phone. "This is ridiculous," I said. "We've got at least a dozen draft dodgers on faculty."

"What are you going to do?" Jenadie asked. "The Committee to Aid American War Objectors called me to see if I knew anyone at the College. I told them I'd call you."

"I'll work on it."

I phoned Thelma Smith, who already had the news. An emergency joint meeting of the Student and Faculty Associations was scheduled for one o'clock.

I got there after my class ended at twelve-thirty. By then the room was already crowded out the doors. Malcolm Carter saw me trying to get in and beckoned. When I pushed through to him, he removed his briefcase from a chair. "I saved you a seat," he said.

"Thanks."

Thelma was at the front of the room together with Peter Hansen from Economics who was also on the Executive, and Dave Marsden and another student leader.

Thelma called through the hubbub, "May I have your attention please! Your attention please!" but the noise stayed high. She needed a mike, and there wasn't one. Finally Peter Hansen stood on a chair and shouted, "QUIET!" This shocked the room into silence.

Looking round at the students present, I spotted Caroline seated a few rows behind me and quickly looked ahead again. As Thelma began speaking, I drifted off to that moment over a year ago in the snow, when I had smelled carnations on Caroline's skin.

I cleared my head and concentrated on the meeting.

"Therefore," said Thelma, "I move that in view of his publicly expressed views concerning conscientious war objectors, this joint assembly of students and faculty shall go on record as having no confidence in Dr. Forrester's leadership of the College."

"Second," a voice said.

I stuck my hand up.

"What the hell good does it do," I objected, "to go on record? Do you think there's a Hansard god up there who keeps tabs on all these bloody motions? I don't think so. If we want to do something, let's actually *do it*! I'm sick of 'going on the record.'"

I sat down, and nobody made any noise. Thelma was looking at me with a steely face.

"Like what?" asked Peter Hansen. "Make a motion."

"We don't need a motion," I said. "We need to show the guy that he's wrong. Why don't we all get up and march from here straight to Forrester's office and tell him so?"

"Right on!" Andrea shouted behind me.

"All right, let's go!" said Peter and he marched down through the crowd, followed by Thelma and the student leaders.

I had never experienced anything like this before. A white boy from a British colony, I had always been on the side of the authorities, at least until the worst of the Mau Mau atrocities, when the settlers stormed Government House demanding action. But I wasn't there then, and here I was now, a sub-administrator, fomenting a riot. I marched along, uncomfortably buoyed with excitement.

About a hundred people began crowding into the second-floor room of the wooden portable building. The two secretaries sat, looking alarmed, at their typewriters, as more and more bodies pressed in on them.

"We're here to see the Principal," Peter announced to Maureen Ingleton, Forrester's secretary.

"I'm afraid he's not available," she replied in a clear voice.

"Then we'll wait," Peter said. "When do you expect him?"

Maureen looked at the other secretary, and then back at Peter. "I believe he's out of town," she said.

"Bullshit!" a woman's voice cried from behind me.

People began sitting down along the walls of the office and squatted in the middle of the carpet.

Forrester's door opened and he appeared, moving casually forward in a blue-grey suit.

"Thank you very much, Maureen," he said calmly. "Good afternoon, ladies and gentlemen. Is there something I can do for you?"

Peter stepped up to him and spoke into his face. "I'm what you describe on the radio as a 'draft dodger,'" he said, "though I don't use that term myself. Because of my moral principles, I took a stand and left the United States of America rather than be forced to serve in an immoral war. I teach here. Now: you going to fire me?" Peter's face was quivering, very dramatic.

"I don't consider this to be an appropriate way to hold a civil conversation," Forrester said. He was tall and well-built, and with his double-breasted jacket hanging open and his hands in his pockets he seemed untidily at ease.

Peter gestured behind himself with his thumb. "There are fifteen of us immigrant American war objectors who work here," he said. And there are student war objectors too. Now you've gone public in the media against us. Is *that* what you call a civilized conversation?"

Forrester frowned and began closing the buttons of his jacket. "There are ways of, if you will, addressing issues here," he said. "I am prepared to meet with a representative group of three people in my office."

Peter looked around, and many people nodded.

"Fine," he said.

"Nine o'clock tomorrow morning," said Forrester.

The demonstration slowly dissolved. I slid off. I had no more classes that day, and I drove home.

No sooner had I sat down than the phone rang. It was Simon Du Lac, Jenadie's Montreal poet. He was polite but forceful and I liked the energetic sound of his voice.

"Come right on over, I'll make a pizza," I said.

I gave him directions from Kits and then I threw the dough up in the air and put the pizza in the oven. I sat at the kitchen table sipping Scotch and reading *Soul on Ice*.

I was repelled by the book but couldn't put it down. Despite my revulsion, I was carried along on Eldridge Cleaver's racist roller coaster: When his prison teacher asked him to write about love, he wrote a list of atrocities committed on black people and asked how he could possibly talk of love? He'd rather be bound in a sack and thrown into the river, he said. Then, as he channelled his rage onto white oppressors, I felt myself raging back. I wanted to get through the book fast, every last word, then give it back to Andrea or burn it.

Today, as I write this in 2012, I see pornography sites on the internet called "Revenge for Slavery" and such, and when I open them, I see that it is Eldridge Cleaver's ideas acted out on film. Black men, who would have been lynched in the past for looking too closely at a white woman walking down the street, now fucking them with huge cocks, and the little white wimp husbands cringing by to watch, and ordered to lick up the excess ejaculate.

Simon Du Lac knocked on the door.

"Come on in," I said. "I hope you like black olives on your pizza."

"My favourite," he said and handed me a bottle of red Mouton Cadet.

"They tell me you're living hand to mouth, and you bring expensive French wine!"

He turned his head sideways and made a "what-can-I-say" gesture with his palms. I liked the man immediately.

"So," I said, laying the pizza down on the Murchie's tea box in the living room, "a job, huh?"

"Wouldn't that be fantastic! Any chance?"

"Not at the moment. We might be hiring next semester. Get your application into the file. Have you finished your master's degree?"

"I was going to ask you about that. I finish my M.A. at the end of this year, in Creative Writing. Do you think my job chances would be better if I took extra time to get the degree in English instead?"

"Not for a college job. As far as we're concerned a master's in the field is the threshold, and then we look at your effectiveness as a teacher. The fact that you have significant publication as a poet is something we would take into account."

Simon cocked his head and smiled at the recognition.

He picked up *Soul on Ice*. "Too much! You're reading Cleaver. We're about to publish an interview with him in the *Straight*."

"Very disturbing," I said. "Have you read it?"

"Not all of it. It's a battle cry."

"It's blatant racism," I said. "Black men raping white women in revenge for all the abuses of the past."

"Well," said Simon with a tolerant tone, "that sexual stuff is all metaphorical, the symbolism of war."

"'Metaphor' my foot! The guy is a self-confessed rapist and he wrote that book in Folsom prison. It's all about the conflict between whites and blacks. Speaking as 'Minister of Information' for the Black Panthers, he quotes Norman Mailer's prediction that 'there's a shit-storm coming.' He practised by raping black women in the ghetto, and then crossed into wealthy neighbourhoods to rape white women."

"But that's not today's Cleaver. That was 'the old Eldridge.' He says so himself: that old Eldridge no longer exists."

"Tell that to his victims!" I said.

"Haven't you read *Technicians of the Sacred*?" Simon said. "Even back in the time of Ptolemy and the great God Ptah the thing was to boast that you had fucked the enemy's women, and that they preferred you to their own men!"

"Listen to me, Simon: if a white guy were to publish the stuff Cleaver's published he'd be in trouble. He has this character Lazarus in the jail telling his fellow inmates how puny white men will hire them to fuck their wives for them. He makes it sound real by dividing them into categories: This type drives the black man to her and leaves him there to 'pile' her, another type watches through a keyhole, or lies under the bed and listens. One guy stands by the bed jerking off as he watches the black guy do the real job. One little white wimp licks up the mixed juices afterwards. And then there's the black guy who gets on the white woman and warms her up, then generously climbs off and lets the pathetic white husband finish up without his help."

Simon was laughing.

"*Listen* to yourself, you've even memorized his categories!" he said. "Don't you understand symbolism? Cleaver's kicking sand in your white man's face, kicking you right in the balls! He's castrating you with words."

"And look at this!" I showed him the gushy blurbs on the back cover by academics and journalists.

"It pisses me off," I said, "and yet you know—I'm astonished to confess this—it turns me on at some base level."

"Of course! It's cunning," Simon said, "yanking on the antagonism between the sexes. But it is war, not sex, Alistair. Soldiers have forever been humiliating the enemy. Look at the British in Scotland and elsewhere."

"What about the British?"

"Uh-ho! Don't get me started. Anyway, Cleaver's coming to Vancouver. The *Straight* is going to publish an article and we've made a big welcome sign. You can come and meet him."

"I'll pass, if you don't mind."

We ate our pizza and sipped our wine. "So, what's it like to work at the *Straight*? All these police busts."

"I'm not on staff there," he said. "Just casual. It's exciting, though. We do some wild stuff. Do you read it?"

"Sometimes. Last issue I saw there was some woman from Chicago who makes plaster casts of rock stars' cocks. There was a picture of her fondling Jimi Hendrix's."

"Cynthia the Plastercaster and the Penis de Milo!" Simon laughed. "We got busted on twelve counts of obscenity for that issue, and you know what? The very same Cynthia is sitting on the shelves in a glossy American skin mag, and the cops are doing *nothing* about that! Zilch!"

"So it's the mayor, uh?"

"Damned right it is. Tom Campbell's the biggest asshole this city's ever seen. He's using the license inspector as a censor. Pretty soon even the *Sun* and the *Province* are going to have to start reporting what's really going on. Meanwhile, it's up to *The Georgia Straight* to let people know what he's doing. Lifting a $12 business licence as a way of closing us down! It's a scandal!"

"I guess I should read the *Straight* regularly. Jenadie's working there."

"Isn't Jenadie great? Tremendous energy."

We finished the pizza and wine and Simon took off, promising to stay in touch and send in a job application. I thought he would be great to have in the department, real vitality. I poured a last Scotch and sat mulling over all that we had talked about.

The phone rang and pulled me out of this reverie.

"Alistair," said Thelma's voice, "we want you on the delegation that meets Forrester tomorrow. Nine a.m."

Oh no! With all the drinking over the past 24 hours, I would be embarrassed to sit in Forrester's sanitary office smelling of booze.

"Can't you get someone else?" I begged.

"The Executive has discussed it," Thelma said. "We feel you'd be good, because he listens to you. I'm going, and so's Peter. But we need someone less confrontational. It was your idea to begin with." 'Less confrontational,' I pondered? Hadn't Norman Bull accused me once of being 'too confrontational'?

"What about the students?" I said.

"They've decided to let us handle this. That way, if he manages to brush us off, they get a second crack at him."

"All right," I said impulsively. "Do we want to meet beforehand?"

"Breakfast at Ripp's at 7:30."

"Fine. I'll be there."

Next morning I got up at six and went for my regular twice-weekly run with Max and Sonia Odegaard and their good-natured Labrador. It was a chilly morning with dew saturating the grass of the park, and I got home as wet as if I'd waded through a river. I left my soggy shoes and old jeans on the back porch, showered quickly, and made it to Ripp's on time. I was buoyed up with excitement.

Peter and Thelma were firm that I should be the spokesperson.

"Forrester can't hear me when I speak," Thelma said, "and Peter will be more effective as a moral presence, being a war objector himself. Now, what do we want from him?" She began doodling on a lined pad.

"He should go back on the radio and withdraw his remarks," said Peter.

"He'll never do that!" I said. "That's like asking him to resign."

"I agree," said Thelma. "Let's leave him room to save face. How about if he goes on the record as saying that the College has no business in the private lives of its instructors?"

Thelma and her goddamned going on the record! I bristled.

"How about," said Peter in a careful voice now, "we ask him to participate in an open forum on the function of a college?"

"What does 'function' mean?" I said. "He'll tell you 'the function of the College is to offer a variety of appropriate academic and career-vocational courses as mandated in *The College Act*,' Where does that get us?"

"I'd like to ask him in public if it isn't the function of a college to provoke moral thought and political debate."

I laughed. "You want to ask Forrester that in public and sit back and listen to a pious sermon?"

"Time's getting on," said Thelma. "I think we should clarify our objectives." Her pad was filled with her trademark doodled faces in space suits.

"Well," said Peter, lifting his head suddenly. "At the very least he has to apologize to us. I'd like it in writing, actually. Plus a written statement from the Council. A policy statement that the College has no business investigating the private lives of its instructors. What if somebody wanted to run for Parliament as a candidate for the Communist Party of Canada, for God's sake!"

"Apology, policy statement," said Thelma, writing.

"And a public debate!" said Peter.

"He'll go for the debate before the other two," I said. "He thinks he's an authority on what's right. He's a pretty fundamentalist Christian, you know?"

Thelma frowned. "We take no interest in his private life or beliefs any more than he should in ours," she said.

"I know," I said. "But anyone who starts out from the premise that death is the beginning of eternal life is coming from a pretty weird place, don't you think? Black is white."

"Sheesh!" Thelma smiled ironically, but whether at Forrester or at me I wasn't sure. Behind Thelma's irony lay a militancy fuelled by the whole history of women's suppression in the West, and the rising feminism of the 1960s. I knew that she herself was a Christian of some sort. I admired her courage but mistrusted her motives. She—divorced, with children; me—divorced with children: what were we but one another's nemesis?

"All right, the apology, the policy statement, and the forum," I said. "Frankly, I think any one of those would be okay."

"*You* think he'll go for the forum?" said Peter.

"I do," I said. "He likes talking. He doesn't like things being written down because then he can't squirm out of them."

"Surely minutes would be kept of the forum?" said Thelma.

"Don't tell him that in advance. Get him to agree to a forum first. If it's a public forum, anybody is free to take notes, right?"

"Sure," said Peter.

We paid our bill and left Ripp's.

Forrester met us at the door of his office with a cursory smile, and a quick glance at his watch.

"Come in," he said. "I must tell you that I have an important budget meeting with Ministry officials at nine-forty-five. I hope we can get done by then."

I could feel Peter about to blurt, and I touched his elbow with mine.

"I'm sure we can," I said.

We went in and sat in the arranged chairs.

Forrester closed the door.

"Before we begin," he said, sitting far away from us across his metal desk, "I want to tell you that I misspoke myself the other day on the radio."

I swear to God, that is what he said! Before Ron Ziegler, Richard Nixon's Press Secretary, used it famously on American network TV to try to hide the President's lies about Cambodia, Dr. Denby Forrester coined the expression at Capilano College, BC: "I misspoke myself."

Thelma was looking down at her doodle pad with a humourless smile. I reached across with my felt pen and ticked the line where she had written "Apology." She smiled and nodded. Forrester meanwhile was blowing soft clichés into the air, and looking back and forth from me to Thelma trying to suss out what communication was going on between us.

"In the context, I was trying, if you will, to express the College's role relative to the unmet educational needs of the community," Forrester said.

I leaned over to Peter. "He's apologised. Okay?" I whispered.

He nodded.

"Look," I said, as Forrester paused. "Perhaps the principle is more important than this particular circumstance. How about getting the Council to develop a policy on academic freedom? We could draft a statement, and then the Council can kick it around until they're comfortable with it and then send it back to us. Eventually both the Council and the Faculty ratify it."

"A memorandum of understanding?"

"That sounds good," I said.

"I don't see why the Council shouldn't pass a policy statement. But why are you bringing up academic freedom?"

"That's what the policy would be about."

"But you already *have* academic freedom. We live in a democracy. We have a Human Rights Act."

"It doesn't mean a lot if someone can be fired for having conscientiously objected to a foreign war."

"I told you, that was a misunderstanding."

"It threatened a lot of people," said Peter.

The two of them glared at one another in silent confrontation. (In the back of my head, Neil Young was singing about words between the lines of age.)

"Well . . ." said Forrester, looking at his watch.

"Why don't we go ahead and draft something," I said, "and send it to you to show the Council?"

"I'm prepared to read anything you send me."

"Fine," I said.

"And there's one other point," said Peter.

With a look I shut him up.

"Dr. Forrester," I said, "we were wondering if it might not be a good idea to have a debate about the role and direction of the College. A forum, you know? Where people could express their ideas."

"I'm *always* open to discussion," he replied. "What are we doing right now? My door is always open."

"Something more formalized," I said. "Set a date. Invite anyone and everyone in the College to come."

"That's the beauty of a democracy," he said. "We're able to speak our minds freely."

"Fine," I said. "Should we set a date in August before the next semester begins."

"Haven't we done this twice already?" he said. "Dean Bull arranged the retreat at Haney and a second one at Paradise Valley. You want another?"

"I think we should do it right here at the College," I said. "More people would come."

"The more the merrier," he replied and looked again at his watch. "But I think we had better get on with the semester. And we're still dealing in committees with the recommendations from the two previous retreats. Why don't we hold it next summer?"

"Next summer!" Peter expostulated.

I grabbed his arm.

"I think you're right. We need to get the committee work done from the past two retreats," I said. "But that won't take very long. How about we hold a forum later this fall?"

"December," said Forrester.

I looked at Thelma, and she nodded.

"Fine," I said.

Outside, as we walked away, I thought Peter would be complaining, but he was jubilant, smacking his hand with his fist. "We got every god-damned thing we wanted! Every god-damned thing!"

"Well," I said, "now you have time to think up questions for him."

On the way home that evening, I stopped to tell Jenadie my success. She listened stony-faced. "You didn't solve the problem!" she said. "You've gone and made a separate peace. There's *no* public announcement. There's *no* retraction. The threat against war objectors remains in force! Shit."

"Get the Committee to call him," I said. "He's admitted to us that he 'misspoke' himself, it was 'a misunderstanding.' So he'll have to admit it to the Committee now."

"Yeah, but you guys should have demanded a public statement from him in the newspaper. You went and chickened out!"

Rashid listened without taking part. He seemed distracted and I didn't blame him, with the worries of his own.

"I must say I like your friend Simon Du Lac," I told Jenadie.

"Isn't he *great*! You know, there's a war going on at the *Straight*, the dopers *versus* the politicals, it's tearing the magazine apart, but Simon's on the right side."

Suddenly there was a knock on the door, and my heart jumped. For one wild moment I thought it might be the police. But it was Richard Duplessis, Rashid's colleague.

"Sorry to come round so late," he said, "I'm down as hell."

"Ah, come on now, Richard," Rashid said gently, putting his hands on his shoulders.

"The stream of abuse in the papers is starting to frazzle me. And now the bills are piling up. This is going to end up costing us each twenty thousand dollars or more!"

"No, no," Rashid dismissed his concern. "Money is not the issue, man."

"Not for Barrington it isn't!" said Richard. "He can spend all the resources of the university going after us. Money that should be providing classes for students. Instead of which it's going to those scummy lawyers with offices on Howe Street and mansions in Shaughnessey."

"Richard! Richard!" Jenadie said. "Have a drink."

"I've had one already," he said. "I've had several as a matter of fact."

"Did you drive here?" Jenadie's voice was alarmed.

"Yes."

"Oh no, you mustn't do this! You can sleep in the study."

Richard fixed his baleful eyes on me, and I noticed now that they were very bloodshot. He extended his hand.

"Alistair," he said.

I took his clammy hand, and he held onto mine.

"Do you know how to tell which is the right side in a guerrilla war?" he said.

"Not really." I wondered if this was a joke.

"Find out which soldiers are getting paid," he said. "The soldiers who are getting paid are in the wrong. The ones who are fighting without pay are in the right. Why else would they fight, you see? Answer me that. Why else?"

I smiled to humour him and looked at my watch. "Got to go." I removed my hand from Richard's and stood up. As I left, I saw Rashid and Jenadie on either side escorting him to the couch in the study.

23

That Friday, I went down to *The Georgia Straight* office on Carrall Street and bought a bunch of back issues for 20 cents apiece, from a kid with hair longer than mine. I took them home and pored through them. One cover had a young woman holding a gun, wearing nothing but an Indian necklace dangling between her big bare breasts and a belt of cartridges around her thighs, while a Victorian gent in top hat and tails walks by outside the window. There were pictures of dressed and naked women protesting the arrival of a *Playboy* PR man on campus with picket signs reading "PLAYMEAT OF THE MONTH," and "GO HOME," and an interview in which they accuse him of promoting the wrong kind of nudity.

Turn the page, and there's a desperate appeal from the editors, announcing that, "In your name and with your tax money the ruling Establishment ordered this paper murdered," and asking for two nickels from every reader for the *Georgia Straight* Defence Fund.

Turn the page and there's George Bowering on "The Indecent Treatment of Indecent Exposure," speculating that "every person in this country has at one time in his life contemplated walking naked down Main Street."

Turn the page: More bare breasts. "Vicki in Love and War."

And then the solid print: Melody Kilian on "Our Duty to Screw," and "Love Letter": she castigates the head-trippers who think they can go off to the islands and make a separate peace, and she castigates Stan Persky for using the term "asshole ideology," to which Persky carefully responds that he's on the same side she is, if she would only realize it.

Turn the page and there's the Manifesto of the Society for Cutting Up Men (SCUM) by Valeria Solanis, who confessed to shooting Andy Warhol and to whom a male professor replies next issue with a "Hail Mary." There's the headline: "C.U.N.T. LOCKED OUT"—the Canadian Union of Narcotics Traffickers kept out of the Arbutus Café by a sign saying "No Hippies 12 noon-1 p.m." so they set up a picket line and went for their lunchtime meeting across the street at the Hare Krishna Café.

Turn the page, and there's Joachim Foikis, Vancouver's official Town Fool, arrested in Toronto for saying "fuck" to a policeman. Next, I came upon the poet George Stanley's "Letter from Berkeley" describing a political demonstration:

> *... And then we joined the great general glow, the main march, which was truly joyous and loving (not "festive" as it would maybe seem to outsiders). Rider was there which made me feel very happy as there is no one I would rather march with. He was carrying one pole of a big tattered American Federation of Teachers banner made out of a sheet with AFT 1928 on it in purple paint. So we moved up Hearst I guess it is, to the first big turn at Oxford, where we caught sight of the National Guard with rifles, bayonets, grenade launchers. We sang, "While the Caissons Go Rolling Along," for the Army. They smiled. The scores of Dept. of Justice types and others in rimless glasses and carefully trimmed grey hair and suits didn't.*
>
> *The best part of the march was on Dwight between Oxford and Telegraph. It took nearly an hour to move these few blocks through clouds of incense, cooling fine spray from hoses, rock music coming from student houses, every one with half nude students hanging from every window, rooftop, gable, etc., and also music from trucks in our midst, rock bands on them, their hoods and fenders carrying little kids ... well, I contradict myself, this was different in a way from other marches and new, in that we didn't only have the concept of moving forward, side by side, towards some goal, the solidarity thing, but also, and I think, predominantly, I think our mood was of turning towards each other, face to face, and at moments it seemed like if we could continue to allow it, time would stop and some kind of breakthrough would occur, not orgiastic or frenzied, but a breakthrough of serenity and invitation, like in the Beethoven*

quartet we heard on Dick's car radio driving back from Berkeley, like endless variations were possible on our simplicity. I found myself dancing, then I found that it was not really possible not to dance, that even the slight effort to return from the dancing mode to the walking mode only made the dance itself more subtle. There was one point where I caught Rider's eyes for a moment that filled me with a feeling of love and beauty, not inexpressible but perfectly expressed, unquestioning. This was at the corner of Dwight and Telegraph, with armed men on the rooftops.

I liked this piece of writing best of the whole stack. Reading all the rest, I understood what Jenadie had meant about the war going on at the *Straight*: you could feel the young, raw, conflicting energies of the potheads versus the political radicals. But I was also feeling a bit jaded with it all. It seemed so naïve.

On Monday at the College, a letter arrived for me from an ex-student. She had spent only one semester with us but it had changed her life. She wanted me to know that something I had said had triggered a revolution in her. "If it feels good, do it!"

I reread the letter, incredulous. *I said that?* Sure it wasn't Timothy Leary? When did I say such a nonsensical thing? I put the letter down, and reflected.

"If it feels good do it." Already, that sounded quaintly old-fashioned. Age of Aquarius turning sour. LBJ's vision of a Great Society with "liberty and abundance for all" had guttered out. The world focused angrily on the Americans: "Go Home Yanqui!"

"Why Are We In Vietnam?" asked Norman Mailer.

I sat down at my typewriter and began to crank out a piece of my own to send to *The Georgia Straight*

"Woodstock is over," I wrote. "Timothy Leary continues to repeat that everybody should get high, and the Beatles scream about doing it in the road. But people are beginning to wonder where the hell the road leads to—if it leads anywhere at all. Mick Jagger can't find satisfaction! Bob Dylan, with his gritty voice and his wailing harmonica, taunts the Establishment that something mysterious is happening down on Desolation Row, and the average citizen doesn't know what it is. Phil Ochs is the only one of the singer poets left with any integrity, and he's reduced to singing 'Rehearsals for Retirement.'"

I scrunched the piece of paper from the machine and fired it into the waste basket.

I thought maybe I'd write them an article on something I knew about: vocabulary. Fresh words were rolling out of people's mouths and I'd been collecting an alphabetical list of all the newly-coined ones: *Acid head* and *be-in, Charley* and *dovish, earthscape* as seen from the moon. *Flower child, groupthink. Handgun* had just entered the dictionary. *IUD, jetbus, kicky* and *lip sync. Macro, the New Left. One-liner,* and *pulsar. Quark,* and *roadeo* (for trucks). *Speed reading. Thalidomide. Uptight. Video recorder, Whitey. Malcolm X.* To *yo-yo.* And to *zap,* meaning to kill.

The alphabet gave me a structure for my article, but what was my main point? Certainly a few people had been zapped. Martin Luther King sang, "I ain't gonna study war no more"; he was killed on a balcony in Memphis. Riots promptly erupted in 126 U.S. cities, 46 people died, hundreds were injured and 21,000 arrested. Two months later, in the middle of his campaign for the Democratic presidential nomination, Bobby Kennedy was shot in the head in California and his body was flown to Saint Patrick's Cathedral in New York for a million people to file tearfully past. Jimmie Hendrix was dead. Janis Joplin dead from drugs and Joan Baez composed a dirge of lamentation for her. Richard Nixon presided over an angry and divided country. Talk about yo-yoing! Nixon was bombing the shit out of "the enemy" even as he pulled back the troops. As for the opposition: "We were grasping defeat out of the jaws of victory," said Robert Ross, founding member of Students for a Democratic Society. "America—love it or leave it," read the bumper stickers. And at the end of April, when I had watched Nixon lie on TV to the world about the bombing of Cambodia, all the while frowning like an angry preacher, I realized we had entered a new age of discontent. When the four white kids were gunned down by the National Guard on the hill above Taylor Hall at Kent State University—white soldiers killing white students—I knew something would have to end soon. But would things have to get worse before they started getting better?

I wasted a whole day at the typewriter with these thoughts and notes, but no article came of it.

A letter arrived from the office of the Dean of Graduate Studies at UBC. He was a new Dean, reviewing his files, and would I please confirm that I had abandoned my Ph.D. so they could close the file? "'Abandoned?' *Oh shit,* I thought. *Finish your thesis before it's too late, then you can try your hand at journalism.*"

The phone rang.
Caroline?
It was Hayley Jones, a student, inviting me to a party at her place the following night.
"Hayley... I—"
"Don't worry, I know you've split up with Caroline. She won't be there. It's just a small party. I want you to meet my boyfriend and a few others, and talk about Africa."

Why not? So, the next evening, I found myself standing in a freak hail storm, ringing the doorbell at Hayley's apartment just off Ambleside beach. I handed her my bottle of wine and came in to a room full of strangers.

"This is Alistair," said Hayley. "He's been around the world and knows everything about Africa!" Her friends tittered and simpered, and I played right along, answering questions and making pronouncements on everything from the continuing Congo crisis to the future of Rhodesia. I began to enjoy myself and swigged back the glasses of red wine as fast as Hayley brought them to me.

Suddenly, I realized there was a conflict. I was standing in the living room holding forth on American offshore oil interests in Vietnam, and this guy to the side of me was muttering. When I turned to face him he said, "Who the hell invited you here anyway?" Hayley gripped his arm and pushed him through to the kitchen. But a few minutes later I was talking about Simon Fraser University radicals, when suddenly the guy again entered the room and, like a dog growling, called across at me, "Bunch of Jewish commies and a raghead!"

I looked at him, a seedy, grey-faced man a few years younger than me.

"You want to try saying that to me outside?" I said.
"You bet I do!"

The next thing I knew, the two of us were swinging away at one another in the falling hail behind the apartment. I was drunk and very angry. My right fist connected with his face and I saw blood, before finally we were pulled apart. I apologized to Hayley as she kept apologizing to me, and I made it to my car and home, wondering what the hell that had all been about.

4 STUDENTS KILLED AT KENT

WASHINGTON (May 4) – President Richard Nixon said today that he hopes the fatal shootings of four students at Kent State University in Ohio will convince American universities that while they maintain the right of peaceful protest they must stand "just as strongly against the resort to violence..."
Vice-President Spiro T. Agnew said he views the killing of the four students and wounding of 11 others by National Guard troops as proof his attacks on revolutionary policies have been justified.

In the bathroom, I dabbed at my bloody face with alcohol, and winced from the sting. I had not been in a fist fight since I was fifteen years old. The next day Hayley called and we apologized to one another yet again, and I resolved to attend no more student parties.

24

A week passed, and no word of a decision in Al Waldie's case.

The day of Rashid's suspension hearing dawned bright and sunny. Vancouver seemed a paradise: snow on the mountains, and clear blue silhouettes of the Gulf Islands on the horizon. Driving over the Second Narrows Bridge, I saw fibreglass runabouts racing on the glassy water, motors kicking up white rooster tails but the boats progressing only slowly against the strong rip tide. Crossing Second Narrows to attend the hearing suddenly felt to me like moving from the private place where I lived in Deep Cove to a public stage where history was happening. When you change the nature of a people's education you change the nation. The bloody war that was being waged in Vietnam with napalm and bombs and body bags had its corresponding ideological battles taking place on campuses: Berkeley, Buffalo, Kent State, the Hornsey College of Art in England, the Sorbonne in Paris, Rosedale College in Toronto, and right here in Vancouver at Simon Fraser University and on the North Shore at Capilano College. I did not realize at the time how much our little college was part of that widespread revolution, but we were actually implementing progressive ideas, some of them Dean Norman Bull's, quietly removing elitist barriers to higher education and shaking up the curriculum, while on the larger campuses the mere theories of those same principles were being fought over and argued about, with implacable boards of governors on one side, and a hard core of leftists on the other. Many of the radical profs in Canada were refugees from the U.S. and poured into their local battles all the anger they felt about the napalm and bombs and body bags on the other side of the Pacific, and perhaps their mixture of pride and guilt for having left their country. I knew which side of the ideological war I was on: above my desk I had pinned a quote from some French *avant-garde* artist: "The fact that there's so much opposition to what we're doing confirms for me that we're on the right track."

I sat in the wood-panelled lecture room next to Rashid's faithful students, Hélène and Ehor. Rashid in the front row turned around and acknowledged me with one quick nod. He looked tense. He and Jenadie were surrounded by heavy political colleagues, and I counted seven men in suits, lawyers presumably, crowded in the front benches. I recognized President Barrington and Dean Marshall from their photos in the paper. There were reporters with tape recorders and notebooks, and a large audience.

The three Hearing Committee members sat at the front table, two in suits and ties and the third wearing a sports jacket and open rosebud shirt with maroon bellbottom pants.

"Good morning," said the taller of the suited men. My name is Dr. Peter Fisher, and I am the Chairman of this Hearing Committee, selected by the Chief Justice of the Supreme Court of British Columbia, following the failure of the two members selected by the parties in dispute to agree on a Chairman. . . ."

It was very sombre. Nobody was having fun. Two years earlier, the Engineers at UBC had distinguished themselves by flinging little Gabor Maté, a reporter for the *Ubyssey*, through the glass of a second floor window down into the shrubbery. That was the worst campus violence we had experienced in BC. But now, only a few short weeks had passed since the U.S. National Guard opened fire on the students at Kent State. Crosby, Stills, Nash and Young mourned on the radio for the four dead. Nobody doubted any longer that campus wars in North America could have fatal outcomes.

The morning was spent in wrangles about procedure. Then Dr. Fisher looked at his watch and declared a recess until 1:30.

"I'll buy you lunch," I said to Hélène and Ehor. We sat down over hamburgers and Cokes in the cafeteria.

"Rashid's such a dedicated teacher," said Ehor. "It's *incredible* that the university would do this to him."

"No it's not!" said Hélène. "This isn't some gentlemanly debate at the Oxford Union. This is out and out war. Did you see Barrington's face? He looks like an army general not an academic. It's war between us and the corporate world."

"More like Oxford Mississippi!" said Ehor angrily.

"'Just be well-behaved little consumers, and don't do any thinking!'" said Hélène sarcastically.

Barrington's lawyer, Craig Barker, outlined his case. The charges were the same as in the suspension letter: failure to perform contractual duties; violation of duty; abuse of trust of students. Barker said he would call evidence to prove each of the three conclusively. He began quietly, "I call Dr. Hassan to the stand."

Rashid rose and went forward, his bare toes sticking out of his Moroccan sandals. A technician lowered the microphones.

"You wish to swear or affirm?" the hearing clerk asked.

"I'll swear," said Rashid solemnly.

"Take the Bible in your right hand and repeat after me. 'I swear that the evidence I shall give—'"

"Excuse me sir," said Rashid.

The clerk looked up in surprise. "Take the—"

"I don't wish to swear on the Bible," said Rashid.

"You wish to affirm?"

"I wish to swear on my holy book."

"Which book is that?" asked Dr. Fisher, looking over his half-moon reading glasses.

"The sacred Qur'an," said Rashid.

A murmur went through the room. The judges conferred and then called the clerk over and sent him to the library.

Twenty minutes later, the clerk returned with a black book. Rashid opened it, turned a few pages, and handed it back.

"This is not the sacred Qur'an."

"It says so on the cover!" The clerk pointed to the gold lettering: "Koran."

"Sir, the sacred Qur'an is in Arabic," said Rashid. "It is the only true copy of The Well-preserved Tablets. Modern translations such as this have no spiritual validity."

Another huddle with the hearing clerk, then the chairman banged his gavel.

"This hearing is adjourned until 9 am tomorrow."

As I drove home, The Jefferson Airplane was singing on the radio: "Stop, children! What's that song? / Everybody look what's going on!"

Next morning, Rashid swore on an Arabic Qur'an, and then Craig Barker began.

"I should like to ask you, Dr. Hassan, whether going quote on strike unquote was in keeping with your professional obligations to your students?"

"Yes it was."

"I see. And do you believe that you had a professional *duty* towards your students?"

"Definitely."

"And by going quote on strike unquote, did you fulfil that duty?"

"Yes. Let me explain—"

"No, no. Just answer his questions please," interjected the chairman.

"I put it to you that by failing to teach your students you violated that duty."

Rashid touched his beard.

"Mr. Barker," he said. "There are two points here. First, I did not fail to teach my students, quote-unquote."

"Ah, well—"

"Allow me to finish, please. Secondly, you have apparently not read the report of MacKenzie Committee Hearing in the case of Professor Duplessis."

"I may have read it. I'm not bound to follow its logic."

"Then how can you—"

"Excuse me," interrupted the chairman. "Dr. Hassan, you are actually the one being examined here by Mr. Barker. You are not the examiner."

Laughter trickled round the room.

Rashid nodded and smiled sheepishly.

Barker resumed: "All right, Dr. Hassan. Never mind MacKenzie. In your own mind, did you or did you not abuse the trust of your students when you failed to appear at your scheduled classes to teach them?"

Rashid's short body circled in the chair, hand forever grooming the beard.

"May I draw your attention, sir, to *Funk & Wagnalls Standard College Dictionary*, Canadian Edition—"

"No, Dr. Hassan! I asked you a question, and I would now like you to answer me 'yes' or 'no.' This hearing does not need to have its attention drawn elsewhere. Yes or no, sir?"

"Some things can not be answered with a yes or no, sir."

"Did you or did you not *abuse the trust* of your students in September of last year when you failed to teach your scheduled classes?"

"Mr. Chairman," Rashid turned and appealed to Fisher, "this places me in a very difficult position. Mr. Barker has asked me a question which appears to confute my understanding of the words he has used. Surely we must refer to a dictionary to establish a common meaning? Isn't it?"

"What does 'confute' mean?" Ehor whispered to me, and I shrugged and whispered back, "Maybe he means 'confuse.' Sounds good, though."

"Do you have a dictionary at hand?" Fisher asked.

"No," said Rashid. "But the dictionary definition is quoted in the report of MacKenzie Committee Hearing. I *do* have that with me."

"Very well."

"I object Mr. Chairman!" said Barker. "The respondent is evading my question."

"Let's hear the definition before deciding that."

Rashid stood up, holding some paper. "Thank you," he said. "It is the paragraph numbered 22."

Fisher called a few minutes delay for the clerk to go and make photocopies, then Rashid continued: "Para 22: according to *Funk & Wagnalls*, 'abuse' means 'to use improperly or injuriously; to misuse,' or 'to hurt by treating wrongly; to injure.' MacKenzie Committee found that none of the actions or inactions of Professor Duplessis fit this definition, because the students knew in advance exactly what was happening. Same thing in my case." Waving his hand behind him at the audience, Rashid declared, "Students knew all along what I was doing or not doing. They knew why. It was all publicly announced. And classes *did* continue in my own house. So this is not abuse, quote-unquote, according to the dictionary. Therefore the charge of abuse is groundless."

He looked around the room. No eye contact. All the lawyers were studying paper, and two of the three judges were writing.

"Leaving aside for the moment, abuse of trust," Barker said, "and I'll retain my right to come back to that, let us look now at the issue of violation of duty. When in September of last year you publicly announced that you were quote on strike unquote, and following that when you did not appear in the scheduled room at the scheduled time to teach your Political Studies 421 class, was that not a *violation of your duty* as a university professor?"

Rashid smiled and shook his head from side to side. "Again, Mr. Barker, I must refer you to MacKenzie at paragraph 29."

"I'm not asking MacKenzie, Dr. Hassan. MacKenzie is not on the stand. You are the witness on the stand, and I'm asking *you*. Answer from your own mind, please, and in your own words."

"Mis-ter. Bar-ker," said Rashid in a sing-song tone of reproach, "when the very same question has already been definitively answered by Professor MacKenzie, in the clearest possible language, and I agree with his answer, it becomes no longer possible for me to answer it in my own words, without reference to MacKenzie. To do so would be a plagiarism, which *would* constitute a violation of my professional ethics. Is that what you are asking me to commit?"

"Thanks for the lecture, Dr. Hassan. Now please answer the question."

"I will read aloud the answer from MacKenzie."

"Hold on! Hold on!" Fisher raised his hand.

The three judges conferred but couldn't agree. Robert Merivale, Rashid's nominee in the floral shirt and bellbottoms, hissed emphatically: "It's an *absolute* violation of his right to freedom of speech."

"I'll call a halt at this juncture," said Fisher. "This hearing stands adjourned until Monday, July 6." But the lawyers' schedules didn't fit that date so it was put over to July 13th.

Back at Rashid and Jenadie's, we held a mild celebration.

"You were terrific, Rashid!" said Hélène.

"They can't win now!" said Rashid. "MacKenzie has given it to us. Not so?"

"You don't think they can make one of those charges stick?" I said.

"The solid fact is that we held our classes. What facts are they left with as grounds for dismissal?" He counted them on his fingers. "One: saying publicly that we were on strike. Who can dismiss a professor for stating what he's doing? Two: failure to write and confirm that we were teaching our classes. Who can be dismissed for not writing a letter? Three, failure to teach classes. Wrong. We were teaching our classes.

But . . ." his confident look flickered, "tell me, Alistair, if you were Barker, which charge would you try to make stick?"

"I guess failure to confirm in writing," I said. "That has a legal tidiness to it."

"I'm hired to teach classes. I *am* teaching classes. How is failure to talk to administration a cause for dismissal? This isn't Nazi Germany! At the most, it would be cause for a reprimand or letter on my personnel file. Not *suspension!* Not *dismissal from the job!*"

"Those bastards," said Hélène. "SFU *is* Nazi Germany. They won't stop till they've completed the purge."

"I don't think they've got a leg to stand on," said Rashid with a wide grin. "We're going to win!"

Ehor looked grim and said nothing.

Over the next few days, Rashid would repeatedly say, "They can't fire someone for not writing a letter, can they? Wouldn't it be extremely unusual, against the rules of natural justice?"

I didn't know how to reassure him. I had a sinking feeling.

When the hearing resumed in July, Barker had refined his attack just as I had predicted: "Would you please give me an answer in a single word, 'yes' or 'no.' Did you confirm to Dr. Marshall, as requested in a letter to you dated September 17th, 1969, that you would teach your classes? Yes or no?"

"You see—"

"Yes or no, sir?"

Rashid held out his palms to the judges in frustration.

"All right Dr. Hassan, I'll try another question. Did you confirm that you were teaching, or that you would teach, your regularly scheduled classes as requested in a letter to you dated September 23rd, 1969, from Dr. J.J.W. Hendries, Vice-President of Academic Affairs? Yes or no?"

"Mr. Barker, if a runner—"

"Objection! Mr. Chairman, you have heard me put two plain, direct questions to this witness, asking for a straight yes-no answer, and he *will not* give it. The witness is not being responsive to my questions. I must therefore ask that you censure—"

"Excuse me, Mr. Barker," Rashid interrupted. "I am trying to respond as fully and accurately as I can to your questions. Would you please do me the fundamental courtesy of listening to my answer before submitting your objection?"

Silence.

"Proceed," said Fisher.

"Suppose you are a runner, running around a track, in full view of the seats in the stadium, okay?"

Barker stared at Rashid in rage, his eyes narrow, lips tight.

"Somebody says to you, 'Please confirm that you are running round the track,' okay? You are very busy running. You don't have time to stop and get a pen, find some paper, an envelope, sit down and write, 'Dear Sir or Madam,' lick a stamp, post it, to confirm that you are running round the track, okay? You just keep running. Openly. In full view. Now would you say that continuing to run like that is a confirmation that you are running?"

Electric silence.

"Or, is that *not* a confirmation in your opinion? Yes or no, sir?"

All three judges were suppressing smiles. Barker had his head down, then pretended to swallow his anger and smile too. He shook his head and came back up like a boxer: "So you admit that you did not in fact write a letter to Dr. Hendries, or to Dr. Marshall, is that correct?"

"I did not *hide* from them or from anyone else the fact that I was continuing to teach my students. Ask any of them!" Once again, he spread his hands behind him to the audience, as though all of us in that room were students of his.

The next day the hearing ended, and the Chairman stated that the report would be released as soon as possible.

"What does 'soon' mean, I wonder?" I asked Rashid.

"Merivale is a pretty dogged fellow. The longer it takes, that means the more he is having to fight for me."

25

I turned my attention back to running the Humanities Division and the English Department and was so busy for the next three months that I had practically no contact with Rashid and Jenadie. Once again, the College over-enrolled, and I had to scramble to hire extra people to cover the additional sections. Simon Du Lac was hired for one class. He was thrilled to be there, and I was excited to have him.

"What exactly do you teach in English Composition?" he asked, at the orientation meeting I held for new faculty. "I never took such a course myself."

"Is it stylistics?" asked Savithri Das, another of the new hires.

"You teach them how to write," I said. "Get them writing essays. I use an aims theory; you can use whatever you like."

"Aims?" asked Savithri.

"Kinneavy's theory. The six aims of writing. Determine your aim, choose appropriate strategies."

"Oh God!" said Simon. "Sounds like Aristotle! Maybe I'll get them to read Blake's *Marriage of Heaven and Hell*."

"Good idea!" I said. "That should start them thinking."

I left the new faculty to their own devices, and whenever I passed Simon's classroom I could see him with his aquiline face and his emphatic hands speaking passionately, and the students intent on his lectures. Norman Bull sat in on his class to evaluate him and told me, "That Du Lac fellow is a born teacher!" And he wasn't just a teacher. After he'd been with us a little while, he asked me once how he could make his position at the College more secure, and I told him to make a significant contribution to the College outside of class.

"Like what?" he asked.

"I don't know. Use your imagination. Found a society of Blake enthusiasts. Start a literary or art magazine."

"*Seriously?*" Simon looked at me with his raptor eyes and did his cigarette act, taking it from his face, holding it at the end of a wave which seemed to contain the dynamic of his thinking process. "How would that work exactly?"

"You tell me, Simon."

He absorbed this turnabout in silence, nodding and his face very serious. He took a drag on his cigarette and then stretched his arm out again so new thoughts could sidle up to him like dance partners. And so sprouted the seed of *The Capilano Review*.

I was very satisfied with the English Department—more than satisfied, I was proud of the energy and independent thinking they were putting into making Capilano College the best place for students to attend for first- and second-year courses. But I felt something was missing: however sure I may have been, there was no objective measure to prove that we were better than the universities. In Kenya, our school students wrote the Cambridge Overseas School Certificate exams, and the results arriving back from England gave us something by which to compare ourselves to other schools. I went to discuss the matter with Dean Bull, and he leaned back in his chair and listened to my concern. Eventually he sat upright at his desk and rotated his silver pencil between finger and thumb: "There's a fellow up at UBC, he said, "John Dennison in the Faculty of Education. Go have a chat with him. He might be able to help us out."

I duly made the appointment and found that as usual, Bull was right on the money: In his gruff Australian accent, Dr. Dennison explained that he was methodically tracking every student who transferred to UBC from the community colleges, and so far he had found that those students who had their first year or two years in a college did measurably better in their senior years at UBC than those who had done the first two years at the university. "Of course, there's a variable here which is hard to compute and put into the results accurately. That is those students who decide to quit their studies after college, and don't transfer. That amounts to a natural self-weeding-out process, whereas the continuing university students who weren't very successful might not have occasion to make the same decision to quit after second year but plod on and possibly bring the upper division results down. Nevertheless, the data that we do have appear to show the colleges in a very good light." He handed me some sheets of statistics and I asked if I could make copies, which I took back and showed to Dean Bull.

"Good man!" said Bull, as he looked at the tables of figures. "This is exactly the kind of evidence we need!" He made his copies of my copies, and over the next little while both he and I went about our constituency making the argument of Cap's superiority for first and second year. In the North Vancouver branch of the Rotary Club, as the lunchtime speaker, I delivered a passionate address to some sceptical looking business leaders, and when I switched on the overhead projector and showed how Cap transferees at UBC had been consistently achieving one full grade higher than the continuing UBC students in third- and fourth-year courses, I think I had them persuaded. "Of course . . .": I added John Dennison's caution about the results possibly being skewed, but if anything that only confirmed for them that I had done my homework. After the lunch, the President handed me a set of leather coasters stamped with the Rotary wheel logo, and in exchange I gave him the Nairobi Rotary branch pennant which my father had instructed me to deliver when the occasion arose. "I too am an immigrant from Africa," the President said. "Seems like you're doing a good job over there at Capilano, boy." I went away elated.

At the end of the fall semester, I had a problem on my hands. Malcolm Carter turned in his four grade books, and there were no semester grades in them. Against each student's name, there was a written comment like school reports, but no columns of assignments, no percentages and no letter grades. I read some of the comments:

"Peter is demonstrating an increased sensitivity to and appreciation of literary genres and is well prepared to enrol in second-semester English courses."

"Margaret's writing has developed considerably during the semester both in self-expressive content and in more formal applications such as writing analytic essays."

"Were Brandon to concentrate more time on study and less on vain and disruptive conversations in class, one might anticipate a vast improvement in his learning curve."

I called Malcolm into my office.

"Listen man, you made it plain to us last year that you didn't want to grade your students, but the department overruled you. What am I supposed to do with these reports? I love your diligent comments, Malcolm, and I'm sure you spent a lot of time writing them. But I need A's and B's and C's for the students' transcripts. The computer can't read your comments."

He stood in the doorway of my office, and I looked up at him and saw his eye and cheek twitching with controlled emotion.

"Okay?" he asked, ignoring my speech.

"You know it's not okay, Malcolm! You have failed to provide grades, which is a condition of employment."

"I don't want to fight with you, Alistair," he said.

"I need a letter grade for each student, Malcolm," I said, handing back the grade books. He looked at them and made no move to take them.

"It says in the contract that I must evaluate students. I have given you a careful personal evaluation of every single student," he said. "I will not label them with grades because I find it unnecessary, educationally irrelevant, and personally demeaning, both to myself and to the student. I have proposed to have the students grade themselves, a method that has worked well before in a university where I was a T.A., and you have rejected that option. For two semesters I have compromised with your system. I will compromise no further. I am a teacher, an educator, not a grading technician."

I got up to open my file cabinet and pulled out the "Memorandum of Understanding" governing our employment. I found the section on "Duties and Responsibilities of Instructors," put it on the desk, and pointed with my finger as I read, "*. . . and to make such evaluation and/or appraisals of students as may be required.*"

"I've given you my evaluations," he said. "Nothing more is required of me."

"Excuse me, Malcolm," I said firmly. "You are to make 'such evaluation . . . *as may be required.*' I could call a department meeting, but there isn't time. The computer at Simon Fraser University is booked for our Registrar at four this afternoon, and I have to have the grades to the Dean by one o'clock. As your Co-ordinator, I am *requiring* you to evaluate in the form of grades, *now.*"

"Then you are quite wrong to do so, Alistair, and you are interfering with my academic freedom. My students do not *'require'* to have a grade stamped on them. They require intellectual stimulation, encouragement, and empathy. Not to be graded like chicken eggs!"

"Malcolm," I said quietly and lifted a warning finger at him, "if Dean Bull doesn't get a full set of letter grades for each of your classes by one o'clock today, I believe your employment at Capilano College will be over."

He stared at me for a long time. Then he snatched the grade books out of my hand, turned about and marched down the corridor.

Ten minutes later he was back. He stood in my open doorway, waiting while I checked off Barnet Nolan's classes on my wall chart, ticking columns for the grade book, the class list, the computer cards, and the grade distribution sheet. When Barnet left, Malcolm came forward and slapped his grade books down on my desk. I opened the top one. Beside his comments he had added an A for every student. Same with the next book. All his students in four classes had been graded A, except for two students who got B's.

"Not acceptable," I said.

He had tears in his eyes and was controlling himself with difficulty. "Alistair," he said, "I like you very much as a person, but I'm feeling *really* upset about this coercion. I'm going to walk out of your room now. Goodbye, and I wish you a fine holidays and a great New Year."

My instinct was to stop him, but I suppressed it. I waited a few minutes to calm down and then walked to Bull's office and knocked on the door.

"Ready?" he asked, lifting his eyes. "I'll be with you in a minute."

The Natural Sciences Division Co-ordinator was in there checking completed grade books. I stood waiting.

"Yes, Alistair?" said Bull, in a break. "Something?"

"Malcolm Carter has refused to assign grades," I said. "When I pressed him, this is what I got." I opened a grade book and pointed to the line of A's. "Four classes," I said. "Ninety-four A's, two B's."

"Who are the B's?" Bull asked sarcastically. "Did they die?"

"Could you maybe contact the students and have them rewrite a final exam?" suggested the Science Co-ordinator.

"Look," I said, "who knows where they are over the Christmas break? And it's English Composition, not an examinable body of knowledge. They've been working all semester. It's a cumulative grade."

"Where's his mark book?" asked Bull.

"There isn't one. Just these comments and the A's and two B's added later."

"Jesus! Who evaluated him?"

"Didn't you?" I said.

"Yes, I suppose I did. It never occurred to me to look at his mark book. In any case, I wasn't planning to re-hire him after Christmas."

"Why's that?" This was the first I'd heard of it.

"He was seen smoking marijuana with students."

I bristled. "By whom?"

"Don't you worry about that. I'm not going into it now," said the Dean curtly, looking at his Rolex. "Well, there's only one thing to do. The College has failed here, so the College is going to have to eat it. These grades'll stand."

"Hell no!" I said. "That would be a mockery of academic standards. You're proposing to send ninety four students out there with A's in English on their Capilano College transcripts, any of whom might be illiterate for all we know? Think of the damage to our reputation!"

"Oh . . ." Bull removed his glasses and leaned back in his chair rubbing his eyelids. He was not now my friendly elder and lunch companion. He was an administrator, on the other side of a divide from me. "In the grand scheme of things," he said, "it probably makes no never mind. The point is that we messed up, and we can't expect these students to pay for that."

"This is terrible, Mr. Bull—" I began to protest, but he held up his hand.

"Alistair," he said patiently, impervious to panic, "every campus has an occasional maverick professor. When I went to university we had a little twerp who failed half the class and never gave higher than a C+. There's nothing to be done, except weed them out whenever you find them. This settles it, though. Mister Carter's career here is history."

I went unhappily back to my office and began filling out the IBM computer cards for each of Malcolm's students. One after another, I reluctantly blackened the oval representing an A with the dark, electro-conductive pencil, and the two B's. When all my division's grades were in, I gathered the pile to carry it down to Bull's office. It was 11:30 a.m. Suddenly, I stopped in my tracks and stared at my wall chart. Good Lord! There was a blank column, with no checkmarks in it whatsoever.

No grade book, no class list, no grade distribution chart, no computer cards. Simon Du Lac's class.

Too late now. I was due at Bull's so I took my stuff down to his office.

"All set?" he asked.

"Except one class. For some reason, Simon Du Lac's stuff hasn't come in yet."

He frowned. "Phone him," he said, and when I got up to go and do so, he pushed his phone across the desk to me.

It took four rings, before Simon answered in a sleepy voice.

"I don't have your grades Simon," I said, feeling my lips tight and dry.

"Yes!" he replied with a yawn and a deep exhalation. "Alistair, you know what? I've decided to do the sensible thing. I'm simply not going to *look* at their research papers until after Christmas. Aaagh!" he yawned directly into the phone, and I pressed the earpiece close so Bull couldn't hear him.

"Simon," I said, "I'm sitting with Dean Bull in his office. I don't know how this could have happened, but apparently you didn't realize the College works on a semester system, not a year system like UBC. The fall semester's classes are over, and all the grades must go to the computer this afternoon. You were supposed to have yours in to me ten minutes ago, so we can check them. I can give you twenty minutes, and then I'll expect a call from you. All right?"

On the other end of the line, there was dead silence. I could picture Simon, shocked bolt upright in his bed, his eagle face fierce, as adrenalin jolted through him. "I'll call you back," he said briskly.

Fifteen minutes later the phone rang in my office.

"Shit *la merde*!" Simon said. "I guess I really screwed this up, man. Have you got the class list and a pen?"

He dictated the grades and I marked them in. When we were finished, I asked, "How did you get them done so fast?"

"I did quick takes on the research papers," he said, "and eyeballed the rest of the columns. I think the grades are accurate."

"Okay. Now, when you mark the research papers and do the arithmetic, if any of the grades turn out different make sure you put through a Change of Grade form."

"Of course!"

"And where it says 'reason for change' just write 'grade book error.' Okay?"

"Jawohl, mein Führer!"

I blackened the IBM cards for Simon's class and walked down the corridor to Bull's office for the last time.

Then I drove away from the College till January.

I bought a bottle of Scotch, and took it over to Rashid and Jenadie's. I knocked on the door, but there was no answer. The Cortina was parked in front. I knocked again, and after a minute, the door opened on Jenadie, rubbing her eyes.

"I thought I heard a knock," she said. "Sorry, we were sleeping."

"Then don't let me wake you," I said pointlessly. "I brought you this." I handed her the bottle. "Hasn't there been any news from the Hearing Committee?"

She stood at the door and yawned savagely. "Both Committees have released their decisions," she said. "Both found no cause for dismissal."

"You've won!"

"No," she said. "Because now it's up to Barrington. And he can do whatever he damn well pleases. Let's discuss this another day."

"Sorry, Jenadie."

I left and went home.

At last I had some time for myself. First I moved from the front bedroom with the double bed to the little dark bedroom at the back of the house. Then I decided to get a new cat. I went down to the animal shelter at Mansfield Place and picked out a grey female kitten and named her Chiquita. As I fussed around, making a bed for her in a cardboard box, and setting out saucers of milk and dry food, I kept worrying over the Malcolm Carter business. Fired because he wouldn't produce grades in the required conventional manner. And there was Simon Du Lac, practically guilty of professional incompetence for not realizing the semester had ended, but *not* fired, because he was willing to scramble and make good his error. Ironically, Simon would now pick up extra teaching sections from Malcolm's former load. How embarrassing if six or eight of Simon's grades had to be changed later. What if twenty did? I felt guilty: was it my fault that he hadn't realized we ran on semesters? Back to Malcolm. Was there *any* way I could save his job? It was wrong that he had no protection. He should have been warned and given an opportunity to correct his error.

No, it was useless: he was going to be fired anyway. The memory of Bull growling at me that it was none of my business where the marijuana allegation had come from was too strong to think of mounting a resistance. I felt humiliated. No administrator should have that much arbitrary power. We needed due process, damn it. The Faculty Association's motion to elect departmental Evaluation Committees was stalled at the College Council and nothing was happening. We needed a Statement of Academic Freedom and Tenure like the universities had. But we didn't even have tenure—Bull had accepted my proposal on contract renewals but it didn't amount to anything like tenure: a one-year contract, followed by a two-year contract, followed by a three-year contract, depending on satisfactory administrative evaluations—and that was only for the few full-time employees. The part-timers, the vast majority of our faculty, were stuck with one-semester appointments forever. We were all just lackeys and could be "non-renewed" without cause. I could feel the gap growing between Norman Bull and myself, and it saddened me. As I had realized earlier, all the Department Co-ordinators he had picked to help him run the College were compromised in certain ways. This fact made us all into yes-men whom Norman Bull could count upon to do his bidding without argument. He, with his bull's neck and bullying ways, had been a perfect administrator to get the College started, against the reluctance of some property-tax payers and the arrogant condescension of the universities. But now that it was up and running, he was becoming outmoded. He was like an imperial governor whose autocratic energies had built a complex and smoothly functioning colony where it did not exist before, but soon it would be time for him to be retired, to allow the evolution of a democratic state.

I stayed home for Christmas. I flea-proofed the house by bombing it with Raid, taking Chiqui out in the car for a couple of hours. In the back of my mind, something was brewing.

Thelma invited the department to an end-of-semester party, and I went with some trepidation, fearing that Malcolm Carter would show up and make a scene. He wasn't there, but the news had gotten out. Andrea cornered me.

"What's this Trevor's been telling us about Malcolm being fired?" she demanded, in a voice magnified by vodka.

"I believe the Dean has exercised his prerogative not to rehire him," I said stuffily.

"Because he's gay?"

"Nothing to do with that," I said. "Bull and I both knew he was gay when he hired him."

"Well then what?"

Conversation in the room had died. People were listening intently.

"This is a party, Andrea," I said. "I'll report on department business at our next department meeting."

"The department doesn't need a report!" she cried out. "It needs to be involved in important decisions! A person's been fired just like that, and no explanation! God! What we need in this college is a faculty trade union!"

My heart beat quickly at her echo of what I had been thinking.

"The very *last* thing I'd want here is a union," said Barnet vehemently. "I worked at a unionized campus once in California, and I can tell you the relations between the faculty and the administration were worse than in a factory. Worse than the Post Office."

"When are we having that open forum with Forrester?" Andrea asked.

"Next Friday," I said. "Ten a.m. in the cafeteria."

"I'll see you there," she said. "We'll find out what kind of mush he has for brains. Merry Christmas everyone." She marched unsteadily out of the house scowling. I went after her and offered to drive her home, but she got in her car and sped off with an angry squeal of tires. I hoped she wouldn't run into a roadblock or have an accident.

I lay in bed that night, with the kitten purring in a soft ball on my blanket, and thought about how fast my world had changed. When I got my first job in Kenya ten years before, I did not even think to question the fact that by becoming a teacher I had forfeited all my electoral rights. I couldn't vote in civic or national elections. As a teacher, I was a colonial civil servant and had to obey orders and be completely neutral on all political issues. In fact, here I was over thirty years old and had never been eligible to vote in any election of government at any level. Now I was on the brink of a clash with our own college administration about participatory democracy.

I wanted to talk to my father. I wanted to show him the news stories of the past months:

Arab guerrillas today blew up three airliners in the desert in Jordan . . .

The trial of the Chicago Seven has been followed by prison riots across the U.S., and Chief Justice Warren Burger today issued a warning that the legal system has been static for 200 years and desperately needs reform if people are to have any faith in it . . .

In an explosion in Montreal today, following years of mailbox bombings, the entire glass front of the Queen Elizabeth Hotel, owned by Mayor Drapeau, exploded into millions of deadly shards . . .

Tanks and soldiers moved swiftly through the streets of Ottawa, today. Following the kidnapping by the Front de Liberation du Québec *of two prominent politicians, a grim-faced Prime Minister Pierre Elliot Trudeau went on national TV to inform Canadians that at four o'clock in the morning he had invoked the* War Measures Act *suspending all civil rights across the nation. "These are strong powers and I find them as distasteful as I am sure you do!" Trudeau said . . .*

In Montreal, sirens wailed and the police vans zigzagged through darkness to arrest some 500 people along with garbage bags full of their papers, people like me, community college teachers, writers—all of this without due process, and only thirty of those arrested were ever charged with any crime—and only four of the charges were connected with the FLQ. So it was not by accident that the Parti Québecois won the next election and a few years later workmen would be climbing stepladders to take down the signs that said "Dorchester Street" and replacing them with signs that said "Rue René Lévesque." Trudeau's attack on the separatists had backfired completely. And the Québec Minister of Labour, Pierre Laporte, was strangled to death. The old Canada of courtesy and trust was disappearing fast. Rashid was right about that.

On my bed, the little cat's motor purred away non-stop.

26

Jenadie invited me for dinner. She handed me a stubby brown bottle of beer, saying, "Alistair, would you kindly persuade this obstinate male that he should come home with me for Christmas?"

"Go home with her, Rashid," I told him with a smile.

"Huh!" he said, unhappily. "First of all, what means Christmas to me? Second of all, I have no desire to go to United States. And third, I have some business to attend to and I have to sit here and wait for the next move, if you have not forgotten?" He said this last with extreme irritation, his face turning from me to Jenadie.

"Oh baby I know you do!" she said, taking his chin in her fingers. "Anyways, it's not about religion, it's about *family*!"

"Of course," he said. "You go! You don't need me. Go, Jenadie Marie MacIlwaine! See your family. Come back happy. You know?"

Rashid usually fronted any discomfort with a grin. I had never seen him quite so upset. His face was pitted with stress.

"But why won't you come?" She was sipping wine as she cooked, and her mood was light.

"I'll stay here," he said firmly. "He can be my Christmas family," pointing to me.

"*Mam-bapu*," I said.

That brought a growly chuckle out of him and distracted him from his dark mood. "Yah! My imperialist Mother-Father. You do still think the British are a power, don't you Alistair? You don't seem to have realized that the Americans have taken over the world. Americans on one side, Russians on the other. British Empire has shrunk to a few old men with mutton-chop moustaches muttering to their dogs as they walk along English country roads, 'By Jove, when we ran the show in India there was none of this Congress foolishness!'"

His Colonel Blimp mimicry was quite good, despite his East Indian accent, and I laughed appreciatively.

So Jenadie flew off to Michigan, and Rashid actually did come and spend time with me. He would arrive at my door around supper time, lonely for conversation but not wanting to talk about his troubles. He played with the new cat while I cooked.

"What is it you teach specifically?" he asked me one day, looking down into the cat's face while he scratched her under the chin.

"English composition and literature courses."

"I understand literature," he said. "Go over the text with the class and discuss content and layers of meaning. But in English composition what do you actually teach them?"

"I try to give them control over what they're doing when they write."

He stared at me with a frown. "What the devil does that mean? Style?"

"No—well, yes, that too. We all have our own approaches. Most people teach them how to develop a topic or prove a thesis. Others are pretty ad hoc and get them writing every day with a prompt. One guy brings an animal to class, or a guitar, and they do free association. Another uses a couple of silent NFB films about nails and chairs. I teach a comprehensive field theory, which enables them to understand their aim in any writing task."

"Sounds bloody complicated, man!"

"It isn't. They get a theoretical introduction, and then they start writing and learn what to do and what not to do. It's a practical course."

"Could I sit in?"

"Sure."

One bright and sunny Sunday, I took Rashid for a hike with my Deep Cove neighbours Max and Sonia Odegaard, up to the big rock that overlooks the Cove.

"Do you believe those dumb bank robbers?" Sonia asked. "Rob the bank in Dollarton, and try to escape going north."

"What's the problem?" Rashid asked.

"They ran out of road! It dead-ends in the Cove. It was right here that they caught them."

Max suddenly turned to Rashid and said out of the blue, "Be sure to let us know if there's ever any way we can help you."

"Thank you!" said Rashid looking startled.

Back at my place, he asked, "Why the hell is Max offering to help me? Is it an any-friend-of-yours-is-a-friend-of-mine kind of thing?"

"I think he identifies with you as a radical. His family were hounded by McCarthy in the 50s in the States. That's partly why he lives in Canada."

"Hmm!" Rashid said, pleased. "Solidarity. Any other so-called radicals in your department?"

"Not really," I said. "The usual bunch of liberal humanists, and a couple of war objectors, a few feminists—Oh, and one full time Canadian now."

"You have only *one* Canadian prof full time in your department! Why is that?"

"This is a raw, young country in the making, man. They've only recently ended the incentive program for immigrants to come and teach here."

"What incentive program?"

"Canada was so short of teachers that for years there was a scheme to attract Brits and Australians and Americans: come and teach in Canada and you're exempt from income tax for the first two years."

"Two years tax free! My God, that's interesting! I never heard about this."

"I don't know if they advertised it in India."

The phone rang and it was Kathy Wardell who had been a grad student with me. She was married with children and lived in a big house in Kerrisdale, where on several occasions she had invited our seminar to hold its meetings.

"Alistair, we're going to Hawaii," she said, "and our cabin on Hollyburn Mountain is going to be sitting empty from now till New Year's. We'd much prefer it to be occupied, and I thought of you."

I looked at Rashid and accepted the offer on the spot. I wrote down the directions, and when I put the phone down I said, "Rashid, how would you like to spend a few days up on a mountain?"

"Sure!" His face broke into a puzzled smile. "Tax free too?"

Next day, I arranged with my neighbour Lil to come in and feed the cat, packed some gear into my army surplus backpack, found another one for Rashid, and then drove to pick him up. He had only sandals for footwear, so we stopped at Park Royal and got him a pair of yellow gorilla-stomper boots at Woodward's. Then we drove to the top of Old Chairlift Road, parked the car in the bushes, adjusted our packs, and started up the path where the chairlift had once been. We entered a grove of tall evergreens and after two hours of steady climbing we reached the skiers' lodge beside the small frozen lake, with the Forest Ranger's log-house on one side and the circle of tiny green cabins on the other. We located the Wardells' and found the key hanging in its hiding place. The cabin was as cold as a walk-in refrigerator, but we threw our packs onto the bunk beds and I soon had a crackling fire going in the stove. Rashid stood chafing his bare hands over the hotplates, and I adjusted the damper and the doors of the stove to get the maximum roar of flame.

"This is exceptional!" he said. "Your friends own this?"

"They lease it. It's about $200 a year."

"Incredible! Maybe we can lease one too."

"Perhaps. Once the university business is all settled."

At the mention of the university, his face fell, and I wanted to kick myself.

After tea and several slices of toast briefly charred on the stove, we dressed up again and went for a walk in the snow. It was the afternoon of a fine, clear day. Smoke was coming from one other cabin, but we saw no one and heard no human noises. There was a short rope tow up a slope, but it wasn't operating. The city had disappeared entirely on the other side of the mountain, and even when we stood still we could hear no sound. We were not ten kilometres from the centre of Vancouver, but we might as well have been way up north or in the Rockies. We walked beside the tracks left by cross-country skiers and climbed eventually to the top of a hill. We sat on our gloves on the snow under a pine tree and peeled mandarin oranges. Instantly, two grey and white birds arrived. I took a peanut out of my pocket and held it out on my palm, and the birds vied with one another to land. The winner stood with his claws curled around my index finger, scooped up the peanut with his beak, and fluttered off to a nearby tree.

"So tame!" Rashid was charmed.

"They're Whisky Jacks. Very trusting."

I handed him the bag of nuts and he held some out.

"Flatten your palm," I said. "That's right."

A bird landed on his hand, and Rashid's eyes looked startled. The bird took a peanut and flew off, and he followed it as it landed on a tree branch, delighted.

"Whisky Jacks!" he said. "How would they get a name like that?"

"Probably an Indian word."

He scowled. "Ah God yes, colonialism! You're right. *Wiz-keejak* probably means 'tame grey bird' in Cherokee or Ojibwa. Along come colonialists and Europeanize it so the bird sounds like an alcoholic. Same with 'Indian.' Portuguese guy crosses the ocean and doesn't know where he is. Thinks he's landed thousand of miles away in India, so for the next five hundred years all native Americans, north and south, are labelled 'Indian.' Ridiculous! That's got to change."

"Take a holiday, Rashid! Besides, Columbus wasn't Portuguese. He was an Italian, employed by the King and Queen of Spain."

We looked at one another unsmiling.

"You know the one about 'kangaroo' don't you?" I ventured, to try and lighten things.

"What is it?"

"Captain Cook ordered his men to find out the native names for all the specimens of flora and fauna they collected round the world and took back to England. So in South Australia they catch a kangaroo and bring it to the ship, and he asks them, 'What's it called?' They say they don't know, so he scolds them and sends them back to find out. They come back and tell him it's called 'kangaroo.'"

"Yah, so?"

"That was in 1770. Now, some Australian aboriginal member of parliament has reported that 'ka-nga-roo,' in his language, means 'What do you want?'"

Rashid chuckled. "Is it true?"

"I don't know, but it makes a good story. Like Kennedy calling himself a jelly donut in Berlin."

"He didn't do that?"

"He said *Ich bin ein Berliner*. But nobody thought he was calling himself a donut. That was a political smear put out by some students in Florida."

Rashid's serious look returned. "Anyway, I tell you, my friend, there are some big developments afoot in this country as far as the so-called Indians are concerned."

"What do you mean?"

"Land claims. I was talking to some progressive lawyers the other day who are working with the native leaders on it. Apparently, by the time they got this far west, the British colonialists grew so arrogant and careless that they didn't even bother to sign treaties with the native people. They just took the land, occupied it, without any legal standing."

"'Possession is eleven points in the law.'"

"Yeah but the twelfth point is going to come back to haunt them. In the past they had gunboats to enforce their arguments, but gunboat strategy doesn't work today. You wait and see. All over this country, the aboriginals are waking up and asserting their rights. Did you see that TV news story about the confrontation in Akwesasne?"

"Are you talking about the Mohawks blocking the bridge in the Saint Regis Reserve?"

"Huh," he gave an ironic laugh. "Okay, Sahib, you use your names! I'll use mine. That guy Jake Swamp—now there's a name to remember for the future—he pulled off that bridge blockade brilliantly. They printed copies of notices published by the Canadian Department of Indian Affairs declaring that Indians own Indian Land and that anyone trespassing will be fined or jailed. Then they blocked the road with their cars and pickups and handed people the government notice—I mean, it's an important international road, connecting the States with Canada!—and they waited for the police to come. Cops arrived and tried to talk them into moving the blockade, but they refused to budge. Okay, next level is force."

I wanted to ask him to shut up. To remind him that I had lived through all this stuff in Africa and eventually found myself kicked out of my own birthplace—or rather kicked myself out before they did it to me. But it was always a pleasure, however distasteful, to argue with Rashid, because he was so polite in articulating his arguments, however uncomfortable I found them, even down to the point of his needing to shoot me.

"Okay," I said, "so who's going to exert force, and what is the objective?"

He began grooming his dark bearded chin between thumb and forefinger, considering his reply. Unlike Jenadie, who would sometimes try to drown me with emotional laughter, and oppose my points with crass slogans, Rashid always answered quietly, with careful and specific forethought.

"In such a struggle," he said eventually, "both sides are going to exert force, and the conflict will escalate. At Akwesasne, Jake Swamp produced a copy of the government's own warning against trespass on Indian land as justification for the blockade, and he demanded that the police enforce the law and charge the people crossing the bridge; the Ontario police answered that by citing another law against blocking highways and dutifully manhandled the blockaders into their cruisers and took them away to jail. All the while, in the TV news footage, you see people looking anxiously over their shoulders, to see if anybody is going to suddenly start shooting. Jake Swamp let a few of the Kanaien'gehaga—'Mohawks' as you call them—be arrested, and then he called his people away to a meeting in the community hall. That was the end of that round. These are matters of strategic advance, one step at a time. They blocked that bloody highway, and it got on the news for everyone in North America and around the world to see. Unlike places here in BC where there were no treaties, at Akwesasne there was a specific agreement, the Jay Treaty of 1794, which stipulated that there would never be a customs post dividing the Kanaien'gehaga nation. So Swamp made his point very effectively. And that won't be the end of it. There are bound to be more roadblocks and other measures ahead."

"And you think that's okay! No peace or agreement is possible? Just throw everything into chaos in hopes of a better distribution of privilege and power in the outcome? Look at what's happening in Africa, Rashid? Is that better than colonialism? At least we wicked colonists kept things operating and didn't slide into corruption, greed and incompetence."

"Oh, Alistair!" he said, as familiar with my arguments as I was with his.

"You didn't answer me on one thing, Rashid," I said, sensing the argument was over. "What are the specific objectives of all these native American uprisings and protests? In Kenya, the Mau-Mau announced they were going to drive the whites into the sea, and to a large extent they have accomplished that. Most of the whites have taken their expertise elsewhere, and Kenya is the poorer for it."

"Specific objectives? I don't know exactly. A first one might be to get a commitment from the Canadian government to enforce the existing treaties, and then, secondly, to negotiate new treaties where they don't now exist. Mineral rights are going to be a big thing."

He stood up and pulled out his cigarette package. He put one in his mouth and was about to strike a match when he stopped, closed the matchbook and slid the cigarette back into the pack.

"Too beautiful up here to smoke," he said. "This air is so clean! What an amazing place. Shangri-La."

"All these majestic trees," I said. "It's like a cathedral."

He looked down at me where I sat. "I don't have much affection for cathedrals," he said. "Fucking Anglican Cathedral in Calcutta is the most disgusting place on the Indian subcontinent. When I was a student, I used to see them carting away corpses every morning. They left the doors unlocked at night so people could crawl in and die."

"What would you prefer to have them do," I asked, "lock the doors so they die out on the sidewalk?"

He shook his head and muttered, *"Acha!"*

I thought of my own cathedral in Nairobi, that big, heavy building of blue stone, with its red-tiled roof and gum trees all around. I was confirmed there, and then joined the Cathedral Youth Fellowship, and later still the choir. And got married to Imogen. It all seemed such a long way away now. Another life. Another planet.

"Shall we go down to the cabin and make supper?" I suggested.

That evening, with full bellies, and glasses of Scotch, we sat in front of the warm stove, and now Rashid lit his cigarette. Outside, snow had begun to fall in big, soft flakes.

"Really an incredible retreat," he said. "No telephone even."

"You said not to mention cathedrals, Rashid, but I was married in one."

"Didn't do any good, apparently! What happened with that marriage, anyway?"

"It came to a point where we just couldn't get along."

"And children and everything!"

"Yes. A great pity."

He sat shaking his head. Then looking at me he said, "You have gone through a lot of changes, haven't you?"

"Not like you, man! Your father's murder. That's *really* incredible."

"In this century, everybody lives through big changes."

"I suppose."

"For you, Mau Mau independence war, change country, marriage ends. Now your father gets out of Kenya—dies! Mother is already dead."

"Yes but she died long ago."

"So! She is your *mother*, man. You dismiss her death like that? 'A long time ago.' Stiff upper lip!"

"I don't feel so stiff upper lip about Caroline."

"Look, I've told you already Alistair: forget her, man. Not the one for you at all."

For a short time, lost in thought, neither of us spoke. The stove crackled and the cabin was warm. I felt the strength of a bond, an unconditional friendship, despite our differences.

Then Rashid said quietly: "You know what was the worst thing for me?"

"What?"

"Being a refugee. At the time of India's partition, when we were so terrified of racial massacres—like had happened with the Sikhs, you know?"

"I've read Kushwant Singh's, *Train to Pakistan*."

"Yah. The atrocities Kushwant describes were absolutely real, I can tell you. Anyway, I wasn't that old, but I knew 'refugee' meant that we could be killed around the next corner of the road. We had to get out of India and across the border into what's now Bangladesh. There was this army truck. We bundled everything in it. My old mother, you know, poor, semi-literate woman, and all the children, and baskets of pots and pans. Just leaving our home, getting out in the most frantic hurry. Everywhere, soldiers with guns. It was a nightmare. I still have bad dreams."

"You've come through."

"For me it's been okay," he said softly. "Not so for others."

I filled the stove with wood and closed it down, hoping the fire might still be alive by morning. Then we crawled into our sleeping bags.

I dreamed my father was driving Cal and me in the blue Wolseley from Nairobi down to Mombasa for a holiday. We have passed through the dry, bushy *nyika* around MacKinnon Road and are beginning to reach the coast through the familiar countdown of names: Mariakani, Miritini, Maji ya Chumvi (salt water). Coconut palms start to appear. White stone houses. Arab men walk in white jellabas and embroidered fezzes in the sweltering humidity. Warm air rushes in through the open car windows, and there's the rank smell of the coast, salt fish and overripe mangoes, and a landscape of coconut palms. Any minute now, at a curve in the tarmac road, one of us will cry out, "I see the sea!"

Oh no! There's a roadblock! A barrier of forty-gallon oil drums, crossed two-by-fours and barbed wire. Several tall, black *askaris* in dark blue woollen tunics with Kenya Police belts stand facing us. A Sikh officer in bush jacket and khaki turban walks up to the car, holding a Sten gun. He looks in the window, dark eyes alert and bright. My father, wearing his navy blue wool beret and a beige cardigan says, "What is the problem Captain? Can you let us through?"

"*Bwana*," the officer says, "Who are you, and why are you here?"

"I belong here," my father says, and there is a silence.

Leaning forward from the back seat, I try my best Swahili: *"Sisi wote ni wananchi, bwana, wote. Nimesaliwa inchi hii!* We're all citizens, sir, all of us. I was born in this country."

The officer stands looking dubious for a moment, then steps back and waves. The askaris lift the barrier and we drive on through.

I woke at five, and the cabin was freezing, the stove cold again. I jumped out of bed, slivered cedar kindling with the hatchet, lit a fire and put coffee on to percolate. By the time Rashid emerged from his bed and stood rubbing his hands over the stove, the cabin was warming and the scrambled eggs were ready

"Get your boots on, boy! We'll go to the top of Hollyburn today," I said.

"Alistair," he said, "this has been great! But I have been thinking. I'd better go back down today, you know? You stay, I'll find my way. There's all that stuff down there I have to get on with."

"No, no. We'll go down together. I'll pick up some thesis work to do."

After breakfast, he packed up and we trekked down to the car.

"Thanks a lot, man. Now don't forget," Rashid said as I dropped him off at his place, "I want to come to your class one of these days."

I went back to my place and collected some of my thesis notes and my Olivetti Slimline Lettera 22 typewriter and returned alone to the cabin. Climbing through the tall trees, I was feeling miffed at Rashid for having bailed when I'd accepted the offer of the cabin mostly for his sake and bought him boots. But later, as I looked up from my books and watched a solitary cross-country skier herringbone up a slope, I realized that Rashid Hassan couldn't possibly have stayed up here in the snow for days on end as I'd planned. There was too much to brood about. It dawned on me that whereas I appreciate solitude, Rashid always needed to be among people. He needed his colleagues. When he went to Oxford to do research, I had imagined him sitting for long hours in a quiet library, as I might have done. Wrong picture! For Rashid, "Oxford research" was probably an endless round of socializing, "struggle sessions," alcohol and cigarettes, laughter. Like the yackety-yack of Jenadie and her colleagues in the smoke-filled Social Science huts at UBC.

When I went back to work at the College, I found a folder of course outlines waiting on my desk for approval. I noticed that the books on Sandra Atkinson's Introduction to Modern Fiction course were all Canadian. I felt embarrassed signing the approval form, because I had read only two of these, Leonard Cohen's *Beautiful Losers* and Ethel Wilson's *Swamp Angel*. I resolved to make up my lack as soon as possible.

The next Fiction outline was Barnet Nolan's, and here I was on familiar ground: Sherwood Anderson, *Winesburg, Ohio*, Ernest Hemingway, *The Sun Also Rises*; William Faulkner, *As I Lay Dying*; Joseph Conrad, *Lord Jim*; D.H. Lawrence, *Sons and Lovers*. I signed this approval form without delay, but before I put the outlines into the basket for the print shop, I went to the photocopier. And next day I began the department meeting by handing out anonymous copies of the two book lists, which I had chopped out of the course outlines and marked A and B.

"Which list would you be inclined to approve as the required reading for an Introduction to Modern Fiction course?" I asked.

"Oh brother! The first thing that strikes me," said Thelma, "is that all the authors on list B are male."

Intense discussion followed, and after a while I cut it off.

"Fine," I said. "Clearly one cannot make a semester's reading list of five novels which are both excellent and also completely representative of every possible ethnic, cultural, gender and political grouping."

"Literary excellence is the only criterion we should consider!" Barnet Nolan interjected.

"In that case, Barnet, how come list B finds literary excellence *only* amongst British and American writers?"

"Male," Thelma reiterated.

"They are first rate books, that's why!" Barnet said, aggrieved.

"I agree. But that's not my question. Listen again. My question is, 'How does it come about' that the list is so restricted."

Barnet looked at me and blinked three times.

"I'm not attacking you," I said. "I'm asking: what is the *process* whereby List B comes into being, with only male British and American authors?"

"Those are the books I happen to know best," he said frankly, breaking the anonymity.

"Why? Because some professor put them on a reading list. Why? Because his professor had them on his reading list? Could that be it?

"Let me end this by suggesting that we should all prescribe books that we find exciting. And we should look around at new authors and new books. And since we do have a small budget for visiting lecturers, you might consider studying Canadian writers you could actually bring to class."

"You mean the College would pay for Leonard Cohen to come to my class?" said Sandra Atkinson excitedly.

"We might not be able to afford Leonard Cohen. Doesn't he live in Greece? And I expect he charges a fortune."

"How about Sheila Watson? She lives in Nanaimo."

"Certainly," I smiled.

"Far *out*!" said Sandra. "I'll write to her immediately. My students are studying *The Double Hook*."

The spring semester started and one of my Composition classes was scheduled at night in the old North Vancouver High School building at 23rd just off Lonsdale. I wondered if I should invite Rashid to visit as he had asked. I thought it might pain him to be in a classroom. Eventually I decided he could make up his own mind, so I phoned him, and he was eager to come. We got to the first meeting and found there were only six students in the room, all women.

"I'll sit at the back," whispered Rashid. "Don't pay any attention to me."

"Hello," I greeted the students. "This class list has eight names on it, so let's give it a few minutes and see if the other two show up."

Across the hallway from us was a Philosophy class with about twenty students. The instructor was a small beady-eyed guy named Glen, with long red hair and a beard, who used to hang around with Malcolm Carter and whose suede jacket smelled of marijuana. I watched through the open door, as he hoisted himself into a lotus position, squatting on top of the table. Then he read off his class list through black granny glasses.

"Please take a copy of the course outline and read it," he said in nasal Cockney, pointing to a pile of paper beside him. The students rose tentatively from their seats and took the outlines.

I looked at my watch. Five minutes was up. Give them a couple more.

In the other room, the students had read Glen's course outline, and were watching him.

"Questions?"

He waited.

"Any questions?"

There was a good fifteen seconds of silence.

"All right," he said, unfolding his legs and getting off the table. "In that case, I'll see you the same time next week. I sincerely 'ope you'll have questions by then, or we are not going to have a very interesting class, are we? See you next week."

He strolled out of the room, leaving the students dazed. Shock tactics. Good, but I also feared for him. Would he last much longer than Malcolm?

I called the roll of my own class and checked off the names of those present. "All right," I said. "At six students, this class may not run, but let's be optimistic. The Dean wants to get this location established, so he may let us run with only six. So, to begin with, write me something."

Silence. The room was filled with tension, and I ignored it.

"What do you want us to write, exactly?" asked Lisa, the oldest student, in her mid-forties.

"Anything you like," I said. "Twenty minutes."

I sat drawing a small diagram of the class and putting their names against each circle. The students exchanged looks, and eventually began clicking open their binders for paper and uncapping their ballpoint pens. I noticed Rashid looking around for something to write on, so I took a pad of college memo paper from my briefcase and slid it onto his desk.

Lisa, Anne-Marie, Sondra, Melanie, Elizabeth, Sally. I wrote out the names till I had them memorised and attached to the faces, easy in a class this small.

"All right," I said after twenty minutes. "Come to an ending of some sort and hand them in, please."

I walked around the room collecting the papers. I offered to take Rashid's, but he shook his head. I quickly skimmed the contents of each paper before I returned to the front table and dropped them in my briefcase.

"Well," I said, "at first glance, I'd say we have an interesting mix in this class. You've told me about being born elsewhere, about sadness, about the ethics of climbing a mountain, about members of your family, and a rare procedure to undertake in the kitchen."

They shifted nervously.

On impulse, I blurted, "How would you feel about getting rid of grades?"

The students looked at one another. Rashid looked up with interest.

"By which you mean what?" asked Lisa.

"I'd give you your grade tonight. You'd have that grade even if you were never to show up again."

"Why would we . . . do that?" Lisa objected. "We've paid fees for this course, we're here to learn something from you."

"It would be great!" said Sondra, a slim woman, about 24, with a lively smile. "It removes the power. It makes us more equal with you, right?"

"Certainly."

"But what about the course?" asked Anne-Marie with a slight French accent. "We don't know if it's going to be cancelled? And aren't there other students you are expecting? What if they don't agree to have no grades?"

"I didn't say '*no* grades.' It's get the grade now, and put it out of the way, and then we can learn."

"How could you tell what grades to give us?" asked Melanie, a freckle-faced tomboy. "Anything we want?"

She brought me up short. ("*Mad plan!*" some inner self was shouting in my head.)

"Obviously I haven't read all through your papers," I said, "but from what I have glanced at, I'd be content to give a B to everyone here."

Again, they looked at one another. Sondra was beaming. Lisa shrugged.

"What about the others?" Anne-Marie insisted.

"You're here and they're not," I said. "It's your decision."

Elizabeth had not spoken a word since answering the roll call. Now she asked quietly, "Why are you doing this?"

"I think you might learn more if you never have to think about your grade."

"Right on!" said Sondra. "I agree with him. Let's do it."

"It would require unanimous agreement," I said. "Are you ready for the vote?"

Five heads nodded.

"Elizabeth?"

"I don't feel comfortable about this."

"All right. Leave it till next week and vote on it then?"

They agreed, and I launched into my opening.

"Writing is a form of communication, true?"

I looked around the room till everyone nodded.

"Then draw me a diagram of communication. And after that, write a definition of 'good writing.'"

For the next hour, I worked them into Kinneavy's theory of discourse, and then wrapped it up: "I'll show you next week how every single decision you make about writing depends on which aim you have. There are only six aims of writing, folks, and every time you sit down to write, whether you know it or not, you are pursuing one of them. And—pay attention—this is the last thing tonight: for each of the six aims we can stipulate which particular strategies of writing are appropriate, and which are not."

"But how can one possibly write anything if one has to stop and think about all this theory!" said Lisa, flustered.

"Good for you Lisa!" I said. "Just go ahead and write. Then use the theory afterwards as a tool for revision, and get it how you want it by the final draft. That's what writing is: getting it down, and then working on it to get it as perfect as possible. That's it for tonight."

I packed up and Rashid strode along beside me to the car, exclaiming, "That was fun! You sounded intense, like a bloody preacher, man! But fascinating to me, as a social scientist."

"Let's go get a beer," I said.

"Lisa has a point, huh? Too theoretical for first year students, isn't it?"

"It gets easier the more they use the theory."

As I drove down Lonsdale, Rashid asked, "Are we going to the College now?"

I turned to look at him. "That was the College," I said.

"That was somebody else's classroom that you are using. Where is Capilano College itself? Where is the campus?"

"We don't have one." I explained to him about the two rooms in the basement of the West Van High School for our office desks, and their classrooms at night, and church basements plus the public library in Squamish.

"You mean to tell me that there is no actual building called Capilano College? It's a college that exists only in people's minds. What a wonderful idea!"

"It's not by choice, man," I told him. "Nobody has a clear idea of where we should be. West Vancouver wants to put us on the garbage dump. North Van is offering us a highways interchange site. Squamish would love us up there, but that's too far away. One of the Council members has a vision of building a skyscraper on the bridge at Park Royal over the Capilano River and putting us in the high-rise there, like Sir George Williams University in Montreal."

"If a college is in people's minds, it can remain live and dynamic and fluid," Rashid said. "Once it becomes institutionalized with concrete buildings etcetera, you have the danger of entropy. You must have read Charles Dickens' novel *Hard Times*? I really like your college in the mind!"

We parked just off lower Lonsdale and walked into the Saint Alice Hotel. In the big old leather couches that lined the west wall of the lounge, we found Simon Du Lac ensconced among students.

"Too much!" he said, raising his hand. "You had a night class too? Come and join us. Did you meet your students?"

"I've been pounding home my writing theory to a class that will probably be cancelled."

"Your Aristotelian bullshit?" said Simon. "'The tigers of wrath are wiser than the horses of instruction.' Teach them Olson, teach them Creely. 'Form is never anything more than an extension of content.' Don't teach them formulas my friend. Waiter!"

I made the introductions.

"Why do you denigrate his approach, Simon?" Rashid asked. "He's giving his students a tool they can use."

"Giving them the tool? That's good!" Simon winked. Then he looked around with bright, animal eyes. "That's what we're *here* for, to *empower* you. Teach you till you don't need us any more. Gotta get rid of your teachers, ladies and gentlemen! Supersede the sons of bitches!"

The young men listened intently. A couple of the women were goners already, their heads canted, their eyes dilating in waves as he spoke.

"But that's exactly what Alistair is saying," Rashid countered. "'Here is the field theory. Take it! Use it.'"

"Theories are reductive," Simon blew out smoke. "They try to shrink the world to fit small brains. Language is a living organism. It can't be contained in theory. 'The cistern contains: the fountain overflows.'"

"You don't think Blake has theory?" I said. "'I must create a system or be enslaved by another man's.' He's got the whole damn universe pinned out in a web of mad theories."

"Exactly!" Simon stabbed a triumphant finger into my face with his cigarette slanted precariously in the crack. He paused for dramatic effect. "It's Blake's craziness that saves him! Total crackpot! Intellectual drunkard. As Baudelaire says, 'Let us get drunk and stay drunk, on wine, or love, or poetry.' Blake only makes sense to the imagination. Your Aristotelian logic is too pedestrian my friend! Sterile!"

Rashid was grinning at him now. "And you Simon," he said, "you're not a bit crazy yourself?"

"Completely off my rocker. How do you know about this aims crapola anyway?" he asked suspiciously. "Don't tell me you teach his theory too?"

"I went to his class tonight."

"Shit *la merde*!" said Simon. "You've been sitting through *that*! Waiter, bring this gentleman a double Scotch, *pronto*!"

In the car, Rashid said, "Lively fellow that Simon! You got more colleagues like him?"

"He's unique," I said. "The students either love him or hate his guts."

"Some of those girls—"

"I noticed!"

When I pulled up at his house, Rashid looked glum again.

"I envy you," he said. "I miss students. Thanks for inviting me to the class, Alistair. It was refreshing. It reminded me what teaching is all about."

"What did you write?" I asked.

"Oh, no." He shook his head and reached for the door handle. "Good night, Alistair."

I drove home feeling pretty sad myself. I picked through my lp's and stacked three albums on the changer spindle, then climbed into bed and drifted off while Gordon Lightfoot mused plaintively about the ice being on the river, and the old folks still being there, and wondering, rhetorically, if she ever mentioned his name.

27

The open forum was eventually called for Tuesday 19th January and well advertised, and the attendance was high. An outside recording secretary had been hired, and the meeting was co-chaired by Forrester and Gillian Alvarez, a Political Science instructor.

"I'd like to point out that there is a problem here," said Thelma Smith, "because we have a lot of part-time people present who will be reluctant to speak their minds in view of the fact that they have no idea whether or not they're going to be rehired next semester."

Forrester gave her a pained look.

"Dr. Smith," he expostulated, "please! Re-employment has no bearing on the purpose of this meeting. We're here to examine and discuss the mission of the College."

Norman Bull took off his glasses and swung them in the air. He said, "The matter of reappointment is being sorted out, and the decisions should be made by early next month. Meanwhile I would be very surprised—frankly disappointed—if any instructor, whether full-time or part-time, felt that their position at the College was in any way jeopardized by their participation in this discussion."

"In theory, that's all well and good," said Thelma. "In fact, many people do feel threatened."

As I watched Norman Bull and Thelma Smith stare each other down, neither one yielding ground by looking away, it felt very uncomfortable. For all his progressive ideas about education, Bull was part of the old guard and I knew he was bound to be superseded soon, which pained me.

After a tense silence, several people made suggestions of how to proceed round the obstruction, and finally Forrester seized the initiative.

"What I think we should do here," he said, "is to frankly state how we see our roles, your role, my role—and our responsibilities. I want feedback from you on what you think I should be doing. And I think we should establish a list of priorities to address."

He looked around optimistically. The faces about him were closed and grim.

For two hours we wrangled back and forth, and by the end of it one thing had become clear: Forrester saw faculty input into governance of the College as merely advisory. Administration had the last say in everything.

"We might as well change the names of all our committees," said Gillian Alvarez. "We don't have a Curriculum Committee—it's really a Curriculum *Advisory* body. We don't have a College Cabinet—it's just an *advisory* panel with a fancy name!"

Neither Forrester nor Bull responded. I saw them both writing notes, and I wondered suddenly how well the two of them worked together. I had never seen them converse. They appeared to ignore one another. Bull seemed so distant from me now, not the friendly father figure who had once frankly discussed public nudity and entertained me with computerised airplane jokes.

"There is considerable dissatisfaction over the Counselling Department," said Mark Meadows the Psychology Co-ordinator. "My faculty have discussed this and we recommend the appointment of people trained in psychology and mental health as counsellors, not the kind of semi-clerical Advisers we have now."

Forrester raised his head like a horse scenting an ill wind.

"We employ Advisers to help students plan their courses. Are you telling me," he demanded in an agitated voice, "that we have students requiring psychiatric counselling on our campus? A significant number?"

"At any one time," said Mark "about twenty percent of our students are mildly disturbed. Over a period of a year most students will have been seriously disturbed in one way or another. One person in ten will require major hospitalization, and the proportion of mentally disturbed will be closer to nine out of ten."

Forrester shook his head in pained disbelief.

Bull took the opportunity of this dead end to speak: "I think we need to have detailed job descriptions for all positions in the College, administrators, faculty and support staff," he said.

This proved a fertile topic, and after some strong opinions were expressed, we agreed to develop job descriptions for discussion of College governance at another meeting to be held after the semester ended. People began to get up and leave.

Gillian Alvarez looked at her watch. "I think, in view of the time," she said—

"No! Wait a minute," Peter Hansen said loudly. "There's something fundamental that we haven't addressed here, and I'd like to hear your thoughts on the matter before we end this." He was pointing at Forrester, who was scowling at the accusatory finger.

"Are you familiar with the ideas of C.B. MacPherson of the University of Toronto?" Peter asked.

Forrester shook his head. "I may have seen the name," he said.

"He's a recognized Canadian authority on politics and economics, and lately he has devoted his thinking to the function of the university within the state. Let me read you an excerpt from his convocation address at Memorial University in Newfoundland. I think this is central to what we're talking about today—well, we are meeting but so far we haven't actually talked about it, and I think we should."

He looked at Forrester, who shrugged. Peter gazed around the room, and several people motioned him to get on with it.

He began to read: "'I am not an ivory tower man, although I know that a case can be made for the university as an ivory tower. . . .'"

Forrester's eyes were downcast.

"'Society *should* be getting its money's worth. But we in the universities must say bluntly that society and the governments which represent society, are not getting, and cannot get, their money's worth *as long as they ask for and get the wrong product*.'" Peter was a slow reader, drawing out the emphases in his Nebraskan drawl.

"Could you not just photocopy—"

"I won't be very long, Dr. Forrester. I want to get a response from you to this. Couple more key paragraphs, if you don't mind."

"'In a healthy and expanding society, such as we enviously see North America to have been in the nineteenth century, it was appropriate for society to ask simply that the universities reinforce and transmit the values and the knowledge on which the society was based and by which it operated, and perhaps to add a little to the knowledge. . . . The main thing was to reproduce the wisdom and to reproduce the people who could use it.

"'Society still asks this of the universities. *But in a sick or distracted society this is no longer enough.* What a *sick* society needs most is *diagnosis*, at every level of its malfunctioning: ecological, physiological, economic, psychological, political, and above all, to use an old fashioned word in little repute these days, moral.

"'It seems to me that the primary function of a university in a sick society, the function which society should be *asking* the university to perform, is *dissent*: dissent from all the received diagnoses which have failed. That is the *only way* that society can get its *money's worth* from the university in our days.'"

Peter stopped and closed his file folder. The room was silent.

"Now, Dr. Forrester," Peter said, "I would like to ask whether or not you see it as the mission of Capilano College to provide a vehicle of constructive dissent to the community it serves?"

Forrester closed the inner and outer buttons of his double-breasted suit and stood up.

"I appreciate your presentation of a very provocative and thoughtful speech, Peter," he said. "I think Capilano College is here not primarily as a therapeutic institution or a voice of dissent. Society may have many ills. We are mandated by the Province of British Columbia to provide first- and second-year courses in University Transfer, and Career and Vocational divisions. So that's what I value your input towards achieving, and I'm sure we'll have further profitable discussions of this."

"Wait!" Andrea Halvorson's voice cut across Forrester's attempted closing benediction. "There's something else I want to talk about!"

He raised his eyebrows at her.

"Ever since I've been at this college, it's felt like a high school to me. Not with my colleagues, not with the students, but with the administration. You come into our classrooms and inspect us! It's like Dickens' England. When are we going to have an adult, professional, peer evaluation process?"

Forrester's Adam's apple moved in his throat. Then he coughed and answered: "Ms. Halvorson, I think you've brought up an excellent topic for our next forum of this sort. I'll put that number one on the agenda. May I suggest now that we move to a coffee situation?"

Coffee was served in the room next door. I mingled for a bit, and Peter Hansen asked me for a ride home.

In the car, he said, "You think one word of the MacPherson stuff got through to that robot?"

"He'll probably read it if you send him a copy. I saw his eyes flicking back and forth. He wished you'd get to the end and shut up. When he took this job, the guy probably thought he was taking charge of a nice, well-behaved institution like a bible college. If he'd known what a bunch of shit-disturbers he was getting, he'd have run a million miles."

"You think we are shit disturbers?"

"In the sense MacPherson would approve of, definitely."

Peter was silent. Then he said: "You know what Forrester said to me last week? He said, 'I hope you don't think I'm too authoritative'!"

"He meant 'authoritarian.'"

"Yes, but he said 'authoritative'! Denby Forrester 'authoritative'!"

Peter laughed exaggeratedly in his seat.

In a way I pitied Forrester for being so out of his depth trying to deal with us. No doubt he did well enough, in his double-breasted grey suit, representing the College to Ministry officials or speaking at Rotary Clubs and the like. But his capacity for relating to the broad range of faculty under his administration was very limited. Unlike Bull, who never flinched from a head-on collision and often opened himself up to argument with the faculty, Forrester preferred to evade confrontation and tried to exercise a godlike and un-negotiable power. He once told me that his young daughter so alarmed him by her dangerous behaviour of going to a nightclub called *The Pink Pussycat* that at 1 a.m. when she arrived home, he bundled her into his car and drove her down to the Vice Squad office at the Vancouver Police Station to get a first-hand look at where she might end up. I looked at him and felt some compassion: what a clumsy and misguided thing for a parent to do! But he had tried his level best—and who was I to make judgments anyway? Where were my kids?

When I dropped Peter off at his apartment, he got out of the car, and then holding the door open said, "Of course you know what the real answer for our college is?"

"What, Peter?"

"Form a union."

Driving home, I thought about my colleagues: we were from different places, geographically, psychologically, politically. But in the short time we had been together we had developed a camaraderie as fierce as that of any family.

I remembered that once Peter, having no transportation of his own at the time, had asked me one day, holding out his hand: "Make you uptight if I borrow your car?" It was like a younger brother asking for the keys.

28

"Rashid, isn't there a good stripper bar around here?"

"Mm, don't know." Rashid shook his head noncommittally.

I was shocked. Jack, a radical Political Science friend and his girlfriend Dawn, had come up from the States and were staying with Rashid and Jenadie for a few days. Jack wanted to see strippers.

Dawn was about ten years younger than Jack, and very good looking. She leaned down over his chair so that her long hair brushed over his, and she nudged his face with a large breast.

"I'll strip for you, Babe!" she said, with a vacant smile.

Jenadie went into the kitchen.

"Bye," she called, and slammed the door as she left for work.

"So I hear this drive up to Squamish is pretty scenic?" Jack asked me.

"It was the first Sunday drive I took when I arrived in Canada," I said. "It's quite spectacular."

"Then I guess we'll steer the Volvo up there. Okay Dawn?"

"Sure, Babe."

Alone with Rashid in his house, I asked, "He wants to go and watch strippers? Isn't he embarrassed? Some political scientist!"

"And they call me a prude!" said Rashid. "It's you who is the prude, Alistair Randall."

"Oh, I can be titillated as much as the next dumb male. But Jack's supposed to be a modern radical. I'm surprised at his being so tactless."

Rashid laughed.

"He's on holiday," he said. "Maybe he dropped his guard."

"And in front of the women!"

"You think Jenadie was pissed off?"

"I know she was. Didn't you hear her slam the door?"

"In that case we'll be hearing more about it. Too bad. She's been calm since visiting her parents. By the way, what happened with that class of yours in the end, did they vote to get rid of grades?"

"The Lonsdale class? Yes! Two more students arrived, so the class ran. We talked it over, and they negotiated me up to B+. I marked their IBM cards on the second day in front of them. I fretted that none of them would show up ever again! But they all did, right to the final exam."

"And did it change the atmosphere?"

"Very much so. Classes were like serious discussions in the pub. Sondra actually called me a fascist to my face one night!"

"So they all got B+. Did they deserve it?"

"Two were a little weak and should probably have got B's at the most. And Lisa, you remember her? She deserved an A. So I gave her one."

"What! You broke the contract!"

"I know. But it was unfair to her. I rationalized that B+ was only the *minimum* we had negotiated."

"Would you do it again?"

"I don't think so. But it was a very interesting experiment."

"Grades. Or no grades. You can't really mix the two systems?"

"It was a lucky accident that they were all diligent."

"But you discovered enough out of it that you would support a no-grade system?"

"I think so. I think they learned a lot."

"That is very far out!" said Rashid.

I was still there a couple of hours later when Jenadie returned to the house.

"You tell that chauvinist pig friend of yours to move his ass on out of here fast," she said.

Pretty soon they were going at it like I had not witnessed before.

"*Pig, pig! Call him a pig! I don't give a shit,*" cried Rashid, thumping on the counter. "*He's a dedicated*"—thump—"*radical*"—thump. "*We have to have people with integrity!*"—thump. "*Jack has it.*"

"Yeah?" Jenadie yelled back. "Well, maybe his fucking *integrity* should extend to his treatment of women. Maybe you could try to *exPLAIN* that to him, Rashid!"

She slammed out of the house again.

How had this storm brewed up so quickly, and to such intensity? How could she lose her temper with him, when he was in danger of losing his job? I knew less about Jenadie's and Rashid's life together now than I had known years before when they were apart and she used to confide in me like a brother. Even though he had become closer and closer to me while she was more distant and wrapped up in her own professional life, Rashid never talked to me about his private life with her. And I never asked. I wondered what had been going on.

Rashid moved around the kitchen, silently preparing food. He set a plate in front of me, and one in front of himself and we sat down. He lifted his hand and spoke.

"So Jack's a chauvinist!" He chuckled nervously to himself and swallowed a forkful of curried fish. "So what! There's a lot of hypocrisy among the radical left. You know what Jack said to me once when we were grad students at Syracuse?"

"What?"

"He asked me to name the four leading radical women on the campus, which I did. Then he bet me fifty bucks that he could sleep with each one of them and get her to serve him breakfast in bed in the morning."

"And you took this bet?"

"And I lost the money!"

"How do you know he did it, man? He might have gone to bed with them, but how do you know they served him breakfast in bed?"

"Come on! About some things you have to trust people to tell the truth."

We ate in silence for a while.

"So," I said, "what's happening with the university? Is it going to be resolved before the fall?"

"It's extremely bitter," he said. He gazed out the window at the cedar trees that enclosed the property. In profile, his face seemed dark and pitted. I wondered if he had ever had smallpox. "I can't see any resolution. Barrington has dug in, and he's not going to back down. He is now taking the initiative. You know what he once said to me—no, not Barrington—that Dean guy, Marshall, you know what he said to me at the beginning of last year? I was alone with him in the elevator and he said to me, 'We're going to clean you buggers out of here in six months.' Looks like he was right, huh? Except it's taking a year and a half."

"But the hearings—"

"They're a sham, Alistair! We are losing the power struggle. Every Hearing Committee has found in our favour. 'No cause for dismissal.' But Barrington continues wielding total power. He's ignored all the findings and places himself above the Academic Freedom and Tenure document. He says AFT is flawed and claims the right to judge for himself whether to follow or ignore it. And it looks like the Board of Governors will support him. At least, finally, the Faculty Association Executive took a stand and passed a motion of no-confidence in Barrington."

"Well, then that's a victory!"

"Yes, but it's only the Executive. It would have to be ratified by the membership. And there are plenty of right-wing faculty who can't wait to lick Barrington's ass. The Executive resolution will be defeated, I'm quite sure."

"You're still on the payroll?"

"Not much longer. Next week the Board considers Barrington's recommendation to fire us, and then it could all be over."

"Christ. What's your next move?"

He shook his head, muttering with a tired grin, "Arrh. Drink Scotch and wait for a better life to suddenly appear."

"Aren't you meeting with your colleagues?"

"*End*lessly, Alistair. Endless meetings with col-*leagues*! I'm getting so tired of it all, man."

There was a bleak silence.

"I'd better be off," I said. "If I don't get on with my thesis really soon, I'm going to lose my degree. I'll call you."

Rashid looked up with an automatic grin.

"Don't worry," he said. "Drink Scotch" ("Drink es-Scotch"—his accent was becoming stronger, as though he had been drinking already, or was still wasted from the night before).

It was a wet June day, and on the Dollarton Highway I stopped for a bedraggled young man with long hair, hitch-hiking in the rain. He laid a box of groceries and his guitar case carefully on the back seat and climbed in the front.

"Groovy man. Appreciate it. Name's John."

We shook hands.

"Where are you headed?"
"End of the road."
"The marina?"
"Yah."
"You live on a houseboat?"
"In a cabin in the woods, about a mile up the inlet."
"You own this cabin?"
"Yah."
"Really!"
"Yah. My buddy and I built it. It's on Crown Land and the government could kick us off any time, so we didn't put much into it. Mostly salvage material. Cost about $250 to build."

"And what do you do in your cabin in the woods? How do you spend your time?"

"Study. Play guitar. Meditation. Right now I'm making raisin wine."

"You study in a school or just on your own?"

"I've been taking courses at Simon Fraser. It's quite a hike to get there, but I like the courses. I might continue, even if it's just at Cap College."

I bristled. When were these damned high school counsellors going to get it right?

"You think the community colleges are inferior to the universities?"

"Well they're not as good, eh?"

"Damn right they are! Better qualified faculty, smaller classes. Plus, first- and second-year are the main clients, the *only* clients. Whereas at a university, freshman and sophomores are the bottom of the totem pole."

"Hadn't thought of it like that."

"So you're at SFU? You know Rashid Hassan?"

"I know who he is. I don't know the dude personally."

"He's my friend. I've just come from his place."

"You're kidding me! He's *real cool*. I'd like to meet him some time."

When we reached the Cove, the rain was coming down so hard that I drove him right to the marina. I watched him load his groceries and guitar into a soggy old wooden rowboat, while squalls gusted in from the north, and the water was rough.

"John!" I shouted down, and he looked up. "That's my boat there in F17. There's a kicker motor on the bracket. You can borrow it and bring it back when the weather's better."

"Thanks!" he shouted back. "I'll leave you some raisin wine. It'll be drinkable in about a month."

I watched him board my boat and take the 3-horse Evinrude and the red gas can. He fitted the motor onto the rowboat's transom and started it with a couple of pulls. As he headed off into the weather, he arranged a green garbage bag over his knees. Turning to look back, he saw me and waved with a beautiful big smile that I could see through all that rain.

Sure enough, when I next went down to the marina, the motor had been put back in its place on my boat, with a note of thanks from John Harron, and a recipe for raisin wine, and the gas can was full. About a month later, there was a bottle of wine inside the cabin, and another note: "Keep the faith." A small thing, but it pleased me that John Harron, whoever he was, had kept his.

By then, things had changed considerably in my world.

29

It was a Saturday morning in early July, and I opened the door to pick up the *Province* from my front porch and stopped dead. Big front page headlines: "TWO SFU PROFS DISMISSED." I took the paper inside, poured a mug of coffee, and read. At a special meeting of the Board of Governors, President Barrington had recommended that the Dismissal section of the AFT document be declared null and void, and the Board had agreed. Then he had recommended that Professors Rashid Hassan and Muriel Meyer be dismissed, and the Board accepted that recommendation too.

I dialled Rashid's number but there was no answer. Over the following few days, I called several times, but the phone rang and rang. I assumed he and his colleagues were busy plotting strategy for the next move.

I got all my old thesis notes and photocopied articles out of the storage box and set up a working office on a spare kitchen table in the front window nook of the house, shielded by the beautiful striped curtains Sonia Odegaard had picked out, the day Rashid first came to stay with me. The cat kept me company, sitting on my lap or the table as I plodded away on Chapter Five, half waiting for the phone.

One evening, I had made dinner and was sitting typing out a clean draft of the chapter, when Jenadie phoned.

"Hi!" I said. "I've been trying to get in touch with you guys. What's happening? Why don't you let me cook dinner for you and you can fill me in on the news? It must be hairy."

There was a silence on the line.

"Jenadie?"

"Alistair," she said, "could I crash at your place for a few days?"

"Of course," I said. "What's up?"

"I'll tell you when I get there."

"You want me to pick you up? Where are you?"

"I'm just out in Stanley Park doing some thinking. I'll get there on my own. See you in a couple of hours."

"The front bedroom's made up. Move in for as long as you want. Are you okay?"

"Yeah, I'm okay. See you soon."

I went back to my thesis and got a couple more pages typed when a Black Top cab pulled up, and Jenadie got out, toting a suitcase.

I showed her into her room. She looked exhausted. Her eyes were red and swollen. "Come and have a drink when you're ready," I said and closed the door and went back to my work.

Jenadie came out of her room and went to the back of the house, where the kitchen and bathroom and my bedroom were. She walked quickly, leaving me my space in the front room. I typed on, until she came back to the living room and sat down. Then I left my work and joined her.

"Scotch or wine?"

"Do you have any tea?" she said.

I made her a pot of tea and poured myself a Scotch.

She sat on the sofa, and I sat in the armchair. She sipped her tea and dabbed at an eye with Kleenex. Then she tucked the Kleenex into her jeans and cradled the mug of tea with both hands.

I waited, thinking how different it was to see Jenadie here alone, when for so long now it had been Rashid and I together in this room, talking. She had cut her hair much shorter than when I first knew her. Her eyes sparkled as usual, but her cheeks seemed flattened with exhaustion.

"This is terrible timing," she said.

She sounded so on edge that I kept quiet and sipped my drink.

"You know," she said, "he's about to go off to India, and if we could have somehow lived out this last week normally before he goes, that might have been.... But I *couldn't* do it, Alistair! I couldn't wait and pretend, and I just, I mean...."

She shaded her eyes with her hand and shook her head.

"Why don't we talk in the morning?" I said.

"I wouldn't mind that glass of wine now."

As I got up to get it, she said, "This really isn't fair to either Rashid or me. It's the *worst* possible timing."

"Relax," I said, handing her the wine glass. "You're here now. You've got some space. Take your time."

"You're probably right," she said and drained the glass.

"More?"

She shook her head. I got up and fetched a front door key from the kitchen drawer.

"I've applied for the Iowa Writer's Workshop," Jenadie said. "Yesterday I got a letter of acceptance. Isn't that great?"

"That's terrific!" I said. "It's supposed to be the best writing school on the continent. When do you leave?"

"Sometime pretty soon."

For a couple of hours we talked about Iowa and other things, avoiding the main issue. She petted my cat, and the cat adopted her—as she did anyone who came into the house. Around midnight, I stood up and said, "I'm off to bed."

The phone rang.

I went into the kitchen and answered it.

"Alistair?"

"Yes, Rashid, how are you?"

"Mm, not very well. Is Jenadie MacIlwaine there by any chance?"

"Yes. Would you like to speak to her?"

"Please."

I put the phone down and walked to the doorway. "It's Rashid," I said.

She got up and went to the kitchen, and I took my glass into my bedroom and closed the door. I emptied the drink in one swallow, and turned onto my pillow. I could hear the phone conversation, animated from time to time, as I drifted off.

Someone was shaking me awake by the shoulder. My bedroom light was on. I turned, and shaded my eyes, and saw a boot and a yellow stripe up black pants. I looked at my watch. It was three a.m.

"What's going on?"

"Sir, my name is Constable Kapuchinsky of the North Vancouver RCMP. Could you please get dressed and come into the kitchen?"

He withdrew and closed my door, and I scrambled into my dressing gown.

Jenadie was sitting at the kitchen table weeping, with the tall Mountie standing erect beside her.

"There's been an accident," she sobbed. "Rashid's—Rashid fell off a br-idge!" She broke up on the last word, ending in a wail.

"*Fell* off a bridge! How is he?"

"He fell in the river. We can't find him."

"Will the lady be all right if I leave her with you, sir?" the policeman asked me.

"Yes, fine."

He left.

"What the hell happened, Jenadie?"

"After you went to bed, Rashid and I talked for half an hour on the phone. He was drunk, and eventually he said he was coming out to talk face to face. I said I didn't want him to come tonight, but he drove out anyway."

"He was here in the house?"

"Yes. We argued, and eventually he began shouting, and I couldn't stand it, and I told him he had to go home. But I thought he was too drunk to drive, so I told him to get in the car and I began to drive him home. I guess he felt humiliated, and when we got to that metal bridge near the Second Narrows, he shouted at me that he refused to be driven by me anymore. He insisted that I stop the car and let him out. So I did. And he walked ahead of me down the road, and across the bridge. But Alistair . . ." she broke into tears again, and I gripped her hand while she sobbed and regained control.

"In the middle of the bridge he disappeared. One minute he was there, and when I looked again he had vanished. I drove onto the bridge, and then I saw fingers. He was hanging on the outside of the pedestrian guardrails. I rushed out of the car to him. His hands were gripping two of the uprights, and he was swinging around, trying to reach something with his feet, but he couldn't. He was dangling.

"I told him to hold on, but he said, 'I can't! I can't hold on!'

"A car coming the other way stopped on the bridge. The woman saw me and got out and ran to help.

"I told her, 'He's losing his grip. He can't hold on.'

"'You hang onto him,' she said. 'I'll go and get help.'

"I reached through and grabbed his wrists. But before she even got back in her car, Rashid took one hand off the railing and tried to grab my hand, and then he fell into the river. I couldn't—he just slipped away.

"We rushed down to the other side of the bridge, and then the police were there, and we called and searched everywhere, and we couldn't find him."

"And that's—I mean, what's happening now?"

"The police are going to get their diving team, and that cop brought me home."

"Where's your car?"

"I think they towed it away."

I held onto her as she shivered and sobbed. When she was calmer, I made a pot of tea, and we sat at the kitchen table drinking it. Dawn began to show on the tops of the mountains above Belcarra.

"This is the worst thing that's ever happened to me in my whole life," Jenadie said.

"Do you want to call your parents?"

She shook her head.

"Do you think they'll find him?" she asked tearfully. "Do you think he's all right?"

"I'm trying to remember how much of a drop it is," I said. "Not very far, as I recall."

"The cop said it was about fifteen feet."

"Well . . . that's not such a big fall."

"But the cop said if he hit his head on a rock. . . ."

"How about you go and lie down for a bit?"

She stared at me with an alien look and eventually got up and walked quietly to her room. I went and lay down for a while too. I knew there was going to be a long day ahead.

In my mind, I replayed that last phone conversation I'd had with Rashid.

"'How are you?'" I had asked him.

"'Not very well,'" he replied.

Rashid, who never complained about anything personal.

I had never before heard his voice sound so upset.

But I hadn't been thinking about him. I'd been giving all my attention to Jenadie.

Oh shit.

30

The disappearance of somebody that close to you either numbs you, or you break down and can't function. Most of us seemed to go onto autopilot. Rashid's colleagues met at Al Waldie's and discussed who to inform and what to do. I stuck close to Jenadie and tried to think of ways to be useful.

At one point she said, "Perhaps I should make my way down to Iowa and start getting on with my life. What do you think? Did I tell you I've been accepted at the Writers' Workshop?"

"Well . . . let me know if you want to go," I said. "I can drive."

One day followed another with no news. Once, when Constable Kapuchinsky was interviewing me at the North Vancouver detachment, he leaned forward and said quietly, "You know sir, if Dr. Hassan's body went into the water and sank, it's going to take approximately ten days for it to bloat and rise to the surface."

The thought of Jenadie hanging around for another week or more in this uncertainty was unnerving. Already, there had been harsh things to get through. The police still had the Cortina and since it was registered in Rashid's name and she wasn't legally married to him, they wouldn't release it to her. The post office wouldn't accept her instructions about mail, and wouldn't even give her own mail to her. Worst of all, when she phoned the landlord and asked him to accept less than a month's notice in view of the accident, he demurred. Weeping, she handed me the phone, and the landlord repeated to me what he'd said to her: "The paper didn't say he's dead. It only says he's missing."

I sat there, trying not to react.

"Nevertheless, in the circumstances, I'm asking you to accept three weeks' notice instead of a month."

"Huh!" he said. "I guess I don't have much choice."

My autopilot kicked in and I avoided screaming at him.

The only family Rashid had in North America was a cousin, Suleiman Hassan, a radical political scientist at Berkeley. Muriel Meyer knew him, and she phoned and they talked for a long time. When Muriel returned to us all waiting in the sitting room, her face was sombre.

"Suleiman has decided to come up and see the situation for himself," she said.

"What does that mean," Al Waldie asked. "Doesn't he trust . . . things here?"

"I don't think he trusts anybody," she said.

We all went to meet Suleiman Hassan at the airport, Al Waldie, Muriel Meyer, Jenadie, myself, Richard Duplessis, and the students Hélène and Ehor.

Suleiman emerged grim-faced from the International Arrivals gate. He took his time and moved carefully. He touched hands with us all formally, with quiet how-do-you-do's. Everything was in slow motion.

Suleiman was to stay with the Meyers at their house in West Vancouver. Muriel had radical connections with him from way back and they had co-authored an academic paper. When he talked with her, his face relaxed. The rest of us he treated with a cold reserve.

We loaded his bag into the car, and then we all took off to West Vancouver. I was driving Jenadie in my car when, on the Oak Street Bridge as the traffic built up to rush hour, she suddenly exploded. She turned angrily left and right and shook her fists against the cars. She was screaming: *"What are all you stupid people speeding around here for? Where do you think you're going, for fuck's sake!"*

I didn't try to quieten her. John Donne's lines on the death of Elizabeth Drury ran through my head: "She, she is dead, she's dead: when thou knowest this, / Thou knowest how poor a trifling thing man is."

Soon Jenadie slumped down in the seat, spent and crying softly.

When I pulled into the driveway of the Meyers' house on Marine Drive, all the others were standing out on the lawn. Suleiman's bag had not been taken into the house but stood waiting on the paving stone.

"Suleiman would like to go immediately and see the bridge where Rashid fell," Muriel said.

"I can drive you there," I said.

"Jenadie needs to go and sign an affidavit about the car," said Muriel, putting an arm around her. "Come, love, I'll take you."

"Then if this gentleman—I'm sorry," Suleiman said, "I haven't got everybody's name yet."

"Alistair."

"If Alistair will take us, I should like an opportunity to look at the bridge."

At the Seymour River, I found a place to pull off the road, and then Suleiman and I, Al Waldie and Richard Duplessis slowly made our way to the bridge. In silence, we walked across it, both sides, and then climbed down to the river, through large boulders. The Donne refrain played over in my head.

Finally, as we stood under the bridge deck looking into the water where Rashid must have fallen, Suleiman began to nod.

"Family members have told me," he said, "that Rashid had a little trick in his youth. You know his father was killed by thugs in India when he was a little boy? He saw it happen actually. He saw them break down the door and kill his father with knives. He was sleeping on the bed with him."

"Oh Jesus!" Al said. "I didn't know that."

"Yes," said Suleiman. "Rashid's father was not liked. He was perceived as collaborating with the robber barons. Even Rashid came to realize that was true. So, later, when he was educated, he came to accept the death from a purely political point of view. But as a seven-year-old child of course he was emotionally devastated. What can you expect?

"In any case, he used to play this game to agitate his mother. There was a bridge beside their village in Bihar. He used to walk across that bridge and disappear. *Acha!* His mother would look for him and become frantic! *Where is Rashidi?* Well, of course, little Rashidi is safe and sound! He has climbed over the side of the bridge and crawled in and hidden himself in the girders. A child's prank on his mother—and also I think he went to the bridge as a place of safety. Climbing like a monkey and curled up hidden in the girders of the bridge, Rashid is safe. No *thuggee* can get to him there. Nobody could see him.

"But look here. Somewhere about here he went over, right?" Suleiman pointed up at the underside of the bridge walkway. "Look what a great distance for his legs to reach the girders! Three, four metres. He couldn't do it. I don't think he was trying to fall in the water. If that was what he had in mind, he could have gone over there." Suleiman turned and pointed to where the Second Narrows Bridge rose high above the inlet.

"Perhaps that bridge in India had no walkway," I suggested.

"Perhaps."

"He must have felt he was on a familiar structure. Over he goes, and he doesn't know that a walkway has been added on to this bridge, so there's no purchase for his feet. And he hangs on till he falls."

"Or, by what I hear," said Suleiman, "hangs on till Jenadie drops him."

"No. He fell out of her hands because he couldn't hang on."

"Too bad my cousin didn't have the good sense to choose a girlfriend with stronger hands."

I looked down at the rocks. Nobody made a sound. What an outrageous thing to say! Then I looked at Suleiman and saw a faint, sad smile on his face. I wouldn't have blamed him for speaking the bitterest words in the world. I wanted to put my hand out to him, but I was afraid he might not take it.

Back at Meyers', we sat in the living room, and Muriel offered drinks.

Suleiman took a neat Scotch and put it on a side table without touching it.

"Friends," he said, "I would like to ask you to join me in conducting a search for Rashid."

"But the police—" I said.

Suleiman raised a palm and cut me off.

"I would appreciate it if we could obtain boats and conduct a search."

Silently, we nodded.

"We can use my boat to search east of Second Narrows up the inlet," I said. "And if we rent another boat some of you can search from Second Narrows to Lions Gate."

Muriel Meyer went to phone Sewell's Marina in Horseshoe Bay.

I took Richard Duplessis aside.

"This is pointless," I whispered in his ear. "If the body's not found immediately, it sinks, and then it takes ten days to bloat and come to the surface."

"It doesn't matter," Richard said. "We have to go through with it."

"All right," I said, "but you come with me. I doubt if Jenadie will want to take part in this."

"Probably she should go with Suleiman in the other boat."

That afternoon, Richard drove with Hélène and Ehor to my place, and we walked to the marina.

"We're not likely to find anything," Richard explained, "but we have to try."

"It's okay," said Hélène.

We slowly searched along the shoreline from Deep Cove to Cates Park past Maplewood Flats to the Seymour Creek and the Second Narrows Bridge, then the other side past the Shell refinery, Ioco, Bedwell Bay and up Indian Arm. After a long, quiet time of searching Richard began trying to regale us with a crude account.

"Richard, I don't think this is the appropriate time and place—"

"Why not?" Richard cut Ehor off. "It's one of Rashid's favourite stories!"

So we listened to him tell about his getting stuck while camping with his girlfriend on Vancouver Island with an erection that wouldn't go down after they'd had sex. I looked across at Hélène, and her smile back told me that she knew all about Richard and his tall stories. I was very moved that she and Ehor had joined us despite the fact that they had split up with one another. "So that's the moral," Richard said, emphatically. "Never come twice on the same erection! Because if that valve gets stuck and stays stuck long enough, it's scar tissue my friend, and that's the end of that. By the time the helicopter got me to VGH I had literally minutes to go. A matter of minutes—that's what the doc said."

He suddenly tossed his cigarillo into the water and blurted out: "Ah God! Do any of you guys think Rashid might be shitting us?"

"What do you mean," I asked.

"You don't think he's maybe laughing at us, hiding out in some motel in Oregon?"

"Why would he do that?" I said.

"He has that kind of humour."

I felt awkward at his use of the present tense for the second time.

Hélène turned her head onto her hand and wiped a tear from her eye.

I concentrated on driving the boat as close to shore as possible without grounding the motor, and the others kept lookouts in different directions.

"What's that?" one of us would say softly, pointing, and the rest would turn and look. But it was never more than a chunk of dark wood floating, or a bird. After covering our half of the inlet, we returned to my place, and I said goodbye to them and sacked out for the night. I couldn't even think about Rashid, I couldn't think of him alive, and I couldn't think of him dead. Closing my eyes, I kept seeing the ocean, kept searching for a head of black hair, a body. This was the worst part of not knowing: having to hold off. I wondered where Jenadie was, and how she was doing.

Next morning the phone rang around eight, while I was in the shower. I answered it, standing naked, dripping on the kitchen floor. It was Al Waldie, asking me to join a meeting of everybody at the Meyers'.

When I got there, Suleiman was standing with his back to the fireplace, looking confident and in charge of things.

"The police have released Jenadie's car," he said. "Would you be free, Alistair, to drive her down to Iowa immediately?"

"If that's what she wants."

Jenadie nodded.

I felt relieved. From Suleiman's point of view I must have appeared very suspect—old friend of Jenadie's, she's staying at my house when he disappears.... Yet since we had been down to the bridge together, he spoke to me more cordially than he had at first.

"When would you like to go?" I asked Jenadie.

"No point hanging around," she said. "Might as well go right away. When are you free?"

"I can go now. How much stuff do you have?"

We figured that we could carry everything if we took both our cars.

"Let's leave tomorrow morning, then," Jenadie said. "I have a friend in Iowa who said I can crash with her till I get a place of my own."

Word went out, and for the rest of the day, people arrived at the Meyers', bringing food, and wine, and later in the day hard liquor. The Meyers' two sons worked dutifully setting out plates of cold cuts and salads.

I stood alone staring through a picture window to the sea and drinking wine. A quiet murmur of talk coursed through the house, now and then a raised voice, even laughter. From time to time, someone else would come silently to the window and look out to sea. I saw Jenadie standing under the archway that led to the living room, with a drink in her hand and a frozen look on her face. *She's holding up*, I thought. *She's holding up amid all these people and she needs to get away from here.*

Kamal Gupta from Simon Fraser University was drinking straight Scotch by the glassful, and eventually he lay down on a sofa and began to make a low, doglike wailing. Then he raised himself up on an elbow and with a baleful lost look began shouting into the room: "Rashid, why you are doing this? Where are you, you *bastard*!" Turning, as though addressing listeners, he cried, "He was going to *cook* for me! That fucking bastard was going to *cook* for me this week! And now where is he?"

People turned away, pretending not to hear.

Muriel touched my arm. "Take him out. Take poor Kamal home," she said. "It's too much."

I found Ehor, and together we lifted Kamal off the sofa and supported him to my car and drove him home. He snored in the back as we drove.

"What do you think, Ehor? Is Rashid. . . ?"

Ehor shrugged.

The next day, I unbolted the front passenger seat of my Austin station wagon and drove to Jenadie's, and we loaded the two cars. The whole company of radical colleagues and a few students were there to see her off. Everybody hugged, even Suleiman.

"Do you like Vancouver?" I asked him.

"Beautiful!" he said with a fixed smile. "Beautiful place, but too small for my liking. I am only comfortable in a very large city." He grinned then without smiling, in a detached, stoical way that reminded me precisely of Rashid.

We waved goodbye, and I followed Jenadie's car south for Seattle, then east across the Cascades on Interstate 90.

31

That was a hideously lonely day of driving. We had decided to keep in sight of one another, but in the flat, dry scrub of Eastern Washington with many trucks on the road, we lost contact. By the time we met up again in Spokane, Jenadie was in rough shape. She had been waiting in a gas station for an hour before we found one another.

"I thought you must have had an accident!" she cried. "I thought you were dead. I was feeling so guilty and wondering what I could do to support your children!"

"Let's find a place to stay," I said.

We drove on to Coeur d'Alene and stopped at a rustic 1950s motel, with white clapboard cottages set back from the lake. We went out for steak and chips, and came back to the motel with a bottle of Scotch. We were both drained.

"You take the bed," Jenadie said. "I'll sleep on the couch."

"No, I need to watch some garbage TV. You take the bedroom."

Next morning we got up early and prepared for another lonely day of driving. It was hot and dry crossing Montana. I couldn't get over how clean it was, and how empty. It reminded me of the beautiful, empty landscape in the John Wayne movie Jenadie and Rashid and I had watched together in Edmonton, years before it seemed, in another lifetime. I tried the radio and could pick up nothing but Bible stations, so I drove for hours listening to hymns and homilies. At a truck stop outside of Billings, there was a tray beside the gas pumps with a sign:

"SOAP - for hippies and other dirty people." We went into the café, and I saw a doorway with a sign saying "Showers."

I asked the woman at the till, "How much is a shower?"

She looked at me.

"They're only ever for men," she said.

"Pardon me?"

"The showers." She stared at my shoulder length hair. "They're only ever for men."

"Let's get out of here," I said to Jenadie, and we walked out and drove to another café.

That night, we slept on the grass in a rest stop to save money. I lay in my sleeping bag and felt completely removed from the events of the past few days. It was like being on a camping trip in a foreign country, sleeping outdoors, with nothing to think about but ourselves and the sky above. I lay and stared up at the clear July night, bright with stars.

"Look, Jenadie, it's like the aquarium."

"You mean the *planetarium*, you dodo."

"Jeez, what a city boy I've become. Sees a sky full of stars and thinks he's in the planetarium!"

Later in the night I heard rustling. Lifting my head, I saw in the bright moonlight a tribe of field mice or shrews searching through the grass for picnic leftovers. They ran right across my sleeping bag in their quest. I watched this small drama and in my mind, the Beatles sang about life going on. . . .

"Are you awake Alistair?"

"Yes."

"Suleiman blames me for Rashid's death," Jenadie said quietly.

"We don't know yet what has happened to Rashid."

"*I* do!" she said firmly. "He's not coming back. Is that what you guys are all thinking? No, he's gone. Suleiman thinks it's my fault."

"Why would he think that?"

She sniffed and didn't answer.

After a while I said, "You know, when we were under the bridge, Suleiman looked up and said, 'My cousin should have chosen a woman with stronger wrists.' First I was appalled and then I thought it was an incredibly bold gesture in the circumstances. I'm certain he doesn't blame you. He's realistic. He was generous enough to risk that joke."

She was silent but I knew she hadn't gone back to sleep.

In the morning we drove for an hour and stopped for breakfast.

"I heard on my car radio that Montana's the fourth largest state in the union," I said. "And guess what its population is?"

"I don't know. A few million."

"Seven hundred thousand. Less than Vancouver. About the size of Burnaby! Isn't that incredible?"

Jenadie smiled for the first time in several days.

In Deadwood, South Dakota, I had to buy a new tire, and the man at General Tire eyed my hair suspiciously, but when I pulled out the green American cash, his face broke into a beam.

"Thanks a lot," I said.

"You bet, and see ya again, and I sure do thank ya now!"

By the fourth day, the absolute vacancy of travel had enveloped us. Apart from that brief conversation in the middle of the night in Montana, neither of us had mentioned Rashid. Everything in Vancouver seemed distant and disconnected from us. We were like self-engrossed tourists, totally focussed on getting ourselves from point A to point B, and it was a numbing relief from the emotional wringer of the previous days.

In Iowa City, we found Jenadie's friend's place, and unloaded, and went to look around the campus. We sat on the steps of the old Capitol building which was the university's administrative centre. Students and faculty strolled under the huge shade trees, oaks and maples, cottonwoods and black willows.

"Quiet city," I said. "You should be okay here, my sister."

"Yes." She lit a cigarette and the look in her eye as she blew away the smoke told me she didn't want to talk. She was gearing up for a tough transition. I spent the night on her friend's couch. Early in the morning, I got up and said goodbye without ceremony and left.

West of Des Moines, I picked up a guy, Bob, hitch-hiking to the coast. We agreed to take turns and drive non-stop, round the clock. As we approached Spokane at dawn on the second day, the red generator light came on.

"Shit!" I said. "Where am I going to get generator brushes for an Austin in Spokane!"

I pulled up on the main street, and there, right in front of us, was a foreign auto parts dealer. "British and European Motors," the sign said, "MG, Alfa Romeo, Lucas Electrical, Magneti Marelli."

"The gods are with us!" I said.

We found a café that was open, and had breakfast, and I dismantled the generator. We waited for the dealer to open, and then I put the new brushes in, and reinstalled it, and we were on our way. I dropped Bob in North Seattle and settled in for the last three hours of driving, with eyelids that felt like sandpaper and would hardly stay open. I arrived home in the early afternoon, picked up my mail off the floor, and was going to put it on the kitchen counter to look through later, when a blue envelope caught my eye. It had a U.S. stamp and was postmarked San Diego.

> *Dear Alistair,*
> *I heard through friends about Rashid's disappearance, and I just wanted to tell you how sad I am. You and he and Jenadie have all had a tremendous influence on my life. Please give Jenadie my love and warmest condolence.*
> *Take care!*
> *Caroline.*
>
> *P.S. I'm really sorry it didn't work out between us, Alistair. That's just the way it happens sometimes I guess.*

I put the letter back it its envelope, drank a glass of milk, and flopped onto my bed. I was dozing off when the phone rang.

It was Constable Kapuchinsky. The RCMP had found a body, and they thought it was Rashid's. Would I be able to come to Lions Gate Hospital to identify it?

I got up and drove straight to the hospital, and the constable was waiting for me and took me down to the basement. A nurse led the way with slow, tired steps. At the door of the morgue she stopped and turned.

"Have you warned him?" she asked the Mountie.

"About what?" I asked.

The young policeman shook his head.

"There's not much left of the poor man," she said to me.

She opened the door, and we went into the cold room. She pulled a sheet right off, to expose a clothed body on a gurney. It was the right size for Rashid. I recognized the gorilla-stompers that we had bought at Woodward's, his S-shaped belt buckle, and his yellow sweater. At the top there was a bare skull, no flesh. Black sea lice were all over the clothes.

"Are you able to identify this body sir?" the Mountie asked.

"These are Dr. Hassan's clothes."

Mechanically he repeated, "Are you able to identify the body, sir?"

I looked at the large empty eye sockets and the perfect teeth, and shivered.

"I can't say legally for sure about the body. I know these clothes are his."

He shook his head once.

The nurse pulled the sheet back over and we left.

"I'm sorry," I said as we walked down the corridor.

"No need to apologize, sir."

"What do you do now?"

"Dental records."

"Maybe one of the others," I said. "Professor Waldie?"

"We've gone through them all," he said. "Waldie, Duplessis, Meyer. They all said the same thing as you. Clothes are not sufficient, sir. We have to have a positive identification before we can release a body for burial," he said. "It'll just take a while longer."

Two days later, it seemed bizarre to be driving to the airport to pick Jenadie up again. We all gathered at Muriel Meyer's. Nobody said much. A process had to be completed. Al Waldie arrived from the airport with Suleiman Hassan, and then we got in the cars and drove down to the Muslim Centre in Kitsilano. There, we found a tense scene. Several unsmiling Centre officials stood in a line blocking the unloading of the hearse.

Al Waldie and Suleiman went to speak with them but soon came back.

"We've assured them the *imam* has given clearance," Al reported, "but they say it's spiritual contamination. We'll have to wait till he arrives." While we waited, he said, "What hassles, man! The funeral home wouldn't even take delivery of the body until it was sealed in a metal canister."

We waited in the tense and sombre silence, until the *imam*'s car arrived, and he jumped out. Al and Suleiman went and conferred with him and soon all was settled. We went inside, and the two men from the funeral home carried the coffin in and laid it on trestles.

I stood beside the *imam*, and he turned to me and asked, "Which end is the head, please?"

I looked down on the varnished wood and thought of the mess of remains in the canister beneath. "Here," I said, pointing to the broader end of the dark coffin. "The head is here."

The *imam* directed the proper alignment of the coffin and began the ceremony, intoning prayers in a high-pitched chant. Then we drove to the cemetery. We watched the two beefy gravediggers lower the coffin into the ground on ratchet straps, and then they removed them and picked up their shovels and began filling in.

Al Waldie stepped up to one of them.

"Would you mind if we did that?" he said.

"Sure!" The big city worker handed him the shovel.

"Let's put our friend to rest!" Al cried in a loud, rabbinical voice and began energetically shovelling earth. He threw the spadefuls high and they fell back into the grave. Suleiman took the shovel from the other gravedigger. One by one we each added a few spadefuls of earth, and by the end most of us were streaming tears.

Back at the Meyers', people had brought lots to drink, and there was a long table of salads and cold cuts. About fifty people were there, and there was hugging, and more tears.

Muriel came to talk to me privately. "I've had an interview at Capilano College," she said. "Perhaps we'll be colleagues."

"Terrific!" I said. "When do you find out?"

"They finish the interviews tomorrow, and then they decide. So I expect to hear . . . day after tomorrow maybe?"

"Good luck," I said. "That would be great."

I hugged Jenadie for a long time.

"We seem to be doing nothing but saying goodbye to one another these days," she said.

The frozen look on her face told me she was still in shock. She was going to stay a few days with the Waldies and wind up Rashid's effects, then fly back to Iowa. If all these journeys seemed unreal to me, how much more so they must have seemed to her.

Now I remember that as I was leaving that night Jenadie handed me something in a brown paper wrapping and I opened it. It was the framed black and white picture of Rashid.

At home I slept for about eighteen hours straight.

Fragments of dream: there is a kerfuffle about putting up a metal plaque for Rashid at the university. Hefty Pinkerton guards stand in a line to prevent its arrival on the campus. Andrea Halvorson grabs the plaque and I drive her with it recklessly across the Second Narrows Bridge to Capilano College.

Then I am at a party in a basement suite in Kitsilano where people are smoking marijuana. I walk into the next room and Rashid is sitting on a sofa, grinning happily, surrounded by listeners. "*Very* subversive!" he says. "Excellent!" I can smell the garlic on his olive skin.

We are going to go out in my boat, and Rashid hasn't brought a warm jacket. I reach into my closet and take out my old duffel coat.

"Fits perfectly!" he cries. "Look," closing the elk horn buttons in their leather toggles, "Fits perfectly! I have exactly the same coat at home!"

32

In the dismal mornings after the funeral, I'd wake up and lie staring at the ceiling before putting coffee on, and the silence of the house would remind me. John Donne ran through my mind: *"All mankind is of one Author, and is one volume."* Rashid's absence became a tangible thing which I had to begin to get used to. But the memory of standing by the coffin with that canister inside was too gruesome. Instead, I'd turn my head to the smiling figure in the frame on my wall. Jenadie had written an inscription across the bottom left hand corner: "For Alistair, whom Rashid respected because political disagreements were always discussed intelligently—for his friend."

Day by day, even the photograph of him began to blend into the wall.

After coffee, back to the books. I picked up the threads of aesthetic theory: Chapter Six. Chiqui purred away on my work table with complacent eyes. I reached out and stroked her, and remembered Rashid playing with her while we talked, then turned back to Shklovsky and re-read his definition of defamiliarization:

The business of the artist, is to impart the sensation of things as they are perceived, and not as they are known, to remove the automatism of knowledge and freshly perceive the world.

"Radical! " I thought, remembering. "I'm going to get this thesis finished. The difference between things as we *know* them to be and things as we *perceive* them. Right, Rashid? 'Systems get rigid and need shaking up.' No wonder the Russians banned the Formalists as decadent, and sent them to Siberia! Communism used to be the leading edge. Now, they're the conservatives. Change terrifies them."

Despite the hollow feeling around talking to the dead, my own life was on the go. I put my Fifth Dimension *Aquarius* album on and cranked out sentences that felt energetic and original.

This excited tranquillity lasted two days until the phone rang.

It was Peter Hansen. Another emergency meeting of the faculty association, this time in a rented meeting room of the Canyon Gardens hotel.

"What's it about, Peter?"

"The College Council is throwing its weight around. They tried to sidestep the Memorandum of Understanding on job security and seniority; now they're interfering in the hiring procedure."

I felt a sudden chill.

"This wouldn't have to do with someone named Meyer, would it?"

"You know about Muriel Meyer?"

"She's an acquaintance of mine. She told me she'd been interviewed for a job at the College."

"All the more reason to come to the meeting, Alistair. I'll see you there." He hung up.

I wanted to stay and work quietly on my thesis. I remembered arriving in Edmonton on Christmas day, and Rashid was away from home at a meeting. Chastened by his dedication, I got in the car, and by the time I reached the Upper Levels Highway, I was pumped.

Peter Hansen worked the meeting skilfully and when he came to the part about the College not having to give reasons for not renewing a faculty member's contract, you could feel the dissatisfaction rumbling. Peter took his time extricating a paper from his briefcase and read out an executive motion, to hold a certification vote for the faculty association to become a trade union. He stopped, raised his eyes, and looked around the room. It was a dramatic moment and he let the motion sink in. No one said a word.

"All right, let's break for lunch," Peter said, "and then we'll vote."

You could hear the hubbub of argument as people filled their plates from the smorgasbord and sat down. When the meeting resumed, Rosemary Campbell, a common-sense, apolitical instructor in Chemistry, raised her hand.

"I attended a College Council meeting last fall and I heard something that truly astounded me," she said. "You know that School

Board representative on Council, the financial analyst?" Well, she said, 'We on the School Board would dearly love to be able to economize by getting rid of our senior teachers, if only we could.' It made me realize how tenuous our position is."

"What's wrong with that?" asked another Chemistry instructor. "Why form a union to protect dead wood?"

"Gretchen," Rosemary said, "she didn't say 'get rid of our *deadwood* senior teachers.' She said 'senior teachers' period! It's fine as long as we're all at the bottom of the salary scale. But what happens after ten years, when they're having to pay you at the top of the scale, and money is tight? 'All right, thank you very much for all your work, senior teachers. Bye!'"

"Are you saying they can fire any of us anytime they feel like it?" another voice asked incredulously.

"You heard Peter," said Rosemary. "'The College reserves the right to discontinue employment.' We don't even have the protection school teachers have, and nothing like the security of tenured university profs."

The question was called and the vote passed by a landslide.

I went up and shook Peter's hand.

"Congratulations! How long have you been planning this?"

He winked. "When we win the certification vote," he said, "it'll become a way better place to work. Collective decisions. No more blind obedience."

Muriel Meyer was hired in Sociology, and whenever she and I passed one another in a corridor or the doorway of a classroom, we would exchange a private smile.

Forming a faculty union did get us out from under the parenting of the Dean and the Principal. From now on there were no more arbitrary decisions and no more bullying. Everything was negotiated in a collective agreement. The campus became a freer and more dignified place to work, and it all began with Norman Bull and the co-ordinator system. Yet his notion of a co-ordinator—*primus inter pares* as he told me in my first interview—did not quite square with the idea of a faculty union.

Bull's power faded fast, and he took semi-retirement with a job in the planning office, before he retired altogether. I regretted that his time ended without fanfare. There should be a monument to him on the campus for the risks he took to introduce progressive ideas.

I went to see him in his planning office, an enclosed cubicle without windows.

"So this is where they've boxed you in now?" I said.

"I'm grateful that they still think I have a role to play," he replied modestly. He wasn't sitting back in his sprung office chair with his hands behind his head as he had done twenty years before, delivering thoughtful judgments.

"Listen, Norman," I said—it was the one and only time I ever addressed him by his first name—"The fact is that the community colleges of BC have delivered a shock of innovation to the hidebound universities and forced them to rethink their curriculum and course offerings. And much of that began in your creative mind, ticking away behind your grey suits and modest ties."

He smiled at me, and I could see the lines in his face becoming fixed with age.

Suddenly, he clasped his hands behind his head and would have rocked back in the fashion I had known, if the chair allowed it. "Well, Alistair," he said, "Every dog has its day, and in regard to a union, I became *passé* and had to go. They still let me do physical planning."

"You did more than anyone to make Capilano what it is today, and I thank you."

We shook hands.

As I walked down the concrete stairs of the new building, I was washed with memories: Bull arranging for us all to retreat off-campus for two or three days, to explore and hash things out. The Haney forestry camp, Paradise Valley, the cabins at Alta Lake, Camp Elphinstone up Howe Sound—anywhere we could feel free from the bustle of work and think outside the box. Once recently, on a visit to Kenya, where the Johnsons were struggling to keep their dairy cows alive on the farm after seven continuous years of drought and a Foot and Mouth epidemic, I tried to explain to Peter and Catherine how vital to my world at Capilano was the co-ordinator system, how we had fought to retain it against repeated administration attempts to sabotage it. They listened politely, and I could see Peter's eye straying onto the hillside where he had a plan to try grinding up the thorny dry *leleshwa* bushes to keep his cattle alive a little longer. When I finished my explanation, his glazed-over eye returned to me, and he said: "So . . . you don't really have any problems to contend with then. It's just a matter of who gives the orders."

"Something like that," I conceded.

How do you convince a struggling Kenya farmer that intellectual stimulus is as important to a country as the survival of cows?

At Capilano, it all goes back to Norman Bull, beginning with the co-ordinator system. Collegiality and innovation. He once showed me a three-part *New Yorker* cartoon of a professor lecturing to orderly rows of note-taking students; the second frame shifted point of view and showed that the "professor" at the lectern was actually a cardboard cut-out with a tape recorder behind it; the third frame shifted again and showed that the "students" were also cardboard cut-outs propped on the desks, with tape recorders behind them.

33

In the Golden Lotus restaurant in Chinatown, I waited at the big round reserved table for the others to arrive. We were having a farewell lunch before Jenadie caught her plane back to Iowa. My ears filled with the modulations of the unfamiliar language around me.

I was watching the doorway, waiting for them, and I kept having this unsettling illusion of Rashid's smiling face coming through the glass door. I wanted to tell him what had happened at the College. Already, I had begun to forget the look of that skull on the gurney in the morgue and instead could picture his vivid white teeth, his grinning lips, his thumb and fingers smoothing down the sleek, black beard. And the dark, shining eyes. "You don't think Rashid might be shitting us?" Richard Duplessis had asked. The skull, the Woodward's boots, that snake-buckle belt . . . did anybody actually make a positive identification, I wondered. They must have done—maybe the dentist—or the police would not have released the body. Part of me still didn't believe it.

Jenadie and the others arrived, breaking me out of this reverie. We ordered, and soon the table was crowded with dishes. Richard Duplessis was there, the Waldies and their children, the Meyers, and those two loyal students Hélène and Ehor. I felt surrounded by family again.

"What are your plans?" I asked Al Waldie.

"I'm going to the People's Republic," he said brightly. "I'm really looking forward to it. Margaret has to stay here with the children, but I'll spell her off on the next occasion."

"What do you hope to find in China?"

"I'm going without preconceptions. It's an important step for Canadians to take. The Americans will have conniptions about our visit. I'm sure the RCMP and the CIA will keep us all under observation—entering the *RED* zone! But I think it will be instructive."

"Send me a postcard," I said.

"Very well," he said, with a strange assessing look. "And what are you doing?"

"I'm battling the universities as usual."

"What does that mean?"

"Transfer battles! The latest involves one of my instructors who requires students in her literature class to do something in addition to writing academic essays. Use their imaginations. Her class was studying Margaret Atwood's novel *The Edible Woman*, and one of the students baked a life-sized cake of a woman and brought it to class and they ate it. They had a discussion about where to take the first bite! The story got out and at the last articulation meeting, this dinosaur from the University of Victoria got up and complained that at one of the 'junior' colleges academic credit in a literature course was being given for baking."

Allan laughed. "If that's the worst you have to face, you're not suffering too badly," he said.

"We've also voted to form a union," I said.

"I heard that," he said. "It was over Muriel's hiring."

"And other things." Al Waldie could have his story, but I had mine.

After lunch, Jenadie took me aside in the back of the restaurant to say our last goodbyes.

"You're going to finish your thesis?"

"Yup," I said. "And maybe one day I'll write something about Rashid."

She just looked at me, too numb to process that one way or another.

As I drove home, I thought about Al Waldie and realized that I would probably never feel as intimate with him as with Rashid. Politics was a wall between us. Rashid could threaten to shoot me one day and maybe even mean it, but he'd laugh meanwhile, and we could continue as friends. With Al, there was a solemnity that ruled out my inclusion. He wasn't amused by my story of Margaret Atwood and the cake, whereas Rashid had hooted with laughter. Al was a kind of priest who owed his loyalty to a higher cause.

A few months later, I did receive a postcard from China. It was a 1934 photograph of the revolutionary writer Luo Shón, standing with his hand on his hip, and a cigarette holder in the other hand, staring cockily out at the world, with a French Colonial brocade curtain behind him. The handwriting on the other side read:

Even when what one sees "confirms" what one has read, seeing provides a profounder understanding. To read about the enthusiasm, energy and optimism of the Chinese people is a particularly pale reflection of what one encounters directly— though in no sense is the reading a falsification. Of course, many things are unclear—particularly the full nature of the Cultural Revolution. Some significant aspects of this revolution are most impressive: sending office and gov't workers at all levels to schools to do manual labour in the most arduous conditions; creative energy and innovation in factories through integration of technical, production and political staff; establishing of factories right in universities; school children working short periods each week in a factory (even primary school age)— not "child labour" but a means to enhance the significance of learning.

Incidentally, Mao's poems are some of the most frequent "decorations" in public buildings.

That was it. No greeting, and no signature, nothing by which to identify the sender. Just the picture of Luo Shón looking out with eyes as confident and determined as those of Al Waldie himself. And the bit about poetry as a thoughtful nod to me. It was 1971 and the Vietnam War was raging intensely. Going to China was a brave step for a Canadian to take then. "Many things are unclear," Al wrote: so he must have had some intuition of the atrocities taking place in secret. I was feeling very alone then and Jenadie's words from Edmonton came back to me like a reproach: "You're a bit of a stoic, aren't you? You seem to have sealed off your emotions and just let things happen to you instead of going after what you want."

"All right," I decided, "it's time to find a new relationship." As though he had read my mind telepathically, Dave Marsden phoned and invited me to a party, saying "There's someone I want you to meet." She was a school teacher, divorced, with two young children, and a violent ex-husband. For a few weeks we dated, and I took her and her kids camping and fishing up at Alleyne Lake, but that soon petered out. I met a legal secretary who was extremely beautiful, and delicate. But that too ended.

I confided to one of the secretaries at the College that I found another secretary attractive, and the next thing I knew the latter was standing in my office in her tall white Nancy Sinatra fuck-me boots, with her hands on her hips and a canting smile that said, "How about it, guy?" She had been married for a while but had left her husband out of boredom. She was a passionate and noisy lover, and on weekends we took the boat and fished for salmon off Bowen Island and across the Gulf in Porlier Pass. But again there was no deep connection—at least not from my side—and the affair fizzled out in a few weeks, despite Conway Twitty and Loretta Lynn singing repeatedly on the radio about never-ending love, as we fished in the warm sun.

The sexual revolution was upon us—the Pill had seen to that, but also the new tide of feminism: women were asserting their sexuality like never before. Books like *The Sensuous Woman* and even unthinkable and today probably illegal titles like *How to Catch a Fourteen-year-old Boy and What to Do with Him* were hitting the shelves. *Playboy*'s many competitors and imitators were on the racks of every corner store, some wrapped in plastic, promising unprecedented revelations, and the serious authors were asserting the right to promiscuous satisfactions. All around us, Henry Green's famous definition of happiness seemed to be happening: to lie in bed on a Sunday morning listening to the sound of church bells, eating buttered toast with cunty fingers. The dark cloud of AIDS had not yet loomed, and lots of women in Vancouver seemed to be paying heed to Melody Kilian's article in *The Georgia Straight*, "Our Duty to Screw."

One day in the Fraser Arms beer parlour, I met a woman who turned out to be the ex-wife of my faculty colleague and office mate Trevor Easton. She had long, blonde hair "down to her ass," and a twinkly smile with Joni Mitchell eyes, and a ready laugh. One day, Trevor Easton said from behind me where his desk was, "Hold still, Alistair, you've got something on your back," and he leaned forward and plucked from my dark green sweater an incredibly long blonde hair, and lifted it carefully above the waste basket and dropped it in. "Thanks," I said and felt like a rat. But for all the romance and excitement of this easy connection, there was no deep feeling on either side, and we drifted apart as casually as we had met.

By now, I was ready to give up on relationships, abandon Jenadie's advice, and retreat to my stoical shell. But men being such idiots, I jumped at two more improbable matches, only to find that one woman was using me to teach her boyfriend a lesson in commitment—they married soon afterwards and are happy grandparents today. The other one assured me that her marriage was over, but as we drove across the Lions Gate Bridge to go for dinner with my old "family," Paul and Viviana, I suddenly spotted her husband's car in my rear-view mirror. I tore around the West End, and managed to lose him, to my relief and surprise for he was a cab driver. I dropped her off at Prospect Point, high above the First Narrows, hoping she wouldn't do something silly.

Even for the promiscuous 70s, these sexual adventures seemed ridiculous and desperate to me, so I vowed from now on to keep my pants zipped up and wait for time to bring me back to sanity. I announced to my colleagues at the College that I was getting married.

"Oh gosh! Who are you going to marry?" my startled colleague Sandra Atkinson demanded, and I replied, "I don't know yet, but it will be next summer."

Jenadie wrote several times over the next few years. I think the fact that we didn't talk much right after Rashid's death was good. She did her talking later, in letters, most of which were too naked and personal to bear repetition. But a couple of them belong in this story:

Dear Alistair,
I must tell you about the most horrible thing that has happened to me since Rashid's death. It was my birthday last week, and I went home, and my parents gave a dinner party. One of my cousins was there, on leave from Vietnam. He's a pilot in the Air Force, and he began talking about bombing raids. Eventually, I couldn't take it anymore, and I said to him, "How can you sit here and talk about this? How can you be involved in dropping bombs and napalm on people—men, women, children, killing them, burning their bodies in the most criminal and inhumane fashion—how can you sit here eating turkey with cranberry sauce, Brussels sprouts and roast potatoes, and talk about it calmly like it's a football game?"

Alistair, he looked at me in amazement. He said, "Jenadie, what're you gettin' all steamed up about? Don't you know those people in Asia have a different concept of life and death than we do in the West. Death is not such a big deal with them."

I couldn't stand being in his presence for another second! I had to get out of the house. I ran and ran, through the cornfield, bawling my eyes out. My own flesh and blood, Alistair! What hope is there for the world? I know he's just an all-American boy who's had his mind fucked over by racist propaganda. But he's my cousin and it so hurts!

Sorry about this. I had to write and get it off my chest.

Another time she wrote to say how ironic it was that Rashid had died young:

He lived because he liked to live. He wanted to know more and more about life. He told me once that he wanted to live to be hundreds of years old, he looked forward to growing old because old was the best time of life. He wanted to live so he could find out and learn, more and more.

And then one day she wrote in response to a letter of mine:

An honours certificate for you Alistair Randall! You have exposed yourself turning from a fascist into a liberal. You start out saying the good thing about radicals is that they call shit shit—Well, I hope you know that shit is defined as a power structure, the Establishment, the system, the ruling class etc. So when you say you are committed to education, let me ask you how the hell education is ever going to change the power structure? Education for whom? Education for what? Sure education—we have to know what causes the evils that oppress us, we have to learn how it can be changed, we have to find out if it's possible—it should be at least a commitment to education for the powerless, with some direction to learning how to change the situation. You know, many a liberal committed to education became dismayed when education about racism didn't eliminate racism, and education about war didn't eliminate war, etc. and they turned to idiots like Robert Ardrey with his "Territorial

Imperative" to explain their failures in terms of human instincts—"human beings are just born that way"... Yeah, well just give me a fuckin' break!

So then I knew she was healing.

My life took a turn for the better just then. I moved out of the shade and firelight of the Deep Cove house to a sunny apartment at 15th and Esquimalt in West Vancouver, with a view out over the ocean to the Gulf Islands. Then, just as I had predicted, I met a woman, Sylvia, and we fell in love into a tide of multiple bliss. I wanted to marry her, but she was only 19 and unsure, and one day at her parents' house for dinner, she got a phone call from some guy who had picked her up hitch-hiking.

"Why did you give him your phone number?" I asked.

"I didn't! We changed one of the numbers."

"'We'?"

"I was hitching with Louise."

Her mother took me aside in the kitchen and advised, "Don't get married! Just live together and enjoy it for what it is. Sylvia's too young for marriage."

That was okay with me, but then a letter arrived which put me into a dilemma: The new Dean of Graduate Studies at UBC wrote saying that he was clearing out old files and asking me to confirm that I had abandoned my Ph.D. *Abandoned! Shit, this was my second warning!* There were quite a few faculty at Capilano who were "ABD," all-but-dissertation, and since it was such a fulfilling place to teach, some of them never did bother finishing their doctorates, which was what you needed to teach at a university. Was I going to abandon mine? No way! I might stay teaching at a community college for the rest of my career, but I hadn't done all this work towards the degree only to abandon it. So I phoned my dissertation supervisor, and asked him to arrange for a year's extension. Next, how to find the time to actually get the dissertation written. The College consumed all my time.

"Maybe we should go away for a year somewhere," Sylvia suggested. "The South Pacific, or your family beach house in Kenya?"

"Yes. And what do we do for income?"

A few days later, a letter crossed my desk offering a teaching exchange to Genesee Community College in Batavia, western New York. We discussed it and I applied for it and got it. I would go as an exchange professor, take no part in committees etc. Just teach and get on with the last chapters of my dissertation and finish the degree in a year.

But as the time approached to go there, I wondered what it would look like to come as a 34-year-old Canadian exchange professor with a 19-year-old unmarried girlfriend in tow. I suspected that Republican rural New York would not be accepting of that. Better if we married. Besides, ignoring her mother's advice, I really wanted to marry Sylvia.

I took her down to Tony Cavelti's jewellery store at Seymour and Georgia "just to look," and by the time she had turned a few artistic gold and diamond creations over in her fingers, I could see she was hooked.

Eventually we agreed to a two-year contract marriage. We wrote and revised the clauses and eventually signed them: "1. Absolute sexual fidelity. 2. No invasion of one another's privacy. 3. Either party may decide not to renew after two years, without fault."

"But this is not a legal document!" Simon Du Lac objected with a frown when he read it.

"Sure it is! Why not?"

So Sylvia and I married and were happily together. Neil Young's *Harvest* was our favourite album, and we would lie on the floor of our high-rise and let the healing strains and the relentless drum beat wash over us. I wrote and told Jenadie my good news, and added this:

> Last Sunday we went to visit Rashid's grave, and Sylvia says, "We must leave flowers." But we couldn't find a place with flowers for sale, so in a flash she ups and scales the barbed wire of a high voltage Hydro substation and picks a handful of red climber roses, and jumps back down again before anybody can see her. We found a Mason jar at the cemetery and left them for Rashid. I think he would have appreciated her going over the wire and defying thousand of volts for him! And she never even met him!

Jenadie wrote back laughing at that picture.

The contract marriage with Sylvia lasted three months beyond its date, and one day I entered the apartment and there were holes where her pictures had been against the walls.

Jenadie finished the writing program at Iowa with honours and got a job as a reporter with the *Washington Post*. She never returned to Canada. From time to time we exchange Christmas cards with a line or two of news—my new marriage, her marriage to a labour lawyer. They live in a collective housing complex in Silver Springs, Maryland, with twin sons and a daughter. She is active in the fight against Wal-Mart and other big box stores.

At Simon Fraser University, the battle dragged on for several years, with still more hearings. Every one of the investigations concluded that Barrington was in the wrong, but his lawyers managed to stall everything in technicalities, and the dismissed professors, although legally exonerated of every charge against them, were never reinstated. Eventually, after SFU had been censured and blacklisted by academic bodies throughout Canada and the rest of the world, it faded from the news for quite a while. Not for me. When I see the name SFU, I think Rashid Hassan.

Of the other five professors who went on strike, I only know what happened to two: Muriel, who continued teaching with us, published three more books, then died of cancer within a few years, and Al Waldie, who is the director of an under-funded society that assists immigrants and refugees. The others I haven't kept in touch with, although Richard Duplessis did send me a postcard from the Yukon once, so he may be working up there.

I often wonder what happened to Ehor and Hélène and the hundreds of other students, teaching assistants, people on the fringes of the drama—naïve bystanders like Caroline's young friends Valerie and Elizabeth, who came down from Kelowna to go to university, only to be confronted by the strike. It wasn't just the six professors that Barrington broke—and they at least had a hearings mechanism for trying to fight back at him. All those other idealists who lay outside the inner circle of solidarity had their futures damaged too, and no recourse to justice.

Sheldon P. Barrington, may you rot in hell!

The College still flourishes in a more tranquil guise than during those heady beginnings and has its own campus and buildings now in the District of North Vancouver, and has become Capilano University. A letter reached me there a few years ago from Caroline: she was in Nicaragua, working on peasant farms with an organization called Tools for Peace. She sent me her "love in Christ."

Times have certainly changed. It's hard today to persuade a single student to sit on any committee, never mind "parity." They're too worried about grade point averages, unemployment and their student loans. If they know the word "parity" at all, it's a technical term to do with computer errors.

As for me, after the contract marriage with Sylvia fizzled out, I found other relationships which didn't last. And I finally finished my Ph.D.

Then I met someone else and married yet again (35 years now and counting— "I'm his last wife," Laura introduces herself sometimes), and I have a stepson and now we have a daughter. My first wife, Imogen, decided there was a better future for her here in Canada than in Africa, so she returned to Vancouver with our kids and her new husband and their kid. All the kids lived in both our households and all went to the College, and her husband ended up getting a job there. The circle of disintegration seemed to close, and everyone got along quite well.

I taught at the College till I turned sixty and took early retirement, but I asked to stay on part-time for a while, teaching just one class. The administration and the union consulted and made me go through a hiring interview. Fortunately I passed and taught on part-time for another six years and now I've handed in my keys.

Towards the end of my time there, I had the job of Faculty Development officer. I would arrange professional development activities for our instructors. Advanced computer sessions were in demand of course, but one day Sandra Atkinson came to me all excited and asked me to lay on an Instructional Skills workshop. I didn't know what this was, beyond the generic meaning of the term, but I looked into the matter and hired an instructor to come and run a week-long workshop in May, after the semester ended. Sandra signed up, along with about a dozen other faculty, and though she had taught continuously at the college for over thirty years, I saw her become totally rejuvenated and energised by the course. You could see it in her eyes and hear it in the noise and laughter coming from her classrooms.

"Tell me about ISW," I asked her.

"ISW and Cooperative Learning are fantastic!" she said. "Thank you a hundred times for the workshops! We learn ways to involve students in discovering the course material for themselves instead of being passive recipients. It's noisy and unruly, but it's way more effective than the old method of the prof lecturing up front while the students copy down notes and later compete with one another on the exam. The saying is, 'The sage on the stage becomes the guide at the side.'"

How very ironic! This is one little piece of the change that Rashid and his radical colleagues were fighting to bring in. I can still hear in my mind Al Waldie's steady voice at the rally: *We wish to replace the one-way monologue of the traditional lecture with dialogue, debate, and cooperative struggles for truth. We believe in constructive mutual evaluation and criticism....* The university governors and administrators went determinedly to war to stop them, purge them, grind those radical bastards down! And now we pay experts thousands of dollars to come and teach our faculty the very stuff they were advocating. Laugh, Rashid! Of course, the radicals would not have stopped at participatory learning and parity. There are always deeper roots to get to, further contradictions to enhance. Meanwhile, parts of yesterday's radicalism become today's orthodoxy, and in the process, people are destroyed. Like building a bridge.

After many years, I heard once again from Jenadie. She was clearing out some boxes and found a piece of writing of Rashid's and sent it. It was a few lines neatly handwritten on a piece of old, green Capilano College memo paper. It must have been the piece he wrote when he sat in on my Composition class:

<u>The Touch of the One</u>
The basic element of any political structure is power and its distribution. How the power is achieved, whether by consensus or by coercion, matters a great deal to some, and not at all to others. Some sociologists define the consensual use of power as mere administration; by their definition, political action requires a fight for control. Other scholars include both cooperation and competition in their definition of the political. I am with this latter group. Political control by any means possible: competition, cooperation, flattery, or outright war. As Mao said: "When the enemy attacks, retreat. When the enemy retreats, chase him!"

I ask only that in the battle for human values and the sharing of power, I shall not lose "the touch of the one in the play of the many."

(Rabindranath Tagore).

envoi

I go to the cemetery occasionally to clean Rashid's marker and leave flowers. The last time I went there, I couldn't find it. His marker had vanished! I searched all around, but none of the headstones was his. I pedalled my bicycle home upset and puzzled. Could it be that in the confusion at the time of his death Al Waldie, or whoever was in charge of things, didn't make permanent arrangements with the cemetery people? It had been many years since he died: had we perhaps paid only for temporary use of that grave and failed to renew a lease? I found the thought that Rashid's remains had been replaced in the ground and his marker thrown away simply unendurable.

Early next morning I rode my bike back and realized I had made a mistake. The Mountain View cemetery in Vancouver straddles ten blocks along Fraser Street, and I had just gone to the wrong section. I crossed the road and, sure enough, there was Rashid's grave, his name and dates on a small brass plaque. I cleaned it up, and later returned with a knife and some flowers, and trimmed back the grass. As I walked away, I felt enormously relieved. His first disappearance was painful enough. I realized afresh how important Rashid Hassan has been to me all these years.

After living in various places, I moved once again to the North Shore, and would frequently drive over the Second Narrows Bridge. I developed a bridge phobia, and crossing Second Narrows in particular, with its meandering roadbed and its historical connotations of catastrophic death, became a problem. I would panic and think I was about to have a heart attack, or imagine the bridge collapsing and my car plunging through the air into the water below. I'd be shouting aloud at the wheel, a danger to myself and others, so I went to a behaviourist at the UBC Health Sciences Centre who got me to make a list of things that made me feel happy: *Listening to easygoing country music*, I wrote, *Thinking about my friends. . . .*

Soon, the therapist's advice was working. The attacks didn't stop but I am able to control them. As I approach the bridge, I punch the radio button to switch to JR Country, 93.7 FM. And I think of my friends.

I often think of Rashid. He had his faults but it doesn't do me any good to think about those. Instead, I remember things like him sitting in the back seat of his big old Chevrolet Impala in Edmonton, evicted from his office at the university, jobless and facing imminent deportation: he grins as I turn his nametag upside down:

Dr. RASHID HASSAN
(shown upside-down)

"Much better!" he says.

Or Rashid with his bare toes sticking out of his Moroccan sandals, waiting for absolute quiet before announcing his entry into the battle at the concrete and steel campus ("Vee can burn it down!"); Rashid, the defenceless little boy whose father was hacked to death in the bed beside him and who would hide in the girders of a bridge, now standing up and braving the Howe Street lawyers at his suspension hearing: "If a runner is running round a track. . . ." It's reached a point for me where I no longer have a problem crossing the Second Narrows Bridge. I think of Rashid Hassan's spirit down there, and I take heart. I remember him standing on my lawn in the Cove with his fist raised to the sky, saying, "We are at a point of no return!" and I'm glad I never voiced my thoughts about the double meaning of that phrase.

"Who's *Rashid*, Dad?" my daughter asked one day when she was about eight. We were coming north over the crown of the bridge onto the down slope, where the stress eases.

"Sorry, did I speak out loud? I was thinking of some friends."

"I know all about your panic attacks—but who's *Rashid*?"

"He died long ago before you were born. See there?" I pointed to the mouth of Seymour Creek. "He fell from that yellow bridge, and his body must have washed into the inlet."

"Omigod! How did he fall, Dad?"

"That's a long story, honey. It was an accident."

On impulse, I took the Deep Cove exit, crossed the Seymour Creek bridge and parked where I had parked so many years before with Suleiman Hassan.

"Let's go see the river," I said.

We clambered down over the rocks below the bridge and sat on a large boulder.

"Look how high the water is," I said.

"I hope none of my friends die," she said.

I didn't answer.

"That's stupid!" she corrected herself with a frown. "Everybody dies in the end." She looked very cross, and I put my arm round her shoulder.

"Yes," I said. "Everyone dies. But if you live your life in a determined way for good that influences other people, then some of the good things you did will go on happening even after you've gone."

"Cool!" she said brightly.

She made her way through the rocks to a stick of driftwood. She carried it to the water's edge and began to play, with cries of delight. She turned her head to me and shrieked as she worked to hold it steady against the changing current.

I watched her play for a few minutes and then called out, "It's time to go now," and started up the bank ahead of her.

For you my friend, this little book. You changed my life. I miss you. Aslaam alequ! Asante sana.

CPSIA information can be obtained at www.ICGtesting.com
Printed in the USA
LVOW121834290513